SEX, SPIES AND SCANDAL

SEX, SPIES
AND SCANDAL

The John Vassall Affair

ALEX GRANT

Biteback Publishing

First published in Great Britain in 2024 by
Biteback Publishing Ltd, London
Copyright © Alex Grant 2024

ISBN 978-1-78590-788-3

10 9 8 7 6 5 4 3 2 1

A CIP catalogue record for this book is available from the British Library.

Set in Minion and Bodoni

Printed and bound in Great Britain by
CPI Group (UK) Ltd, Croydon CR0 4YY

FSC
www.fsc.org
MIX
Paper | Supporting
responsible forestry
FSC® C171272

To my daughter, Alice, with much love

'What the hell do you think spies are? Moral philosophers measuring everything they do against the word of God or Karl Marx? They're not. They're just a bunch of seedy, squalid bastards like me. Little men, drunkards, queers, henpecked husbands, civil servants playing cowboys and Indians to brighten their rotten little lives.'

ALEC LEAMAS IN THE FILM ADAPTATION OF JOHN LE CARRÉ'S *THE SPY WHO CAME IN FROM THE COLD* (1965) SCREENPLAY BY PAUL DEHN AND GUY TROPSER.

CONTENTS

Prologue   xi

Chapter One   "A Secret World"   i
Chapter Two   "Never Ruffled, Always Helpful":   23
                 Vassall in Moscow
Chapter Three   "The Suitable Candidate": Vassall in London   77
Chapter Four   "VINE LEAF"   123
Chapter Five   "The Wretched Galbraith"   209
Chapter Six   "Why the Devil Did You Catch Him?":   279
                 Vassall in jail
Chapter Seven   "Hope and Confidence": Vassall after release   357

Conclusion: "Out in the cold"   391
Acknowledgements   421
Sources and Bibliography   425
Index   441

PROLOGUE

AS IF NOTHING HAD HAPPENED

It was the men in white overalls that first sent a shiver down his spine.

Throughout the first eight months of 1962 John Vassall, a 37-year-old clerk at the British Admiralty in London, 'had a strong premonition that something was wrong'. After seven years of handing defence secrets over to the Russians, both in Moscow and in London, he sensed that his time was up. 'It was a most unpleasant sensation, feeling that time might be running out,' Vassall later recalled. He could not make up his mind what was worse: the agony of carrying on with his double life, or the fear that at any moment he might be unmasked.

In the spring, a number of odd incidents at Dolphin Square, the apartment complex in Pimlico where he lived, made Vassall fear that he was under surveillance there. In February his neighbours at 806 Hood House, Mr and Mrs Kitchen, installed a spy hole in their front door, directly opposite Vassall's flat, number 807. At eight o'clock one Monday morning, after Vassall had been on one of his regular weekends out of London, his doorbell rang. Vassall was woken up and approached his front door in his dressing gown. A 'solemn, civil service sort of voice' announced, through the locked door, that there had been 'an accident upstairs'.

When Vassall opened the door he found three men in white overalls, carrying a ladder, who told him that they needed to check his kitchen because someone had spilt acid down the sink in the flat upstairs. When the men entered his flat they had a good look around, not just at the kitchen, but the other rooms too, all elegantly furnished with Queen Anne antiques. After they left Vassall contacted Dolphin Square's maintenance staff, who told him that they knew nothing.

Vassall was convinced that the men were British spies, who had wanted to search his flat and were disappointed to find him at home. 'I had not the strength to do anything but wait for one side or the other to come and collect me', he later recalled. In fact, it can't have been a police or MI5 operation, as the visitation was in February or March 1962, and Vassall wasn't under suspicion until April at the earliest. The men were indeed workmen investigating the plumbing, and the square's maintenance department had simply not been informed they were coming. But in a sense Vassall was right: the authorities were now on the lookout for a spy who was passing secrets from the Admiralty to the Soviet Union, and it was only a matter of time before he was caught.

For Vassall, Dolphin Square had changed from a party palace into a castle of Kafkaesque paranoia. For three-and-a-half years he had lived there alone, in a small but pleasant flat on the eighth floor, overlooking the square's large internal garden. Little did Vassall know that his tenancy there had proved to be his undoing: once his name was on a shortlist of four men suspected of being Soviet spies in the Admiralty, suspicions about how a poorly paid clerk could afford the rent on his Dolphin Square flat, and to decorate it with expensive Queen Anne furniture, were the major reason why his name rose to the top of the list, and why MI5 put him under surveillance there.

Early in the morning on Wednesday 12 September, Vassall looked out of his windows and saw a 'strange face' – a burglar, he assumed – peering out of the window of a nearby flat where he'd once had drinks. Vassall left a note for his cleaner, who was due to come the following day, warning her to keep an eye out for an intruder. It was 'an awful premonition of disaster'. John Vassall was now at the epicentre of one of the Cold War's most serious spy scandals.

As always, Vassall dressed carefully, wearing a grey suit and green hat, and picked up a document case, yesterday's newspaper and a rolled umbrella as he left his flat. At about 9.15, as he walked from the lift through the ground floor lobby of his block, he saw a 'large, burly man who watched me intently as I passed'. At a nearby bus stop he caught the number 24 bus to Whitehall, as he did every weekday. But on this particular day Vassall sensed, as someone got off the bus behind him at his stop, that he had been tailed all the way from Pimlico. The man followed him towards the Admiralty building's main entrance on Horse Guards Parade.

A few months earlier, Vassall had invited his cousin Nancy, her husband and two sons to join him in his Admiralty office, watching through a window as the Queen rode on horseback at the Trooping of the Colour ceremony on Horse Guards Parade: a rare perk of his job. But today he felt that he was no longer a spectator, but the spectacle. He was being followed, and watched. As he entered the Admiralty building at 9.46, Vassall thought he spotted a tall man, playing with a waste-paper basket, through one of the windows of the Naval Intelligence division, where he'd worked a few years earlier.

His working day passed like any other: a mundane mixture of writing up notes, fetching files, copying them for distribution, and then returning them to cupboards. Towards the end of the afternoon Vassall glanced out of a window and saw a strange car parked in the Admiralty's quadrangle. Whenever anyone came out of the building, its occupants seemed to jump up in their seats, to check if it was the person they were waiting for. Vassall opted to leave the building by a different exit, at its north-western corner on Admiralty Place, a short street that runs from the Mall to Spring Gardens.

He had traveller's cheques to pick up at the post office on Trafalgar Square, which he needed for a forthcoming holiday in Italy. A flight to Rome was already booked for Friday 15 September. From the Admiralty Place entrance, it was a short walk down the eastern end of the Mall, under Admiralty Arch and across Trafalgar Square to the post office. He would avoid the strange car and its even stranger occupants.

What Vassall did not know was that the Metropolitan Police's Special Branch had stationed an officer with a telephoto lens in New Zealand House, a tall building under construction on Pall Mall, which overlooked the shortcut he was taking. There was now no chance of escape. He would never enjoy his Italian holiday.

Vassall finished work and left his office just before six, as usual. As he crossed the Mall at 18.05 'two men in mackintoshes came forward, *Third Man* style, flashed me a warrant and asked me to accompany them to a car waiting by the statue of Captain Cook'. The statue was on the south side of The Mall's red tarmac, facing away from the Admiralty's stately red-brick and Portland stone façade. Vassall had been thinking about his forthcoming holiday so intently that he had not noticed the parked car he had walked past moments earlier.

Many key events of the twentieth-century Cold War, and the Cold War that restarted in the second decade of the twenty-first, took place in central London – including two audacious assassinations. In September 1978 a Bulgarian defector called Georgi Markov, who was working at the BBC World Service in Bush House, was assassinated (probably with a pellet containing ricin at the end of an umbrella wielded by a member of the Bulgarian secret service) as he walked to work over Waterloo Bridge. In November 2006, the former Russian Federal Security Service (FSB) officer Alexander Litvinenko was poisoned with polonium at the Millennium Hotel on Grosvenor Square, just yards from where the American embassy then stood (he died of radiation poisoning at University College Hospital three weeks later). But neither Waterloo Bridge, nor Grosvenor Square, are as iconic as the spot where Vassall was arrested.

The eastern end of the Mall, London's equivalent of Paris's Champs Élysées and Washington's National Mall, is in direct sight of Buckingham Palace, and just 200 yards from Nelson's Column. It is within a stone's throw of 10 Downing Street and many government departments. It is just yards from Waterloo Place, which is dominated by a high column topped by a statue of Prince Frederick, Duke of York, commander-in-chief of the British army during the Napoleonic Wars. Vassall was arrested right on the ceremonial route that many royal coronation, wedding and funeral processions have taken over the last 200 years, from Buckingham Palace to Westminster Abbey or St Paul's Cathedral.

Vassall recognised one of the men who approached him as a special branch detective who had guarded Nikita Khrushchev and Nikolai Bulganin during their stay at Claridge's Hotel in April 1956. Suddenly, the sequence of bizarre encounters at Dolphin Square over the last few months – mysterious strangers in corridors and lifts, bogus maintenance men gaining access to his flat by subterfuge – made sense.

Vassall was bundled – 'panting with fear,' one policeman noted – into the car. A female special branch detective spoke into its radio. A few minutes later two more senior officers, a superintendent and a chief inspector, climbed in, and asked Vassall to give them his briefcase so they could search it. Vassall complied, but inside it they found only personal papers. Vassall said 'I suppose this is because I have been in Russia', as if he was hoping, in vain, that this was a routine stop of a civil servant who had once worked behind the Iron Curtain. In fact, it was anything but routine.

On the car's back seat, Vassall was flanked by two officers who were already well known as Britain's foremost 'spycatchers'. The older of the two was Chief Supt George Gordon Smith, who had helped to unmask a string of Soviet spies in the 1950s and early 1960s – among them Klaus Fuchs, Alan Nunn May, the Portland spy ring and George Blake. George Smith had been waiting at the main exit of the Admiralty building to apprehend Vassall, but he rushed round the corner to the Mall as soon as he heard on his radio that Vassall had been arrested there. He later said that Vassall had 'the face of a fox he had once seen trapped in a gin-trap'.

While George Smith was only a few weeks away from retirement, the other man, Detective Chief Inspector Ferguson Smith, was still on the up: in 1966 he would become the Metropolitan Police's Deputy Assistant Commissioner, and the *de facto* head of Special Branch. Born in Aberdeen in 1913, Ferguson Smith had flown with Bomber Command and won the Distinguished Flying Cross in January 1944, during the Battle of Berlin. Like the older Smith, Ferguson had helped to unmask Klaus Fuchs, a German theoretical physicist who had supplied information from the Manhattan Project to the Soviet Union. In 1950 Ferguson Smith had hidden in a cupboard at Brixton prison to eavesdrop on an incriminating conversation between Fuchs and another German scientist.

Ferguson Smith later recalled that not long after he and George Smith joined Vassall in the car, he told them 'I know what you are after'. Even before the car reached New Scotland Yard, only half a mile away, Vassall had told them much of what they had hoped to hear, and confirmed much that they already knew. When George Smith asked Vassall whether he owned any cameras, Vassall immediately told him that the police would find Minox and Exakta cameras, in brown leather cases, and several films (both used and unused) in a drawer of the mahogany desk in his Dolphin Square flat. He did not know that MI5 had already searched it after he had left for work that morning and found them all.

Vassall also told the police about a crucial hiding place that MI5 had failed to unearth: a bookcase in the corner of his bedroom, whose base had a hidden compartment full of more films. The bookcase had been given to Vassall by the Russians in late 1959 or early 1960. Like Vassall himself, it had hidden in plain sight. Later on, Vassall even provided the police with useful advice on how to prise the compartment open – with a steel blade, kept in an oblong box on another piece of furniture in the bedroom.

As Vassall began to spill the beans, he was driven slowly past numerous symbols of British prestige: under Admiralty Arch, clockwise around Nelson's Column in Trafalgar Square and down Whitehall, past Admiralty House – where Harold Macmillan's government was being run from – past the entrance to Downing Street (which Macmillan had temporarily vacated for reconstruction work), the Ministry of Defence, the Foreign Office, and the north-eastern corner of Parliament Square. Vassall arrived at New Scotland Yard, on the Victoria Embankment, at 18.25. He was taken up several flights of stairs to a large room and asked to sit down. One superintendent there seemed breathless with anxiety, Vassall recalled, but the other officers were silent like the night.

Vassall was asked to hand over the keys to his flat, so it could be searched again – officially this time – and he did so immediately, without complaint. Then, Vassall himself was searched. On his person were found two combs, a fountain pen, a book of stamps, a few pounds in cash inside a brown leather wallet with the initials J. V., an official Admiralty pass (number 05600), three Admiralty keys – and a return ticket from Victoria to Streatham Hill. Only later did MI5 discover the significance of another scrap of paper, inscribed with a diagram and indecipherable letters: handwritten instructions on how to operate his Minox camera, which only made sense to the initiated.

The police could not believe their luck. Not only had they arrested Vassall: he had confessed immediately to all the spying that he was suspected of, and more. In both the big spy cases that the detectives Smith had worked on in 1961, the men and women they arrested had protested their innocence. The five Portland spies had denied everything, and despite overwhelming evidence, four of them pleaded not guilty at their Old Bailey trials in March 1961. Likewise, it was only after three days of what could be described as a very British interrogation of George Blake – at MI6's offices in London, at the legendary molehunter Harold Shergold's country cottage in Hampshire (where Blake made pancakes for his interrogators), and at a house in suburban East Sheen – that Blake finally confessed to being a Soviet spy. It has been claimed that if Blake had not confessed when he did, his interrogators would soon have run out of questions, and as they only had circumstantial evidence, they may have had to release him.

Vassall was very different: the evidence against him was strong, and he confessed everything immediately. The sense of triumph felt by the police and MI5 would be short-lived, however. Little did they know that within a few months, the aftershocks of Vassall's arrest would lead to a ministerial resignation, newspaper headlines about a vast network of homosexual spies across Whitehall and Westminster, reporters being sent to jail and the near demise of Harold Macmillan's government. The worst part of John Vassall's ordeal may have been over, but for the British establishment the nightmare was just beginning.

CHAPTER ONE

"A SECRET WORLD"

John Vassall's surname always suggested divided loyalties. A vassal is (or was) a feudal tenant in medieval Europe – a man who was obliged to fight for a king or landowner whenever they were needed, in exchange for land to live on. A vassal state is one under the control of a more powerful country, to which it must give money, or military support, when ordered. But most of the Vassalls have been anything but underlings. Instead, many of them were colonial adventurers, statesmen and senior military officers. Most English families remain in the same part of England for generations, or even centuries, on end. The Vassall family is different: from the sixteenth century onwards they were nomads who constantly moved between France, England, the American colonies and the West Indies.

Ultimately the Vassalls are not English anyway: their earliest certain ancestor, the first John Vassall, was a French Huguenot, of the house of Du Vassall in the Périgord (present-day Dordogne), which could trace its roots back to the eleventh century. This John Vassall arrived in England in the 1500s to escape 'dissensions then prevailing in Normandy'. His son, another John, is said to have fitted out, at his own expense, two ships that he commanded in battle against the Spanish Armada in 1588. He was granted arms by

Queen Elizabeth with the motto 'Often for the Throne, Always for the Country': an ironic maxim for an ancestor of one of Britain's most notorious twentieth-century spies.

John Vassall the spy was descended from William Vassall, the fifth child of John Vassall the Armada hero. William was born in Stepney in 1592, but in 1635 he went to New England and later settled in Barbados, where he died in 1655. For several further generations, the Vassalls owned swathes of land in New England and sugar plantations in Jamaica, maintained by slave labour (several Vassall wills bequeath "Negroes, Cattle, Utensils and Stock" to the next generation). But from the late eighteenth century onwards most of John Vassall's ancestors lived and died in England.

Back in their native land, the Vassall family remained nomads: over the next 150 years they constantly moved between Somerset, Gloucestershire, Leicestershire, Yorkshire, Devon and Bedfordshire, and one member of the family worked and died in France. One Vassall ancestor served as a staff surgeon in the Peninsular War, but John Vassall's paternal great-grandfather, grandfather and father were all Anglican churchmen, and all three of them were called William. The first William was born in Wigston, Leicestershire, in 1824 and studied at St John's College, Cambridge before being ordained in 1851. He was rector of Hardington Mandeville, a small village in Somerset, where he died in 1883. This William had no fewer than fifteen children by his wife Martha (née Skelton). Their eldest son, another William, was born in Yorkshire in 1858 and educated at Cheltenham College and a theological college in Gloucester, where in 1884 he married Alice Maud Holland. After ordination he became rector of Weare Giffard, in Devon. But from 1891 onwards he was a British chaplain at St Servan, a village just south of St Malo in Brittany, where he died in 1896, aged only thirty-eight.

Despite his often tense relationship with his father, John Vassall was always keen to boast about the paternal side of his family. As a child one of his proudest possessions was a forty-page book, entitled *John Vassall and His Descendants* (after his sixteenth-century ancestor and namesake), written in 1920 by Charles Maclear Calder (another Vassall descendant). Vassall's memoirs make much of the distant relatives who were Members of Parliament and Aldermen of the City of London. As an adult he constantly talked about Elizabeth Vassall, one of Georgian England's most scandalous women. In 1786 Elizabeth, then a wealthy heiress aged only fifteen, married a 38-year-old baronet, Sir Godfrey Webster. Although their marriage quickly produced five children, it was a disaster from the start. After persuading Webster to take her on a Grand Tour, Elizabeth met Henry Richard Fox, 3rd Baron Holland of Foxley and nephew of the Whig politician Charles James Fox, in Naples in early 1794. At first Elizabeth disliked his suntan – and wrote that he was "not in the least handsome". But they soon became lovers, and she scandalously gave birth to Henry's son, Charles Richard Fox, in November 1796.

Even more shockingly, on 4 July 1797 she was divorced by Webster. He was awarded Elizabeth's fortune of £7,000 a year, £6,000 in 'damages' from Holland and custody of their children. Two days after her divorce she married Henry Vassall-Fox and became Lady Holland, and a legitimate son, another Henry, was born in 1802. Elizabeth became one of Regency and early Victorian England's most renowned hostesses. At Holland House, on the western outskirts of London, Elizabeth Vassall-Fox entertained the Prince of Wales, Henry's Whig friends, and writers including Sheridan, Byron, Dickens, Disraeli and Wordsworth so that by the time of her death in 1845 the 'Holland House set' was considered one of the great political and literary salons of the age and her scandalous youth was almost forgotten.

John Vassall the spy's connection to Elizabeth Vassall and the 'Holland House set' is tenuous. Thousands of English families can boast of obscure connections to aristocracy, but few do so. John

Vassall, however, could never stop boasting about his. He constantly bragged that two of his great-uncles had played rugby for Oxford University and England, and that they had been housemasters at Harrow and Repton. He once boasted that one of his aunts was a friend of the writer and broadcaster Malcom Muggeridge.

The historian Richard Deacon once wrote that Vassall's family background was 'about as highly respectable an entourage into which anyone could be born'. Respectable, maybe, but certainly not rich. John Vassall was not in the wealthiest of the Vassall family's many lines. Church of England vicars were (and to some extent still are) people of high social standing but unlike many clergymen, Vassall's father and grandfather do not seem to have received remittances from wealthier brothers or cousins.

John Vassall's father, yet another William, was born on 10 July 1885 at 132 London Road, Wotton, a district on the eastern side of Gloucester. He was ordained in 1910 and began his career as curate of St Barnabas, Bethnal Green. Like his son, his early life was disrupted by a world war. In 1917 he went to the Western Front with the YMCA, and according to some accounts he was a Temporary Chaplain to the Forces (TCF) in Mesopotamia as well as France. He married Vassall's mother, Mabel Audrey Sellicks, on 12 July 1923.

Mabel had been working as a nurse at St Bartholomew's Hospital when she met William, who worked there briefly as a chaplain. She was from a different strata of England's rigid interwar class structure. While the Vassalls were a family of plantation owners, statesmen and senior military officers, the Sellickses were very much 'other ranks' and not from the officer class.

Mabel was born on 13 November 1895 at the South Front Barracks in Hougham, near Dover, where her father (a sergeant in the 2nd Queen's Royal Regiment) was stationed. Vassall described her fondly as 'sweet-natured and sympathetic', with a 'streak of non-conformity'. By the time he reached adulthood Vassall was far closer to his mother than his father but in his 1975 memoirs, he spurned the more humble Sellicks side of the family. He made no mention whatsoever of his maternal grandparents, and only remarked that his mother 'was born in Kent, but preferred London'. His mentions do not even contain the Sellicks name.

● ● ●

William John Christopher Vassall was born at St Bartholomew's Hospital, where his mother had been a nurse, on 20 September 1924. While the name William was used on his charge sheet in 1962, he reportedly always hated it. From birth he was always known as John, no doubt to distinguish him from all the other William Vassalls.

Some accounts of Vassall's childhood claim that it was happy, but his parents' marriage was miserable from the start. Apart from class differences, there was a substantial age difference of eleven years. Around the time of John's birth, William became the vicar of St Peter's, Stepney, though he only stayed there for two years. He finally settled down in 1926 as vicar of Christ Church, Hendon, a town that was well on its way to becoming a London suburb. William stayed there for fifteen years, until 1941, but Vassall's memoirs contain no reminiscences of a childhood in a Middlesex vicarage. He grew up heavily dependent on the generosity of relatives, particularly three unmarried great-aunts, the Misses Vassall – Kate, Nellie and Amy (born in 1866, 1868 and 1869 respectively) – who lived in some grandeur at Hurst Manor in the village of Martock, Somerset.

At Hurst Manor the three great-aunts 'entertained lavishly, had an army of servants, tennis courts and a huge garden'. But they were also terrible snobs, with the unflattering nickname 'The Tartars'. One of them once walked out of a draper's shop as soon as she spotted Vassall and his mother inside it. None of the great-aunts seem to have approved of Vassall's Kentish mother, presumably because she was the daughter of an army sergeant, not an officer. Vassall told MI5 in the 1960s that his father's sisters had never been on speaking terms with his mother, and that one of his aunts, Molly Wickham, 'behaved as if she were the bride' at his parents' wedding.

From an early age Vassall was always on the fringes of wealth and privilege, but was never quite a beneficiary of either. He can at best be described as being at the 'shabby genteel' end of the middle classes. A vicar's job is poorly paid, and as William would later discover, precarious.

John first attended The Hall (one of Hampstead's foremost prep schools, founded by an Anglican clergyman in 1889), followed by Lee House in Hampstead Garden Suburb, whose headmaster, and his wife, often took pupils on trips to Angmering, Sussex. Before long he was, like many middle-class boys, sent away to boarding school: Seaford House prep school in Littlehampton. Even in early childhood, he seems to have been on the lookout for famous people or those who would later become famous: his memoirs happily note that at Seaford House he used to bathe in the English Channel under the supervision of a schoolmaster named Derek Farr, who later became an actor and played the part of Group Captain John Whitworth in the 1955 hit film *The Dam Busters*.

Vassall's memoirs contain a strange list of excuses for why he did not attend a prestigious public school. He was not sent to Trinity College in Perthshire because of the cost of travel, Marlborough was spurned because its boys never wore overcoats, and Charterhouse was ruled out because his mother disliked 'fagging', and the headmaster's wife. The real reason he ended up at a much less prestigious school – Monmouth, near the border of England and Wales – is probably because it was all that the impecunious Vassall family could afford.

Monmouth School was founded in the 1600s. Today it is a growing institution, but in the late 1930s it was a tiny school, and almost unknown beyond the Welsh Marches. When Vassall arrived in

September 1938, just before his fourteenth birthday,[1] Monmouth's headmaster was W. R. Lewin, a First World War pilot who had become the school's Modern Languages master in 1937. When hostilities began in 1939, Lewin enlisted and became a lieutenant-colonel in the Royal Armoured Corps, 'but in reality, given his linguistic prowess, [he was] almost certainly in Military Intelligence', the school's history notes.

Vassall's memories of Lewin, sent to the Radcliffe tribunal in 1963, are in sharp contrast to his school contemporaries. He had heard that in School House there was 'sexual impropriety between boys' and that Lewin – who was School House's housemaster as well as the school's head – 'had gone into a boy's or prefect's room at night and that one of the boys had told him to get out. He used to creep around at night for immoral purpose.'[2] Vassall was told that Lewin had agreed to resign 'of his own will and take up a post in the Intelligence Corps' soon after 'the incident in the boy's room'. Although Lewin can have barely known Vassall, who was still a very junior pupil when Lewin left Monmouth in 1939, Vassall sought his help in the 1940s. In the early 1960s, when Lewin was working alongside Vassall at the Admiralty, the connection between them prompted much tabloid speculation that Lewin had been Vassall's 'protector' there.

Vassall seems to have put a brave face on being sent to a 'minor' public school. He may have appreciated being away from his parents' dysfunctional marriage, and he seems to have had little to do with his younger brother, Richard Henry Holland Vassall, born on 10 March 1926. Although Richard was barely eighteen months

---

1   Some accounts claim that Vassall did not arrive at Monmouth until the outbreak of the war a year later. The school's own records suggest otherwise.

2   Vassall's own housemaster in New House was Ross Irvine, a geography teacher. Irvine's advice to pupils was "write short sentences, read a good newspaper every day, noting down any words not understood which, once their meaning is clear, should be used in the next composition, and read the *Book of Common Prayer* to acquire a feeling for style and cadence". This appears to be advice that Vassall, whose writing style was often mannered and stilted, always followed.

younger than John, he barely features in Vassall's account of his childhood.

Vassall developed an artistic streak and had precocious ambitions to become a concert pianist or a sculptor. He spent much time walking the Wye Valley between Monmouth and Tintern Abbey. He later recalled that he had enjoyed rugby, hockey and cricket, and that he had even boxed for his house. Above all, it was at Monmouth that he had his first sexual experiences – with other boys.

Accounts of nineteenth- and early twentieth-century public schools are full of homosexual fumblings. As W. T. Stead said, during the trial of Oscar Wilde, 'Should everyone found guilty of Oscar Wilde's crime be imprisoned, there would be a very surprising emigration from Eton, Harrow, Rugby and Winchester to the gaols of Pentonville and Holloway.' Yet for Vassall, school was not an experimental phase but a genuine sexual awakening. He later wrote that he was 'addicted to homosexual practice from youth'.

'The first person I had a really deep experience with was a rugby football player,' he recalled.

I first noticed him in the fives courts: a massive, well-built, tough man. I watched him play in the first XV, in scrum-cap and white shorts, and found him very earthy and sexually stimulating. I never dreamt that we should meet, but one day we did, when I was practising the piano in one of the classrooms.

Soon after his imprisonment in 1962, Vassall reminisced in the *Sunday Pictorial* about the grip of this 'sturdy rugger type' on his shoulders as he played the piano. 'I knew it was prompted by the sexual urge … an urge to which I had to respond. This was the first time I experienced it' – and by no means the last.

The rugby player was one of several boyfriends. In his early teens Vassall began 'to form secret and intimate friendships with older boys, whom I thought of as mature beings, strong, masterly and physically attractive', and whom he looked up to as 'Greek Gods'. 'I was drawn to them like iron filings to a magnet,' he recalled.

But some other boys were far less pleasant to be around. Unlike most of the farmers' sons Vassall was at school with, he was not 'from' anywhere: for three generations his family had moved around England, from one parish to another. Vassall's bragging about being 'well-connected' and his fawning over the school's grandest pupils meant that he was quickly nicknamed 'serf'. Norman Lucas, a *Sunday Pictorial* journalist who wrote much about Vassall in 1962 and 1963, claimed that "Monmouth, famous for its rugby players and its rowing fours, was not much to his taste". He seemed happiest singing in the choir and playing the piano on his own. Lucas also contended that Vassall was soon labelled as 'queer', and that he often sobbed into his pillow after lights out, until an older boy crept into his bed to 'caress' him: 'his first step into the world of homosexuals'.

Like every other aspect of Vassall's life, journalistic accounts of his schooldays are often steeped in supposition, stereotype and homophobia. Richard Deacon wrote that while most public schoolboys 'throw off these [homosexual] proclivities when they go out into the world' and 'adapt to the company of women ... Vassall's tragedy was that in his case the metamorphosis did not take place and subsequent events prevented any such development'. Deacon, like others, suggested that Vassall was simply an immature Peter Pan who never grew out of his teenage aberration.

Monmouth is not the kind of school whose 1930s and 1940s class lists read like a roll call of the Great and Good. Victor Spinetti (a Welsh actor best known for his roles in the Beatles films *A Hard Day's Night*, *Help!* and *Magical Mystery Tour*, and the 1971 film of *Under Milk Wood*) was a pupil at Monmouth in the 1940s. In his autobiography Spinetti recalled that he once saw 'a boy bouncing up and down on another boy' in a locker room. 'To me, then, it was almost meaningless. I closed the door and went off to the game'

Spinetti wrote. Vassall's only exact contemporary of note was John Gwilliam, later a well-known rugby player who played for (and often captained) Wales in the late 1940s and early 1950s. Gwilliam was born in 1923 and was in the year above Vassall, but there is no evidence that he was the "sturdy rugger type" who propositioned Vassall while he was playing the piano.[3]

One of the perversities of the British class system is that on top of the educational gulf between state and private schools, there is another, equally deep, chasm between the top public schools and more minor ones. Even today, writers look down their noses at Monmouth and mock Vassall for having gone there. As Simon Kuper, George Blake's biographer, says, Vassall went to a 'boarding school so minor that it had run out of money and turned into a grammar soon after his time there'. In turn, Monmouth remains ashamed to have had Vassall as one of its pupils. Fifty years after his conviction, the school's official history, published in 2014 to mark its 400th anniversary, was ungenerous. 'Mercifully, there are few notorious villains among Old Monmothians,' it said. 'It is true that just as Marlborough had Anthony Blunt, so Monmouth had a traitor in the person of the spy who worked in the Admiralty Department: John Vassall. But this is the exception in a list of alumni of whom the school can be proud.'

Overall, Vassall recalled that he was 'both lonely and unhappy' at Monmouth, but he showed the school a curious degree of loyalty in later life. For nearly twenty years after he left, he provided updates for 'O.M. News', the alumni section of the school's magazine. In December 1942 *The Monmothian* reported that 'John Vassall (1938–41) has a post in the Victualling Department at the Admiralty' and in July 1954, the magazine carried the news that

---

3   The Russian–British actor Richard Marner (best known for playing the Nazi colonel, Kurt von Strohm in the sitcom *'Allo 'Allo!*) was at Monmouth in the 1930s, but as he was born in 1921 he would only have overlapped with Vassall for a year or two.

W. J. C. Vassall (1938–41) was recently appointed Secretary to the Naval Attaché in Moscow for two years. He writes that although life behind the 'Iron Curtain' is fantastic, he is thoroughly enjoying himself [*sic*]; but he would be most interested to hear from any contemporary O.M.s, if they would write to him c/o The Bath Club, 74 St. James's Street, London, S.W.1.

In January 1959 there was a further update: 'W. J. C. Vassall (1938–41) has now left the British Embassy in Moscow. ... He is now Assistant Private Secretary to the Civil Lord of the Admiralty, a post in which he finds a pleasing absence of routine.' As often happened, Vassall's account exaggerated his status. He was only ever a clerk, never a secretary or an assistant private secretary. From 1954 onwards, sending these boastful and embroidered updates to his old school's magazine appears to have been a way of blotting out the awful truth: he had been trapped into treachery, with no escape. Less than four years after Vassall's final update he was in prison, beginning an eighteen-year sentence for espionage. If there were any 'O.M.s' in Wormwood Scrubs, Vassall was not keen on letting them know that he could be found there.

• • •

Vassall left Monmouth in the spring of 1941, aged sixteen-and-a-half, before he could sit his school certificate exams. His departure was not voluntary, but he was not expelled as some have speculated. Vassall later claimed he was never told why he left school suddenly but it is clear that it was because of an insurmountable problem: lack of money. Vassall's father had lost his living in Hendon because of the Anglican parish's disapproval of his mother's conversion to Catholicism in 1932, and he could no longer afford to pay the fees.

Mabel's conversion meant that the Vassalls' unhappy marriage was further tainted by resentment. Vassall claimed that his father could have become a bishop had it not been for the problem that her conversion caused. Instead, William was forced to assume a more poorly paid and insecure position as a Royal Air Force (RAF) chaplain, while Mabel found war work in the Mechanical Transport Corps. Vassall made no secret of his anger that he could not fulfil his ambition of studying at Keble College, Oxford, as his father had. Still only sixteen, he had to settle for work as a clerk at the Midland Bank's Poultry branch, in the City of London, for a few months in summer 1941: the first of a lifetime of clerical jobs.

As with all his other jobs, Vassall made his time at the Midland Bank sound much more prestigious than it really was, and he also extended the time he spent there from a few months to a year. 'On leaving school I spent a year in Banking in London … I liked the atmosphere … but the work was all to do with paper, nothing to do with people,' he wrote in his memoirs, implying that he was "something in the City" – a kind of management trainee, rather than a bank cashier.

At just seventeen, Vassall left the Midland Bank and became a temporary clerk in the Admiralty's records office: the first of many jobs there. The Admiralty had been the administrative cornerstone of the Royal Navy ever since its establishment by Charles I in 1628. Until its absorption into the Ministry of Defence in the 1960s the Admiralty was, according to Nigel West, Whitehall's 'Holy of Holies'. As an island nation, Britain's Royal Navy was always the senior service, and normally the one in which royals served. Vassall's jobs at the Admiralty were always lowly, but it was an institution that radiated power and prestige and Vassall always seemed proud to work there, even after he began spying for the Soviet Union.

Vassall applied for flying duties in the RAF on 25 November 1942, just after his eighteenth birthday. He later claimed that by that stage of the war aircrew were not needed, but in fact he was turned down, without any reason being given. His application, Norman Lucas later wrote, was 'surprising' because Vassall was a 'timorous youth and not at all of the stuff from which heroes are made'. Vassall then started, possibly with help from family friends, another temporary posting as a 'clerk Grade III' in the Admiralty's victualling department – effectively its catering corps. Although he insisted to *The Monmothian* that his job there 'puts him in contact with many Naval Officers from abroad', and that it was 'most interesting', even his fertile imagination struggled to gild this lily. After the war, he admitted in a letter that he had dealt with nothing more exciting than 'rationing documents and post'.

Although they had rejected him as a pilot, in January 1943 the RAF called up the restless Vassall, still aged eighteen, for wartime service. Vassall went to a reception centre at Cardington, Bedfordshire – famous for its huge airship hangars, which remain to this day. He never became a pilot as he had wanted, but he did serve as a Leading Aircraftsman (Photography), and he soon became an expert with Leica cameras. Photography – both the compromising photographs that were taken of him, and the photographs that he was forced to take – was to haunt Vassall for the rest of his life.

Vassall's memoirs are vague about the details of his wartime service, saying only that he worked at 'airfields in north-west Europe' and 'served on the continent under active conditions'. He added that 'I remember being with the Tactical Air Force with fighter and medium bomber aircraft ... We worked hard, irregular hours; emergency operations were announced at a moment's notice'. These ambiguous sentences imply that Vassall was taking photographs from aircraft flying on dangerous bombing missions. In fact, most wartime RAF photographers were on the ground, processing and printing photographs taken by aircrew, or taking photographs of people and events at RAF stations in Britain. With hindsight, it seems that Vassall was probably only sent to Europe well after VE Day: in his October 1962 confession he said that he had 'served in France, Belgium and the Holland after the finish of the war', not before.

It is certain however that after 1945, Vassall lived for a while in Holland, on an estate of modern 'Strength Through Joy' houses that had been built by the country's German occupiers. He travelled extensively in Belgium and northern France and he was particularly fond of Antwerp, where he met 'at least two Americans who I liked a great deal'. 'The first was of Polish origin, serving in the American army. We used to talk and have a quiet drink together, and wander happily about the city. The other man was called Robert. When he finally left Europe it took me two years to forget him.'

Most Old Monmothians would have avoided its former headmaster W. R. Lewin like the plague, given his reputation as a nocturnal prowler of dormitories. But before the war was over, Vassall had written to Lewin. This was the beginning of a lifelong habit of writing fawning letters to powerful people, soliciting their help, which would later prompt questions about whether he was seeking to become their lover.

While Vassall was on leave from the RAF he visited Lewin at his home in Cobham, Surrey. He asked his former headmaster for advice on getting on the 'aircrew list', without success. When Vassall was in Belgium after the war, he and Lewin corresponded again, and Vassall went to see Lewin in Brussels, where he worked in the Intelligence Corps. Lewin was 'extremely helpful in every way' and 'made no improper advances'. When Vassall was "demobbed" in March 1947 Lewin worked at the Civil Service Selection Board at Stoke D'Abernon, Surrey – a country house at which the leaders of the post-war civil service were nurtured. Vassall said that he visited Lewin at Stoke D'Abernon, but he did not join this elite group as he may have hoped. If Lewin was Vassall's lover and "protector", as some newspapers later implied, any help he gave Vassall seems to have ceased by 1947.

According to Norman Lucas, Vassall's RAF career was an ignominious failure. If journalism is the first draft of history, Lucas's book shows that the second draft – bad books written by journalists

– is often no better. 'His family background and public-school education might have helped him to gain a commission, but he had none of the qualities of leadership needed in an officer and he remained in the lower ranks', where he was apparently 'ashamed of the menial tasks he had to perform'. In fact, there is no evidence that Vassall ever sought to become an RAF officer. As Lucas reluctantly acknowledges, he was a success with 137 Wing, his photographic unit, and when he was demobilised his service record read that he had shown 'V.G. [very good] conduct throughout service'.

Lucas comments that Vassall was 'obviously drifting', but so were many young Englishmen whose education had been curtailed by the war. He portrayed Vassall as a uniquely troubled young man, rather than just one of hundreds of thousands (if not millions) of young gay men who were pondering their sexuality. Although Vassall never completed his secondary education, he tried to gain admission to Keble, his father's old Oxford college, after the war. He was interviewed by its warden, Harry Carpenter (later the Bishop of Oxford), who told him that they 'were looking for undergraduates who would get first-class honours degrees and nothing less'. Young men, like Vassall, whose university admission had been delayed by the war, were forced to compete with new cohorts of school leavers, and Vassall's application failed. 'At least I attempted the ascent, even if I did not reach the summit,' he later mused. It is hard not to admire his chutzpah.

Having been rejected by Oxford, in 1947 Vassall's 'main desire was to find a good job and start a new career'. His memoirs vaguely refer to going into 'some international concern with the backing of my father', but instead he ended up back where he had started. The Cold War was now in full swing, and the Admiralty still needed many clerks. From 1947 to 1954 Vassall held a number of jobs there, but he was never promoted, which Norman Lucas argues 'was a constant irritation to his snobbish vanity'.

To begin with Vassall worked in the Admiralty's Air Equipment

Division, and from November 1949 onwards in its Naval Law branch, where he spent his time drafting 'letters and reports on court martial procedure' and 'checking summary punishment returns'. Vassall moved on from Naval Law to the Admiralty's War Registry – its communications hub – in June 1952. The Admiralty appeared to tolerate, or turn a blind eye to, Vassall's homosexuality. Staff reports say that he was considered as 'defective in the power of judgment and of limited intellectual capacity', but also 'a discreet, reserved, and obliging young man, well-spoken and in appearance neat and well dressed'.

Vassall's working life from 1947 to 1954 is glossed over in his memoirs, which provide only scant details of his domestic and social life. By 1947 his parents were living at 1 Addison House, a ground-floor flat in a red-brick Edwardian mansion block in St John's Wood, and John and his younger brother Richard (who had completed his National Service in Singapore) moved in with them.

Outwardly, Vassall led a conventional life in the late 1940s. He became a member of the Young Conservatives Association in Marylebone and joined the Conservative Club at 74 St James's Street. It is not clear exactly when Vassall joined the club, or who his sponsors were, because many of its records were destroyed after its merger with the Bath Club in 1950. But Vassall was definitely a member by the time of the merger, and well before he went to Moscow in early 1954.[4]

One reason why Vassall's expensive tastes did not arouse much suspicion after his return from Moscow in 1956 was that he had started living beyond his means well before he went there, wearing 'velvet-collared, waisted overcoats, well-tailored suits and carefully selected accessories'. He probably paid little or no rent to his

---

4   The Bath Club, which was one of the few London clubs to allow women to join, placed a strong emphasis on sport; its indoor swimming pool is said to be the inspiration behind the fictional Drones club in P. G. Wodehouse's Jeeves and Wooster novels. After its Dover Street clubhouse was destroyed by bombing in 1941, the Bath moved in with the Conservative Club at St James's Street, ahead of the two clubs' formal merger in 1950 (which led to jokes about the new club being known as the 'Lava-Tory').

parents, and seems to have sought out the best clothes, restaurants and clubs to compensate for his lowly working life. By the late 1950s the Bath Club was far from being in the upper echelons of London's gentlemen's clubs, but Vassall's membership was certainly unusual for an Admiralty clerk. By 1962 the Bath had relocated to 41–43 Brook Street (next door to Claridge's and 900 yards from Leconfield House, MI5's headquarters), and Vassall appeared to 'spend quite a lot of his time' there, MI5's surveillance officers noted.

'For a short while, life was tolerably pleasant' for Vassall in the late 1940s, Lucas acknowledged. Yet it was only tolerably pleasant, because Vassall had to live a double life. Many of his friends and colleagues knew that he was gay, but like almost all gay men of his generation he never explicitly 'came out', and lived in constant fear of rejection, ridicule, or even prosecution. 'It is a secret world, a kind of masonic society to protect oneself from mankind because they can be so cruel', he wrote, decades later.

Vassall was coy about his post-war love life, but documents in MI5 files are much more forthcoming. They suggest that he met a 'discreet' Admiral called Bedford at a house party near Alton, Hampshire, in the late 1940s, and that he subsequently went to stay with him in Torquay. They also provide details of his first long-term relationship. In 1941 Vassall had met a young man called William Campbell while they were both temporary clerks in the Admiralty: for the first three or four days they shared the same desk. They lost touch later in the war, but had clearly made an impression on each other. In 1947, when they were both back at the Admiralty as clerks, they began an 'affair'. MI5 believed that they slept together at Campbell's flat in Newburgh Street, Soho, (these were the days when Admiralty clerks, even without money from the Russians, could afford to rent flats in Soho). They went to the theatre and in the coffee room of the Cumberland Hotel Campbell introduced him to another William, who also worked for the Admiralty. William Wilby had heard derogatory talk about Vassall from others and his 'unfavourable impression … was in no way dispelled' on meeting him. MI5 concluded that Wilby may have seen Vassall as a rival for Campbell's affections.[5]

Vassall seemed fond of Campbell, but he derided Vassall's pretentions behind his back. Their affair lasted only three months, and by the end of it Campbell was 'fully occupied with someone else'. Although the pair stayed in touch when Vassall went to Moscow, and they met socially a couple of times in the late 1950s, Campbell told MI5 that he had found Vassall to be an 'immature schoolboy'.

Vassall gave his double life a third dimension in the early 1950s. Having shown little interest in religion at school, he began turning to Christianity after undergoing a course in 'moral leadership' while in Belgium with the RAF. Remembering his childhood visits to Westminster Cathedral with his mother, it was to the Catholic Church, not his father's Church of England, that he turned. By the early 1950s, he was worshipping at the Church of the Immaculate Conception in Mayfair, commonly known as the Farm Street Church. Rather than worship in St John's Wood, Vassall seems to have deliberately sought out one of the capital's most prestigious Catholic parishes, in terms of both its Gothic revival architecture and its congregation – many of whom, Vassall included, lived far from Mayfair.

Once Vassall made it known that he wished to convert, he was assigned a layman – a sort of churchwarden – at Farm Street, a young barrister named Robin McEwen. Little did Vassall know that

---

5   Like Vassall, Wilby was entrapped by the Russians in 1959, while on holiday in Moscow. He had befriended a male ballet dancer called Sigerov and the KGB photographed them together in the Bucharest Hotel. Bravely, Wilby reported what had happened to his MP. With Wilby's agreement an MI5 tail was put on him when he went to meet a Russian contact at a pub on Tottenham Court Road, although the Russian never turned up. Given that Wilby had told him that his only important acquaintances were his MP, the singer Joan Sutherland, a costume fitter at the Royal Opera House and an art critic, clearly the KGB had decided he was not worth recruiting. MI5 later speculated that Vassall may have given the Russians Wilby's name as a potential target for blackmail, or even that Wilby had given the Russians Vassall's name ahead of his arrival in Moscow in 1954. Incredibly, MI5's files show that as late as 1971 they were investigating the details of Vassall's love life in the late 1940s, several years before he had started spying for the Russians.

his mentor would not only become a good friend, but one of his defence barristers at his Old Bailey trial in 1962.[6]

Vassall was received into the Catholic Church in 1953.[7] According to Norman Lucas, 'His religious beliefs had failed to subdue his homosexual proclivities and many of his weekends were spent at the homes of wealthy men who entertained him lavishly in return for his favours'. In fact, there is little certainty about Vassall's sex life before he arrived in Moscow and no evidence that he hired himself out as a high-class male sex worker as Lucas implied. Even his memoirs, published long after the decriminalisation of homosexuality, name none of his lovers. He had however very good reason to be discreet: although homophobia ebbed slightly during the war and in the immediate post-war years, in the early 1950s a crackdown began.

The shift in British attitudes was not a linear progression from prohibition to tolerance. Until 1885 only buggery (anal sex between heterosexual and homosexual couples) was a crime: in theory all other homosexual activities, as long as they were conducted in private, were not criminalised. Yet the 1890s saw a wave of homophobic prosecutions, most famously of Oscar Wilde, for "the love that dare not speak its name". But for much of the early twentieth century, prosecutions of gay men were relatively unusual and male gay couples, along with lesbians, often cohabited quite openly.

This tolerance ended soon after the Second World War. Between 1951 and 1954, with the rabidly homophobic David Maxwell Fyfe as Home Secretary, the police and judiciary began to actively seek out homosexual 'offences', often by lying in wait in public lavatories to entrap men seeking sex there. Maxwell-Fyfe declared that

---

6   After Eton, McEwen did his National Service with the Grenadier Guards, during which he reported on the Nuremberg Trials for *The Tablet* magazine. He studied law at Trinity College, Cambridge, and was called to the bar in 1951. He was always a polymath: alongside helping to write a new constitution for Pakistan, he was a skilled illustrator, producing topical cartoons and drawings for several books by Gavin Maxwell, including *Ring of Bright Water* and *Raven Seek Thy Brother*.

7   Some accounts say that Vassall's reception into the Catholic Church was in 1951, not 1953. It is generally agreed, however, that he was not confirmed as a Catholic until the 1960s, while in prison.

"homosexuals in general are exhibitionists and proselytisers and a danger to others especially the young" ... so long as I am Home Secretary I shall give no countenance to the view that they should not be prevented from being such a danger." By the mid-1950s, as David Caute puts it, "police, prosecutors and judges were on a homophobic rampage".

At the same time, the defections of the openly gay Guy Burgess and Donald Maclean (who was possibly bisexual) to Moscow in 1951 seemed to confirm many prejudices about gay men being naturally unreliable and unpatriotic.[8] MI5 began to take a particular interest in the sex lives of communists, such as the Marxist academic Arnold Kettle. Throughout the 1950s, the service monitored Kettle's 'homosexual tendencies' and "contact with homosexual friends in St Martin's Lane and Soho". The academic was part of what the scholar Maurice Bowra – who was himself gay – called the 'Homintern': a network of gay communists. While Bowra used the term partly in jest, from the early 1950s onwards MI5, and the Federal Bureau of Investigation (FBI) in America, became convinced that the Soviet bloc was devising a 'lavender conspiracy', using other gay travellers in the West to proselytise left-wing views. By the 1960s, some American conservatives even claimed that a Hollywood 'Homintern' was deliberately reducing the West's masculine resolve by producing 'camp' television series such as *Batman*.

Even the foremost hero of the Bletchley Park codebreakers was not exempt from the crackdown. After the mathematician Alan Turing was convicted of 'gross indecency', he was forced to undergo hormonal treatment and lost his job at GCHQ. He committed suicide in June 1954, possibly by eating an apple laced with cyanide. That same year, Lord Montagu of Beaulieu received a twelve-month prison sentence, having been found to have engaged in 'abandoned

---

8   Maclean had once been found drunk and naked with a gay Englishman in a flat in Alexandria, but rather than face disgrace, he was promptly promoted as head of the Foreign Office's American department. Before his defection, the unwritten rules about homosexuality were flexible and arbitrarily applied.

behaviour' with a journalist friend, a cousin and two RAF service-men in a beach hut. The year before, the actor John Gielgud was fined £10, after being found by police 'cruising' for sex at a public lavatory in Chelsea.

By the mid-1950s around 1,000 British gay men were being im-prisoned each year. If Britain's aristocrats, one of its most renowned actors and its most gifted codebreaker were not immune to the homophobia of the period, what hope did a humble Admiralty clerk like Vassall have?

Bored with his menial job, living with his parents and frustrated by the lack of privacy, it is hardly surprising that Vassall sought to escape London. In late 1953 he saw a circular advertising the post of clerk to the naval attaché in Moscow, and jumped at it. His timing was spot on: 1955, the only year he spent entirely in Moscow, was the peak year in Britain for prosecutions for gross indecency and other homosexual 'offences'.

'It all comes back so clearly. I was sitting in the Kremlin-like [Admiralty] building … when I saw a post in Washington and a post in Moscow were to be filled shortly,' Vassall remembered. 'The Washington post had just been filled, so with much trepidation I applied for the Moscow post, being ready to try a position which promised a completely new world of excitement and danger'. Just how exciting, and how dangerous, he could scarcely have imagined.

CHAPTER TWO

"NEVER RUFFLED, ALWAYS HELPFUL": VASSALL IN MOSCOW

John Vassall was never a civil service high-flyer. An annual personnel report from January 1954 said that he was "a difficult man to assess. So willing and courteous but has his limitations … [and] not yet ready for promotion". Vassall had been seeking an overseas posting for some time. During September 1953 he wrote a begging letter to John Carter, assistant to the new British ambassador in Washington, Sir Roger Makins, enclosing his photograph and asking for advice on emigrating to the US or finding a job there. Having received no reply, on 6 November Vassall wrote another ingratiating letter to the ambassador himself, saying that he had admired a speech that Sir Roger had recently made in Kentucky. "I can think of nothing more pleasant than marrying in the United States so I do hope you can help me", Vassall concluded.

On 10 November Carter replied on Sir Roger's behalf, to say that his original letter had been lost. Carter, himself married to an American, wrote "I am afraid the ambassador has no concrete suggestions to offer for enabling you to achieve your matrimonial and other designs on the United States". Postings to the US embassy were made via the Foreign Office, Carter reminded him, signalling that it was no use writing to embassies directly. Vassall wrote to Carter again on 30 November, to say "If by any chance you do hear of a friend wanting a young Englishman to work for him I do hope you will remember my name".

By now Vassall was writing to all and sundry: his final letter to Carter said that he had written directly to Lord Ismay, NATO's first Secretary General, but had been told that NATO "have no vacancies at the present".

Despite his lowly position and eccentric letter-writing, Vassall was sometimes successful at impressing interview panels. The field for the job of clerk to the naval attaché at the British embassy in Moscow was not, as some have suggested, weak: Vassall was one of forty applicants. Bachelors were actively encouraged because their housing costs were lower; only two of the forty applicants were married men.

Vassall now wrote another begging letter, to the First Lord of the Admiralty, J. P. L. Thomas, a fellow member of the Bath Club, to ask for his help in securing the Moscow appointment. In 1963 Lord Radcliffe found no evidence that Thomas (who had become Lord Cilcennin in 1956 and died in July 1960) had intervened on Vassall's behalf, though the precise nature of the friendship between the two men was not examined further.[9]

After a skiing trip in Zermatt (with David Marine, an American friend he first met in a Paris restaurant in 1951), in January 1954 Vassall faced an interview panel who considered his mediocre annual reports, interviewed him for 20–30 minutes, and observed him in his current role (mostly watching him type up documents). A longlist of eight was reduced to a shortlist of five. With or without Thomas's help, on 20 January Vassall was told that he had been successful.

---

9   J. P. L. (Jim) Thomas, MP for Hereford since 1931, was widely rumoured to be gay. As Simon Heffer, editor of "Chips" Channon's diaries, has written, "He and Channon were very close friends for a time, with quite possibly a closer relationship even than that." Channon himself was told by Thomas in 1947 that "no man who wasn't at least a touch homosexual would ever stand for Parliament".

At Vassall's final interview he was open about his religion and asked about "the availability of an American Roman Catholic priest at the embassy". It does not seem to have been a very robust interview. A report later shown to the Radcliffe tribunal said that because of his faith, Vassall "should therefore prove a politically reliable clerk and [a] steady character".

The espionage historian Nigel West has said that, with hindsight, Vassall was a "fairly obvious security risk" and that giving him a job in Moscow was "one of the worst appointments of all time". Vassall did not undergo the sort of positive vetting (PV), commonplace later, which could have uncovered his homosexuality. At that time, PV only applied to those with access to classified atomic secrets, or information that "would be of crucial value to an enemy or potential enemy". Vassall had access to neither. PV was later extended to all posts that provided "regular and constant access" to top-secret information, but this was not judged to apply to Vassall's position until March 1958, almost two years after he had returned to England.

Vassall's name seems to have been merely checked against a database of people who were known to have "subversive beliefs". The Radcliffe report later noted that on 28 August 1952 the Foreign Office had told Captain D. C. Ingram, a deputy director of naval intelligence, to take special care when hiring service attachés and "their subordinate staff". A memorandum was duly circulated, on which Mr H. V. Pennells – chair of the panel who appointed Vassall for Moscow –wrote "Noted. I will see that clerks, etc for Moscow and Warsaw [the only two cities behind the Iron Curtain which had naval attachés] are duly briefed". But the document was then filed away and forgotten about. Rightly or wrongly, Vassall had evaded the unwritten rule that gay men should not be posted abroad.

The day before he left London for Moscow Vassall saw, on the front pages of the evening newspapers at the Bath Club, headlines about Lord Montagu's arrest on indecency charges. He recalled that

"I thought to myself, thank goodness I am leaving the country". Vassall's eagerness to escape meant that when Thomas Crawley, an Admiralty official, offered advice on what to take to Moscow, and to put him in touch with someone who had been posted there before, Vassall replied "No, that is not necessary, I have a friend who has just come back from Russia and I can get all the advice I need from him".

Although Vassall left London on 2 March, he did not reach Moscow until five days later. En route he spent several days in Stockholm, whose "aroma of cold electricity" captivated him, and in Helsinki, where he saw Miss Finland being photographed in an airport departure lounge. The flight from Helsinki to Leningrad, where Vassall had to change planes to reach Moscow, had only three passengers: Vassall, the sister of the American ambassador's wife, and the French ambassador Louis Joxe (later a minister of justice under de Gaulle), who Vassall claimed to have had a friendly chat with. It was just the kind of elite passenger list that Vassall loved.

Richard Deacon and Nigel West have argued that if Vassall had arrived in Moscow a year earlier, before Stalin's death on 5 March 1953, he may have never been "compromised", as "he would have been virtually a prisoner within the British embassy compound with hardly any opportunity of meeting Russians". In the early 1950s the Foreign Office had even debated whether it was worth the trouble and expense of keeping a Moscow embassy at all. But under Stalin's successors – Georgy Malenkov, Nikolai Bulganin and Nikita Khrushchev – relations gradually thawed.

The British ambassador, Sir William Goodenough Hayter, had arrived in Moscow only five months before Vassall in October 1953, having been minister (in effect number two) at the British embassy in Paris. When his wife, Lady Iris Hayter, had suggested that his next posting might be Moscow, he had replied "Much too senior for me". But Moscow it was.

Aged forty-six in late 1953, Hayter was the youngest British ambassador anywhere in the world – and Moscow was a fascinating post so soon after Stalin's death. Back in the 1930s a London *Evening Standard* article had concluded that ambassadors were little more than "mere office boys ... handling only second-rate questions; all really important international matters were treated directly between heads of state". But now that the "Dark Night of Stalinism was over", 1953 to 1955 was a period of political turmoil in Moscow. Beria was executed, Molotov outmanoeuvred, and Malenkov gradually sidelined. Hayter was horrified by Churchill's 1953 speech advocating greater dialogue with the Soviet Union and he lamented that the Soviet Union "talks of coexistence, but they visualise it as the coexistence of the snake and rabbit". But Hayter soon found that he was "able ... to see more of Russia's rulers than perhaps any British ambassador since Lord Malmesbury became the confidant of Catherine the Great".[10] He also got to know Molotov, Gromyko and the loquacious Khrushchev, who reminded Hayter of Ernest Bevin and other old-school union leaders, as his shoulder "retained its chip". During the Tushino Air Show in 1956, Hayter and other members of the Presidium "settled down to some heavy drinking around a table in the open" – the only occasion when Hayter saw Khrushchev the worse for drink.

Crucially, the slight thaw in the Cold War meant that security at the British embassy was relatively light in the mid-1950s. The embassy did not have its own dedicated security officer: it was covered by a security officer in Vienna, 1,000 miles away, who seems to have only visited annually. During Hayter's post a man armed with a revolver once wounded a Russian policeman standing guard outside the embassy and took refuge in Hayter's dining room, until Hayter himself handed him over to the Russians.

There was hardly any "British colony" in Moscow in the 1950s,

10   Malmesbury was Great Britain's Envoy-extraordinary in St Petersburg from 1777–83.

other than a few journalists. Embassy staff "inevitably lived un-comfortable and generally confined and dull lives", Hayter recalled. If anything, fraternisation between Russian locals, embassy staff and British visitors was encouraged. "But … We never got to know any of them really well, never could make the kind of genuine and lasting friendships we had achieved in all our previous diplomatic posts, and were never once invited inside a Russian home".

Hayter said "it was rare that any attempt was made to force un-willing foreigners to drink more than was good for them … The bonhomie, so laboriously engendered, always seemed a little syn-thetic". By that score, John Vassall's tenure at the embassy, during which he befriended many Russians, was invited into their homes, and was rendered insensible by spiked drinks, was an unqualified success.

● ● ●

The British embassy that Vassall reported to on his arrival in Moscow in March 1954 is a palatial building. Standing on Sofiys-kaya Naberezhnaya with a superb view across the river towards the Kremlin and the onion domes of St Basil's Cathedral, the man-sion was built in 1893 for the "sugar king" Pavel Kharitonenko and designed by Vasily Zalessky. Externally it looked much like many other classical buildings in Moscow, but internally, British restraint was thrown out of the window. Its public rooms, still used for dip-lomatic events today, were designed by a well-known art nouveau architect, Fyodor Schechtel, and included a rococo white and gold ballroom with First Empire furniture, a galleried library and a pan-elled Renaissance room with British naval scenes on its walls.

If John Vassall had hoped that he would be allocated living quar-ters in this palace, he was quickly disappointed. While all Ameri-can diplomats in Moscow lived in their embassy, or at an American club, only a favoured few British diplomats lived in Kharitonenko's mansion, and Vassall was not one of them. Most embassy staff were scattered in apartments across the city to save money.

The officials who greeted Vassall seemed ill-prepared: they had been told he was married, not a bachelor. Vassall was told that he must share a flat in a utilitarian block (sometimes known as International House because of the mix of diplomats living there) at 13 Narodnaya Ulitsa. The block, which had been built by German prisoners of war, was near the north bank of the Moskva River and two miles south-east of the embassy. The flat was hardly spartan: it had parquet floors, double glazed windows and even a maid, Elizabeth, who cleaned and cooked lunch on weekdays (Vassall seems to have returned home for lunch sometimes), but it was far from the splendour that Vassall may have hoped for.

To begin with, Vassall shared the flat with John Richardson, a member of the Joint Press Reading Service, and Thomas Banks, the military attaché's clerk. When Vassall first arrived, Richardson (who was considered by some at the embassy to be "queer") seemed indifferent, going to have a bath without greeting him. Banks made him a cup of tea (or offered him a glass of whisky in some accounts). In 1963 Banks told MI5 that Vassall "alluded to incidents in the RAF which Banks interpreted as homosexual overtures", but that he liked Vassall and they stayed in touch.

Vassall was put in a small dining room by the kitchen. At least he was not made to sleep on a sofa, as newspapers later claimed, but he was still disappointed with the meagre flat. "We all agreed it was stark and unsuitable for entertaining," he recalled. Banks and Richardson soon moved out and another member of the Joint Press Reading Service, Stanley Jennings, moved in. Vassall now had a proper bedroom, and before long he and Jennings relocated to another flat in the same block.

The flatmates never asked each other about their private lives. Jennings was a "complete introvert" and "temperamentally ... almost a recluse", Vassall remembered. Unusually for an Englishman, he spoke fluent Russian. Vassall assumed that Jennings was gay, and that he spent nights with a Russian "man friend", but it later turned out to be a woman.[11] For his part, Jennings heard lots of embassy gossip about Vassall being gay and had jokingly been told to "watch out", though he told MI5 that Vassall had never made a pass at him. Jennings asserted that Vassall's "girlish titter" and "coy gestures" meant that almost everyone suspected he was gay. But "far from finding it embarrassing to share a flat with Vassall, Jennings found it was convenient", MI5 noted in October 1962. "Vassall was very meticulous in his ways and kept the flat looking very nice", giving its drab Ministry of Works furniture a new élan by tastefully arranging lamp shades and draping a travel rug over a settee.

The flat was still "rather dismal", Vassall recalled, but now that it was just the two of them he and Jennings seem to have become uncommunicative soulmates. Jennings often went out all night, not returning until 5 or 6 a.m., and on Saturdays and Sundays he spent most of the day in bed, catching up on sleep. This meant that the flat was often empty, or at least silent, for Vassall to do his own entertaining. He moved his divan into the sitting room so that Jennings no longer had to go through Vassall's room to reach his own. Eventually, Jennings returned to England and was replaced by Stanley Ford: another straight man who had been told that Vassall was gay, but did not mind living with him.

While Vassall found solace in his new home, the embassy was another matter. On his fifth day in Moscow Vassall was part of a group invited to lunch with the Hayters, a standard invitation for new staff. At first, Vassall thought that he and Lady Hayter had hit it off: it turned out that she and Vassall's mother had a mutual friend in London, "a woman doctor". Lunch was served on a mahogany table with placecards. There was caviar on crushed ice "with toast

---

11 Jennings was still unmarried when MI5 debriefed him in 1963, but no doubt because of his bragging about his Moscow girlfriend, Olga, MI5 concluded that he was probably not gay.

Melba and minute thimble glasses which held Vodka" – the first time Vassall had drunk it.

After the final course everyone retired to a small drawing-room for coffee, where Lady Hayter talked about bridge, and Vassall dropped a hint that he would like to be included in her parties. "Although I mentioned I enjoyed playing I was never taken up on it", he lamented.

Vassall later told MI5 that he came to view Lady Hayter as an "intolerable snob and totally lacking in feminine softness". Afterwards Vassall sent her a thank-you note, but "this apparently was not necessary and all it achieved was embarrassment for myself". Vassall had not realised that giving lunch to him and other new arrivals was not a pleasure for Lady Hayter, but a tiresome duty. Her diary merely recorded that "a new Mr Vassall" had come for lunch. Vassall himself seems to have been curiously resentful that the Hayters never paid a visit to his flat. "Perhaps it was reticence on their part", he ponders in his memoirs.

His relationship with his new boss, Captain Geoffrey Bennett, got off to an even more disastrous start. Bennett took his job, as the naval attaché at the British embassy in the capital of Britain's most deadly foreign foe, very seriously. Although the Royal Navy was shrinking rapidly, it was still the third-largest navy in the world, after the Americans' and the Soviets'. Bennett was tasked with discovering all he could about the development of the Red Navy. At times he acted like a spy: Bennett's wife later told their daughter-in-law, Perdita, that when she joined him on "recces" of Russian military installations she would carry a tape recorder in her pocket.

Vassall's job, however, was purely administrative: collecting keys and documents, returning them to the registry each night, and sealing envelopes with sealing wax. Roy Smith, the assistant military attaché, later told MI5 that "all that was required of the naval attaché's clerk was typing with two fingers, operation of a simple adding machine and the ability to shake a cocktail". Going through the diplomatic bags, which arrived by Queen's Messenger every Wednesday evening, was "the event of the week", Vassall later recalled. This did not however dampen his usual enthusiasm for making any job sound more important than it really was: he soon started flourishing business cards carrying the words "Mr W. J. C. Vassall, Junior Attaché, British Embassy, Moscow", printed in the sort of florid script normally reserved for wedding invitations.[12]

For several months in 1954 Vassall and Bennett worked in the same room, until a restructure gave Bennett his own office. Bennett was not impressed by his new clerk. Because Vassall had not heeded advice about what to bring to Moscow and basic household items such as blankets, linen, crockery and cutlery could not easily be bought there, they had to be ordered from London, at great expense. As expenses claims were settled, an irritated Bennett wrote to London "I don't think it is unfair to suggest that if a kick, major or otherwise, is deserved by anyone the only eligible candidate is Master Vassall himself". The handwritten memo is barely legible, but the message is clear.

One morning, three months after Vassall arrived, Bennett called him into his office, and told him frankly "that he was not pleased with me", Vassall recalled. It had been "brought to his attention that I was moving in circles too high for my position or station in the embassy", that he was lazy and careless, and that he might be sent back to England if his work did not improve. Later, Norman Lucas alleged that Vassall had "continued to lead the gay life to such an extent that his work began to suffer". But Bennett's dressing-down seems to have had little, if anything, to do with Vassall's sexuality and everything to do with social class. Vassall believed that Bennett had been told to give him a "rocket" by Lady Hayter, after a diplomat called John Morgan (who Vassall described as a "ruthless careerist and thoroughly double-faced") told her that Vassall

---

12 Vassall seems to have remained proud of the cards he had printed in Moscow: an image of one is on the dust jacket of his memoirs, published twenty years later.

was enjoying a busy social life on other embassies' cocktail party circuits.

A distraught Vassall thought it was "the most unkind thing that anyone could say about another person in the same embassy", and it "hurt me a great deal". At about the same time, the assistant naval attaché – then a Lieutenant-Commander Davidson – shou-ted at Vassall in the office for having made a trivial mistake. Bennett did not raise Vassall's effeminacy with him directly, but on a visit to London in August 1954 he did mention it to Mr Pennells, the chairman of the panel who had appointed him. That autumn he raised it with Hayter himself. But Hayter later told MI5 that he believed Bennett had alluded to Vassall's sexuality "only in the vaguest way" and "half-jokingly". The ambassador advised Bennett that no further action was required. Having been rebuffed, Bennett seems to have done what any modern employer should do: realised that Vassall's sexuality was none of his business.

After nine months, Bennett's judgement of Vassall had mellowed slightly. "He made a bad start, arriving in Moscow in March [1954] with an unjustified excess of confidence in his abilities and a wrong conception of his social position" wrote Bennett in a report from January 1955. "He has small conception of the meaning of the word 'work.' On the social plane he made a number of bad gaffes. ... I gave him a severe warning, which I am glad to report had the desired effect. Although his work is not outstanding, it is now in general satisfactory. And on the social side he is no longer a misfit, despite the handicap of an irritating effeminate personality." Back in London, Pennells spoke up for Vassall in an endorsement attached to Bennett's report: "I believe Vassall is quite sound. ... Now that his rosy-coloured spectacles have been removed I suspect he will do quite well".

Bennett's relationship with Vassall gradually improved, helped by the arrival in the spring of 1955, of Bennett's wife Rosemary (known as "Bud"). Mrs Bennett had had a serious mental breakdown after the war and Bennett was always "in a great state of worry" over her health. Bennett's mood lightened, and Vassall found Rosemary to be "a very kind woman" who he accompanied to the Bolshoi ballet. During Vassall's trial, *The Times* implied that he and Mrs Bennett had had an affair. Later, Vassall said he could have turned to Mrs Bennett for help after his "compromise" began, but she did not arrive in Moscow until it was too late.

While Vassall got on well with Rosemary, he still found Captain Bennett unapproachable. "He was always in a hurry to do other things and I am afraid we never really got to know each other", Vassall recalled. "At brief moments he would smile and say something nice to me over a drink", but for a long time Vassall seems to have refused to forgive Bennett for the reprimand.

Like Vassall, Bennett was old enough to have served in the Second World War, but not the First. But Bennett was fifteen years older than Vassall and he had served as an illustrious naval officer, not as a lowly RAF photographer, and received a Distinguished Service Order (DSO) for his service in the Mediterranean.

Bennett was not just a stuffy martinet: he was also a precocious and prolific writer of naval history, and fiction, with some commercial success. In the late 1920s, while still in his teens, he began writing articles for *Jane's Fighting Ships* and other publications.

His novels have long been out of print and are now seldom read. No one would argue that they are literary masterpieces. Like many naval officers, Bennett enjoyed telling naval stories, but he wrote them with skill under the *noms de plume* 'Sea Lion' and 'Walrus'. He wrote his first novel, *Phantom Fleet*, in 1942 "to while away the blackout hours". It was published in 1946 and quickly turned into a BBC serial on the Light Programme. He had more success with radio plays about the adventures of two midshipmen, "Tiger" Ransome and "Snort" Kenton, for the BBC's *Children's Hour*.

Between the mid-1940s and mid-1960s Bennett produced novels on an almost industrial scale: *Sink Me the Ship* (1946), *Cargo for*

Crooks (1948), *Sea of Troubles* (1949) and in 1950 *When Danger Threatens* and *This Creeping Evil* (about a giant octopus with tentacles three miles long that appears out of the Devil's Cauldron, a waterfall on Dartmoor).[13] In 1951 Bennett wrote *The Pirate Destroyer* and in 1952 he wrote *The Diamond Rock* (set in the Caribbean during the Napoleonic wars) and *The Secret Weapon*, a children's book about the attempt to foil "an international gang bent on stirring up revolution in Egypt and Greece".

By the time Bennett met Vassall he had started to pivot from naval yarns towards a rather different genre: spy thrillers, and he seemed to have hoped to rival Ian Fleming by producing a trio of novels about a secret agent in the Foreign Office's "Special Duties Department", Desmond Drake, who is "dark of hair and eye, blue-jowled, broad-shouldered and muscular". The second and third Drake novels are firmly set in the Cold War and in *Desmond Drake Goes West* (1956) Drake outwits "foreign powers" by bringing a vital roll of microfilm from the American President to London. Yet Bennett, who must have spent every moment of his spare time writing, never suspected that from the spring of 1955 onwards he had perfect source material – an actual Russian spy – under his nose, working as his clerk.

Bennett was an admirer of Russian intellectualism: in one of his pseudonymous articles he praised the "level at which Soviet culture is officially maintained: to put it in a nutshell, there is no Light Programme, no I.T.V., nor other pandering to moronic tastes". But Bennett was not just a Cold warrior or a pious prig as this gripe implies. He was genuinely a man of high culture. In November 1956, a year after leaving Moscow, he wrote a lengthy article in *The Listener* (an intellectual magazine published by the BBC), under his own name, about the many performances of the Bolshoi ballet he had

---

13   *This Creeping Evil*'s plot was similar to a third-rate Hollywood B-movie, but it received surprisingly good reviews, including from publications like the *Naval Review*, while other reviewers praised its message that only a return to religion and morality can thwart evil.

attended, and the company's imminent performances in London. He also discussed the Bolshoi's ballet and opera repertoire on the BBC Third Programme.

Bennett did not hide behind pseudonyms: most of his novels' covers explained that "Sea-Lion" was his pen name and that he was a serving Royal Navy officer. But Vassall seems to have had no knowledge of, or interest in, Bennett's literary hinterland or their shared love of opera. Bennett's double life as a prolific writer is never mentioned in Vassall's memoirs. Like two ships passing in the night, Vassall did not appreciate Geoffrey Bennett. More importantly, Bennett never understood John Vassall.

●   ●   ●

"To enjoy diplomatic life in Moscow you must be one of two things, a bachelor secretary with no ties or responsibilities, or an ambassador, luxuriously installed in an Embassy with plenty of people to look after you", Vassall wrote in his memoirs twenty years later. As usual, Vassall looked on the bright side. His interviews with MI5 after his arrest in 1962, and MI5's own interviews with his contemporaries, paint a fascinating picture of embassy life in the mid-1950s. The embassy was a den of vice, full of resentment, thwarted ambition, drunkenness and adultery.

Vassall told MI5 of a drunken Mrs Hayden and an Air Commander called Donkin (whose awful wife had a chip on her shoulder and a voice that was a "nauseating screech"). Douglas Ash, an embassy transport manager, married an East German woman but she was not allowed to join him in Moscow, where Ash started an affair with a female archivist, Irene Carpenter. A Major Marshall turned to Lady Hayter for matrimonial advice after his wife lost interest in him.

A Harry Hayward was sent home in the summer of 1955 for "habitual drunkenness, culminating in a fierce argument with the

Soviet militia". Edward Johnson, clerk to the air attaché, was sent home in April 1957 for black marketeering, while John Charles Luck, the Hayters' butler from October 1953 to June 1954, was compromised by the Russians for having made "indecent proposals". MI5's files reveal that in 1955 compromising photographs of a Mrs Fickle, a British diplomat's wife, were found in the luggage of Michael Alan-Smith, another black marketeer and amateur photographer. The photographs were subsequently found not to be of Mrs Fickle herself, but part of an elaborate Soviet dirty trick to get Fickle and his wife transferred from Moscow. An internal inquiry then discovered that many British diplomats were sleeping with their colleagues' wives. "Operation Fickle," as it was known, was of such interest to MI5 that they were still asking Vassall about it as late as 1969, although the operation never seems to have turned its attention towards him.

Vassall did not admire most of his embassy colleagues, and in return most of them formed an instant dislike of him. Lisa Lewis (personal assistant to the embassy's minister and the wife of the air attaché, Squadron Leader P. H. T. Lewis) told MI5 that Vassall was seen as a "misfit", whose "rather pathetic attempts to impress his colleagues tended to make him the object of derision". Olive Perry, an archivist, described him as "rather odd", an "incorrigible social climber" and "an old woman". In 1957 she bumped into him on Horse Guards Parade back in London, and Vassall "spent five minutes telling her of the many important people he had recently seen". Assistant military attaché Roy Smith found Vassall to be a "glib, lazy and fanatical social climber to such an extent that his homosexual tendencies were quite submerged by the lesser defect". Among Vassall's few real friends at the embassy, the only common ground was their shared dislike of the Hayters.

Five foot ten inches tall, with blue eyes and dark brown hair, Vassall was, everyone would admit, a good-looking man. June Denby, a typist, was "promiscuous" and prone to "fun and games with men".

Vassall told MI5 that Denby was "sexy and not unattractive". Denby was possibly the unnamed young woman in Vassall's memoirs who asked him to marry her – and was disappointed when he turned her down (Vassall explained that his mother "wanted me to go far in my career and not sacrifice it to marriage").

"I liked talking to married women much better than single girls", Vassall recalled. Most, though not all, of his colleagues immediately sensed that he was gay. As the espionage writer Ronald Seth once wrote, "though a man does not go about with a label declaring his deviation from the sexual norm, Vassall was the type of homosexual whom experienced men could and ought to have recognised".[14] In contemporary terms, he was the sort of man who aroused the "gaydar" in most observant people, both gay and straight.

One Moscow contemporary, Kinloch, told MI5 that while he hadn't thought Vassall was homosexual, his wife and Mrs Chamier (the wife of the military attaché) had seen Vassall trying on hats owned by an embassy secretary, Beryl Price, which "left no doubt of his inclinations". Price herself told others that "when Vassall is around we are all girls together". A Mrs Petty said that Vassall's manner was always "rather 'airy fairy' and that he would wave his hands about during a conversation" (clear proof that someone is gay in Mrs Petty's world). After Vassall left Moscow, his place in Stanley Ford's flat was taken by a Frederick Whittaker, who told MI5 in 1965 that most people knew that Vassall was gay and that many of them referred to him as "Vera".

To avoid the embassy's boredom and back-biting, Vassall soon sought new company. He was much more popular with the staff of foreign embassies. Moscow's only tennis court – or at least the only one that foreigners could use – was at the British embassy,

---

14   Seth, a Second World War Special Operations Executive (SOE) veteran, had a colourful double life even by espionage standards. As well as writing about spying using his real name, he used a pseudonym, Robert Chartham, in his parallel career as a sexologist, writing booklets with titles like *Mainly for Wives*, *Sex Manners for Advanced Lovers* and *The Sensuous Couple*, and lecturing British students on "How to Enjoy Sex".

and it was sometimes made available to junior staff. Vassall seems to have used it to get to know other embassies' diplomats in early 1954. He was soon invited to their parties and absorbed into "la vie diplomatique".

His Catholicism also gave him an entrée. By the end of March 1954 he'd met Father Georges Bissonette, an American Augustinian priest who acted as an unofficial Roman Catholic chaplain to Moscow's diplomatic corps.[15] That autumn, Vassall met a Dutch diplomat called Bob Van Den Born at a mass, where Vassall was helping Bissonette to serve. Van Den Born and his wife lived in a flat above Vassall's own, and he soon began going to theirs for dinner and drinks. The Dutch couple's home had "gracious furniture, beautiful objects to decorate the rooms, and an air of welcome and warmth" – everything that Vassall's own flat lacked. Van Den Born told MI5 that Vassall was a "typical cocktail figure" who was "not taken seriously" but was "unperturbed" when mocked. He added that Vassall was a man who "when kicked out by the front-door, would happily come in again by the back-door".

Once, Vassall invited the Van Den Borns into his flat so he could show off a new dressing-gown and at Christmas he boasted that he had sent 500 cards, seeming disappointed that he had only received 496 in return. But despite his vanity, the Van Den Borns liked him. Bob was flattered when Vassall heard that he was a painter and asked him for some lessons, and by Vassall's comment that he did not really want to be an Englishman, but "typically continental". The couple never suspected that he was gay, let alone a gay spy, even after he visited them in the Netherlands around 1958, bringing Bob "a fairly expensive tie", and mysteriously asked them to wait outside in the cold while he sent a telegram to Hamburg from a post office. When the couple came in, Vassall "ostentatiously bent over the telegram form" so they could not see what he was writing.

---

15   Bissonette was in Moscow from 1953 until March 1955, when the Soviets asked him to leave. He later wrote a memoir entitled *Moscow Was My Parish*.

Half-jokingly, Bob asked Vassall if he was in the "secret services". "Maybe", he replied.

Vassall kept a detailed, 25-page account of his social engagements in Moscow, which MI5 found in his London flat in 1962. "One certainly does not get the impression of a neglected waif that he has given in his statement to police", the MI5 officer Charles Elwell wrote. It is clear that his life there was much more glamorous than anything he had previously known. From 1954 to 1956 he existed in a social whirl: a constant round of cocktail parties at the Mexican embassy, games of bridge, tennis parties thrown by the Argentinian ambassador, and a party at the Swedish embassy in honour of the Swedish Opera Company. He got to know two Swedish military attachés, who lived on the same floor as the Van Den Borns. One of them, an air attaché, lived in a flat with wall-to-wall carpeting ("no longer was the cold atmosphere of our own Ministry of Public Buildings and Works at play", Vassall recalled). The Swede later told Vassall's mother, when she joined Vassall on a visit to him and his wife in Stockholm, that he "liked John because he was not aloof or wanted to be important or impressive, as did so many in our embassy", which was the exact opposite of what most of the British embassy's staff thought about him.

Unlike in London, Vassall's modest salary could go far, and if there were no parties to attend, he filled every moment of his spare time with trips to the opera and ballet. He saw Prokofiev's' *Romeo and Juliet*, Tchaikovsky's *The Queen of Spades*, Mussorgsky's *Boris Godunov*, Chekhov's *The Seagull* (performed in Russian), Wilde's *An Ideal Husband* and *Lady Windermere's Fan* and Shakespeare (in English), and he went to one of the first performances of Shostakovich's Tenth Symphony.

In September 1954 he travelled to Stockholm, where he met his mother (his father seems never to have ventured abroad to meet him). Together, they went to see *Tristan and Isolde* and dined at the Grand Hotel to mark Vassall's thirtieth birthday. At the Strand

Hotel, where they stayed, Vassall clearly exaggerated his professional status: its bill, in MI5's files, was addressed to "Herr Attaché Vassal [*sic*]".

After a week in Stockholm, Vassall flew back to Leningrad, via Helsinki. On the plane he befriended a Finn, who Vassall soon guessed was from "the twilight world". The Finn showed Vassall some erotic photographs and invited him to stay at the Valkuna Hotel in Helsinki. "It was with great reluctance that I boarded the plane for Leningrad at Helsinki airport ... If I had stayed with him in Finland I might never have been involved in espionage", he later recalled.

Vassall returned from Stockholm on 26 September 1954. A long, harsh Muscovite winter lay ahead. His next leave was not until 27 January 1955, when he was due to visit England. He then made the most fateful decision of his life: that winter, on top of the diplomatic party circuit, he would spend as much time as possible mingling with Russian men.

Many have claimed that Vassall was criminally stupid to fraternise with Russians. A few decades later, such fraternisation would have been out of the question: Rodric Braithwaite, a later British ambassador in Moscow, recalled that by the late 1980s "junior staff were instructed to keep well clear of Soviet citizens. The rest of us had to report even the most innocent and accidental contact." The embassy assumed that all its rooms were "microphoned" and that all Russian servants were spies. But in 1954 it was very different. Vassall said that when he arrived he was told by the embassy's Head of Chancery, a Mr Rouse, that "it was only all right to speak to Russians in a theatre, a restaurant or public place", and that while friendships with Russians were not outlawed, Vassall should tell the embassy about any. But this rule was regularly flouted by several embassy staff. In any case, the events that led to Vassall's "compromise" mostly took place in public or semi-public places: restaurants and hotel dining rooms. As Richard Deacon has explained, in the mid-1950s the divide between "dips" and "non-dips" at the British embassy was "very marked". Non-dips like Vassall faced "very lonely lives indeed" and understandably, many "set out to mingle with Russians and people from other embassies and missions".

Many observers later blamed the embassy for not stopping Vassall's fraternisation with Russians, but if anything, Geoffrey Bennett and others not only permitted it, but actively encouraged it. Bennett lent Vassall his car, and its chauffeur, so he could visit Archangelskoye, the ancestral home of Prince Yusupov (who participated in the botched assassination of Grigori Rasputin in 1916) and the former homes of Tolstoy (which Vassall went to with the wife of a Swedish military attaché) and Tchaikovsky.

Bennett himself regularly mingled with Soviet military men, and ordinary Russians. In a February 1955 article in the *Naval Review*, 'Walrus' wrote about a recent visit Bennett had paid to the Frunze Naval Academy in Leningrad,[16] where he had lunched with the academy's deputy-superintendent and six of his staff officers. Another piece in the *Naval Review*, published three months earlier, recounted a three-week tour of Russia, during which he socialised with Russian students learning English. In an ancient railway carriage, "swarming with workers and peasants", the words "'On Her Britannic Majesty's Service' printed on the writer's luggage labels excited a naïve curiosity. When explained, the reaction was friendly", Bennett recalled. It is clear that the British naval attaché in Moscow felt it was entirely appropriate to travel around the Soviet Union in crowded railway carriages, openly advertising his identity.

● ● ●

---

16   The academy's library, Bennett noted approvingly, contained a large display of novels by Henry Fielding (the Soviet Union was, remarkably, holding a series of events in 1954 to mark the 200th anniversary of Fielding's death).

Gradually, Vassall's taciturn flatmate Stan Jennings had become more gregarious. He and Vassall once lunched in a restaurant and got talking to an attractive Russian woman, who asked Jennings "Who is this good-looking young man with you?" Only in retrospect did Vassall realise that this was probably his first encounter with the Russian Secret Service. It would not be his last.

It was Jennings who introduced Vassall to his first two Russian acquaintances. Volodya Semenov was a university lecturer in his late twenties, about five foot seven with dark brown hair brushed back. Boris Kavotsov (sometimes referred to as Khrostov) was a research worker at a state enterprise, also in his late twenties and five feet nine, burly and with blond hair. Boris seems to have tried to entrap, or at least seduce, Jennings: in his memoirs Vassall recalled that Kavotsov told Jennings he liked Oscar Wilde, and once "locked Jennings in an iron embrace and kissed him", but that Jennings managed to resist his advances.

When Volodya and Boris invited Jennings and Vassall to dine in a Russian flat, Vassall was wary, as neither of their hosts spoke much English. But Jennings pressed him to join him at the party. They were "received at the front door with open arms". Vassall's main memory of the evening was meeting a "tall, blond young man of strong physique who obviously found me attractive". But the feeling was not mutual: "My opposite number got me in corner and made advances to me. I resisted". After a small banquet and many toasts, it was Jennings – not Vassall – who said that their Russian hosts must visit their own flat soon: they soon did. Vassall said that he did not enjoy the evening, avoided political conversation and hoped that their guests would leave quickly. Their two visitors – probably KGB stooges – were never seen again: "They were just two pieces in a game of chess", Vassall recalled.

This sort of encounter was common for many embassy staff: contrary to later newspaper reports, Vassall was far from being the only person to fraternise with Russians. Vassall knew that Jennings had not reported his trips to the theatre with Boris and Volodya, or the dinners in their flat. Later, Jennings told MI5 that, like Vassall, he had not been explicitly warned against social contact with Russians until August 1955. By then such a warning was much too late.

One of Vassall's duties was the maintenance of an "Impest Account": a petty cash stock, from which embassy staff paid for taxis, restaurants and concert tickets. It was through obtaining his own tickets that Vassall met Sigmund Mikhailsky, an embassy interpreter-cum fixer, and his sidekick Nikolai Costakis, who helped British staff with maintenance of their offices and flats (his nationality is unclear, though he was nicknamed "the Greek"). Vassall said that they expressed surprise that he wanted concert tickets, but quickly obliged.

Mikhailsky had started working at the embassy in early 1954, at about the same time as Vassall. Born in Poland around 1930, he fled the invading Nazis with his mother at the beginning of the war, and after a period in Moldavia he'd ended up in Moscow. Nothing was known about his previous career and many embassy staff were wary of him: MI5's files describe him as "greasy, oily, shifty, ingratiating, effeminate and servile", dressed in "Teddy boy style". But he was very useful at procuring theatre and travel tickets for diplomats, or helping them skip the interminable queue outside a popular restaurant, the Kiev.

Vassall soon fell under Mikhailsky's spell. When he went to a production of Prokofiev's *Romeo and Juliet* he discovered that the ticket Mikhailsky had procured was in the sixth row of the stalls, not the seventh row or further back, where other diplomats sat. Mikhailsky was a Catholic who worshipped at the same church as Vassall, and he made "disarming criticisms of the Soviet regime". He told Vassall that he was Polish, and later that he was partly Romanian, which may have reassured Vassall, as he had met many Polish officers through his mother's war work in the Mechanical Transport Corps. Mikhailsky was a constant source of diplomatic gossip: he told Vassall that the Egyptian embassy's First Secretary was having an affair with a male Russian driver. Later, the Radcliffe report asserted that Mikhailsky "indulged at least intermittently in homosexual acts", and was suspected of blackmailing two other diplomats, one of whom had to be sent home.

Although Mikhailsky claimed to hate the Soviets he was, almost certainly, a KGB spy. All of the embassy's "local staff" were employed through Burobin, a Soviet Foreign Ministry agency and effectively a branch of the KGB. If any potential employee put forward by Burobin was vetoed, there would be a substantial delay before another was nominated. Burobin held the whip hand, and the British embassy seems to have turned a blind eye to whatever Mikhailsky was up to.

Several historians have argued that the KGB may have known about Vassall's vulnerability to blackmail – his sexual tastes, his love of luxury and desire for a higher standard of living – before he arrived in Moscow. If they didn't, they probably soon found out, thanks to Mikhailsky. As Vassall himself wrote later, "The Russians must have found the chink in my armour before anyone else".

Many of Mikhailsky's invitations seem innocuous: he once invited Vassall to an agricultural exhibition, a proposition Vassall declined. But Mikhailsky's name was missing in Vassall's 1954 and 1955 diaries, "for reasons which were fairly obvious", he later told MI5. Vassall and Mikhailsky may not have had an affair, as some have claimed, but Mikhailsky certainly gave Vassall an entrée into a livelier social scene where he could meet Russian gay men. As Vassall and Mikhailsky dined at a restaurant one evening, two men at an adjoining table asked if they could join them. As Vassall was brushing his hair in the cloakroom, one of them "looked at me with fire in his eyes and showed me with his smile how passionate he felt". They met again a few days later at the Bolshoi Ballet.

At the Aurora restaurant in early autumn 1954, Mikhailsky introduced Vassall to another Russian who told him that he was "a skier" – a nickname that stuck.[17] MI5 later declared that the skier "may be addicted to drink, women or boys". In fact, Vassall didn't believe that the "skier" was gay, and they do not seem to have had a sexual relationship, contrary to many claims. But Vassall undoubtedly found him attractive. They often met outside metro stations or the Bolshoi Theatre. When the "skier" arranged a series of dinners for Vassall, he enthusiastically accepted all the invitations. They were typically part of a group of six, and the skier once urged Vassall to tell another Russian, who had introduced himself as a journalist, that he was an Estonian who was visiting Moscow on business. Vassall seems to have enjoyed the roleplay. But the "skier" and the other diners were playing roles themselves: most, if not all, were KGB agents.

Before long the skier introduced Vassall to a forty-something man who spoke perfect English and reminded him of a psychiatrist, though he talked more than he listened. He was probably assessing Vassall's suitability for the role the KGB had in mind for him: as a secret agent at the heart of the British defence establishment.

Sex and espionage have always been bedfellows, from 'Wild Rose' Greenhow (the Washington hostess who extracted information from Union commanders during the American Civil War and passed it to the Confederacy) to Mata Hari, the fictional James Bond and beyond. Russia had a long tradition of sexual blackmail, predating the revolution. Before the First World War Russia blackmailed Colonel Alfred Redl, an Austro-Hungarian chief of staff, into handing over a complete list of spies, some of them Redl's friends who were summarily shot by the Russians. It transpired that Redl had long been a "compulsive homosexual" with a secret wardrobe full of "women's dresses, perfumes, cosmetics … and a

---

17   MI5 later decided that the 'skier' was probably Aleksey Volkov, born in the 1920s, who was five foot eleven in height, blond haired, with a ruddy face and grey eyes. MI5's files say that Volkov was indeed an accomplished skater and skier, that he spoke German and English and that in the mid-1950s he was working in Moscow for the Soviet Ministry of Fisheries, which could well have been cover for a KGB role.

large assortment of whips". Rather than face public disgrace and execution Redl committed suicide in a Viennese hotel room in 1913, leaving a note saying: "Levity and passion have destroyed me. Pray for me. I pay with my life for my sins".

Sexual espionage was also used by the West in the twentieth century. But British and American security agencies normally avoided outright sexual blackmail. During the Cold War it was the Russians who perfected the art of 'Son et Lumière' – espionage jargon for recording sexual encounters using hidden cameras and/or microphones. Since the end of the Second World War – or even before – the KGB's Second Chief Directorate had used male and female agents, known as "swallows" or "ravens", to entrap Western diplomats and politicians. It has been claimed that the Labour MP Tom Driberg was entrapped when he visited Moscow to interview Guy Burgess for a biography of the spy in 1956, and willingly "compromised" himself with a number of men at an underground urinal behind the Metropole Hotel. Driberg, who became Chairman of the Labour Party in 1957, is said to have carried on handing over intelligence until the late 1960s, and possibly right up to his death in 1976. In 1959 the *Observer* journalist Edward Crankshaw, who had close links to MI5 and MI6, was photographed indulging in what the KGB called "sexual frolics" while he was also in Moscow to interview Burgess, though as the frolics were probably with women rather than men, he managed to resist the KGB's pressure.

Vassall was not the first man to be sexually blackmailed by the KGB, and nor was he the last. Dennis Amy, who was in charge of security at the British embassy in Moscow in the early 1960s, has said that even five years after Vassall had left, the KGB would "set up middle-aged old ladies … in bed with people, take pictures of them, which was absolutely inexcusable. It blighted their lives". Amy also claimed that a University of Manchester maths professor had a "hard time" on a trip to Moscow and committed suicide soon after returning home. Sir Ian Orr-Ewing, Civil Lord of the Admiralty from 1959 to 1963, said that after Vassall's conviction in 1962 there were "thousands of Russians, … all trained to detect weakness in character, weakness for drink, blondes, drugs and homosexuality".

"Some people are born spies, some become spies and others have spying thrust upon them", Richard Deacon and Nigel West once wrote. They rightly concluded that John Vassall was in the latter category. His blackmail was not an isolated incident but a carefully choreographed sequence of events. In short, Vassall was groomed.

It began on the night of Saturday 30 October 1954.[18] Vassall's diary records that he was due to attend a masquerade ball at the American Club that evening. Instead he ended up at a different, and much more sinister, form of pretence. Winter arrives early in Moscow, and in October there was already snow on the ground. Vassall met his "skiing friend" outside the Bolshoi as usual, but the "skier" said that he wasn't able to accompany Vassall that evening. Instead, he introduced Vassall to a friend who wanted Vassall to join him and some "comrades" for dinner.

Alarm bells should have been ringing loudly, but Vassall seemed charmed by the stranger. He "looked at me … with a Mona Lisa smile and black penetrating eyes" under a fur hat. The "skier" soon said farewell, and Vassall and the dark-eyed stranger took a taxi to the Hotel Berlin, which Vassall had never visited; only later did he work out its name and location.

At first, Vassall felt at home in an internationally renowned hotel with a distinct "cosmopolitan taste". The Berlin seemed to be "humming with life and vitality" as Vassall's "fur-clad mystery man" took him up a grand, carpeted staircase to a private dining room, furnished in red and gold. The men already in the room – Vassall did not recall any women – were strangers, but Vassall was

---

18   Vassall did not keep a proper diary in Moscow. It was thus difficult for MI5 to work out exactly when events took place. Vassall initially thought the "blackmail party" at the Hotel Berlin took place in about April 1955 and that he was forced to work for the Russians in July, but eventually he and MI5 agreed it had probably been on 30 October 1954 and that he was confronted with the photographic evidence four-and-a-half months later on 19 March 1955.

greeted as if by "old and civilised friends". Over dinner the wine, and conversation, flowed liberally and after the meal Vassall was "plied with a very strong brandy".

Around two hours later, Vassall was told he must be very warm under his jacket, which one of his companions immediately removed. It was then that events took a sinister turn. Vassall insisted that there was no "drunken orgy". But after dinner, some guests drifted away and he was left with the dark-eyed stranger and two other men. One of them suggested that Vassall looked unwell and urged him to lie down on a divan in a recess in the room's walls. Later, Vassall said that from this point onwards, he "was not responsible for my actions". His 1962 confession made no direct reference to being drugged, but it did make it clear that he "was helped out of his clothes" and elsewhere in the confession he was more explicit: "my clothes were removed". In his memoirs from 1975, Vassall recalled that he was asked to "take off all my clothes including my underwear". This was an order, not a suggestion, and he later realised that the wine he had been drinking must have been spiked.

Vassall was indeed unwell: he could hardly stand up. The next thing he remembered was "having my underpants in my hand and holding them up in the air at the request of others. Then I was lying on the bed naked, and as far as I can recollect there were three other men on the bed with me. I cannot remember exactly what took place [but] suddenly everything became very painful." Vassall's memoirs do not categorically state it, but it is clear that he was anally raped.

He remembers seeing the dark-eyed man taking photographs. "When I called out to someone that what was going on was painful I was told it would not last much longer, but it felt endless to me," he recalled. Strangely, he seemed grateful to the men who had just attacked him. "Everyone treated me like a young person who needed looking after very carefully. When they had finished … I asked if I might go to a bathroom to tidy myself up … On my return I was dressed properly, and we all behaved as if nothing had happened. It was like a painful dream, a period that one had to pass through before being allowed to go back to normal routine".

Yet later, Vassall told MI5 that he had been so insensible that the Russians had supported him on the way to the bathroom as he was "unable to walk". At about 3.30 a.m., "my hosts asked me how I would like to go home and could they take me. I said I would make my own way to my flat, but they insisted on arranging for a taxi to collect me. I cannot remember whether I left by the front entrance or a side door". Vassall had been due to go to an organ recital at a conservatoire that Sunday morning, with a friend of Stan Jennings called Gwen Parker. He never made it.

How should Vassall have responded to these events? Many have suggested that he should have immediately contacted his superiors and told them that he had been raped, or at least sexually coerced, and that photographs had been taken. After all, several embassy employees had reported their attempted entrapments in the 1950s and 1960s, and managed to nip any blackmail in the bud. In March 1963, the KGB made what Nigel West has called a "rather heavy-handed" attempt to "honey trap" Ivor Rowsell, a 47-year-old transport clerk. After the Russians "threatened to disclose an incident in his private life", Rowsell and his wife were withdrawn to London, and on 20 March Ted Heath, in his capacity as Lord Privy Seal, proudly told the Commons that Rowsell had done the right thing by telling the ambassador everything, and that the embassy had made an "oral protest" to the Soviet Foreign Ministry, followed by a "formal note".

But Rowsell was a straight man caught in a heterosexual honey trap, while Vassall was a gay man who had been raped. "To me it was an evening to be lost and forgotten as quickly as possible," he wrote. Ambassador Hayter was "cold and aloof" and the last person he would have spoken to about his ordeal, Vassall said. As for Lady Hayter, her only words to him were to enquire about the mutual friend of Vassall's mother: "And how is the dear doctor?" Having been snubbed from joining her bridge parties, and rebuked by the naval attaché for having aspirations above his social station, Vassall was unwilling to approach the Hayters, or Geoffrey Bennett. "Unfortunately I never had a close relationship with the naval attaché: our worlds were quite different", he later recalled.

He said he would have turned to the military attaché, Brigadier Chamier,[19] who "was the only person I could have spoken to in a completely uninhibited way". The trouble was that Vassall hadn't got to know Chamier as well as he wanted, because Bennett didn't get on with him. Vassall liked and trusted David Peck, the embassy's visa officer (who secretly worked for MI6), and he felt closer to Peck's wife than anyone else at the embassy. But, like many rape victims, Vassall only blamed himself at first. "I felt so ashamed … that I was unable to lift my head and eyes to speak to her", he recollected twenty years later. Vassall once spent an entire night in March 1955 talking to Mrs Peck. But Mikhailsky had told him that the Pecks were "something to do with counter-espionage, and he avoided them like the plague". Vassall heeded this advice and told the Pecks nothing.

After the publication of his memoir about his time in Moscow, in 1966, Hayter told the press that the Soviets had made three attempts to blackmail officials between 1953 and 1957, and only Vassall had fallen for it. Elsewhere, he said of Vassall: "I remember him dimly as an obliging little figure who was useful at tea parties. There was no excuse for him. If he had come to me or to the naval attaché and told us that he was being blackmailed by the Russians he could have been sent home at once without any opposition from the Soviet authorities."

"Vassall's timidity or folly amounted to a crime, and though I have always doubted whether he was a really useful source of

---

19　Brigadier Chamier is referred to as "D Chamier" in Vassall's memoirs, even though his full name was George Deschamps Chamier. Vassall seems never to have learnt his Christian name.

intelligence to the Russians he certainly caused a great many people a great deal of trouble in the end", added Hayter, who seemed to regard the inconvenience to himself as greater than anything that Vassall endured.[20]

Why didn't Vassall tell anyone that he was entrapped, and later blackmailed? The answer is simple: all homosexual activity was illegal, and he feared prosecution (or even imprisonment), in London if not in Moscow. "And what would happen to me when I went home? The incident could be hushed up, but at that time it was a serious crime in England. Had attitudes been different then, I might have been more courageous in dealing with the events in Moscow". But they weren't, and he couldn't.

After being raped Vassall's social life continued as normal. On 6 November 1954 – a week after the "compromise party" – Vassall met his assailants again at the Aragvi restaurant. He went to a physical training display at the Dynamo Stadium and to football, ice hockey and boxing matches. He went skating with a Russian friend and to the sauna at the Moscow Central Baths where he was beaten with twigs, had buckets of cold water thrown over him by a "burly Russian" and "enjoyed every moment". He went to supper parties at the Military Officers' Club, which were above his station, but where Vassall felt at home. He was asked to tutor junior diplomats at the Indonesian embassy, and a more senior official at the Iranian embassy, for which he was well paid in US dollars. Vassall became close to the Iranian, who took him to a concert where Vassall met another young diplomat, with whom he had an affair. This was known to the Russians. "Their ability to spot me in private quarters,

---

20   Ironically, the only Briton to have emerged from the British embassy in Moscow of the 1950s as a committed communist was not John Vassall but the Hayters' only daughter, Teresa, born in 1940. Although she went to an English boarding school "of an exceedingly conventional kind", she was a regular visitor to Moscow in her teens. In her memoir, *Hayter of the Bourgeoisie* (1972), she recalled having her pockets stuffed with sweets by Khrushchev's deputy, Mikoyan, at the Bolshoi ballet but she does not mention Vassall. Teresa Hayter declined to be interviewed for this book, saying that she had no recollection of ever meeting John Vassall. This is unfortunate, as she is one of the few people still alive with clear memories of the British embassy in Moscow in the mid-1950s.

having dinner or going into a bedroom, was truly amazing," Vassall recalled.

Christmas 1954 was a petty affair. After dinner at Bennett's residence, Vassall went to a ball thrown by the Hayters, with carols around the Christmas tree and dancing in the ballroom that was "more of a duty than a pleasure". A New Year's ball at the American Club, however, was much more fun.

It was common for the KGB to leave blackmail targets alone for a few months after they had been photographed: to reflect, and to panic. In January 1955 Vassall spent a few days in London, but the night after he returned to Moscow "the skier" called him. Their friendship resumed, despite what had happened at the last party the skier had arranged.

On Saturday 19 March the trap was sprung, as Vassall wrote in his memoirs. Unwisely, he turned down an invitation to a St Patrick's Day Ball at the American Club. It was a fateful decision. Instead, he accepted another invitation from the skier, to go to the theatre and then dinner. But at the Kursky railway station the skier introduced Vassall to a uniformed military officer, who was in Moscow on leave, he explained. The officer was a "tall, slim man, upright and fair of face and complexion" with a longish face, and he appeared to speak no English.

Rather than go to the theatre, the skier and the officer took Vassall by taxi to a nearby flat, where they had drinks and chatted in comfortable armchairs. Then the skier took Vassall into another room and told him that the officer "liked me and wanted to come in to see me alone. I was of course, excited and stimulated by such a proposal," Vassall recalled. He waited, "butterflies in my stomach", until the officer entered, embraced him and then kissed him. Matters soon escalated, and "there was nothing faked about our love-making".

Twenty minutes after this sexual encounter began, the lights were suddenly switched on. Then they suddenly went out, and there were the sounds of chains, bolts, and whispered voices. Then the lights came back on again, and a voice asked Vassall to enter the next room when he was ready. The officer dressed and left without a word, along with the skier. Vassall never saw either one again: both had clearly been tools of the KGB.

Vassall put his briefs and shirt back on, but apparently no other clothes. In the next room he found two figures in dark overalls, and two others guarding the front door in the hall. One of the men motioned for him to sit at a table, and Vassall recognised another as a man who had claimed to be a journalist at a previous dinner.

The men in overalls were polite, but sinister. They asked Vassall whether he had a diplomatic card (Vassall said he didn't; presumably they were checking to see whether he would claim diplomatic immunity if threatened with prosecution). When Vassall was permitted to go the lavatory he tried to rush out of the flat's front door – which was now unguarded, but locked. The lavatory itself had only a tiny window. Once back in the room, Vassall began to ponder throwing himself out of its larger windows, but he knew that as the flat was on an upper floor he would certainly die in the attempt. It would be difficult anyway, as there was a large table between him and the windows. Again, he felt strangely grateful to the men who had imprisoned him. "I owe my life to the Russians who saved me from suicide by protecting me", he wrote later.

Vassall was interrogated from 9 p.m. until 4 a.m. the next day. Was he a spy? No, answered Vassall. Was he a homosexual? Yes, answered Vassall. He was then shown a box of photographs of the "party" he had attended at the Hotel Berlin four-and-a-half months earlier. Vassall's memoirs describe the pictures: "There I was naked, grinning into the camera: naked, holding up a pair of men's briefs which must have been mine. The first photograph showed my face with a terrible sick expression. Another showed me on the bed with a Russian. After about three photographs I could not stomach any more. They made me feel ill … If you were a man and saw photographs of yourself having oral, anal and a complicated array of sexual activities with a number of different men, what would your feelings be, especially when these photographs were exposed by the Russian Secret Service?"

It was now clear that Vassall had engaged in a greater range of sexual activities than his dim memories of that night at the Hotel Berlin had contained. It was only now that he realised that he had not just been raped: he had been gang-raped, both anally and orally, by at least two men.

The Russians warned Vassall that if he did not assist them, he would not be allowed to leave Russia and would be thrown into the Lubyanka jail. Worse still, the photographs would be shown to his colleagues, and to Lady Hayter, "as an example of what members of embassy staff did with their leisure" (the thought of a woman seeing the photographs seems to have appalled Vassall the most). The KGB do not seem to have specifically threatened to send the photos to Vassall's parents, as some have claimed, but they did say they could be published in newspapers that Reverend and Mrs Vassall read.

Vassall was then told that he had "committed a grave offence under Soviet law and that I was in serious trouble with the State". At one point, the interrogators' calmness disappeared and they "kept on deliberately throwing the photographs in my face", calling him a "disgrace to the embassy". Vassall refused to sign a confession, fearing that it would consign him to a long sentence in the Lubyanka, or worse. But his warning that he needed to head home fell on deaf ears: the Russians knew that the party at the American Club, which Vassall had told friends he might go on to, would last well into the small hours. No one would miss him until much later in the morning. Only at 4 a.m. did they let Vassall go, driving him home in a limousine with tinted windows, on the condition that he met them again at seven the following evening, Sunday 20 March, at a railway station. "If, in the meantime, I dared to speak to anyone about this night, I was assured of the high jump", Vassall later remembered.

Once again, Vassall did not report what had happened to his employers, as he sensed that his honesty would not be rewarded. At best, his civil service career would be over. At worst, he could end up in jail, either in London or Moscow, even if he had refused to hand over any secrets to the Soviets.

He may well have reflected on what had recently happened to a Commander Geoffrey Phillips, the Canadian naval attaché, who had been "sent home" after only a few weeks in Moscow. The ostensible reason was that Phillips had been spotted taking photographs of a Russian ship on a Leningrad slipway, and handed over to the Soviet militia. But Bennett had told Vassall – who barely knew Phillips but had heard on the grapevine that he was gay – the real reason. As Bennett's successor, Captain Adrian Northey, later told MI5, the Canadian was a "bit pink" – a phrase that neatly evoked both communist sympathies and homosexuality. Bennett told Vassall that Phillips "was naive, homosexual and inadequately briefed", that he never had girlfriends, and that he had been removed partly because Bennett himself had made "vigorous representations" to London.

For all these reasons, Vassall felt he couldn't talk to Bennett. Even going to confession was out of the question: he was told that Father Bissonette was under surveillance, in case Vassall told him about his "compromise" and Bissonette then told the Americans, who would tell the British. From then on, Vassall went only to mass, not confession. Likewise, Vassall was told that if he tried to enter the British embassy he would be turned away by the Russian militia who were stationed at its entrances.

Vassall spent Sunday morning lying in bed, afraid to do anything: he was convinced that the flat was bugged and the telephone was tapped. Later that morning, Mikhailsky turned up on the doorstep. Vassall decided that Mikhailsky was the only man he could confide in, but predictably he advised Vassall to tell no one, and to keep his appointment with the Russians that evening. Mikhailsky seems to have repeated the warning that if he didn't, the incriminating photographs might be sent to the embassy, and to Lady Hayter specifically.

By now, Mikhailsky was the Iago to Vassall's Othello: a Machiavellian manipulator who posed as an honest friend but was in fact plotting his downfall. It appears that his visit was deliberately timed to ensure that Vassall did not attempt to contact anyone at the embassy, and the tactic worked. Mikhailsky stayed with Vassall, as a sort of minder, until the latter caught a taxi at 6 p.m. for his appointment. Ominously, Vassall slipped on some ice as he left the flat: the spring thaw had not yet begun.

At the station, dark figures in "long black coats and fur hats" appeared at 7 p.m. as if from nowhere. They drove Vassall to a side entrance of the Hotel Sovietskaya, where he was taken to a private suite upstairs. Vassall feared being "stripped again and having all kinds of tricks played on my body, or being tortured, or made to drink so that I would give in easily to my desires." Instead, the Russians wanted to continue talking. They showed him the pile of photographs again, and "the most unpleasant member of the group started to harangue me about what I had done ... and tore up some of the photographs in my face. But they were far too shrewd to use any physical torture, and when I realised this I began to feel better," Vassall recalled. Then they let Vassall go, on condition that he met them again in three weeks' time. On the following night, Monday 21 March, Vassall saw Prokofiev's *Romeo and Juliet* again and didn't want the performance to end. Two days later, he dined with his Dutch friends, the Van Den Borns, but told them nothing.

So began Vassall's regular rendezvous with his Soviet handlers in Moscow, every two or three weeks from early 1955 until June 1956. All the appointments were made verbally but never on the telephone. He would take a taxi to a designated place and then walk back and forth, looking in shop windows. A chauffeur-driven car would then appear and a Russian in a long, dark overcoat and fur hat would beckon him inside. Vassall would talk to a senior intelligence officer on the back seat, via an interpreter, and then be driven to an anonymous apartment for two or three hours, where Russian brandy – which he hated – would be served. At other times Vassall would be taken on walks in the countryside or by a river: treachery disguised as a pleasant outing.

Unlike his initial interrogators, the men that Vassall met now were mostly polite, like "a sort of league of father-figures, concerned for my welfare". At first, Vassall was only asked to give them general impressions of embassy colleagues and "whom I liked and disliked" – nothing illegal (unlike his homosexuality), he was told. The Russians asked Vassall about homosexuality in Britain, and he willingly discussed the recent Lord Montagu scandal with them. Gradually, they started asking Vassall which diplomats might be gay. They were fascinated when Vassall told them of a visit by a Labour Party delegation from London, including Barbara Castle. Vassall had been asked by the First Secretary, Sir Thomas Brimelow, to help entertain the politicians. Much wine was drunk and Castle had a long chat with Vassall about life in Russia, before joining him in a game of musical chairs. Little did Castle know that Vassall was a KGB spy who quickly told the Russians about everything they had discussed.

Adjacent to Vassall's office was a "silent room" in which the ambassador conducted confidential conversations with Bennett and others; the Russians expressed great interest in it. But they seemed uncertain about who was a spy at the embassy, and Vassall could not help them identify any. Among the staff in the mid-1950s was the former SOE operative Daphne Park, though she was barely mentioned in MI5's debrief of Vassall. He recalled that "the Russians were not particularly interested in her but were amused by her attentions to Deverill", a squadron leader and air attaché, who the Russians knew she was "running after". The Russians seemed unaware that Park worked for MI6 and was well on her way to becoming one of the giants of post-war British intelligence.

These discussions were friendly at first. Vassall often reassured the Russians about the "word of an Englishman" when they asked him to comply. Nigel West, who befriended Vassall in the late 1970s, says that he was reassured that the KGB's "bad guys" would be kept at bay if he gave them snippets of information now and again – a classic "good cop, bad cop" routine. "Please remember," the Russians told Vassall, "that we have had just forty years to evolve a new society, whereas your country has had centuries". If anything, Vassall grew fond of the Russians, naively believing that they cared "for my welfare and tried to make life as relaxed as possible in spite of the constant strain I was under" – strain that they had created in the first place.

In fact, the good cops and bad cops all belonged to the same team. The defector Anatoliy Golitsyn later told MI5 that Vassall's recruitment was overseen by General Oleg Gribanov (known as "Little Napoleon"), head of the KGB's second directorate and in charge of internal intelligence. Vassall's Moscow handler was, MI5 concluded, a KGB officer called Vladimir Aleksandrovich Churanov (codenamed HARRISON by MI6). Churanov was about the same age as Vassall, and married with one son.[21] His Moscow sidekick, identified only as Nikolai, was very short with a round face, fair hair and blue eyes. He could not speak a word of English, but he seemed to be superior in rank to Churanov.

In September or October 1955 Churanov and Nikolai took Vassall on a drive through Moscow. Churanov told him that they required more. They "thought it was in my own interest to produce

---

21   Churanov is believed to have later received the Order of Lenin for his work in recruiting, and managing, Vassall, as did his next handler, "Gregory".

something in the way of paper or files", rather than just embassy tittle-tattle, Vassall later recollected. If Vassall did not, "it would be necessary to take him in front of the General" (possibly General Serov, the head of the Secret Service, whose office Vassall believed was in the Lubyanka). It sounded like a threat, not an enticement. Vassall was fixated upon physical torture: "I was terrified of being sexually and psychologically assaulted ... and I had fearful dreams of hooks, spikes and instruments being placed on my body and private parts", he later wrote. He felt he had no option but to comply.

Having led a double life as a gay man in an era when homosexuality was punishable by imprisonment, leading a triple life did not seem such a challenge. Vassall started taking documents from Bennett's office at the end of the day, hiding them under his coat or amongst other papers and books. "I remember the first time, taking an envelope with me, ... thinking that I had not the remotest reason for doing this and that I was betraying sacred trust", Vassall recalled. In fact, he had a very clear reason: survival.

When Vassall tried to fob the Russians off with "innocuous items", he was warned that if he didn't hand over "more important matters" he would be "dealt with" in the headquarters of the MVD (the Soviets' Ministry of Internal Affairs). Then, for the first time, the Russians offered him the carrot of financial reward. Before Christmas 1955 they gave him a painted Palekh box with 2,000 roubles – about £50, the equivalent of several weeks' pay – inside. Vassall initially refused to accept it, but relented when the Russians said they would be shocked if he didn't. He was always coy about how much he was paid in Russia, saying only that "from time to time the KGB had pressed money on me". In fact, there was little to spend it on in Moscow: most of it was saved, or spent on lavish travels, or on winter clothing and goods from England. Vassall certainly accepted his first chunk of money, but later gave the Palekh box to his brother Richard, as if it was a cursed object he did not want to hang on to.

• • •

Just as Vassall started spying, his social life began to look up. In the autumn of 1955 he enjoyed cocktails at the American embassy, an independence day garden party at the Indonesian one, and more trips to the Bolshoi. Shortly before his thirty-first birthday, on 20 September, he threw a party for twenty friends at his flat, followed by another for "forty-five friends from many different embassies" on the day itself. Vassall celebrated his birthday officially and unofficially, more like a head of state than an office boy.

However aloof Vassall thought the Bennetts were, they invited him to join them on a trip to the Tsaritsyno Palace and on 24 August 1955 he accompanied them to Soviet Navy Day in Leningrad, joining Mrs Bennett on a tour of the Winter Palace's galleries. Less than two months later, he returned to Leningrad by air with the Bennetts, for one of the most important events of Geoffrey's Moscow posting: the visit of a squadron of British warships on 12–15 October 1955. It was the first such Royal Navy visit to Russia since 1914.

Nothing must go wrong, and in the best traditions of the Royal Navy, nothing did. As Bennett proudly flew the flag for the British navy and fraternised with their Russian hosts, little did he know that the clerk standing beside him was entering his sixth month as a spy for them. Vassall was more than just Bennett's bag-carrier: he went to a reception on board *HMS Triumph* and a dinner on board *HMS Decoy* and he even helped Mrs Bennett to entertain an admiral's wife, Lady Denny, and Mary Thistleton-Smith, the wife of Denny's chief of staff.

Norman Lucas claimed that when Vassall was taken aboard a British warship to exchange its sailors' pounds into roubles he could have confessed all to an officer, and asked to be taken back to Britain before the Russians could stop him. "But he was too much of a coward to do so," Lucas argued. "His fear of exposure to the

British authorities was by then matched by his fear of his Russian masters". For once, Lucas was at least half-right: Vassall knew that he was now in too deep, and any passage back to England would ensure a prosecution for espionage, buggery, or possibly both. Instead, he obediently returned to Moscow at the end of the fleet's visit, and he doubtless told his masters everything that he had seen and heard on board the British ships.

Geoffrey Bennett still didn't suspect a thing. Indeed, he seemed impressed by Vassall's performance in Leningrad. A month later, on 15 November 1955, he wrote a staff report that was positively glowing compared to his first, damning assessment. "After a poor start, he has developed into a first-rate clerk ... a pleasant young man of first-class appearance and manners, never ruffled, always helpful. His moral standards are of the highest".

Soon afterwards, Vassall was given permission – both by Bennett and his Russian masters – to go on another holiday to Sweden. "No monkey business or we shall be after you", the Russians warned. But they must have been confident there was no risk of Vassall returning to Britain and spilling the beans. Vassall spent most of his time dining with a "Swedish sportsman I had met previously in Stockholm", and sunbathing outside his parents' summer house on the Baltic coast, until it began to snow.

Back in Moscow, in the run-up to Christmas 1955, Vassall was "drawn into the diplomatic whirlpool again" and befriended the Ethiopian delegation, which appeared to consist of two brothers who took it in turns to be ambassador. Vassall listened to records and sat on their fluffy wool carpets, "talking well into the night". At Christmas another bridge was crossed: the Russians funded an expensive holiday to Rome. Vassall was desperate to escape the formality of another embassy Christmas, but he could not return to England as "local leave" was permitted only within a certain radius, which excluded Britain but luckily included central Italy. Just before his departure, his

Russian handlers gave Vassall another expensive cigarette box. Inside, there were no cigarettes, but "a large sum of roubles".

Vassall flew to Rome via Hamburg, and on his arrival he took the aircrew he had befriended to midnight mass at Santa Maria Maggiore. On a whim, he caught an express train to Florence, but spent most of his time in and around the Vatican.

On Christmas morning Vassall went to see Pius XII on the papal balcony in St Peter's Square. Some accounts claim that he had applied for a semi-private audience with the pope, to confess all to His Holiness, until he realised that he was being watched by MVD officers based at the Soviet embassy in Rome, who had been alerted to his arrival. "In a sweat I turned my back on the Vatican and hurried away," Vassall was quoted as saying after his conviction in 1962. This detail was not mentioned in Vassall's later memoirs. It is more likely that Vassall never planned to tell the pontiff anything.[22]

On New Year's Eve 1955, the cream of Moscow's diplomatic community, including Sir William Hayter, were at an enormous state dinner in the Kremlin's St George's Hall, with 1,200 guests. Amid the long speeches there were many champagne toasts, and much music and dancing, into the small hours: the *New York Times* reported that Nikolai Bulganin, then Premier, "pranced about surrounded by a ring of girls".

The Soviet Politburo was letting its hair down. And so was John Vassall – at a very different kind of party. He and Amy Sanderson, Bennett's naval coding clerk and one of the few colleagues Vassall liked, saw in 1956 at a New Year's Eve ball at the American Club. After midnight Vassall drank champagne with Orville L. Wilson, from the US State Department's coding unit, before going to Wilson's room upstairs.

---

22   Pius XII was in his early eighties and in failing health; in 1954 he had undergone cellular rejuvenation treatment that led to hallucinations, "horrific nightmares" and "blood-curdling screams". It is not clear what he would have done if Vassall had told him that he was being forced to spy for the KGB and required the Vatican's protection.

Vassall later recalled that it was Wilson who undressed him, not the other way around. Wilson was married, but his wife and two children were in the US and his Moscow life was in turmoil: Vassall once saw Wilson head off to work at midnight, "drunk and with a full glass of whisky in his hand". The Russians soon told Vassall that they knew all about his dalliance with Wilson: they clearly had spies at work, even in the American Club.

As 1956 began, no one in the British embassy seems to have suspected Vassall was a spy – or taken very much notice of him at all. He was even trusted to take superfluous confidential papers from the naval attaché's office to an incinerator in the embassy's grounds. There, under the watchful eye of Russian labourers, it sometimes took Vassall three hours to get an ancient stove, with a defective chimney, to burn all the papers thoroughly: not a pleasant occupation in the Russian winter. But he later insisted to MI5 that he had never extracted waste from the sack before it was burned.

This lack of suspicion is all the more surprising given the strong precedents for Vassall's treachery. In the mid-1930s, a cypher clerk, John Herbert King (codenamed 'MAG'), worked at the British Delegation to the League of Nations in Geneva, where his financial problems made him vulnerable to an approach by Henri Pieck, a Dutch citizen working for Soviet intelligence. From 1935 to 1937, King was paid to provide the Soviet Union with Foreign Office communications, but he was discovered and in October 1939 sentenced to ten years in prison. In 1952, William Marshall, who had just returned to Britain after two years as a wireless operator at the British embassy in Moscow, was unmasked as a spy and sentenced at the Old Bailey to five years' imprisonment.[23]

King was motivated purely by money, and there is no suggestion that Marshall was gay or subjected to sexual blackmail, but,

---

23   Like Vassall, Marshall carried on meeting Soviet handlers after his return to London, in Kensington Gardens and Richmond Park, though he proved to be an inept spy who quickly aroused suspicion in the Foreign Office.

like Vassall, Marshall had been seen as a social misfit in Moscow. He later said that "when I came back from Moscow … I was as friendless as when I arrived there", that he had felt shunned by the embassy's diplomats, and that snobbery in the diplomatic service contributed to his treachery.

Three years after Marshall was unmasked, the Moscow embassy was, according to the espionage writer Rebecca West, "a prison where people served out their terms with a hostile climate, an alien culture, and an incomprehensible language as their jailers". But no one seems to have been on the lookout for clerical spies. The embassy's main pre-occupation was not persecuting gays, but speculating about who was sleeping with who (heterosexually), who was hitting the bottle, and who was making money on the black market.

Incredibly, over Easter 1955, Vassall went on holiday to the Black Sea at the KGB's expense, without anyone at the embassy seeming to bat an eyelid. He had been due to travel to Finland for a few days to stay with a Mr and Mrs Smith, friends at the British Embassy in Helsinki. But on 28 March, his Russian "masters" told him unambiguously that he would not be allowed to leave, and that if necessary they would cancel all flights from Leningrad (the only Russian airport offering flights to Scandinavia). He was encouraged to go to the Caucasus instead, and he arranged to fly to Tbilisi in Georgia with two British embassy secretaries, Frances Hay and Mary McCallum.

Vassall thought that Hay and McCallum readily agreed to him joining them. He already knew McCallum, who was "a bit amorous with Stan Jennings", and he had once lunched with Hay, soon after her arrival in Moscow in September 1954. But McCallum later told MI5 that she and Hay thought Vassall was "foolish, feminine and a homosexual", and that his "penchant for gossip [was] unwelcome in the small Moscow embassy community". Both women were "rather annoyed" when Vassall asked if he could join their holiday, as they felt they hardly knew him, yet they could not find "reasonable excuses" for saying no.

They were relieved when, after their first day in Tbilisi, Vassall announced that he was "fed up" and going on without them. Vassall caught a sleeper train to the resort of Sochi – the Russian equivalent of St Tropez – where he was met by his "Secret Service host": Churanov. Vassall seems to have had no qualms about accepting a free holiday from his captors, and even seems to have been excited by it. Incredibly, Vassall and Churanov stayed at a hotel that an American naval attaché had only just checked out of: courting risk seemed to be half the fun.

Vassall came to loathe Churanov, whom he regarded as a "Soho type", and it seems there were no sexual relations between them in Sochi. But it was presumably Churanov who took photos of Vassall in his hotel room wearing only a pair of boxer shorts.

Churanov drove Vassall to Lake Ritsa – normally closed to foreigners – where he was taken out on a speedboat, before being put on a plane back to Moscow. A year later, the Pecks told Vassall that they had visited Lake Ritsa: Vassall decided not to inform them of his own visit, with the KGB.

After Vassall parted company with them, Hay and McCallum had an eventful holiday of their own. An RIS[24] operation to compromise Hay, who was due to become the embassy's acting archivist, began. Walking in the hills near Tbilisi, Hay and McCallum met two men – a Georgian called Nodarim and a Russian named Peter Terpsikhorov. MI5's files do not elaborate upon what ensued, but presumably the Russians seduced Hay or engaged her in something that left her open to blackmail. Although the embassy immediately heard about an "incident" between her and a Russian, she was not "flown home" until August 1955 (or March 1956, by another

---

24   RIS (standing for Russian Intelligence Services) was commonly used by the British as shorthand for the KGB and the alphabet soup of other security agencies the Soviet Union ran – from the GPU (state political directorate) to the GRU (Main Intelligence Directorate), the NKVD (People's Commissariat of Internal Affairs), the NKGB (People's Commissariat of Stater Security), the MGB (Ministry of State Security) and of course the KGB (Committee of State Security). In 1993 the KGB morphed into the Federal Counterintelligence Service of the Russian Federation (FSK), which in turn became the Federal Security Service of the Russian Federation (FSB), which still exists today.

account) because she seems to have had friends in high places: Vassall said she had been taken skiing by Lady Hayter. When Vassall returned to Moscow from Sochi he was summoned, with others, to see the embassy's chargé d'affaires, Sir Cecil Parrott. He told them that Hay "had been very lucky to get away with it". "The way he confided to us ... made it quite clear to me that no one would dare admit a thing to anyone in authority in future", Vassall later recalled.

Bennett asked Vassall – in the embassy garden, for fear of bugs – whether he had ever done anything that might land him "in possible trouble". Vassall said he hadn't, of course. He was not interviewed about his own mysterious trip to Sochi, and the incident involving Hay then seemed to be brushed under the carpet.

The archives suggest that far from being wary of Soviet infiltration, the embassy wanted to downplay the risks. In December 1955 a Mr Slater, its head of chancery, wrote to all staff, warning of the dangers of social contact with locally engaged employees, and mentioned Mikhailsky by name. In early January 1956 Miss M. J. Wynne, a typist, reported that Mikhailsky had said he was "under Russian control", and that Vassall was one of four recent "targets", along with Michael Mullett, the military attaché's clerk, a Mr Bedworth in the engineers' department, and Arthur Barklamb in the wireless department. On 13 January 1956 Brigadier Davidson-Houston, the military attaché, passed a minute to a Mr O'Regan (deputising for Slater, who was on leave) with details of what Wynne had told him. O'Regan wrote "I have at any rate several times observed him [Mikhailsky] going to Narodnaya [where Vassall's flat was] and Sadovaya on Sundays and after hours. H M M [His Majesty's Minister] has informed H E [the ambassador]."

What O'Regan did with Davidson-Houston's memo is not clear: by the time of the Radcliffe Tribunal in 1963 he was dead. But the ambassador was certainly not informed and Vassall never seems to have been interviewed. Captain Adrian Northey, who had

succeeded Bennett as naval attaché in November 1955, had no recollection of being told that his clerk was a "target" of an embassy
employee, who many suspected was in the pay of the KGB. Nor was
Northey's assistant, Commander Humphrey James, interviewed.
James was probably working for MI6 and should have been well-
placed to make further enquiries about Vassall. The commander
remains a shadowy figure: Northey told MI5 in 1962 that he was "a
very odd naval officer ... very untidy in his dress, with his long hair,
had artistic inclinations and spoke Russian, as did his wife". James
is not mentioned in Vassall's memoirs, even though they worked
together on a daily basis, and it seems that suspicions about Vassall
never crossed his mind.

By January 1956 Bedworth and Barklamb had both left Moscow,
leaving only two names to investigate: Mullett and Vassall. The
former was later found to be involved in selling clothes on the
black market with Mikhailsky. He kept his job, though he was never
given another posting behind the Iron Curtain.

While Mullett's links to Mikhailsky were investigated in 1956,
for some unknown reason Vassall's weren't. By then "security had
obviously gone down the drain", Rebecca West wrote. If there was
a conspiracy, it seems to have been to protect Mikhailsky as much
as Vassall or anyone else. Mikhailsky was not fired until September
1956 – some eight months after Wynne's warning – when he tried
to ensnare another wireless maintenance engineer in "black market
offences".[25] One embassy official, David Whyte, suggested to another, John Street, that Mikhailsky should be "interrogated" before his
dismissal, but Street "concluded that this would not be possible",
MI5 later found.

Charles Elwell, the MI5 officer who interviewed Vassall more
than a dozen times after his imprisonment, wrote that if Mikhailsky

---

25   One possible reason why Mikhailsky survived is that he traded on being a Pole, not a Russian. In June
      1956 Soviet-Polish relations were strained by the Poznan uprising, where protesters chanted "Down with
      Soviet occupation!". The revolt was soon brutally suppressed with Soviet help.

had been questioned properly "Vassall's career as a spy might have been nipped in the bud". Mikhailsky "had left a trail of mischief behind him in the embassy" but somehow, that trail never led anyone to John Vassall.

● ● ●

In November 1955, a few days after writing his glowing "Never ruffled, always helpful" report on Vassall, Geoffrey Bennett left Moscow. Vassall was one of thirty guests at a farewell dinner party that Hayter threw. Bennett told his successor, Captain Adrian Northey, that Vassall was a "possible latent homosexual" but left it at that. Later, Northey did not recall being told this and he insisted that although he had found Vassall "rather a pansy little man", he never suspected he was gay.

Soon afterwards, Vassall started to seek his next job. His two-year posting in Moscow was due to end in March 1956. Over the winter, Vassall spoke to a kindly Swedish neighbour, Major Hallstrom, about the possibility of a job in Sweden, but Hallstrom only gave him the address of the Swedish Chamber of Commerce in London. Vassall may have also written to the United Nations in New York, without success.

On 10 December 1954 Vassall had written to H. V. Pennells, who had landed him the job in Moscow, and lied through his teeth. "I like working for Captain Bennett and don't mind in the least the odd things that have to be done in such a post," Vassall wrote. "It is good to know that one is doing something worthwhile. The work and the people one comes into contact with are immensely interesting". The letter's purpose seems to have been to keep Pennells sweet for when Vassall's posting ended. In January 1956, Vassall wrote again to ask for another overseas job – but not behind the Iron Curtain. "One hears of jobs in NATO and the British Joint Services Mission, Washington, but I don't know how one should apply unless it is through the Ministry of Defence," he wrote. If Pennells could not secure Vassall another foreign posting, could he at least work for a British civil servant who "travel[s] abroad occasionally"?

"I shall never forget the many unusual and extraordinary happenings that go on here," Vassall's letter concluded. Read one way, Vassall appreciated his exciting Moscow posting. Read another, he was admitting that he had been to hell and back, and that he couldn't wait to get home. Pennells replied cordially, but added "While I sympathise with your wish to continue the exotic life, I must advise you that you are reaching the stage [when] people will undoubtedly prefer you to have a term in the Admiralty".

Early in 1956 Vassall went on another trip to Leningrad with Northey and the assistant military attaché, Roy Smith. His main duty was to guard documents in their train compartment en route. Vassall told his handlers about the upcoming trip but they already knew about it. They ordered him to meet them there and leave the suite of hotel rooms he shared with the attachés unoccupied, so they could be searched. During a meeting with a KGB man Vassall appears to have been drugged again: "All I remember ... was that I was given a drink, then everything is a blank", he recalled. But when he returned to their rooms, nothing was out of place. Northey and Smith seem not to have suspected a thing.

Far from being sent home early from Moscow as a security risk, Vassall's tour was extended beyond the usual two years. His return to Britain was delayed from March until June because his successor, a Miss Tidmarsh, could not yet leave her current post in Berlin. Tidmarsh, who spoke both German and Russian, had applied for the same job in 1954 but been pipped to the post by Vassall, apparently because her Russian parentage counted against her.

While Vassall was keen to head home, and hoped he could then escape the Russians' demands, he was probably somewhat happy to be in Moscow for a few more months during spring 1956, just as things got really interesting there.

On Saturday 11 February 1956, British journalists in Moscow were invited to a mysterious press conference in a private lounge at the Hotel National. Only two, a Reuters man and the *Sunday Times* correspondent, turned up. They were astonished to see Guy Burgess and Donald Maclean – the two British spies who had defected to Moscow in 1951 but had not been seen since – sitting in easy chairs. Burgess and Maclean refused to answer questions but handed the two reporters a typed statement, written in Russian and badly translated into English, which explained that they had come to Moscow "to work for ... better understanding between the Soviet Union and the West". The same statement was published in the Soviet newspapers *Pravda* and *Izvestia* the following day, and broadcast continuously on Radio Moscow's English programme.

Coming two months before Bulganin and Khrushchev's planned visit to Britain,[26] and hot on the heels of the former's offer to forge a "pact of friendship" with Eisenhower, Burgess and Maclean's reappearance sent shockwaves through London and Washington. John Vassall got closer to the spies than many reporters did: on 12 February he went to a cocktail party, thrown by the incoming Canadian naval attaché, in the very room they had appeared in twenty-four hours earlier. Vassall seems to have fantasised about meeting both men. "I expect Maclean may have known about me, although I don't believe the Russians wanted us to meet to tell them that I had been compromised", he later wrote Delphically.

A few days after Burgess and Maclean emerged, Nikita Khrushchev delivered his so-called "secret speech" at the Twentieth Congress of the Communist Party of the Soviet Union at the Kremlin. In the early hours of 25 February, after most delegates had gone home, Khrushchev dropped a bombshell on fellow members of the Presidium. Over four hours, he denounced Stalin for having orchestrated a "whole series of exceedingly serious perversions

---

26 Bulganin, as chairman of the Soviet Union's council of ministers, was at the time technically senior to Khrushchev, but he was soon eclipsed.

of party principles, of party democracy, [and] of revolutionary legality". Stalin had been, Khrushchev thundered, a "distrustful and sickly suspicious man" who had "made possible the cruellest repression". Khrushchev even denounced Stalin as "a coward", reminding the Politburo that "not once during the whole war did he dare to go to the front". The speech, which was greeted by stunned silence, was not a secret for long: by the end of March it had been reported around the world, causing jubilation in the West and consternation in the East.

No doubt wanting to get closer to the man of the moment, as he always did, Vassall asked Northey if he could accompany him on Khrushchev and Bulganin's official visit to Britain in April: the first visit by Soviet leaders since the 1917 revolution. Vassall also asked the Russians if he could go, but they and Northey refused him. Northey would be the only Briton accompanying the Soviet delegation on their crossing on the *Ordzhonikidze*, a Soviet cruiser, and Vassall had to settle for seeing Northey off at a Moscow railway station, en route to Konigsberg where he joined the ship. "Capt Northey would have taken me, had I been allowed to go", Vassall later claimed.

Vassall thus narrowly missed having a ringside seat to one of Britain's most embarrassing moments in the Cold War: the mysterious disappearance of a veteran Royal Navy diver, Commander Lionel 'Buster' Crabb, who mounted an unauthorised examination of the *Ordzhonikidze*'s hull after she docked at Portsmouth harbour. A furious Anthony Eden soon had no option but to issue a humiliating apology to the Russians for a frogman's examination of the cruiser's hull, which he said had "occurred without any permission whatever".[27] Vassall recalled that he was fascinated by Pathé News footage of the Soviet leaders being driven through the streets of Mayfair to Claridge's, next door to his gentlemen's club, the Bath.

---

27 MI6's director Sir John Sinclair left his post soon afterwards, and while he may have planned to retire anyway, the incident hardly did the service's credibility any good.

But Bulganin and Khrushchev's visit had turned into a diplomatic disaster. Just as the Vassall scandal was later overshadowed by the Profumo affair, Khrushchev's visit was soon overshadowed by an even greater crisis: Suez.

Back in Moscow, Vassall embarked on a final affair in early 1956, with a Czech man he had met at one of Mikhailsky's dinners at the Metropole Hotel. "My social life flourished. There was never a spare day or night", he later wrote.

He attended a performance of Verdi's *Requiem*, and on the following night the Verdi opera *Il Corsaro* with a delegation from Manchester, Leningrad's twin city. Over Easter 1956 Vassall went on another holiday in the Caucasus with three embassy friends: Mary Hill, his flatmate Stanley Ford, and Angela Winder. As with Frances Hay and Mary McCallum the previous year, Vassall informed the others that they were being followed, and when Russian students invited them to a party, Vassall and Ford urged caution and the girls did not go. Hill and Winder were being warned of possible entrapment by a man who knew only too well what the costs could be.

Yet Vassall's Russian handlers almost seemed to court discovery, buying him tickets to the Bolshoi Ballet, and shortly before his departure from Moscow in June they took him on a final holiday to Yalta, on the Black Sea. Again, Vassall went on an expenses-paid trip across Russia, arranged by the KGB, which appeared to raise no eyebrows in the embassy.

By the end of his time in Moscow, Vassall's flat appears to have been bugged: after he expressed some criticism of other Brits to Stanley Ford, the Russians quoted some of his remarks at a subsequent meeting. To his horror, Vassall soon learned that they expected him to continue spying when he got back to London, even though he was not sure what his next job would be. At his final meetings in Moscow, he was introduced to someone he had not seen before. Vassall was told that his name was Gregory, and that they would meet regularly in London. "My heart sank; I had imagined that on leaving Moscow my troubles would be all over, and that I could forget about the whole beastly business" Vassall recalled. Gregory told Vassall when they would have their first London rendezvous, and where: outside Frognal Station on the Finchley Road. Ominously, Gregory asked Vassall if he had ever used a Minox – a miniature camera invented by the Nazis during the Second World War.

At their last meeting with Vassall in Moscow, Churanov, Nikolai and Gregory "enfolded him in a simultaneous hug". Churanov said "Do not forget that we will meet again". But Vassall had no wish to return to a city that was indelibly associated with his sexual humiliation. It was the last time that Vassall ever saw Churanov or Nikolai. But Gregory was to haunt him for the next five years.[28]

The night before Vassall left Moscow for good, Captain Northey and his wife threw a big party for him at their flat. After a buffet supper, Northey made a speech that included a weak attempt at a pun, describing Vassall as "his best vessel". Vassall was asked to say a few words himself, telling guests that the occasion was a "culmination of a most extraordinary tour of duty", before the carpets were rolled back for dancing. At a table in a corner of the drawing room, he played roulette with Baroness Akerhielm, a Swedish aristocrat.

As with Vassall's journey to Moscow in 1954, his return to London in early June 1956 was not direct. In fact, he went on an extraordinary odyssey via Sweden, Norway, the US, Canada, Mexico, and then Sweden again. He met his mother, who had flown out from London, in Helsinki. Together, they sailed across the Baltic

---

28   The Russians do not seem to have given Vassall a "golden goodbye". In his last few weeks in Moscow Vassall sold many of his possessions to a diplomat called Huse, the secretary archivist of the Norwegian embassy. In 1962 MI5 pondered whether the payments from Huse to Vassall were in fact monies from the Russians, channelled via Huse, who later opened a Barclays Bank account in London and made unusually large deposits into it. In fact, it seems that Vassall was only ever paid in cash, not via any bank account, and Huse was entirely unaware of his spying.

to Stockholm, where they saw the Royal Yacht, *Britannia*, moored for the Queen and Duke of Edinburgh's state visit. It was the closest that Vassall came to the royals, as Baroness Akerhielm told him that the ticket she had promised him to a royal ball could not be had for love or money.

Vassall and his mother then caught a train to Oslo, where a Norwegian naval attaché suggested to Vassall that he should go to America by ship, not plane. Having said goodbye to his mother, who flew back to England, Vassall sailed from Bergen to New York on the SS *Oslofiord*, enjoying the *dansants* with three single American women, one of whom described Vassall as her "chaperone".

In New York, Vassall said that "everything seemed so sleek and 'with-it'". After a few nights he and his friend, David Marine, went down to Baltimore and then Delaware, where Vassall was introduced to Marine's parents. The Americans only seemed interested in the bottles of whisky he had brought with him, Vassall recalled.

In Los Angeles, Vassall stayed with a friend of a friend, a Dr R. Koons, and then spent a night with his own friend, Ken Rolfe in Beverly Hills. Then, he flew to Vancouver to see another friend called Grant, explored Mexico, and flew back to Stockholm via Los Angeles to collect his luggage and return to England.

This "extensive tour would have gone far to wiping out" Vassall's modest earnings in Moscow, Nigel West argues. But no one seems to have asked Vassall how he spent the few weeks between leaving Moscow and reaching London. And no one asked how he had paid for them.

CHAPTER THREE

"THE SUITABLE CANDIDATE": VASSALL IN LONDON

After returning to London in July 1956, John Vassall's instinct was to "keep away from the Russians." But he knew that he had no choice but to keep his first date with his new Soviet handler, still only known to him as "Gregory", outside Frognal station at 7.30 p.m. one summer evening.[29]

For this first rendezvous Vassall was told to wear a "Tyrolean hat with a brush of feathers" so that Gregory would recognise him. But while Vassall may have seen this encounter as an opportunity to dress up, the Russians treated it with deadly seriousness. "Gregory" was not a minor Russian functionary, but none other than Nikolai Borisovich Rodin, a KGB general who had also used the cover name Korovin from 1953 onwards.[30] "Gregory" was to be Vassall's main handler in London, living at a flat in Pelham Court, Kensington, until he suddenly left the city in April 1961.

Outwardly, Vassall led an innocuous life back in London. For

---

29   The station is officially known as Finchley Road & Frognal, and is now on the London Overground network.

30   Born in Moscow in 1907, Rodin was married with three children. After working in Moscow as an aeronautical engineer, in 1939 he went to New York to work for the Autrog Trade Corporation – a cover for his real job in Soviet military intelligence. In 1944 Rodin returned to Russia and in 1947 he re-emerged in London. Again, his official job – as a scientific adviser – concealed his real one, as "resident" (head) of the KGB's London section. Apparently Rodin met George Blake in 1953, and again in 1955.

the next two-and-a-half years he lived with his parents in St John's Wood, as he had before his posting. Many writers have argued that Vassall was a simpleton who was lucky to carry on spying for another six years without arousing the suspicions of his family, or his employers. In fact, he was a resilient spy. Unlike many other victims of blackmail, he did not commit suicide, emigrate, reveal himself and beg the British to spare him from prosecution, or hit the bottle and drunkenly confess all to a friend or colleague.

John Vassall was disciplined and obedient: when told to lie low for a few months he would. He and his handlers never used "dead drops" (leaving documents in public places to be picked up), but instead handed them over in person. Such tactics seem risky today, given the ubiquity of CCTV and phone tracking, but in the late 1950s these technologies were unheard of. The pitch was tilted in the spy's favour, as the authorities could only determine whether anyone was meeting people they shouldn't through physical sur-veillance, which was labour intensive. Unless he was on a list of suspects, Vassall was safe, and until the summer of 1962 he never seemed to be under suspicion.

Vassall was considered much more competent than many other westerners who spied for the Soviets.[31] Vassall's methodology was similar to that followed by Anthony Blunt and John Cairncross during the Second World War, and almost identical to several other post-war Soviet spies, such as the Canadian Hugo Hambleton, an academic recruited in Ottawa in 1952 by a KGB officer called Vladimir Borodin.[32]

From July 1956 onwards Vassall regularly left the Admiralty at the end of the working day with any documents he could lay his hands

---

31 Yuri Andropov, who became chair of the KGB in 1967, once complained about a lack of American agents "of the caliber of the Britons Kim Philby, George Blake and John Vassall".

32 Hambleton's regular rendezvouses with his handler, "Paul", in and around the 18th and 19th arrondisse-ments, and his use of dead drops behind tombstones in the Père Lachaise cemetery are a Parisian equivalent of Vassall's assignations in London. Like Vassall, Hambleton was a Catholic convert who was ordered to lay low in 1961 and like Vassall, he was regularly given cash for "travel expenses" around Europe.

on. These were then copied during his meetings with Gregory and returned to him, so that he could replace them before they were missed. The Russians advised Vassall to always carry a briefcase or newspaper to work so that he could conceal documents and avoid "snap checks", which they felt wouldn't involve a thorough search of bags, or newspapers. In fact, "snap checks" of staff leaving the Admiralty, or other Whitehall departments, were almost unheard of.

Meetings with Gregory were always at 7.30 p.m. apart from emergency ones which were at 7.50 p.m. If Vassall was late, Gregory would check every 15 minutes until 8.30 p.m.; if Vassall could not attend at all he was to return to the same place at 7.30 p.m. the following evening. Vassall and Gregory typically went to a restaurant or pub while an assistant copied the documents that Vassall had brought, but from the middle of 1957 onwards, Vassall often took photographs of the documents himself, at home. Then, rather than hand documents over to Gregory he simply gave him films to be developed, in a small box sealed with Scotch tape. Despite the change in Vassall's methodology, the dinners and drinking sessions continued but they would finish by 9.30 p.m., as a car would pick Gregory up at 10 p.m. to drive him home. Vassall would travel home by train or tube.

Vassall always wrote details of his assignations with Russian contacts in pencil in his diary and erased them later, in case his diary was ever found. Once he had access to information of real importance, including atomic secrets, Vassall was trained in spycraft and taught how to lose a tail: taking a tube train in the opposite direction to his destination, getting off at the last minute before the doors closed, and then doubling back. He was told that if he suspected being followed to a rendezvous point he should stop, bend down and tie his shoelace, to warn Gregory to stay away. But he never felt that he was being followed.

Soon they devised a system of secret messages in London telephone boxes – one outside St John's Wood tube station, and later, one on Grosvenor Road outside Dolphin Square, where Vassall lived from 1959 onwards. On a painted strip above the telephone itself Gregory or Vassall would write, in pencil, a 1 in a circle if they needed to meet at a pre-arranged spot the next night; a 2 if they were to meet at 7.30 p.m. on Monday the following week, a 3 if they were to meet the week after next and a 4 if they needed to meet urgently. An x in a circle meant that Vassall was not to make contact for another month. An Ø (later changed to +) indicated that they should only meet monthly for the next six months. An O indicated that Vassall feared he was at risk of imminent arrest, and square brackets meant that Vassall should watch out, as the Russians believed that the police or MI5 were watching him.

Eventually, signals in phone boxes were abandoned as there was no sign of any interest in Vassall, so there was no need to depart from meeting every three weeks. Vassall later told MI5 that he only wrote symbols in the phone box outside Dolphin Square twice, both after he had been kept late in the office by Tam Galbraith, the minister he worked for. Vassall felt uneasy writing signals in a phone box outside Dolphin Square, even if the Admiralty may not initially have been aware that he lived there.

Gregory had another system, sending Vassall a motor car catalogue in the post if he needed to meet him urgently at a designated spot – a quiet suburban street called The Drive, a short walk from Brent tube station,[33] at 7.30 p.m. the following Monday. Sometimes Vassall turned up there on time and found no one to meet him: the Russians were observing him from a discreet distance, to check he was being obedient. During the Suez crisis Vassall skipped some meetings because he claimed to be too busy. Gregory was lenient, but highly professional: when he bumped into Vassall and his mother at a performance of the Bolshoi ballet, he completely blanked him.

---

33   Brent station has since been renamed as Brent Cross, after the nearby shopping centre.

Vassall sometimes met Gregory on Church Road, Richmond Hill, where Gregory said there was a British intelligence "training school" nearby. Gregory and Vassall went for long walks after they met at Frognal station, as far as Heath Drive where they would separate. Walking through residential streets in Hampstead, an area teeming with MPs, civil servants and journalists, was inherently risky. The Labour leader, Hugh Gaitskell, lived on Frognal Gardens then, just a few yards from Vassall and Gregory's walking route.

In time, the pair abandoned Frognal station and opted instead to rendezvous at near stations (which the carless Vassall could easily travel to) in more obscure, far-flung suburbs of north and west London: Worcester Park, Streatham, Southfields, Alperton, Edgware, Harrow, and at a Greek restaurant on Cockfosters Road, Barnet.

These suburban meetings were still not without risk. In November 1958 Vassall and Gregory dined at the Kings Head Hotel in Harrow-on-the-Hill, an upmarket inn just yards from one of England's foremost public schools.[34] Vassall claims that the Russians always "checked" meeting places to ensure they were not bugged or frequented by the security services, but there was always a risk of bumping into police officers, on or off duty. After dinner Vassall found that another diner had mistakenly taken his coat (a navy blue Crombie) from the cloakroom, leaving a similar coat behind. Vassall contacted the Kings Head the next day to ask if anyone had reported picking up his coat. It had been picked up by a Scotland Yard policeman, who was dining at the hotel at the same time. They met in Trafalgar Square to exchange their coats. Vassall was very relieved that he had not left any microfilms, or anything else incriminating, in his pockets. Gregory was "furious", Vassall later claimed, and argued that Vassall should have forgotten about the coat and not contacted the hotel. "Talk about playing with fire – this was

---

34   The pub is, like many of Vassall's old rendezvous points, now closed and converted into flats.

more like T. N. T.", said Vassall. It never occurred to Vassall and Gregory that it might have been best not to go out for dinner together at all.

Vassall seems to have been more cautious than the reckless Gregory, and early on he vetoed one communication method. Gregory told Vassall that in "a grave emergency" he should go to the Duchess of Bedford Walk, a footpath on the eastern edge of Holland Park, not far from the Soviet embassy. He had to mark a pink cross (or a circle) in chalk, on a plane tree outside Plane Tree House, to signal that he wanted to meet Gregory at 7.30 p.m. the following evening. Gregory probably did not know that the spot was just a couple of hundred yards from what was left of the seventeenth-century Holland House (wartime bombing had destroyed much of it), where Vassall's distant cousin Elizabeth Vassall had created her salon in the early 1800s.[35]

Vassall found these rituals humiliating, not exciting, and so risky that they seemed like madness. After making use of the Holland Park system, twice at most, Vassall "rebelled at the insecurity" and refused to do it again. He also rejected the idea of making chalk marks on the pavement outside Addison House, where he lived with his parents. Eventually, the whole system of chalk marks on pavements and fences was abandoned as too insecure.

Vassall also disliked another emergency measure, calling Gregory's home phone number – KEN 8955 – at 8 a.m., 1.30 p.m. or 10 p.m., and asking for "Miss Mary", to signal that he needed to meet Gregory urgently: a tactic that was bound to raise suspicion if MI5 tapped the line.[36] "The whole business was utterly revolting but it was all part of the elaborate safety precautions that were taken by

---

35   One of the iconic images of the London blitz is a photograph of well-dressed Londoners browsing in Holland House's library, whose shelves had miraculously survived even though its roof had been destroyed. See: https://commons.wikimedia.org/wiki/File:Holland_House_library_after_an_air_raid.jpg.

36   The number KEN 8955 was later reallocated to Mrs Norah Reeve, the widow of an Indian Army brigadier who moved into Gregory's flat in Pelham Court after he left. She complained in the autumn of 1962 that she wanted the number changed, but also told newspapers what she thought of "Gregory's" interior design: "It was tastefully furnished, but I didn't like it, so I sold the lot.".

the Russians" he later rationalised. In fact, the Russians' "safety precautions" only increased the risk of discovery, and Vassall seems to have told his Russian handlers to be careful as often as they reminded him.

Gregory and Vassall did not have an equal relationship. Photographs from the Hotel Berlin were always lurking in the background. "It was made quite clear to me, in the most polite terms, that if I did not fulfil my task something would happen to me", Vassall recalled. But like his predecessors, Churanov and Nikolai, Gregory's menace was mixed with charm. Nigel West says that Vassall "developed a reliance and even friendship with his Soviet contacts" in London. Vassall felt that he was obliged to carry on handing over secrets, lest Gregory's career suffered. "I even felt that his success as a diplomat depended upon me: if I did not hand over the goods he too would be in a very awkward position", Vassall explained. In 1962 Vassall told MI5 of Gregory's "hypnotic charm and personal magnetism".

Gregory was seventeen years older than Vassall. He was, MI5 later surmised, a "father figure who satisfied his emotional needs". Gregory once told Vassall that "he liked me because I was unlike his other contacts who were always talking about money or complaining about their wives", Vassall said. "He was a man of the world ... We had quite a lot in common and used to talk about travel, painting, music and human nature".

Gregory always said he wanted to be more generous than security considerations permitted. He claimed that he would have liked to take Vassall out to dinner in the West End "but this would have been insecure". Once, he suggested a holiday in the Bahamas or Bermuda – presumably at the KGB's expense – although Vassall never accepted the offer. Gregory told Vassall that he was not spying at all, but merely sharing "information needed to brief a possible future Summit conference", that would broker a lasting peace between Russia and western powers.

Gregory was not, of course, a friend in any way, but a manipulative spymaster who merely said what Vassall wanted to hear. Out of sheer self-preservation, and to avoid going mad, Vassall seems to have persuaded himself that Gregory was sincere.

● ● ●

Soon after he returned to London in July 1956 Vassall met a civil assistant at the Admiralty and was offered a job in the office of the Director of Naval Intelligence (DNI). He began working there on 25 July.

Vassall was back in the Admiralty building, a grand edifice of red brick and Portland Stone. As a symbol of the imperial Royal Navy's power and prestige, it couldn't be beaten. Vassall's new office overlooked Horse Guards Parade, with a view extending to St James's Park and the garden of No. 10 Downing Street. After the stuffiness of the Moscow embassy it was a definite step up. Soon, Vassall had a ringside seat to the Suez crisis in October 1956, during which "our office became a hive of industry with uniformed staff coming and going from the Ministry of Defence and other agencies".

Although some have claimed that his move to the Naval Intelligence Division (NID) meant that he must have had a "protector" or "sponsor" inside the Admiralty, it was, in fact, common for a clerk returning from a foreign embassy to be allocated to the NID. As in Moscow, Vassall was still a very junior clerical officer, but he later said that from July 1956 to June 1957 he was "acting as a secretary" to the deputy director of naval intelligence, a Captain Best (Vassall never told the Russians that he thought Best did not like him and was rude: some secrets were too intimate to divulge).

Incredibly, within two weeks of Vassall starting work at the NID, the DNI himself (Vice-Admiral Sir John Inglis) placed him on a list of staff who were allowed access to classified atomic information, before Vassall's positive vetting was complete.[37] Vassall was made the NID's "atomic liaison officer" and was given the combination for a steel cupboard in another secretary's room, which he said contained "top secret nuclear matters". Technically, Vassall's "atomic clearance" lapsed in 1959, but this seems to have made no difference to what he was and was not allowed to see. Most cupboards and cabinets in the offices that Vassall had access to were kept unlocked, during the day at least.

Vassall claims that he did not resume handing over documents, including the minutes of Admiralty Board meetings, to Gregory until after the Suez crisis of October 1956. But once he did, he sometimes put them in an "On Her Majesty's Service" foolscap envelope, as if tacitly goading the Admiralty for its woeful security measures.

He was now subjected to a new regime of "positive vetting", designed to identify employees with extremist views, and those vulnerable to blackmail because of alcoholism, heavy debts, homosexuality or other vices. Throughout the 1950s Whitehall was constantly "tightening up" security: especially after Maclean and Burgess's defection in 1951, and after rumours that their old friend Kim Philby had been their "Third Man" emerged in 1955. A "Statement on the findings of the Conference of Privy Counsellors on Security," published in March 1956, said that "There is a duty on departments to inform themselves of serious failings such as drunkenness, addiction to drugs, homosexuality or any loose living that may affect a man's reliability". Department heads had a "duty to know their staff and they must not fail to report anything which effects security."

In 1961, after the jailing of George Blake and the unmasking of the Portland ring, Prime Minister Harold Macmillan established

---

37   Richard Deacon said that Vassall's work for the NID was "almost exclusively concerned with highly classified material". Vassall "dealt with the in-trays and out-trays of naval officers and civilians of the highest ranks", Chapman Pincher claimed.

another committee led by Sir Charles Romer (a Lord Justice of Appeal) to get to the bottom of what was wrong with British naval security. In 1962, Lord Radcliffe conducted a similar review, only to chair yet another inquiry in 1963 after Vassall's conviction.

In theory, positive vetting was robust and foolproof. But in practice it was absurdly superficial. Until 1960, the process did not even involve a criminal records check. The novelist Muriel Spark once said that during the Second World War she secured a job in MI6's Political Warfare Executive, a secret propaganda unit, largely because she was seen bearing an Ivy Compton-Burnett novel at her interview, which evidently marked her out as "one of us". Vassall's experience shows that the system had not changed much by the late 1950s.

The vetting system was handicapped, not just by class discrimination, but by a lack of trained staff. Neither interviews nor field enquiries were carried out by MI5, because its deputy director Graham Mitchell had recommended that the service was too secret to be exposed to the public. Instead, legwork was done by a "procurement executive" in the Ministry of Defence (MOD), and MI5's only role was to "cross-check": to see whether those being vetted appeared on lists of people already deemed to be a security risk.

It is clear that the authorities did not even attempt to look into Vassall's homosexual relationships, which he had never been very discreet about. Vassall's vetting began on 7 August 1956, and clearance was granted on 10 December. What exactly happened in the intervening four months is not clear. Incredibly, no one spoke to any of Vassall's colleagues or acquaintances in Moscow. Geoffrey Bennett, who had in effect been Vassall's line manager for almost two years, was never spoken to, because it was supposed that he was on his way to the Far East. One of the world's biggest military powers seemed to have no way of establishing communication between Whitehall and the Far East. In fact Bennett was in Portsmouth, barely sixty miles from London. Adrian Northey was not contacted in Moscow either.

Vassall was surprisingly honest in his vetting questionnaire, which he completed on 23 August 1956. In the "Foreign Travel" section he almost ran out of space listing all his foreign holidays in the last decade: to France, Spain, Switzerland, Finland, Sweden, Norway, the USA, Canada, Denmark and Germany. In the days before budget airlines, this was an extraordinary number of foreign holidays for a poorly paid clerk, but no one seems to have queried them.

Vassall was asked to provide two character references. To begin with he gave Rear-Admiral R. M. King DSO and a Doctor W. L. Dunlop, living in London NW4. But King, who Vassall later said was a friend of his mother, told the Admiralty that he had only known Vassall well during the Second World War, and had barely seen him since. Dunlop – previously the Vassall family's doctor – said he had not seen Vassall since about 1944. Vassall was told he had to supply new referees who had known him well over the past three years. Rather than people he'd worked with in Moscow, the two referees he supplied were both elderly women, and neighbours of the Vassalls: Dr Agnes Francklyn (a part-time, semi-retired doctor), and Miss Elizabeth Roberts, a retired civil servant living at 3 Addison House, adjacent to the Vassalls' flat.

"It might now appear as if [Vassall] were trying to exclude from the field of enquiry any close men friends that he had," the Radcliffe report concluded in 1963. But Vassall had been overseas for two years, so it may have been concluded that he simply didn't know many men who could be interviewed in London.

In 1956, vetting questionnaires asked referees whether candidates were "free from pecuniary embarrassments", whether they had communist or fascist associations, and whether there were any "further circumstances which would tend to disqualify the candidate from Government employment of a secret nature". But the form did not directly ask about blackmail, or sexuality, and both Roberts and Francklyn gave Vassall a clean bill of health. Francklyn said that she had "known him to attend Conservative meetings", while Roberts said that Vassall was "most conscientious" and "decidedly discreet", and that he "disliked both" communism and fascism.

Roberts "was careful to point out that he took little interest in the opposite sex," wrote Rebecca West, but "the Royal Navy was, however, too innocent to take the old lady's point". Roberts's subtle hints that Vassall was gay do not appear to have prompted any suspicions (while being gay would not automatically make him a security risk, in the 1950s, many believed that it did).

Vassall later told MI5 that in the summer of 1956 he spent two hours with "the JIB" – the Joint Intelligence Bureau, part of the MOD – as part of his vetting. This was not an intrusive interrogation, as Vassall implied. Instead, it seems to have been a friendly chat with Mr E. S. Sherwood, a former deputy commissioner of police in Nigeria, who seemed impressed that Vassall was from a respectable family, and that he was a member of the Bath Club. The vetting included background checks on Vassall's closest relatives, but the fact that his father was a former Church of England vicar and RAF chaplain still working as a curate, and his brother Richard was a "heating and ventilation consultant", still living with John and their parents at Addison House, reassured Sherwood that no further checks were necessary. Sherwood concluded that, as Norman Lucas put it, Vassall was a "reserved, sober and reliable young man of good character and unquestioned loyalty ... [who] appeared to possess a strong dislike of communism and the Soviet way of life". Sherwood's report said, "He spoke to me at some length regarding his stay in Moscow and has no wish to return there" but Sherwood does not seem to have asked Vassall, or himself, why not.

On 10 December 1956, Vassall was "cleared for security for access to classified atomic information up to and including Top Secret, and for regular and constant access to Top Secret defence information". He was "white-carded" for five years, with a subsequent check due on, or before, 7 December 1961 but this did not occur because of a "heavy backlog". In addition, there was no automatic revetting after a major change of circumstances – such as when Vassall moved out of the family home and into a rented flat at Dolphin Square in 1959.

• • •

In early 1957 cuts in defence expenditure caught up with Vassall. He was effectively made redundant from Naval Intelligence, as when it did not need so many clerks preference was given to ones that were more competent or experienced. Vassall was obliged to look for a job elsewhere in the Admiralty or beyond.

If Vassall did have a "sponsor" in the Admiralty it was a bureaucrat called P. N. N. Synott, its principal establishment officer. Vassall had first approached Synott in 1951 or 1952 to seek his help in escaping the Naval Law branch, which he found "boring". Synott helped Vassall to move to the War Registry, and possibly helped him to land his new job at Naval Intelligence. In 1957 Vassall asked Synott for help again, but Synott told him that he had "to go up the hard way and earn his promotion to executive officer". However, Synott did mention Vassall's name to another bureaucrat, W. J. E. Attwell, and stressed his "good appearance, manners and background".

Later, Vassall told MI5 that he had only reapproached Synott because of pressure from the Russians, who wanted to see him promoted. Lord Radcliffe concluded in 1963 that Vassall had not been "given any special or indulgent treatment at all" and "the problem seems to have been to find work that he could do [rather] than to find attractive work for him". But in early 1957 good words from Synott, and Attwell, did land Vassall his favourite job: in the private office of an Admiralty minister.

At the beginning of 1957 Thomas (Tam) Galbraith, the Conservative and Unionist MP for Glasgow Hillhead, was promoted from the whips' office to become the Civil Lord of the Admiralty, with responsibility for civilian staff, its works and buildings departments and naval lands.

After Suez, J. B. Priestley wrote, "abroad we cut a shabby figure in power politics and at home we shrug it all away or go to the theatre to applaud the latest jeers and sneers at Britannia." But the Admiralty was still one of the most respected departments in Whitehall. Even if he had not been officially promoted, working for a minister – any minister – delighted Vassall, who was always obsessed with status. Unlike his previous bosses he found Galbraith congenial and friendly – a friendliness that was to have fatal consequences for Galbraith's career.

As soon as he became Civil Lord, Tam Galbraith felt that his private secretary, John Peters, needed more support. An extra clerical position was created, and Vassall came in for an interview with Galbraith. "I took an immediate liking to him and I think he must have for me, for he asked few questions and merely told me about his office", Vassall recalled. The job as clerk – or "assistant private secretary" as Vassall described it, was his: he could start whenever he liked, and in May 1957 he did.

His new office overlooked the Mall and he had a direct view of Admiralty Arch and a statue of Captain Cook. Always wanting to move in higher circles, Vassall took to lunching at the Treasury Solicitor's Luncheon Club and eyeing the senior civil servants there wistfully. His duties in Galbraith's office were, Ronald Seth once quipped, "to act as a kind of Nanny to the chief, a job which suited his temperament very well". Vassall was effectively a personal assistant, typing up Galbraith's correspondence, managing his diary, and scanning newspapers for any stories that would be of interest to him. Vassall seems to have loved every minute of it.

He soon found himself going to the House of Commons, sometimes in a ministerial car, with a black box containing official papers for Galbraith to read and sign. Vassall sat in the civil servants' box in the Commons chamber during one late-night debate, though he is silent on whether he ever had to pass an urgent note to Galbraith at the despatch box. Naturally, he loved seeing all the household names milling about. "The person I most liked to see was Lord [Rab] Butler" (who was then Home Secretary and widely seen as Macmillan's heir apparent), Vassall later recalled. You can sense that Vassall would have been beside himself with joy if Butler had deigned to speak to him.

Vassall once needed to walk to Galbraith's London home (a small but elegant Queen Anne house on Cowley Street, five minutes' walk from the Commons) bearing a black box whose contents the Civil Lord had to see immediately. On the way, Vassall bumped into Galbraith, who told Vassall to press on and drop the box at his house. He was, to his joy, invited to stay for sherry with Galbraith's Belgian wife Simone and her sisters, who were visiting from Belgium. Before long, Galbraith invited Vassall for lunch at Cowley Street: an "invitation I cherished, for I liked doing anything with Mr Galbraith". Upon his arrival, he was ushered into an upstairs sitting room, where he met Simone again. After Galbraith arrived, they had sherry, and then lunch. "I felt very much at home in this atmosphere". Indeed, suddenly Vassall felt like he was being treated as an equal, not an underling who had to be entertained through gritted teeth.

Vassall frequently took urgent papers up to the Galbraiths' main residence, Barskimming House in Ayrshire, Scotland: an elegant neo-Georgian pile that had been built in 1882. Galbraith normally went up to Barskimming on Thursday night or Friday morning, and if papers that he needed to see arrived after then, it was Vassall's job to take them up on a night train from Euston.

It appears that Vassall himself first suggested these long rail journeys, rather than have papers sent by another messenger, but Galbraith readily agreed, as did Sir Clifford Jarrett, the Admiralty's permanent secretary. Jarrett once gave Vassall urgent papers for

Galbraith and offered to write him a second-class railway warrant then and there, but Vassall felt that first class was the appropriate way to convey classified Admiralty documents. He always paid the difference between the second- and first-class fare himself.

On one of these visits, Vassall recalled, Mrs Galbraith took him upstairs to a sitting room, where he was given tea and something to eat. At 10 a.m. Galbraith himself appeared. Galbraith went through the black box as Vassall read newspapers, before calling Vassall in to discuss its contents. By now, Galbraith's mood had softened: he asked Vassall to stay for lunch with his parents, Lord and Lady Strathclyde, who lived in a converted stable block adjacent to the main house. Naturally, Vassall was "delighted to stay" to meet them, and two of their daughters (Tam's sisters). After lunch Vassall was asked "where he was going to spend the weekend", and he replied that he might go to Turnberry, the nearby golf course. Instead, he found himself invited to join one of Galbraith's sisters at a gymkhana. The Galbraiths gave Vassall "ideas for sailing on the Clyde" the next day, before one of the Galbraiths' horsey friends gave him a lift from the gymkhana to Turnberry. After a night in a hotel there, Vassall spent the Sunday on a steamer going to the Kyles of Bute and back, before returning to London by train on the Sunday night.

One of Vassall's rare slips came when he took his parents to a production of *My Fair Lady*, just before Christmas 1958, and accidentally left some papers, which he was due to give to Gregory, in the theatre's cloakroom. He picked the documents up after the show, and took them with him to Euston where he saw the Galbraiths off to Barskimming. Vassall seems to have regarded taking Admiralty documents up to Barskimming as a sacred duty, beyond the reach of his espionage. He always insisted that he drew the line at removing any documents from the black boxes and that he never opened them, even when he was entrusted with the keys.

Much to his annoyance, Vassall did not accompany Galbraith on his official trips to South Africa and the Far East, but he regarded himself as a vital conduit for information between Galbraith and his wife when the former was away. Ship-building was in Galbraith's remit, and in the summer of 1959 Vassall handled invitations for Galbraith to join Lady Nancy Astor at the keel-laying of the frigate *HMS Plymouth*, and to join the Duke of Edinburgh at the keel-laying of *HMS Dreadnought*, Britain's first nuclear-powered submarine (later launched by the Queen in 1960). In 1961 one of the Portland spies, Harry Houghton, told MI5 that the Russians were getting information on *HMS Dreadnought* from another spy in the Admiralty. Whether this was Vassall or not – and the evidence is unclear – it is obvious that a Russian spy helped to arrange the ceremonial event to mark the start of her construction.

At other times Vassall drew up guest lists for official receptions and seating plans for dinners at Lancaster House, attended by the First Sea Lord and the Chief of the Defence Staff. He arranged Galbraith's visits to displays of new guided weapons, and in November 1958 to the Royal Observatory at Herstmonceux Castle in Sussex, where Galbraith lunched with the Astronomer Royal and the Duke of Edinburgh (who would be "in a lounge suit", Vassall told Galbraith in a handwritten note).

Vassall effectively had access to all safes, cupboards and cabinets in Galbraith's private office: if they were locked, he knew where the keys could be found. But the Russians had little interest in the documents there. Vassall first told Gregory that he was moving from the NID to a minister's office at a meeting near Ealing Common. Gregory did not share Vassall's excitement. "I don't think Gregory was very pleased with the change," said Vassall. "The Russian authorities were not particularly impressed or interested by anything I took them while working for the Civil Lord ... Gregory was still upset that I had transferred from naval intelligence".

Later, Vassall told MI5 that Gregory had asked whether he liked John Peters and a fellow clerk, Jennifer Hall: the Russians obviously had access to an Admiralty staff directory to know who Vassall worked with. But Galbraith was not a senior minister and the reports that came across his desk were about building maintenance, dockyard industrial relations, pay scales and surveying. Vassall recalled that only a handful of documents he extracted from Galbraith's office were of interest to Gregory. He was, Vassall said, "interested in anything to do with Berlin, Christmas Island [in the Pacific, used for nuclear tests in 1957 and 1958] and atomic weapons in aircraft carriers". But few such documents crossed Galbraith's desk.

In October 1959 Vassall was effectively made redundant again. The posts of Parliamentary Secretary of the Admiralty and its Civil Lord (which Galbraith was vacating to head to a new job at the Scottish Office) were amalgamated. This reduced the need for clerks in the ministers' offices, and it was Vassall who was eased out because he had recently failed to pass a promotion board.

"I was very sad when I heard that Mr Galbraith was about to be moved", Vassall recalled. If Galbraith had taken Vassall with him to the Scottish Office, Vassall might have been able to extricate himself from spying for the Russians. "I had a good talk with him and told him I would much rather go with him, wherever he was going than stay behind", said Vassall. But Galbraith either didn't take the hint, or didn't want to take Vassall with him.

Gregory hoped that Vassall might soon work for the First Sea Lord, Peter Carrington, 6th Baron Carrington, but Vassall was told that "it was impossible to hold two such similar posts one after the other". Vassall approached Mr Synott again, and with his help he secured a job which he may have found dull, but which the Russians found very interesting indeed: as a clerk in the Fleet Section of the Admiralty's Military Branch, where he remained until his arrest in September 1962.

"Though the papers I dealt with were of great interest to the Russians, I was not happy there", Vassall recalled. But while he found the work "extremely boring", Gregory, and his successor Nikolai, often told Vassall how impressed they were by the material he brought them – especially anything with an American angle.

Despite its dull name, the Fleet Section was the secretariat for the Admiralty's naval officers, "through which passes a large volume of highly classified material" on "radar, communications, torpedo and anti-submarine, gunnery trials, Allied Technical Publications, Fleet Operational and Tactical Instructions and … general matters concerning naval liaison with Commonwealth countries". Vassall told MI5 he also saw documents about salvaging stricken submarines: in other words, pretty much everything related to the Royal Navy's ships, and their technology.

Vassall seemed unimpressed by Lord Carrington, who once did a walkabout in Military Branch "to find out exactly what they did". When Vassall was introduced to Carrington as part of a trio of civil servants, he explained that his work was different from what the other two did. The First Lord replied that "I must be the cuckoo in the nest". A few days later, Vassall saw Carrington at L' Aperitif on Jermyn Street, London's first "cheese bar" and a smart restaurant that few clerks could afford to dine at. "I felt almost compelled to go up to him and say how strange that only the other day we had met formally and now informally," Vassall recalled nearly twenty years later. Born in 1919, Carrington was only five years older than Vassall, and maybe he saw the First Lord of the Admiralty as his social equal. It is unclear whether he did go up to Carrington or not: either way, it would have been typical networking by Vassall. While Carrington might have been startled, he clearly would not have suspected that he was talking to a spy for the Soviet Union.

•   •   •

Vassall's parents' downward social spiral continued throughout the late 1950s. In 1960, William and Mabel were forced to move out of Addison House, after more than ten years, because of a steep increase in rent. They moved to live near Mabel's relatives: a house "on the borders of Middlesex and Hertfordshire", Vassall recalled (just the kind of quiet suburban setting that he loathed). The day after Vassall visited his parents' new home, and before they had fully moved in, on 21 October he got a phone call from his brother Richard to say that their mother had died of a coronary thrombosis, having suddenly fallen ill while visiting her sister, Alma, in Pinner.

"It was a terrible shock, from which I have never really recovered", Vassall wrote. Mabel was in her mid-sixties and had been in poor health for some time, but it must have been a surprise that she predeceased Vassall's father, who was more than ten years older. Vassall received a legacy of only £100 from his mother. The only consolation, Norman Lucas once suggested, was that she had died "mercifully unaware" that her son was a traitor.

Two days after her death, Vassall received a letter of condolence from Tam Galbraith, who liked to stay in touch with people who had worked in his private office. Soon afterwards, Galbraith paid what was probably his only visit to Vassall's Dolphin Square flat, accompanied by his wife, on a fifteen- or twenty-minute call to console Vassall. Galbraith later claimed that he had kept a taxi waiting outside while he made a brief appearance, which suggests that he was keeping his stay as perfunctory as courtesy allowed. The event was certainly not a "cocktail party", as newspapers later claimed.

Gregory was also "genuinely sympathetic" after his mother's death, Vassall recalled. As if trying to keep up with Galbraith, he gave Vassall "a present from Harrods". For once the convivial Vassall chose to spend Christmas 1960 alone, at Uplands, an upmarket guest house in Aldeburgh (where he had stayed briefly in early October 1960, and where he would stay for a final time in August 1962).[38] He had declined an invitation to spend Christmas with his aunt Alma but received generous gifts from the Galbraiths: a silver penknife, inscribed with his initials, from Tam and a set of white linen handkerchiefs from his wife. "Oh, John, handkerchiefs are

---

38 Aldeburgh is a town on the Suffolk coast that was already popular with gay visitors, since the composer Benjamin Britten had started its music festival in 1948.

unlucky," Vassall was told by a lady friend. "I hope it was not an omen", Vassall reflected.

Perhaps it was a bad omen, but as 1961 began, Vassall could marvel that he was entering his seventh year as a spy for the Soviet Union without once coming under suspicion. Incredibly, civil servants were never searched on their way in and out of the Admiralty, or other Whitehall departments, because of "a resistance to this technique which is based on class-feeling," wrote Rebecca West. Whitehall quaintly assumed that it was not the 'done thing' to subject senior mandarins, or their underlings, to the random security checks that are now routine. It later emerged that many Admiralty documents were kept in cupboards with "common keys", so Vassall had access to all of them, not just those he was authorised to open. Throughout the late 1950s and early 1960s he seems to have bragged to work colleagues about his European travels but kept his trips to the United States, Canada and Egypt more secret.

At the very end of the 1950s, Vassall may have come close to telling a friend everything. In 1966 the *Mirror* newspapers received an anonymous letter from Germany enclosing several letters that Vassall had sent to a Verner Hauffman (who he had befriended in Capri) between October 1959 and March 1960. Vassall apparently told Hauffman that he had been compromised by the KGB in Moscow, but not that he had started spying for them. Vassall was playing with fire: an MI5 report from 1971 said if "the KGB had learned of Vassall's insecure behaviour, it might have influenced their subsequent handling and disposal of him". Even in the early 1970s, MI5 were obsessively trying to trace Hauffman's identity and whereabouts, without success.[39]

Something of Vassall's inner turmoil can be glimpsed in his Admiralty personnel assessments of the late 1950s and early 1960s.

---

39   Vassall told MI5 that he had first met Haufmann in Capri in September 1959, just after "almost tripping over Aristotle Onassis and his then escort Maria Callas" on the way into the Eden Bar ("a nice Vassall touch", an MI5 officer noted).

Despite his good looks, well-spoken manners and fast typing, his only promotions were in the late 1940s.[40] After that, his career was stuck. In those days the civil service had three divisions – clerical, executive and administrative – and Vassall remained stuck in the bottom clerical division. He twice applied for promotion to become an executive officer, but was unsuccessful on both occasions.

Rebecca West once alleged that by "playing the dumb gazelle" Vassall deliberately avoided promotion, because if he had become more senior his specialised remit would have meant he only had access to a limited range of documents. Although Vassall was in a very junior position, post-war technological changes meant that a much wider group of people gained access to security secrets. "In this era of ciphers, code-rooms, computers, tapes, hidden micro-phones and other paraphernalia of espionage, thousands, if not tens of thousands, of ordinary people have become targets for the spy recruiters to exploit if they can", Richard Deacon and Nigel West explained.

Others have exaggerated Vassall's incompetence and suggested that he was lucky to keep his clerical job until 1962. In fact, Vassall may have never been bright enough to be promoted, but he was certainly never incompetent enough to be at risk of dismissal. The Russians were keen for Vassall to seek promotion, and while his appraisals show that he was never deemed ready, they also suggest that he was a borderline case and that he would probably have been promoted in due course. His staff reports read like a poignant record of mediocrity – the legacy of a man who never quite made it off the bottom rung.

"If his professional competence and zeal matched his pleasant manners and smart appearance he would be outstanding", was the wounding assessment in a report dated 31 January 1957. Another superior wrote in the same report that Vassall "can work very well,

---

40   In September 1947 Vassall was promoted from a clerk grade III to clerk grade II, and in January 1948 he was promoted to clerical officer.

but I suspect he always wants to run before he can walk properly, and is a day dreamer". In February 1958, Vassall's boss John Peters judged that the "Civil Lord, who is very keen on detail, is always satisfied with his work" but that "on one or two occasions [Vassall] has not appreciated (political) importance of a paper".

A few months later, in October 1958, Peters was more effusive: "If it were not for occasional blind spots in judgement and under-standing, Mr Vassal [*sic*] would deserve a higher assessment in section D [fitness for promotion]". Yet, hopes of promotion were quickly snuffed out. A promotion board in late 1958 placed Vassall in category "F" –"Not yet fit for executive officer but may develop, and should be considered again in the longer term, i.e. not less than three years". Galbraith later told the Radcliffe inquiry that while Vassall had "many attributes necessary for promotion, he lacked sufficient perceptive intelligence to be advanced".

A January 1960 report found that "Mr Vassall is a very presenta-ble officer personally and shows plenty of zeal. He still shows some immaturity ... however". In January 1961 he was judged to be "no more than average in ability, but he looks, and sounds, a cut above the rest and these could be useful assets in some posts". But again, Vassall was only judged to be "satisfactory" in terms of fitness for promotion. When he appeared before another promotion board in 1961 he was placed in category D – "Marginal, worth looking at again in one year's time" – by which time he was in jail.

•   •   •

Just as Vassall was trying to attain promotion, he underwent a big change on the domestic front. Having lived with his parents at Ad-dison House since 1947 (apart from his two years in Moscow), in 1959 – a year before his mother's death – he finally moved into a flat of his own.

William had stepped down as an RAF chaplain in 1953. In 1955 he had turned seventy, but had carried on working part-time at St James's, Piccadilly, a fashionable church designed by Christopher Wren. He was a mere curate, with "permission to officiate" but only a modest salary.

Vassall later said that he always concealed his conversion to Catholicism from his father. He seems to have been less careful, however, about keeping his sexuality secret. Norman Hutchison, a civil servant who was gay himself, was a friend of Vassall's and met his father several times. Hutchison later told MI5 that by the late 1950s his parents "knew all about" Vassall's "style of living … and appeared not to disapprove". David Marine, Vassall's on–off American lover from the early 1950s onwards, met his parents and brother in London. Marine doesn't seem to have been introduced as a boyfriend but like many British families in the 1950s, the Vassalls seem to have quietly accepted John's sexuality without ever discussing it, and without any formal "coming out".

Vassall's mother may have once asked whether he was going to marry a secretary in Moscow, but this is not inconsistent with knowing he was gay: after all, many of Vassall's gay contemporaries had marriages, which in many cases produced children. Some were happy, and even lifelong. "Throughout the 1950s, some friend we met as a fully-fledged queer would announce with an apologetic giggle that we would shortly be invited to his wedding," the gay writer Ben Duncan recalled.

Vassall's love life seems to have become increasingly busy after he returned from Moscow. He became friendly with Derek Warne, who he worked with for eleven months in 1959–60 in Military Branch, until Warne was promoted and became private secretary to the Admiralty's secretary (its most senior civil servant). Warne, who was unmarried and lived with his brother, sister-in-law and their two children in Cricklewood, was close to William Campbell, with whom Vassall had a brief affair in 1947. Throughout the 1940s and 1950s Warne and Campbell regularly went to the opera and theatre and in the early 1960s they told MI5 that they had holidayed with Warne's friends in Ilfracombe, Devon in 1945 or 1946, taken a coach tour of Portugal in 1960 and gone to Italy together in 1954. These were brave admissions to make before decriminalisation.

Vassall's relationship with Campbell was distant after 1950, but he seems to have been closer to Warne, and Vassall entertained Warne at his Dolphin Square flat at least once. Vassall claimed he was also pursued by Commander Geoffrey Marescaux, who held an "important position" at the Admiralty. The commander once "invited him to dinner and pressed him to stay" overnight at his flat, but Vassall said he was "suspicious of his motives and declined the invitation". But they were later reconciled, and Vassall said that the commander came to his flat about once a week (presumably when his brother and parents were out, while Vassall lived with them). Vassall later told MI5 that he knew the commander was gay, even though he was married.

However tolerant his parents might be, sharing a small flat with them and his brother did not afford Vassall much privacy. In 1958 Gregory began encouraging him to move out. Vassall later claimed that Gregory offered him £5,000 to buy a suburban house and to buy Vassall, who hadn't yet learnt to drive, a car. Vassall refused both offers: he did not feel the need to drive, and "the idea of a house depressed me ... the idea was ghastly". As a bachelor who loved going to his club and West End theatres and restaurants, a house in a quiet suburb was the "last thing he wanted".

At first, Vassall was not enthusiastic about moving out of his parents' flat because, his memoirs explained, he "felt sorry for his mother" and feared she would be lonely without him (his father was not mentioned). But it appears that once Vassall was in his mid-thirties, his parents gently encouraged him to rent his own flat.

Vassall was lucky. Firstly, he had the chance to live on his own – a freedom that many gay men simply couldn't afford. A 1960 study by the sociologist Michael Schofield found that only a minority of English gay men lived alone and a full third of Schofield's respondents – most of them middle class – lived with a landlady or landlord: hardly a recipe for a carefree sex life.

Some gay couples lived together fairly openly. The playwright Joe Orton and his lover Kenneth Halliwell cohabited in West Hampstead from 1951 onwards, although they lived with other drama students at first. Schofield also cited a discreet homosexual couple: D, a successful businessman, lived with H, the editor of a trade paper. Schofield wrote that "Although they are careful to keep their relationship secret from their business associates, they have a number of heterosexual friends". It was not unheard of in the 1950s for gay couples to "come out" to trusted straight friends and live together openly. But their social lives were largely conducted at home, not in nightclubs or bars. While the rate of prosecutions for homosexual "offences" was falling in the late 1950s, they were still common.

If gay men and women could find "digs" without a landlord or landlady living on the premises, they were often tiny bedsits or overcrowded flatshares, where cold and damp were perennial challenges. The population of inner London was still sharply falling in the late 1950s: between 1931 and 1961 it fell from 4.4 million to 3.2 million, as more and more people moved to the suburbs or satellite towns. Many London districts had been decimated by wartime bombing and slum clearances, and in those that hadn't gentrification had yet to begin.

The most "gay-friendly" district in the 1950s was considered to be Notting Hill, which one of Schofield's interviewees described as a "kingdom within a kingdom".[41] Many memoirs of gay London life in the 1950s centre on boarding houses there, where gay tenants were actively welcomed, or at least tolerated. Alan, interviewed in

---

41   *The L-Shaped Room*, a 1962 film based on a 1960 novel by Lynne Reid Banks, features a heterosexual white woman, a heterosexual white man and a homosexual black man living happily alongside each other in Notting Hill bedsits.

Matt Cook's book *Queer Domesticities*, found a room in a boarding house through Flora McDonald, the "matriarch" of Notting Hill's queer community. Flora called Alan "Nelly Bagwash" and greeted other gay men with the words "hello sexy". She was "quite eccentric, looked like Cat Weasel, hair and all ragged beard and god knows what else, [and] rattled along the road with her bike", Alan recalled.

Vassall's memoirs feature no such characters. Not only did he avoid having to live with a landlady, he also managed to avoid the squalor of a bedsit or flatshare and the excesses of Rachmanism (whereby tenants in furnished rooms could be evicted with only a week's notice). His Russian money meant that he could afford to rent a flat of his own in a more salubrious area than Notting Hill. By the end of 1958, Vassall "had my name down for" four places: Cranmer Court and Swan Court in Chelsea, Grove End Gardens in St John's Wood and Dolphin Square, a huge complex of flats by the Thames in Pimlico.

Cranmer Court and Swan Court are red-brick blocks, very similar to Dolphin Square, and not far from the Kings Road; Grove End Gardens was a similar red-brick block, five minutes' walk down Abbey Road from Addison House. Vassall said that his parents would have preferred him to live there, to stay close to them. He did not consciously choose Dolphin Square: it was simply that a flat came up there before the other options.

In February 1959 Vassall signed a seven-year lease on 807 Hood House,[42] an eighth-floor flat with windows looking westwards and southwards over Dolphin Square's courtyard garden. The rent was £325 a year, including maintenance and service charges but not rates and lighting, which brought the total up to about £400.[43] The square's managers later told the Radcliffe inquiry that they took

---

42   One of the ironies of Vassall's story is that the twelve blocks of Dolphin Square are named after British naval heroes, most of whom defeated Napoleon's navy. Vassall's block was named after Admiral Samuel Hood, 1st Viscount Hood (1724–1816).

43   Some press reports, keen to exaggerate the cost of Vassall's lifestyle, claimed that his rent was £500 or even £700 a year by 1962. In fact, in a time of low inflation the rent seems to have risen modestly.

references from Vassall's bank, solicitor and a letting agent, and obtained a personal reference from a doctor. A Pall Mall estate agent, Fladgate and Company, said that Vassall had been "introduced to us from [*sic*] most valued clients", while the Cox's and King's[44] branch at 6 Pall Mall said that Vassall was "respectable and considered trustworthy for your figures and purposes". Dr Gerard Lang said "I have known him for a number of years and am confident that he is in a position to undertake the tenancy". But it was not then Dolphin Square's practice to take references from employers and for a while the Admiralty may have been unaware that Vassall lived there.

His tenancy began on 6 March but he did not move in until a week later, Friday 13 March 1959.[45] If the date was a bad omen, Vassall did not realise it at the time.

Vassall's tenancy may have ended dramatically but it began quietly. He appears to have been a model tenant ("Vassall always paid his rent promptly", the square's general manager, Gerald Rhodes, later told the Radcliffe inquiry). The only blot on his copybook was a complaint from G. C. Gover, of 710 Hood House, about a "noisy party with loud music" until 3 a.m. on the morning of Sunday 12 June 1960 in Vassall's flat upstairs. Vassall quickly apologised and the incident seems to have been forgotten. Newspapers later alleged that such parties were almost nightly occurrences, and some accounts of Dolphin Square have implied that life there has always been one long sexual orgy. It was a "great pleasure" to be able to "entertain my friends from abroad and return some of the generous hospitality I had received", Vassall wrote. He certainly enjoyed an active sex life there, but many of the people he entertained were old ladies with whom he played bridge. "He had a genuine liking for the society of old ladies, and as some of them were rich he was

---

44   Cox's and King's was a banker to the armed forces, acquired by Lloyds Bank in 1923. Its name was still carried by some Lloyds' branches after that.

45   There is some confusion over when Vassall moved in: some accounts wrongly claimed that he lived there after his return from Russia in 1956, while the Radcliffe report asserted that he moved there in April 1959.

suspected by the malicious of legacy-hunting," wrote Rebecca West. One regular visitor was Hilda Knowles, an elderly neighbour of the Vassalls in St John's Wood.

In any case, his flat was not really big enough for large-scale entertaining. It was, the Radcliffe report said, "not a striking affair". Newspapers from 1962 and 1963 described it in exotic terms, as if it was a suite of staterooms at the Palace of Versailles. In reality, it was very small. Although described as "two-roomed" in Dolphin Square parlance, this only indicated that it was somewhat larger than a bedsit. As Vassall himself said, all it had was "a sitting room, a small bedroom and a small kitchen" (or "kitchenette"); it did not have a separate dining room.[46]

Vassall compensated for the flat's size by cramming it full of antiques. It was, as Matthew Parris has said, a "gaudy residence". Vassall's interior design tastes avoided the fads of the late 1950s: Formica, abstract patterns, metallic lampshades and gramophones on slender tapering legs. "It was the first time I had ever had a flat of my own, and I lavished great care on it, taking eighteen months to furnish and decorate it as I wanted," Vassall recalled.

Most of the furnishings were bought with Russian money, but not all. In 1958 Vassall received a small legacy from a Mrs Macnaughten, the widow of a Monmouth rector, and he may have received a legacy or two from aunts. The Macnaughtens had befriended Vassall and his brother Richard when they were pupils at Monmouth, and seem to have acted as unofficial guardians during termtime. After her husband died, Mrs Macnaughten moved to Bexhill, Sussex, where Vassall visited her until her death and in return, a female friend of Mrs Macnaughten stayed at Dolphin Square sometimes.

Vassall's flat never had a £400 Queen Anne wardrobe and a £150 Persian carpet, as newspapers later claimed. But by 1962 it

---

46   A floorplan in the National Archives shows the living room was 13 feet by 20, the bedroom ten feet by twelve, its bathroom ten by four, and the kitchenette only five-and-a-half by seven.

did contain several pieces of silver that Mrs McNaughten had bequeathed him, and several pieces of furniture he had bought from her estate, while its table lamps were a present from Mademoiselle Buca Bowinkel, a friend who lived on Capri, and the fine Swedish glasses in the drinks cabinet had been bought in Moscow from a journalist, Stanley Johnson. The flat was very grandly furnished given Vassall's modest clerical salary. But he could – and did – plausibly claim that its contents had either been inherited, given by friends or cannily bought at bargain prices.

Vassall was keen to show off his new flat. After he moved in – probably in 1959 or 1960 – he was spotted by his old Farm Street friend Robin McEwen, and his wife, at a Chelsea restaurant. After befriending Vassall at the beginning of the 1950s, McEwen invited Vassall to his wedding to Brigid Laver – the Anglo-Irish daughter of a Victoria and Albert Museum curator – in the chapel at Marchmont, his family's house near Duns in the Scottish borders, in September 1954. Vassall could not go as he was in Moscow, but he sent the McEwens a wedding gift (a Russian wooden cigarette box with a snowy scene painted on its lid) which Brigid owns to this day. But McEwen was also aware of Vassall's social flaws. "There's Vassall," he told Brigid. "Quick, let's go. He's an awful bore". But it was too late for them to leave the restaurant unnoticed. Vassall had spotted them and he quickly came over and invited them to visit his new flat. When they did so Vassall proudly showed off his china in a display cabinet, which he was delighted to hear was the same service as the McEwens themselves owned in their Wiltshire home.

Vassall may not have selected Dolphin Square: if anything it had selected him. But it is easy to see why, trapped in a dull job and eager to break free from his parents, he liked living there. While his parents had wanted him to rent a flat in St John's Wood, Vassall seemed to prefer the loucheness and privacy of Dolphin Square. It must have seemed the perfect place to try and exorcise unpleasant memories of Moscow.

In the late 1950s Dolphin Square was not "in one of London's most exclusive and expensive areas" as Ronald Seth claimed. It has often been described, inaccurately, as being a "stone's throw from Westminster": in fact, it is more than a mile from Parliament Square. In Vassall's day, Pimlico was still considered a down-at-heel and dull place, but Dolphin Square is near the ill-defined border with Chelsea, which had long been an area where gay artists and writers (including Oscar Wilde, C. R. Ashbee, Osbert Sitwell and Quentin Crisp) lived.

For three-and-a-half years Vassall "neatly weaved his way every evening down Whitehall to his flat on Dolphin Square, with an envelope in his overcoat full of secret documents, spending fussy and capable evenings photographing them nicely for the Soviet government," Rebecca West once wrote, before neatly weaving his way back the next morning "to spend five minutes fussily and capably replacing the documents in their files". There were a few near misses. An MI5 intelligence report, typed up on 5 June 1959, said that a Russian man (probably a Soviet embassy employee) named Chizhov had been seen "hanging around in a nervous fashion on the Embankment just past Dolphin Square going towards Chelsea. On another occasion ACHIEVE [codename for an MI5 surveillance officer] saw the same man also waiting around in Jermyn Street" – which runs behind St James's church, where Vassall's father was a curate. Was this Russian on his way to or from meetings with Vassall? He may well have been, but clearly MI5 never connected him to Vassall.

Gregory seemed delighted when Vassall moved in to Dolphin Square, as it reduced the likelihood that his spying would be discovered by his parents. He probably did not realise that the square had been known as a place of intrigue and spying ever since its construction in the 1930s by the New York real estate developer Frederick Fillmore French – the Donald Trump of his day.

To understand the Vassall story, and why it is such a landmark in modern British history, the stage is as important as the main player. In the 1950s and 1960s Dolphin Square was not the preserve of the rich but an organic community and what was probably a unique social experiment. To this day, all of its flats are rented, not bought, and it has been described as a "bourgeois council estate" where the wealthy lived alongside much humbler Londoners – taxi-drivers, market stallholders and clerks – whose rents were effectively subsidised by the higher rents paid by richer tenants who used their flats as second homes.

Remarkably, Vassall was now living in the very block where the British fascist leader Oswald Mosley had lived, and where the MI5 spymaster Maxwell Knight had worked and still lived. Like a microcosm of Europe at large, Dolphin Square was home to many of the different factions involved in the Second World War. Mosley and his wife Diana rented 706 and 707 Hood House from December 1939 until Mosley was arrested there in May 1940, prior to his internment for most of the rest of the war. His recent presence did not however deter Charles de Gaulle's Free French movement from taking over one of Dolphin Square's thirteen blocks as offices during its enforced exile in London in 1941–43. According to de Gaulle's biographer, Jonathan Fenby, the Free French were a "motley band who resembled medieval knights pleading themselves to a baron who had put himself forward to the rank of Constable of the kingdom". If they were a band of knights, then Dolphin Square was their Camelot.

Both before and during the war, Maxwell Knight ran a top-secret MI5 operation, M Section, from 308 Hood House, five floors below Vassall's flat, and Knight remained living at 612 Hood House until January 1964. Knight is believed to have worked with Ian Fleming, and the character of "M" in his James Bond novels was largely based on Knight.[47]

Anthony Blunt once claimed that Maxwell Knight was a

---

47   In late 1940, John Cairncross – later exposed as the fifth member of the Cambridge spy ring – lived briefly at Dolphin Square until his block was bombed and he moved in with his brother, elsewhere in London.

homosexual who "pretended to be a near-hysterical homophobe". Indeed, by the late 1950s Dolphin Square was already known as a place where lesbians and gay men could live in relative freedom. Marguerite Radclyffe Hall, author of *The Well of Loneliness*, a ground-breaking lesbian novel that was labelled "corrupting and obscene" and banned, lived at the square until her death in 1943. In the late 1940s it attracted Angus Wilson, author of *Hemlock and After* (1952), which was arguably Britain's first modern gay novel. From 1949 onwards, Wilson shared his one-bedroom flat with a sixteen-year-old British Museum attendant, Tony Garrett. They lived happily at Dolphin Square without any professional or legal repercussions until 1959 and moved just after Vassall arrived there. Wilson's biographer, Margaret Drabble, wrote "it was and is inhabited by a wide range of characters – diplomats, politicians, con men, artists, spies, call girls, minor royals and many others with good reason to wish for trouble-free, well-run anonymity ... and Angus liked it".

In the 1950s Dolphin Square was also home to the womanising Peter Finch, one of the most prolific screen actors of the day. By the time Vassall moved in his neighbours included the singer Shirley Bassey (one of Finch's many lovers), Winston Churchill's daughter Sarah (who was struggling with alcoholism) and her friend April Ashley – Britain's first transgender actress and model.[48] Vassall also lived alongside the racing driver Donald Campbell, the singer Bud Flanagan and the *Carry On* actor Sid James (who was already well known for playing a recurring character in the radio sitcom *Hancock's Half Hour*).

These showbiz stars lived among a growing number of Members of Parliament. Many of them were obscure backbenchers but others were heavyweights, like Hartley Shawcross – the glamorous former lead British prosecutor at the Nuremberg War Crimes tribunal,

---

48   Ashley was born in Liverpool in 1935 and moved to the square in 1960 immediately after undergoing gender reassignment surgery in Casablanca.

Attorney General and a Labour MP until 1958 – who lived at 201 Beatty House with his second wife Joan from 1950.

By the late 1950s, the square was also the weekday home of many scientists and defence officials far more senior than Vassall, who benefitted from its proximity to Whitehall and Westminster. Vassall seemed unconcerned that Dolphin Square was almost at the heart of London's political and defence apparatus, only half a mile from the Broadway offices of MI6 and quarter of a mile from Thames House, where MI5 had been based before the war (and where it returned in the 1990s).

Patrick Blackett, who was one of Britain's top nuclear physicists and the Admiralty's director of Operational Research from 1942 to 1945, lived at the square shortly after the war, and Vassall's neighbours also included Air Vice-Marshal Sir Conrad Collier – one of the RAF's most senior officers – who lived at 901 Collingwood House from 1957 to 1962. At no other point in the Cold War did a Soviet spy, who was supposedly lying low, choose to live so openly at the heart of London with so many MPs, civil servants and celebrities as his neighbours. Sometimes spies enjoy hiding in plain sight and find it exciting to take extravagant risks that almost invite discovery: Vassall took this tendency to a new extreme.

•   •   •

Vassall's social life took off after he moved to Dolphin Square. His stomping ground was neither Notting Hill, nor Soho (generally considered to be the centre of bohemian and gay London by the late 1950s), nor the King's Road of Mary Quant (who opened her shop Bazaar there in 1955). Instead, Vassall preferred the more staid and refined streets of "clubland": Mayfair and St James's. Vassall's father was still a curate of St James's Church on Piccadilly and Vassall soon adopted its parish, as well as Dolphin Square, as his social territory.

Vassall was following in the footsteps of an older generation of London gay men, such as George Ives: the Victorian writer and the model for E. W. Hornung's "gentleman thief", Raffles. Ives lived, as did the fictional Raffles, in a "bachelor apartment" at Albany, an exclusive eighteenth-century building just off Piccadilly. Vassall and Ives saw the nearby streets as "the inner sanctum of the masculine city" owing to its many tailors' shops, barbers' shops and Turkish baths. So did Vassall: he frequently shopped on Jermyn Street, Savile Row and Bond Street, where Admiralty clerks could not afford to buy luxuries without remittances from the Soviet Union. Likewise, Vassall's liking for Queen Anne furniture conformed to an older template of homosexuality exemplified by Noël Coward and Somerset Maugham. In Mary Renault's 1953 novel *The Charioteer*, the flamboyant and self-consciously modern interiors of a "discreditable queer", Bunny, are contrasted with the "restraint of the model, respectable and subdued homosexual", Ralph. By opting for conservative décor, Vassall was choosing to be like Ralph, not Bunny.

The *Daily Mail* later alleged that Vassall dined at Simpson's in the Strand and was a regular at the Royal Ballet. "Vassall was not merely a spy: he was a conspicuous consumer in the class of James Bond himself," the historian Dominic Sandbrook has said. "In the heady atmosphere of the hire-purchase boom, however, nobody noticed". One reason why Vassall was not apprehended earlier is that he was well-spoken and the son of a respectable clergyman. If anyone ever asked Vassall how he could afford his expensive lifestyle, his explanations about a legacy from "an old lady living near Eastbourne" (Mrs Macnaughten), or an aunt, cut the necessary mustard.

Vassall was not normally expected to be in the office until 10 a.m., allowing him to enjoy a hectic social life at night. Yet he was never a mod, a rocker or a Teddy Boy and nor was he an "angry young man". Nowadays, he would be termed a "preppy" or a young fogey.

He avoided the "youthquake" of the late 1950s because he was of the generation that was old enough – just – to have served in the Second World War. Nonetheless, he was young enough to be sexually liberated, resentful of a more repressed older generation and frustrated by the limitations of life in London before homosexuality was decriminalised. As the historian John Davis has pointed out, London was, if anything, a slightly boring place at the dawn of the 1960s: it had not yet started "swinging" and even when it did, the swing was largely concocted by inventive journalists.

Although many of his Admiralty colleagues would later tell MI5 that they had suspected that Vassall was gay all along, he seems to have been careful not to tell colleagues, either directly or indirectly. Ann Miller, who worked with Vassall in Naval Intelligence in 1956–57, said that she thought Vassall was a "neuter" sexually, even though a naval officer had told her that he was "as queer as a coot". Miller found that Vassall was "rather tiresome about his 'in' friends and the importance of visiting people in 'in' counties". Nonetheless, she got on well with him, in part because she sensed that their friendship would never lead to any kind of "emotional entanglement". From 1957 onwards Vassall regularly took Miller to the theatre and out for dinner. After 1959 he invited her to parties at Dolphin Square where other guests included an army general, a Home Office official and Vassall's father. In the run-up to Christmas 1960 Vassall was invited by "a girl friend" to cocktail parties at the NID, where he had previously worked. Vassall accepted the invitation, as he always did, and saw the new DNI – Admiral Denning, brother of the judge Lord Denning – standing with a drink in his hand.

The real epicentre of Vassall's social life was not Whitehall cocktail parties like these, but in Continental Europe, and beyond. Vassall's memoirs, diaries and passport records show that after his return from Moscow he travelled extensively: to Hamburg, Corsica, the French Riviera, Brussels, Venice, Capri, Egypt, and even a skiing trip to Zermatt – with a string of male companions, often travelling by first-class train.

An MI5 minute states that Vassall "must have spent every possible moment abroad" when not working at the Admiralty. Later, Vassall boasted that he'd always kept a leather suitcase packed in case. He once received a call one afternoon – presumably on a Friday – and was invited to Brussels for the weekend. "As I never said no to such an invitation" he set off at once. Vassall had travelled as much as he could before his "compromise" by the Russians but now that they were giving him money he travelled further, more frequently and in greater comfort than before.

Vassall's trips were both with established male lovers, and expeditions to meet new ones. While drinking with Dutch friends in a hotel bar in Zermatt, Vassall's memoirs claim that he was beckoned over by a "distinguished looking man", an advocate from Bern, who asked him to swap room numbers. The next evening, Vassall found an invitation to visit the mysterious man's room on his pillow. "Our relationship blossomed rapidly," Vassall recalled breathlessly. "He was exceptionally nice to me and treated me as his best friend". Vassall seemed heartbroken when the lawyer suddenly had to return to Bern and left a valedictory note on Vassall's pillow while he was out skiing.

Although the Russians had vetoed a foreign holiday in Helsinki while Vassall was in Moscow, now that he was in London, Gregory actively encouraged tourism and gave Vassall the money to pay for it. "He never turned a hair when I suggested going to Brussels, Nice or Rome, as long as I met him every three weeks and was not too extravagant," Vassall recalled. He once took his mother to the World's Fair in Brussels at Gregory's suggestion.

Gregory seems to have been indifferent to what Vassall might say to strangers on these holidays or whether he might be recruited by spies from other countries as a double agent. At some point in 1957 Vassall travelled to Corsica, via Brussels, where a friend joined him for the rest of the journey. On the way back from Ajaccio they stayed in Cannes for a few days, meeting two more friends from Brussels, and took tea at a house with a fine view over the Mediterranean near St Tropez. Their host, "a most charming and amiable Frenchman", invited Vassall and the Belgians to dinner, and then to stay the night. The Frenchman was "only the second person who seemed alive to the dangers of my position," Vassall recalled: he told Vassall that he knew he was gay and that he had worked in a defence role in Russia, before telling Vassall that he had been "very unwise" to take the Moscow job. Did this man know that Vassall was a spy or did Vassall confess all to him? Vassall's memoirs are unclear, but as usual, Gregory seems to have been happy for his protégé to sail close to the wind.

One of the holidays authorised and financed by the Soviets had a very clear purpose. At Christmas 1957 Vassall was told to go to Hamburg to purchase an Exakta: a 35 mm camera made in Dresden, East Germany, and ideal for close-up photography. From now on, Vassall was expected to photograph documents himself rather than hand them over to Gregory. Once the camera was purchased, Vassall was "brought down to earth with a bump. It made me realise that gradually I was becoming more and more deeply involved". Increasingly, Vassall avoided seeing friends in London or "leading a very energetic social life" there, as he feared that he would be followed by "our men". He relied on visits from foreign friends and more trips abroad.

While he was in Hamburg Vassall seized the opportunity to mix business with pleasure. He met up with an unnamed friend for a skiing holiday in the Harz Mountains. One night, in a Hamburg bar, Vassall's companion left early but told him "you won't be alone for long". Soon, two German men in leather jackets who said they were "from the sea", befriended him. "One of them, with pale blue eyes, came over and said his friend and he would like to have a drink with me," Vassall recalled. "We walked along the famous Reeperbahn and then went to another bar".

Vassall also seems to have picked up another German, identified only as Baumgartel (or Baumgarten), who worked at a gentleman's outfitters in Hamburg. After Vassall bought some clothing there he wrote to Baumgartel at his shop to thank him and a "halting correspondence" began. Vassall met Baumgartel four or five times in the next few years: they spent Whitsun 1960 together in Amsterdam and Baumgartel stayed with Vassall at Dolphin Square in May 1961.[49]

Vassall never told Gregory about picking up the two German men in a bar in Hamburg. "He never asked and must have believed I would not do anything foolish," Vassall said, as if spying for the Soviets was the most sensible thing in the world.

When Vassall arrived back in England he had a shock: he was ordered to pay more than £60 in duty when the Exakta was discovered by Customs. No one seems to have wondered why an impecunious Admiralty clerk was coming back from Hamburg with an expensive camera that was ideal for taking accurate photographs of small type.

Why did the Russians ask Vassall to buy his own camera rather than supply one? Maybe it was a psychological ploy, rewarding Vassall with another overseas holiday. But the journey soon turned out to be a waste of time: when Vassall practised by taking photographs of newspaper stories, the Russians judged them a failure and he had to be supplied with another camera.

There was more travel in 1958; that October Vassall travelled to Italy, by train, with "an English doctor of my own age". They stayed in a "hidden-away hotel at Santa Venere beyond Pompeii and Paestum" for a week (later, Vassall gleefully told MI5 that the hotel was also a favourite of Peter Thorneycroft, a Tory minister

---

49   After Vassall's arrest the Federal Intelligence Service (BND) (West Germany's security agency) found Baumgartel hard to track down. When they did, he told them that he had found Vassall "restless and nervy" in 1961. Vassall had asked Baumgartel to buy him a Varex camera in Hamburg, which struck Baumgartel as odd. Why did Vassall not buy a camera in England, and why did he want Baumgartel to buy it on his behalf?

who defended the failure to detect Vassall in 1962, and the Duke of Rutland). Vassall and his doctor friend went on to "incomparable Venice", where Vassall had to wear sunglasses because of a spot, which turned out to be a carbuncle. "It must have been a kind of reaction to the tense double life that I was leading", Vassall noted.

The spring and summer of 1959 were busy times in Tam Galbraith's office but in the autumn of that year Vassall went on his first trip to Capri. He'd been inspired to visit the island "by a chance conversation with two foreigners at a theatre" in London. As usual, Vassall "made friends quite effortlessly", and began a chaste relationship with a Mademoiselle Buca Bowinkel, who invited him to stay at her villa on Capri whenever he liked. On his second night at the Quisisana Hotel, Vassall descended its marble staircase to have a nightcap in the small bar. As he supped a peppermint liqueur over crushed ice, Vassall spotted a man at an adjacent table "staring at me endlessly". Vassall played things cool, not following the man's "distant smile" on to the bar's terrace but he then found the stranger by his side in the lift. He invited Vassall back to his room for a drink. Once there, Vassall saw a diplomatic passport on the tallboy. He found the room to be "just the place to chart unknown waters". The two men "sat on the bed, revealing all kinds of inner secrets to each other until it was morning."

A "fortuitous meeting [had] led to a new and happy friendship", Vassall reminisced. After seeing off a German lady friend who was catching a boat to Naples, Vassall met his new lover again for a "heavenly swim" at Faraglioni after lunch. They drank Campari and soda several nights running before Vassall went to stay at the Hotel Excelsior in Naples with another "diplomatic friend".

Vassall's new lover in Capri was, MI5 later found out, Dr Francesco Gentile (Franco for short), a diplomat at the Italian embassy in Egypt.[50] Franco invited Vassall to spend Christmas 1959 there

---

50   Vassall later provided a slightly different version of his first meeting with Gentile: at a café in Capri at about 1 a.m., drinking coffee. Vassall told MI5 that he saw Gentile in Geneva and London, as well as Cairo.

("all you have to do is arrive at Cairo and I shall look after you", he promised). Vassall told his parents about the invitation, which they urged him to accept. At a party in Cairo, Vassall met a Scandinavian diplomat and later, they met again "in another foreign capital and in London". Yet Vassall still found the time to send a postcard to Tam Galbraith and his wife at Barskimming, offering them "Greetings from Egypt".

The sexual freedom that Vassall enjoyed on these holidays could not be replicated in London. Attitudes to homosexuality may have started changing, but only slowly. By the time Vassall returned from Moscow in the summer of 1956 David Maxwell Fyfe was no longer Home Secretary and the rate of prosecutions of homosexual "offences" had passed its peak. In 1955 Donald West, an academic psychiatrist (and a gay man himself) wrote *Homosexuality*, an academic study of sexual orientation that nevertheless argued that homosexuals "were not just a tiny minority, or a bunch of psychopaths ... but ordinary individuals capable of contributing to society [if] given a chance". West was brave to write such words, but his academic status clearly gave him a degree of leeway.[51]

In the Royal Navy and the Admiralty, it was another matter: anything that was interpreted as a gay overture could be career ending. In March 1956, shortly before Vassall left Moscow, a young lieutenant-commander, Christopher Swabey, was accused of rubbing the leg of a fellow officer, Timothy Havers, in a taxi at the end of a drunken night out in Malta. Despite protesting his innocence, Swabey was court-martialled, found guilty of indecency and "dismissed from Her Majesty's Service". It took sixteen years of letter writing by respectable supporters in politics and the Navy, two applications to the court martial appeal court, a petition to the Queen

---

51   Born in June 1924, West was the same age as Vassall and like him had served in uniform at the end of the Second World War, though only in the University of Liverpool's Officer Training Corps. In his memoirs he recalled that on overnight train journeys during the war he found that "surreptitious groping ... and the like were by no means uncommon and excited me greatly" – until one soldier told him "'I've killed men for less than that'".

and three debates in the House of Lords, before Swabey (who was represented by Jeremy Hutchinson QC, almost a decade after he had defended John Vassall at his trial) finally had his 1956 conviction quashed as "unsafe and unsatisfactory" in 1972. Even then, Swabey never received the MOD pension he was entitled to.[52]

Working in the Admiralty in London from the summer of 1956 onwards, Vassall would have heard much about the Swabey case. What clearer reminder could there be of the power that the Soviets held over him? Swabey's fate showed that even a hint of homosexual activity could end a promising career in the Royal Navy or the Admiralty, and Vassall's Soviet handlers did not just have the power to offer a hint: they had photographs of Vassall, apparently willingly, engaged in anal and oral sex with a number of other men. The furore over the Swabey case shows just how toxic allegations of homosexuality in the Royal Navy still were in the 1950s, and beyond. If an officer with first-class family connections and an excellent service record could be destroyed, what hope did John Vassall have?

• • •

In 1957 the Wolfenden Report recommended that some – though not all – homosexual activities should be decriminalised, but it was almost ten years before the modest changes in the law that Wolfenden called for were finally enacted, in the summer of 1967.[53]

Vassall's prosecution in 1962 fell exactly halfway through this

---

52   Like Vassall's spying, the story of Swabey's disgrace, and eventual exoneration, appeared in the headlines for several years in the 1960s and 1970s but has since been almost forgotten. One reason may be that unlike Alan Turing, John Gielgud or Peter Wildeblood, Christopher Swabey was not a gay man who stood up against the homophobia of the times. He always insisted that he was heterosexual and that he had been falsely accused of making homosexual advances.

53   The Report of the Departmental Committee on Homosexual Offences and Prostitution (better known as the Wolfenden report, after the committee's chairman, Sir John Wolfenden) was published on 4 September 1957. It recommended that "homosexual behaviour between consenting adults in private should no longer be a criminal offence" and that "homosexuality cannot legitimately be regarded as a disease, because in many cases it is the only symptom and is compatible with full mental health in other respects."

ten-year period. During it, some attitudes changed from outright derision to a form of pity. In Ian Fleming's 1959 James Bond novel *Goldfinger*, Fleming observed "pansies of both sexes were everywhere ... Bond was sorry for them, but he had no time for them". But "homosexual" rarely appeared in newspapers: many internal style guides dictated that the word should only be used in court reports on men who had been convicted of having sex with other men. "Homosexuality" was treated like a pathology or an illness and gay men were mostly referred to, in newspapers and everyday conversation, using derogatory terms: "pansy", "faggot", "fairy", "brown hatter" and "queer". Although "gay" had long been used as a synonym for homosexual, to most people's ears the word still meant jolly, colourful and cheerful.

In November 1958 a junior Foreign Office minister, Ian Harvey, was "caught in bush" (as the press put it) with a young Coldstream guardsman, Anthony Plant, in St James's Park, yards from Harvey's ministry (and the Admiralty, where Vassall worked).[54] Unlike Vassall, there was never any suggestion that Harvey or Plant were spies. Although an indecency charge was dropped and Harvey was only fined £5, his political career was over. After his conviction Harvey closed his diary with a single line – "The Rest is Silence". Rather than hang on until the next election, he resigned his seat in Parliament immediately and it was ten years before he felt ready to return to his Harrow East constituency, "and then only to a private lunch with friends".

"I never met Vassal [*sic*], though I knew something about him", Harvey later wrote, implying that they had moved in overlapping social circles. "It always surprised me that no one in the services seems to have suspected him, including the highly intelligent Sir

---

54   Harvey's successor at the Foreign Office was one John Profumo.

William Hayter under whose eye he came in Moscow".[55] But until 1958 no one had suspected Harvey of being gay, either.

Harvey was an establishment Tory MP, married with two daughters, but in 1958 his life fell apart. He resigned from the Carlton Club and even in the early 1970s he was told that he couldn't rejoin, as some members had said they would resign if he was readmitted. The War Office nearly "cashiered" him from the Territorial Army, in which he was a lieutenant-colonel, until a fellow MP, Hugh Fraser, intervened. Ahead of the 1959 election, H. Montgomery Hyde, a respected barrister, prolific writer and Ulster Unionist MP for Belfast North, was deselected by his party, merely because he had the audacity to call for the swift implementation of the reforms that Wolfenden recommended.

Until decriminalisation the threat of blackmail hung over all gay men, particularly those in well-paid or public positions with the most to lose. The Wolfenden Report had found that out of 71 blackmail cases reported to police in England and Wales between 1950 and 1953, 32 – nearly half – were connected to homosexuality. Of course, the vast majority of blackmail cases were not reported. The 1964 pamphlet *Towards a Quaker View of Sex* claimed that 90 per cent of blackmail cases involved homosexuality.

Elite gay men of the generation before Vassall – such as the MP and diarist Henry "Chips" Channon, born in 1897 – had so many friends in high places that they did not worry too much about blackmail or public exposure. But in the 1950s humbler gay men lived in constant fear of a letter or phone call threatening them with blackmail. "When a friend, as happened, killed himself in despair, or was blackmailed, robbed, beaten up or arrested, the ranks closed," Ben Duncan wrote. "We offered what help we could to the

---

55   Harvey also wrote that "The only way around this problem would seem to be to make it plain that the punishment for a homosexual relationship will not involve dismissal if it is admitted, whereas it will if it is not". Harvey did not seem to appreciate that Vassall's main predicament had not arisen from a consensual homosexual relationship, but rape.

victim or to the survivor. Above all we went on with our lives [but] kept in close touch."

The 1961 film *Victim*, starring Dirk Bogarde, was one of very few plays or films to shed a sympathetic spotlight on the predicament.[56] Bogarde played Melville Farr, a successful London barrister with a childless "lavender marriage" (arranged to mask his homosexuality) to Laura, a judge's daughter, played by Sylvia Syms. On the verge of "taking silk", Farr is receiving regular and unwanted phone calls from a mysterious young man, "Boy Barrett" (played by Peter McEnery), a wages clerk on a building site. It transpires that Barrett used to accept lifts to and from work in Farr's car, which had led to a brief affair. The men had been caught on camera, embracing in Farr's car, by a mysterious blackmail gang who regularly issue "summonses" and order victims to hand over cash. Accused of stealing money from his employer to pay off the blackmailers, Barrett is arrested and then found hanged in a police cell.

Farr turns amateur detective, trying to obtain the letters and photographic negatives that the blackmailers depend on. Along the way there are poignant cameos by some of the gang's previous victims. One is Henry, an elderly hairdresser who has been imprisoned four times for homosexual offences, and is on the verge of selling his salon and emigrating to Canada. Other victims include Calloway, a flamboyant actor played by Dennis Price[57] and clearly based on Noël Coward, who wants to pay the blackmailers off rather than expose them, and a car dealer who fears being cut out of his father's will.

Farr himself tracks the blackmail gang down in a bookshop off the Charing Cross Road, and its members are arrested by a surprisingly sympathetic group of policemen, yet Farr knows that it is only a matter of days before his sexuality is revealed in the press. There

---

56 Tellingly, although there is no sexual activity or nudity in *Victim*, it was still given an X certificate. Bogarde was apparently offered the part of Melville Farr after it was turned down by two other actors, who feared that playing a gay character would damage their careers.

57 Price was himself bisexual and is best known for his role in *Kind Hearts and Coronets*.

is no point testifying in court as "Mr X" as his identity is bound to be leaked. The scandal "will destroy you utterly," Laura warns him. "They're going to call me all sorts of filthy names", he replies. In the film's closing scene, Farr burns the negatives and letters in his fireplace. Although it's unclear whether his marriage will survive, it is obvious that he will lose his legal career, and quite possibly his liberty.

Like Melville Farr, the anti-hero of *Victim*, John Vassall was a man trapped by the moral climate of the early 1960s. While money from the Soviets meant that he could lead a colourful social life, it was hardly a large fortune. Vassall couldn't give up his job at the Admiralty as this gave him his only access to the secrets that the Russians coveted. For six years John Vassall must have existed in a feverish state of fear, or resignation to, being unmasked and ruined at any moment. His flat in Dolphin Square may have been comfortable and well furnished, but it was a gilded cage.

CHAPTER FOUR

"VINE LEAF"

On 6 January 1961 a middle-aged English couple and a middle-aged Canadian man were arrested, by officers of the Metropolitan Police's Special Branch, outside the Old Vic theatre, near Waterloo Station.[58] They were not theatregoers or old friends meeting up for a drink or a meal. Four secret Admiralty files, including information on HMS Dreadnought, Britain's first nuclear submarine, were found in a basket carried by the woman.

The police had caught a spy gang red-handed and within a couple of days they arrested two more accomplices, "lock, stock and barrel". The middle-aged English couple were Harry Houghton and his mistress, Ethel Gee. Born in Lincoln in 1905, Houghton was almost twenty years older than John Vassall, and firmly heterosexual, but he had a similar career history. He had worked as a pay clerk in the naval attaché's department at the British embassy in Warsaw from 1951 onwards, three years before Vassall arrived in Moscow. While in Warsaw, Houghton fell for a "deliciously attractive" Polish girl named Katrina and deserted his long-suffering English wife, Peggy. "He drank, broke his wife's leg, worked the black market and got involved with Polish girls," the American writers David Wise

---

58   The senior officer who arrested them was Chief Superintendent George Smith, who arrived on the scene of Vassall's arrest as soon as he could in September 1962.

and Thomas B. Ross later recounted. The impressionable Houghton was soon persuaded by Katrina to sell coffee on the black market. This funded his expensive tastes in alcohol, food and luxury goods. His supervisors soon became fed up with his constant hangovers and suspicious about how he lived beyond his means. Later, there were suggestions that he may have taken secret papers home. After fifteen months in Warsaw, Houghton was recalled to London in October 1952.

Back in London, Houghton met up with Polish contacts, supplied by Katrina, at a pub in Earls Court and started selling them secret Admiralty documents. These helped to fund a new love affair, with Ethel Gee (known to all as Bunty), a 38-year-old clerk at the Naval Research Establishment in Portland, Dorset. Despite being a "blatant and prodigious drunk", as Rebecca West said, Houghton landed a job at Portland himself, in a repair unit which gave him little access to secrets of interest. He had to obtain them via Bunty, who seems to have been unaware that she was an accomplice to a spy.

Houghton spoke freely to his Polish "friends" (who were in fact KGB agents) of his love for Bunty, his dissatisfaction with his loveless marriage to Peggy and his constant money worries. Details of his spycraft seem to belong in a Graham Greene novel, but they are remarkably similar to Vassall's. Vacuum cleaner brochures in the post were a secret signal that Houghton should attend assignations at Dulwich Picture Gallery with a Polish handler codenamed Nikki. Houghton was told he had to wear brown kid gloves and carry a copy of *The Times*. He also handed over documents at a pub on the Kingston bypass, the Toby Jug, from which his handler would take them away to be photographed using a Minox camera.[59]

Houghton was not a cosmopolitan jet-setter like Vassall: much of his money was wasted on drinking sessions with Bunty at the Elm

---

59   The Toby Jug (now demolished) has a place in rock music fame as the venue where David Bowie played the first night of his Ziggy Stardust tour on 10 January 1972.

Tree, a pub in the small village of Langton Herring. Houghton soon walked out on Peggy and lived with Bunty in a caravan in Warmwell, ten miles from Portland, and in the grounds of a hotel on Portland itself. Later, they lived with Bunty's widowed mother and a bedridden aunt on Hambro Road, a terrace of modest red-brick houses on a Portland hillside. Houghton and Gee's MI5 codenames ('Reverberate' and 'Trellis' respectively) suggest that they were seen as trivial spies: a drunken bore and his petty bourgeois mistress.

The hapless Houghton was almost rumbled by Bunty, who once opened a brown paper parcel containing confidential Admiralty documents (she had suspected it contained a gift for, or correspondence with, a rival lover). Houghton flashed enough cash around in Portland to arouse suspicion and by the spring of 1960 he was being tailed by MI5.

By now, Houghton had been introduced to a new handler, a Canadian man called Gordon Arnold Lonsdale. Lonsdale had arrived in Britain from New York in March 1955. He was outwardly a respectable businessman selling switches for burglar alarms, juke boxes and bubblegum machines. He had an office on Wardour Street in Soho and he lived at the White House, a huge 1930s apartment block on Albany Street, very near Regent's Park.[60] Nine storeys high and clad in pale cream faience tiles, it was a more prestigious address than Dolphin Square where Vassall lived. Like Vassall, Lonsdale was a member of a respectable club, the Royal Over-Seas League.

What Houghton didn't know was that Lonsdale was not as he seemed. He was in fact Kolon Molody (codenamed BEN), a Russian KGB officer. The real Gordon Lonsdale had been born in Ontario on 27 August 1924, but was last heard of in 1932 when his Finnish stepmother took him to Finland. It seems that the real Lonsdale

---

60   The White House was built in 1936 and converted into a hotel in 1959, though one wing was kept as apartments. Today, it is a four-star hotel with 450 rooms, called the Meliá White House.

died in the early 1950s and that Molody used his identity after he materialised in Vancouver in 1954.

Houghton, and later Gee, were introduced to a Russian handler called "Nikki" – none other than Nicolai Korovin, alias "Gregory", who was Vassall's handler until 1961. Lonsdale then upped the ante. He told Houghton to start handing over secrets about submarines if he wanted to carry on receiving money. Houghton introduced Bunty to Lonsdale (who he said was a US naval commander named Alex Johnson, who was blackmailing him because Johnson knew about Houghton's previous black marketeering in Warsaw) at a performance of the Bolshoi Ballet in London. He also seems to have told Bunty that he was handing over documents so that the Americans could check that the British were "playing fair" and abiding by the NATO agreements they had with their allies. The gullible Bunty agreed to play ball, and she and Houghton began coming to London regularly to stay at the Cumberland Hotel and hand over secrets to Lonsdale outside the Old Vic theatre. In Houghton's memoirs he admitted, "I did it for the money – there is no question about that".

Houghton, Gee and Lonsdale were not the only members of what became known as the Portland spy ring. They were assisted by a mild-mannered couple from New Zealand called Peter and Helen Kroger. The Krogers had rented a bungalow, 45 Cranley Drive in Ruislip, Middlesex, since October 1955. Peter Kroger was an antiquarian book dealer, operating from an office on the Strand, and Helen was known locally as "Cookie", because of her habit of throwing parties for children on the street.

Like Lonsdale, the Krogers were not what they seemed. They were really Morris and Lona Cohen, an American couple who had secretly worked for the KGB for years. The son of a grocer in the Bronx, Morris Cohen had fought with the American Abraham Lincoln Brigade in the Spanish Civil War, during which he was recruited as a Soviet agent, and then served in the US Army during the Second World War. Lona had worked as a teacher in Manhattan and as a nanny to the children of Harry Winston, a New York diamond dealer and alleged KGB paymaster. Both Cohens were close to a Soviet intelligence officer, Rudolf Abel, who was born in England to Russian émigré parents (he was later sentenced to a long jail term in the US, before being exchanged for the captured American U2 pilot, Gary Powers).

In July 1950, shortly before the arrest of the American spy Julius Rosenberg, the Cohens vanished from New York. Morris told friends that he had secured a screenwriting job in Hollywood. They did not go to California and instead, re-emerged in Middlesex five years later.

Special Branch and MI5 soon discovered that the secrets Houghton and Gee had given to Lonsdale were being communicated to Moscow from the Krogers' residence in Ruislip. On 7 January 1962, the day after Houghton, Gee and Lonsdale were arrested, the intrepid Chief Superintendent George Smith knocked on the bungalow's front door and announced to the Krogers, "I am a police officer making certain enquiries. May I come in?", as if he was making a routine call about a neighbourhood burglary.

The bungalow turned out to be an "arsenal of espionage" at the cutting edge of early 1960s technology. Hidden inside a Ronson lighter, and other hollow places, were lenses that reduced 35mm film to microdots, two microdot readers, six one-time cipher pads, a high-frequency transmitter and an automatic keying device for Morse transmissions (which reduced the time that the Krogers had to spend on the air to Moscow, thereby reducing the risk that their frequency would be listened to by the British). Later, an antenna was discovered, hidden beneath the kitchen's linoleum floor. Photographic paper was found hidden in the pages of a family bible and KGB call signs were hidden in a tin of Three Flowers talcum powder.

The tip-off that led the British to the Portland spy ring came from a defector called Michał Goleniewski (codenamed Sniper), a former Polish intelligence officer. Goleniewski had probably known about Houghton since his Warsaw days, when Houghton had been recruited as a spy by the Poles or identified as a potential recruit given all his "baggage". In late 1960, Goleniewski told the CIA, in letters written in bad German, that there was a spy in Portland, codenamed Lambda 2, whose real name was "Huppkener", "Happkener" or "Huppenkort". Although none of these names are particularly similar to Houghton, they helped the British to narrow their search.

The Portland ring had been exposed more by Goleniewski, and Houghton's stupidity, than by MI5 and Special Branch's spycatching skills. But the British could take some pride in the rare feat of catching Russian "sleeper" agents masquerading as western civilians. Chief Superintendent Smith did a lot of the legwork in the Portland case, gaining access to a box in a Midland Bank safe, where he found a suitcase containing a Praktina camera. Despite the overwhelming evidence, all five suspects pleaded not guilty at their Old Bailey trial in March 1961. Houghton claimed that Polish agents had forced him into spying by threatening his life and that they had once hired "London thugs" to "prove that they meant business". Ethel Gee admitted removing files from the Portland base to pass to Houghton, and then to the Russians, but denied receiving any money. The Krogers denied everything, and Lonsdale covered for them, claiming that he had installed transmitters in their cellar and hidden other tools of spycraft in the bungalow while the Krogers were on holiday. Nonetheless, they were all found guilty. Gordon Lonsdale's real identity – Molody – was only publicly revealed eight months later.[61]

The capture of the Portland spies was not the end of the story:

---

61   Molody was only in jail for three years: on 22 April 1964 he was returned to the Soviets at the Heerstrasse checkpoint in Berlin. He was exchanged for the British spy Greville Wynne and fêted as a hero in Russia. The Cohens, meanwhile, returned to Poland in 1969.

if anything it was the beginning. In May 1961, Houghton told the court of appeal that the Russians had told him that they were receiving information from another Admiralty source – possibly Vassall. It was also claimed that one mysterious microfilm found in the Krogers' bungalow had not come from Houghton and Gee but another source, elsewhere in the Admiralty.

On 26 March 1961, the *Sunday Telegraph* reported that "Scotland Yard has not yet closed the file on the spy ring operating around Gordon Arnold Lonsdale. Papers found in the house of the Krogers implicate two more undiscovered agents. One is believed to be a diplomat at the London embassy of an Iron Curtain country who has since been sent home. The other is thought to be a minor civil servant. ... There is no clue to his identity".

Vassall had never met, or even heard of, the Portland spies, but his first reaction to news of their arrest was panic. It was, he said, a "shattering experience". He was having dinner with friends when the news broke and he "had to be terribly careful not to get involved in any conversation on the matter".

On the Monday or Tuesday after the Portland arrests, Vassall was due to meet Gregory again.[62] When he got to The Drive at 7.30 p.m. no one was there. A few minutes later, an unfamiliar man, with fair receding hair and a round face, greeted him with the ominous words: "I know you because I recognise your face from photographs". In a panic, Vassall at first assumed he was a Special Branch officer. In fact, it was his new Soviet handler, who introduced himself as Nikolai.[63]

---

[62] There is confusion about where and when Vassall was "deactivated". Vassall once said it was in January 1961, but on another occasion he said it was on a May evening in 1961 at Princes Park, off Golders Green Road.

[63] Nikolai told Vassall that he had a brother in Siberia and that he had worked in the Soviet embassy in Rome, which made it easy for MI5 to work out his full name: Nikolai Karpekov. He was born in 1914, served in the Red Navy during the Second World War and spent 1944–46 in New York, working for the Soviet Government Purchasing Commission. Between 1948 and 1955 he worked at the Soviet embassy in Rome, acquiring a reputation as a "frivolous womaniser" and became a colonel in the NKVD. In 1958 he was posted to London, where officially he was a first secretary of the Soviet embassy. He was assigned to Vassall as his controller in December 1960, though he did not meet him until several weeks later.

Gregory had told Vassall, shortly before the Portland news broke, that he was being recalled to Russia. "I had grown to understand Gregory, a serious and stern agent but with an apparently warm sympathy for me," Vassall recalled naïvely. Nikolai seemed to know all about Vassall's movements and his active love life. "I said I felt awful and very nervous," Vassall later recalled. But Nikolai assured him that Soviet espionage was "foolproof" and whatever the Portland spies said, he would not be detected. He reassured Vassall that he should not "worry at all". But as a precaution, Vassall was to "cease operating at all until further notice". Nikolai lived in a flat in Fulham and did not lie very low in London: MI5 later discovered that he was a member of the Feltham Piscatorials Angling Society. He told Vassall that he was moving his emergency rendezvous point to a railway bridge in Headstone, as The Drive had "been used too much".

For the next fifteen months, from January 1961 to the spring of 1962, Vassall did very little espionage. In fact, it seems that he was without a functioning camera for almost a year. In June 1961 Vassall sold his Exakta camera (model number 821939) to a branch of Dollond & Aitchison on Royal Arcade, Bond Street, for £30 or £35. Nikolai bought a new Exakta (model number 971296) and gave it to Vassall in April 1962. In-between times, Vassall does not seem to have extracted, or photographed, any documents at all.

The espionage historian Keith Melton once said, "Agents are among the loneliest people in the world". For Vassall, the fifteen months of his "deactivation" from 1961–62 must have been the loneliest of all, waiting to see if the Russians would quietly forget about him or ask him to start spying again.

"In my mind I had visions of undercover agents floating around Whitehall looking for me or anyone who had been in Eastern Europe", Vassall recalled. In the Admiralty there was much talk about the Portland spy ring, and Vassall even found himself the butt of jokes, as so many people knew that he had been in Moscow.

For Vassall, the office banter was no joke. "Somewhere in London, or more probably Moscow, a leak must occur", he feared. But in the months that followed, Vassall was not hauled in for questioning by the British authorities and he began to relax.

That summer he went travelling again. On 7 August 1961 Vassall sent the Van Den Borns (now at the Dutch embassy in Lisbon) a postcard from Scotland, proudly announcing, "Hello, John Vassall calling from Edinburgh. Have just been visiting the home of the Marquess of Linlithgow ... Leaving for Italy at the end of September". In late September, he did indeed flee to Capri where he took up Buca Bowinkel's offer to stay in her villa. To celebrate Vassall's thirty-seventh birthday, they drank champagne at the Eden II Club, a "smart little night club" near the Quisisana Hotel, where Vassall had stayed previously.

Increasingly bored and unhappy in the Admiralty, Vassall wrote to Tam Galbraith to seek careers advice in the autumn of 1961. Galbraith, who was now a junior minister in the Scottish Office, called him at Dolphin Square one morning when Vassall was taking a day off suffering from a cold.[64] Galbraith invited Vassall for lunch. Vassall was delighted, and suddenly forgot about his cold. "Immediately I felt better and said I would very much like to".

Vassall arrived later than expected but was soon chatting to Galbraith and his wife Simone in their house on Cowley Street, "which reminded me of the world that I felt most at ease in". Over lunch, Vassall breathlessly told Galbraith that he would much rather be working for him than at the Admiralty, even if the Scottish Office "would hardly be very exciting".[65] Galbraith may have been taken aback by his honesty, but he suggested a role as a Queen's Messenger

---

64   There is uncertainty about the date of Vassall's second, and final, lunch at Cowley Street. Galbraith said it was early in 1961. Vassall said it was around Christmas 1961, and the Radcliffe tribunal concluded it was probably in April 1962, through others suggest it could have been in May of that year. Vassall's letter to Galbraith to say that he would stay at the Admiralty is dated 27 May 1962, which suggests that the lunch must have been before then.

65   Galbraith was Parliamentary Under-Secretary of State for Scotland, from October 1959 until his resignation in November 1962, in the wake of Vassall's conviction.

(a Foreign Office courier), which would have provided Vassall with a lot of foreign travel – this time at the taxpayers' expense. "Nothing very specific was suggested, but we did have a good talk before he had to hurry back to a committee meeting", Vassall recalled. He stayed on to drink coffee with Mrs Galbraith, but the normally talkative Vassall was rendered speechless when she expressed her "disgust" at the Portland scandal. Vassall found himself "in a maze", became incoherent, and quickly said his thanks and left.

A new job could have been a way out for Vassall – either to avoid detection or to stop spying altogether if the Soviets were uninterested in a Queen's Messenger – but it seems that Mrs Galbraith's comment on the Portland spies made him reconsider. Soon afterwards, he wrote to Galbraith to say that he was resigned to staying in the Admiralty after all. The lunch was a "poignant incident" said Rebecca West, and probably the last time that Vassall saw either of the Galbraiths until catching a glimpse of them at a Radcliffe tribunal hearing in early 1963, after he was jailed.

Incredibly, rather than keep a low profile, Vassall's next move in the winter of 1961–62 was to begin new friendships with not one but two backbench Conservative MPs. He seems to have been indirectly introduced to the first by his American friend Dr Bartels, who gave the MP Vassall's number at a party in New York.[66] Vassall's memoirs recall that in the late autumn of 1961 he received a strange phone call at home. The voice asked Vassall to confirm his name and then to say whether he knew "X, who worked in the secretariat at the United Nations in New York". Vassall replied that he did know "X". The unidentified caller said he had recently met X at a cocktail party and that Vassall's name had come up. What were Vassall's political views? And would Vassall like to come for dinner at the House of Commons?" The call was not an intelligence

---

66   British Treasury solicitors later misunderstood this and thought that Vassall himself had first met the MP in New York.

operation, as Vassall first thought, but simply a pick-up: a gay friend in New York had recommended Vassall to a gay MP as a good date.

A few hours later, Vassall met the MP in the Central Lobby before an "enjoyable evening chatting about our mutual friend and various other matters". As they dined, another MP joined them, and later that evening both MPs went back to Vassall's flat at Dolphin Square for brandy, tea, and then more brandy. "They came with great pleasure," Vassall recalled.

Over the next few months, both MPs continued to see Vassall, taking him out separately to dinner, the theatre or the cinema. "They were very curious about each other, longing to know if the other was 'gay'. I was rather surprised that they were not aware of it immediately," recalled Vassall. In due course Vassall met a young American, Dr Douglas Bushy, through one of the MPs, and one evening Bushy and both MPs came to Dolphin Square for tea.

Bushy – identified only as "the American" in Vassall's memoirs – was "tall, good-looking and very scholarly". He worked at the National Council of the Protestant Episcopal Church (the Anglican Church in America) and was "known to Lord Fisher of Lambeth" (a former Archbishop of Canterbury), MI5 later noted.

Soon, Bushy was visiting Vassall's flat frequently and he invited Vassall to spend Christmas 1961 with him, either in New York or on the Caribbean island of St Thomas. In the end, they spent it in New York, "exchanging feelings and presents", before going to High Mass at St Patrick's Cathedral on Christmas Day. After visiting other friends in Baltimore, Vassall returned to New York for a few more days with Bushy. It was the last Christmas he would spend as a free man for twelve years.

Vassall continued to see his "M.P. friends" throughout early 1962, and on 26 May – or 26 June, according to other accounts – Vassall got chatting to another American, Robert Eiserle, at Francis Bacon's first retrospective exhibition at the Tate Gallery. Eiserle was a "young Ivy League type" with whom Vassall was soon breakfasting at Dolphin Square every morning, his memoirs note delicately. He was clearly wealthy and staying at Chesham Place, Belgravia, on business. "He seemed somewhat naïve but exceedingly nice and gentle with thoughtful eyes and a masculine bearing," Vassall recalled. It was Eiserle who Vassall arranged to meet in Italy in September 1962, but three days before Vassall was due to fly to Rome he was arrested in London.

For sixty years the identity of the two MPs has never been officially confirmed, although one did reveal himself. In January 1996, nine months before Vassall's death, the backbench Conservative MP Fergus Montgomery revealed that he had "had a close relationship" with him in 1961–62. In 1975 Montgomery had been forced to resign as parliamentary private secretary to Margaret Thatcher (then Tory leader) after Humphry Berkeley – a former Tory MP who left Parliament in 1966 and later switched to Labour via the SDP – told the Cabinet Office about his links to Vassall.[67]

"Yes, I knew Vassall," Montgomery told the *Sunday Times* reporter Maurice Chittenden. "He was very grand. I thought he was a sad, lonely person. I felt sorry for him. In the short time I knew him he posed as a Conservative." Montgomery added that Vassall became "obsessive" and he had "had to disentangle himself from their friendship". But Montgomery insisted that he had only met Vassall for drinks in the House of Commons, that he had never gone to his flat or had "an intimate relationship" with him and that he "knew nothing about Vassall's treachery ... If he had any plans to involve me he was barking up the wrong tree". "I have not seen him for 30-odd years," he insisted. "I have had no contact. Nor in fairness would I want any contact". Montgomery strongly implied that he was the victim of a smear campaign by Berkeley (who had

---

67   Montgomery was MP for Newcastle-upon-Tyne East when Vassall met him, having been elected in 1959. After losing his seat in 1964 he re-emerged as MP for Brierley Hill in the West Midlands from 1967 until February 1974. He was then MP for Altrincham and Sale from October 1974 until 1997.

died in 1994). He added that Berkeley had befriended Vassall after his release from prison in 1972, but that Berkeley had never been his own friend.[68]

Only recently have newly declassified files shown that in 1962 MI5 concluded that Montgomery had visited Vassall's flat seven or eight times and that Montgomery introduced Vassall to Douglas Bushy. Montgomery not only spent a lot of time at Vassall's flat: he also introduced Vassall to a new boyfriend.

After his arrest in 1962 Vassall told MI5 that his relationship with Montgomery had not been physical, but he did tell them that he believed that Montgomery (who was unmarried until 1971 and never had children) shared a London flat with the television newsreader Kenneth Kendall.[69] Certainly, Westminster gossip was that Montgomery (who died in 2013) was bisexual.

The identity of Vassall's second "MP friend" has always been a secret. Some have speculated that it was Tam Galbraith, but it cannot possibly have been: in his memoirs, and elsewhere, Vassall made it clear that he first met the two MPs in autumn 1961, while he had first met Galbraith in 1957. Only recently have MI5's files revealed him to be Sir Harmar Nicholls, Conservative MP for Peterborough from 1950 to 1974.[70]

Nicholls had been made a baronet in 1960, the year before he met Vassall. He was seen in Westminster as a straitlaced and low-profile backbencher, best known for holding on to his seat with improbably small majorities (144 votes in 1950, 373 in 1951, 3 in 1966 and 22 in February 1974).

---

68 There is little firm evidence of a friendship between Vassall and Berkeley, although he was thanked in the preface of Vassall's memoirs. Berkeley's own memoirs make only one short reference to the Vassall affair – revealing that Berkeley had shared a flat with Peter Tapsell at the time of the "Do a Pontecorvo" scare of November 1962 – but none to Vassall himself.

69 From 1989 onwards Kendall lived in Cowes on the Isle of Wight with his partner Mark Fear. They entered into a civil partnership in 2006. Kendall died on 14 December 2012 after a stroke and in April 2013, Mark Fear was found hanged aged fifty-five.

70 Nicholls had little time to seek high ministerial office in Westminster, though he was parliamentary secretary to the Ministry of Agriculture, Fisheries and Food from 1955 to 1958 and to the Ministry of Works from 1958 to 1961. He was given a life peerage as Baron Harmar-Nicholls in 1975. From 1979 to 1984, he served as Member of the European Parliament for Greater Manchester South.

Roy Lakey, Labour's agent in Peterborough in the early 1970s, recalls that Nicholls was widely rumoured to be gay because of his "foppish dress" and his habit of "flouncing in" theatrically at election counts just before the declaration. Lakey remembers seeing his daughter Sue Nicholls – the *Coronation Street* actress – at election counts, but never his wife. "He's our Jeremy Thorpe," one local Conservative told Lakey. Unlike Montgomery, no whiff of any connection to Vassall emerged in Nicholls's lifetime. He died in September 2000, aged eighty-seven.

Soon after his conviction in 1962, Vassall told MI5 that Fergus Montgomery was the MP who had contacted him by telephone in the autumn of 1961 and that Montgomery had introduced him to Nicholls. In 1962, with legal bills to pay and a story to sell to the *Sunday Pictorial*, it might have made sense for Vassall to drop as much innuendo as he could about love affairs with men in high places. But Vassall never publicly named either of the MPs, in his memoirs or in press interviews. It seems that he did indeed have a close relationship with both of them, and a sexual relationship with at least one, just as he entered his most fruitful period as a Soviet spy.

● ● ●

The Russians never forgot about Vassall. In the spring of 1962 he was "reactivated" after his fifteen-month hibernation. The Cold War had grown even more tense since Vassall had been told to "cease operations" in January 1961. On 17 April, 1,400 Cuban exiles launched a botched invasion at the Bay of Pigs on the south coast of Cuba, which heightened Soviet–American tensions considerably; in August, after the USSR issued an ultimatum demanding the withdrawal of Western forces from Berlin, East Germany hastily started building the Berlin Wall. The Conservative MP Bob Boothby wrote that four Eastern European countries he had recently visited (Poland, Czechoslovakia, Hungary and Romania) had one thing in common: "the political power of the communist party". By 1961, they were all "solidly behind Mr Khrushchev" and "the political power of the communist party is nowhere seriously in doubt".

Nineteen sixty-two was set to be one of the most important years in the Cold War, when the world came closer to nuclear conflagration than at any time before or since. Appropriately enough, Chapter 17 in Vassall's memoirs is entitled "1962 – The Fatal Year". "Shortly after Christmas [1961] I was informed by Nikolai that I could start bringing them material again, as they said the all-clear had been given by Moscow", Vassall recalled. He was asked to buy another new camera, but he told Nikolai that doing so would draw too much attention. Instead, on 17 February, Nikolai gave him a new Minox, at a meeting in Grovelands Park in Winchmore Hill. The Minox proved difficult to use and he apparently never mastered it but in May, Vassall picked up a new Exakta that Nikolai left in a phone box on Grosvenor Road, outside Dolphin Square. It is clear that the Soviets did not think that Vassall would be unmasked only a few months later.[71]

Vassall recalled that he called his brother from one phone box, as Nikolai dropped off the camera in another. After collecting the camera, "I was nervous, but as I walked along I did not feel anyone was watching me." But at another meeting with Nikolai, Vassall had a narrow escape. Soon after they parted company, Vassall was standing on a platform at Southgate railway station and bumped into a man called Seymour, an Admiralty official he knew, who was with his wife and daughter en route to a pantomime. Nikolai was waiting on the opposite platform. If Seymour had arrived a few minutes earlier, he might have caught Vassall in the company of a mysterious Russian.

---

71   MI5 later found that the Exakta had been imported by K. G. Corfield (a camera shop on Charlotte Street) and bought by Karpekov there, not at a shop in Fulham as Vassall believed.

Vassall now started photographing documents in greater numbers than ever. He was "up to his elbows in material", claimed Rebecca West. Rather than smuggle documents out to photograph at home, he seems to have started taking photographs at the Admiralty itself. In July 1962 Nikolai started asking Vassall questions he simply could not answer: about the recent reshuffle that had seen the Chancellor of the Exchequer, Selwyn Lloyd, dismissed and whether Captain Henry Kerby's "friendliness to the Russians was genuine, or if Kerby was a British agent", Vassall later told MI5.[72] Nikolai also asked him about John Osborn, Conservative MP for Sheffield Hallam, who Vassall had once met in Moscow (Vassall recalled that Osborn had been very rude, and that the embassy had wanted little to do with him as he talked too much). Vassall could tell the Russians nothing more about any of these men. In his final few months of spying Vassall was told to look out for information in four very broad categories: "Anything to do with American activities, anything to do with NATO, Atomic subjects [and] the DEATH RAY", he later told MI5.[73]

Just as Vassall resumed his spying, and fraternising with Tory MPs, he found time for much more socialising. His diary records that on Sunday 4 February 1962 he went to the Guards Club, to the Brompton Oratory with his father (without telling him he had converted to Catholicism) and met Humphrey (probably Humphrey Hicks) at a restaurant called Chez Ciccio. Over the next few days he had a 2.15 appointment with a Chester Barrie on Heddon Street, lunched with the Pecks, his old Moscow friends, at their home in Wallington, Surrey and dined with 'Hilda' at Au Jardin des Gourmets, a restaurant on Greek Street. On 21 February he went to an event at Caxton Hall at 8 p.m. and on Saturday 3 March he lunched

---

72   Captain Kerby was Conservative MP for Arundel and Shoreham in Sussex.
73   "DEATH RAY" appears to be a reference to the "teleforce" that the Serbian-American physicist Nikola Tesla claimed to have invented in 1934. Throughout the Cold War, both the USSR and the US feared that the other was developing such a superweapon that could "end all war". See https://www.sciencehistory.org/distillations/the-undying-appeal-of-nikola-teslas-death-ray.

at 55 Park Lane and went to the wedding of the daughter of a Mr and Mrs Lang at St James's, Spanish Place (a Catholic church in Fitzrovia).

In the winter of 1961–62 he also found the time to renew an old friendship. Despite their initial mutual dislike, Vassall and Geoffrey Bennett had begun to get on by the time Bennett left Moscow in late 1955. Bennett had clearly tolerated Vassall's homosexuality. Back in London, "it is evident that Capt Bennett felt no lasting disapproval", the Radcliffe report noted. They did not just stay in touch, but became unlikely friends. After Vassall's arrest, Bennett's name was found in his address book. Vassall sent Geoffrey and Rosemary postcards from Capri and other European holiday destinations, and after 1959 the Bennetts visited Dolphin Square at least once. Geoffrey later told MI5 that he had probably last seen Vassall at a cocktail party there three months before his arrest.

After returning from Moscow Bennett served on the staff of the Royal Navy's commander in chief, Portsmouth, until he retired from the navy in February 1958. He then worked as the City of London's Marshal (an organiser of events behind the scenes and a ceremonial factotum in front of them), and from 1960 as secretary to the Lord Mayor of the City of Westminster. Bennett became "an authority on civic protocol" and organised events such as the inauguration of the Norwegian Christmas Tree in Trafalgar Square each December.

Bennett's productivity as a writer had dipped slightly during his two years in Moscow but he now made up for lost time, writing a string of naval histories and biographies as well as more spy novels. Nineteen fifty-eight saw *Death in Russian Habit*, a Moscow "whodunnit" set at an international trade commission, which is solved by a holidaying British detective inspector, Paul Snell, whose mother was born in Russia. *Operation Fireball* (1959) was about the "misadventures that befall the first attempt of the Navy to fire a long-range rocket with a nuclear warhead" from the fictitious

HMS Mandalay, which has to contend with "would-be wreckers" on board and a mysterious submarine. This was followed by *The Missing Submarine* (1960) (in which Snell hunts down the *Orchid*, a British submarine that has vanished from anchor in Rothesay Bay), *Down Among the Dead Men* (1961) and *Death in the Dog Watches* (1962).

Bennett never knew that while he was writing these books, Vassall was still handing over details of real-life British warships and submarines to the Russians. In 1961 he wrote *By Human Error*, an account of catastrophic accidents, most of them naval. He was unaware that a year later, he would find himself at the centre of a disaster of his own.

Bennett was close enough to Vassall to invite him to his son Richard's wedding on 3 February 1962 at St Mary Abbots church, not far from the Soviet embassy on Kensington Palace Gardens.[74] It was a very literary wedding. The 22-year-old Richard married Perdita Watt, the 19-year-old great-granddaughter of Alexander Pollock Watt, who was widely considered to be London's first literary agent in the 1870s.[75] Perdita had been "the first deb of 1961 to become engaged", a press announcement explained.

At the reception, at the Hyde Park Hotel, the well-known humourist and former MP Sir Alan Herbert proposed a toast. In the 1930s Herbert had composed a light-hearted advertising pamphlet for Dolphin Square's developers and John Vassall must have loved it. He was one of 300 guests, many of them Geoffrey's diplomatic and naval friends, at the reception, but Perdita still remembers the wedding present that Vassall gave: a ceramic saucepan from

---

74   With his interest in family history, Vassall must have known that his uncle Henry Vassall had married Gwendolen St Clair Chase Morris at St Mary Abbots in 1910.

75   In 1973 Geoffrey's younger son Rodney wrote *The Archer-Shees Against the Admiralty*, a book about the Royal Navy cadet who was the inspiration for the Terence Rattigan play *The Winslow Boy*. Like Geoffrey's books, it made no mention of Vassall.

Asprey's, an expensive gift out of all proportion to their acquaintance. Like Vassall's life, it was broken soon after the honeymoon.

More than sixty years on, Perdita still clearly remembers the handful of times she met Vassall in the early 1960s.[76] She saw him at drinks parties at the Bennetts' house on Argyll Road, Kensington – only 300 yards from Holland Park, where Vassall had been told to leave chalk markings to communicate with his KGB handlers. A grand piano in the Bennetts' through reception room would be played by guests, but never by Vassall, even though newspapers later claimed he was an accomplished pianist. Rather than being the life and soul of the party, Vassall was always in the background. "He was very personable and charming ... but also slightly smarmy" recalls Perdita. She would acknowledge him, and chat, but they weren't friends. She thinks that the last time she met Vassall was only a few weeks before his arrest. Everyone assumed that Vassall was gay, but nobody had the slightest suspicion that at the same time as his attendance of Richard and Perdita's wedding, he was embarking on the final part of his seven-year spying career.

By 1961 Vassall worked in Room 56A of the Admiralty, overlooking Horse Guards Parade, which he shared with a Mr Munson and a Miss Dunstall. A Mr Mowat later took Munson's place, and Miss Dunstall was succeeded by a Miss Prior. Their paperwork was "very dull and dreary and of no interest to the Russians," Vassall recalled. He recollected only one document with a classification higher than "secret". By early 1962 he shared Room 56A with a Mrs Royal and Miss Elizabeth Paterson. His working hours were relatively short – 10 a.m. to 6.30 p.m., with an hour's break for lunch – and logs showed that he rarely arrived much before 10, or stayed much beyond 6.30.

Vassall's most prolific period of his seven years of espionage appears to have been at the very end, from May 1962 onwards.

---

76   Perdita is now called Perdita Campbell-Orde. After divorcing Richard in 1976 she married Peter Campbell-Orde. The couple divorced in 1992.

Whenever a Miss E. E. Turner was sick or on holiday, Vassall moved to Room 52 and "acted up" as personal assistant to the head of the Fleet Section, Mr Tupman, which gave him much greater access to documents. Mr Marshall, one of Vassall's bosses in 1962, later told the Admiralty's director of security, a Royal Marines colonel named Jack MacAfee (nicknamed "Black Jack"), that Vassall had access to "Ward Commission papers" (about plans for a Joint Operations Centre in Cyprus) and "the COSMIC file" of secret NATO documents.

Vassall was later found to have taken photographs of seventeen documents, more than half of them marked as "Top Secret", in the six weeks before his arrest on 12 September. Even the Radcliffe report, which did its utmost to minimise the seriousness of Vassall's spying, acknowledged that for brief periods in 1962 he was "in a position to handle a volume of documentary matter which carried a very high security classification", and that the films found in his flat "do not suggest that he was either slow to seize his opportunities when they came or … reluctant to obtain for his masters the richest spoil that he could put in their hands". Behind the Whitehall verbosity, the truth is clear: Vassall had access to the crown jewels and he handed over whatever jewels he could lay his hands on.

By 1962 Vassall's annual salary was still only £908 gross, or about £700 after tax. According to his Admiralty friend, Jennifer Hall, his only other real friend there was Ann Miller. Vassall was considered "somewhat stand-offish" by most colleagues, especially men, Hall recalled. A staff report from January 1962 judged his overall performance to be no better than "adequate". The reporting officer added the scathing comments: "a puzzling, disappointing person. Has all the superficial attributes of a success [sic] but little real ability to achieve it".

That summer Vassall played a small role in Operation Shop Window, a NATO exercise. He led a group of surgeons on a tour of the aircraft carrier HMS Centaur. One of the surgeons, J. W. Cope, had once operated on Vassall's father. Vassall later wrote to several officers, including a lieutenant-commander Barton, to thank them for their hospitality and invite them to visit him at Dolphin Square, though only Barton replied and it seems that none of them ever visited. But Mr Marshall, the head of Vassall's section, told him that several officers had written to thank Vassall for his efficiency. Vassall later told MI5 that the Russians were aware of his visit to the *Centaur* but had not asked him for further details. Nonetheless, his diary was later found to have a note on the page for 29 October, reminding Vassall that the *Centaur* was due to return to Portsmouth that day. By then, however, the *Centaur's* movements were the least of Vassall's worries: he was entering his second week at Wormwood Scrubs.

In 1962 the Admiralty was even closer to the seat of British government than usual. In 1960 Prime Minister Harold Macmillan moved out of No. 10 during its extensive renovation, and until August 1963 Macmillan's residence and offices were at Admiralty House, towards the north end of Whitehall: an elegant mansion that had been built in 1788 as the official residence of the First Lord of the Admiralty. Admiralty House was adjacent to the Admiralty itself and Vassall had worked there continuously for more than six years. He was, both figuratively and literally, a spy at the very heart of the British state.

•　•　•

Failure is an orphan, but success has a thousand fathers. While no one would later admit to failing to catch John Vassall sooner, many people claimed the credit for his unmasking in the spring and summer of 1962.

There are several competing claims. The first is that Vassall's capture was a logical extension of Michał Goleniewski's exposure of the Portland spies in January 1961. Tim Tate's biography of Goleniewski, *The Spy Who Was Left Out in the Cold*, says that "although some accounts state that a later defector [Anatoliy Golitsyn] exposed Vassall – and MI5's files on the case remain under lock and key – Goleniewski aways claimed the credit". Goleniewski himself always claimed that it was microfilms recovered from the Portland spy ring that led to Vassall's arrest. There is some merit in this: after all, if the Russians had given Harry Houghton the code-name Lambda 2, it would be logical for the British to wonder if there was a Lambda 1 at the Admiralty.

Officially, the British always denied that the Portland spies led them to Vassall. But the Americans disagreed: in an article in the 1963 edition of the *Britannica Book of the Year*, the outgoing CIA director Allen W. Dulles stated that "Microfilms found in their [the Krogers'] apartment [*sic*] eventually led to the apprehension of John Vassall". "It would seem that either the Radcliffe tribunal or the former CIA Director was wrong on this point", David Wise and Thomas B. Ross noted drily. Given that Dulles was a well-respected CIA director, first appointed by Eisenhower in 1953 and retained by Kennedy until after the Bay of Pigs débâcle in 1961, it is clear who they believe.

This is a double-edged compliment: while it places the credit for Vassall's detection largely in British hands, it also prompts questions about why it took the police and MI5 twenty months after the arrest of the Portland spies in January 1961 to apprehend Vassall.

MI6 and the CIA tried to boost Goleniewski's credentials, planting stories in the press claiming that he (identified only by the codename 'Martel') had helped to expose spies in France (including Georges Pâques),[77] Germany (Heinz Felfe and Johannes

---

77   Georges Pâques, Deputy Head of NATO's press service, was a former French resistance fighter who was sentenced to life in prison in July 1964, having confessed to passing information to the Soviets between 1944 and 1963. Charles de Gaulle lowered the sentence to twenty years, and Georges Pompidou pardoned him after only seven years. Like Vassall, Pâques was apprehended after the French intelligence service received information from Golitsyn, via the CIA.

'Hans' Clemens), Sweden (Stig Wennerström)[78] and Britain (John Vassall). The British certainly showed Goleniewski much gratitude. MI5 once gave him a silver George III tankard as a thank-you present and British intelligence continued to seek his help. But Goleniewski became an unreliable source. One of his more outlandish claims was that Vassall's name had been on "a list of candidates for agents", drawn up by Houghton. The list had been known to MI5, and by James Angleton (the fanatically anti-communist head of counter-intelligence at the CIA for two decades from 1954 to 1974), since Houghton's arrest in January 1961. This suggests that MI5 had deliberately failed to investigate Vassall for at least a year.

A second theory is that while Goleniewski may have helped to identify the Portland spies, their capture (and John Vassall's) was all down to British detective work, without any foreign help. In his fawning 1973 biography of Chief Superintendent George Smith, "Britain's number one spycatcher", Norman Lucas insisted that "Smith picked up the trail of Vassall … in early April 1962, as rumours swirled that Burgess and Maclean might be about to return to Britain".[79] Lucas also claimed that the tip-off that led to Vassall's arrest was "in a letter sent in the Diplomatic bag from the British embassy in Moscow" after "officials at the embassy had learned that British naval secrets had been communicated to Russian naval chiefs". John Bulloch's 1963 book *MI5: The Origin and History of the British Counter-Espionage Service* claimed that Vassall was detected after someone overheard a Russian naval officer bragging about

---

78   Colonel Stig Wennerström was a Swedish Air Force officer, convicted in 1964. Vassall always denied having met, or even having heard of, Wennerström but the latter's arrest, on the morning of 30 June 1963, is a Swedish equivalent of Vassall's. Wennerström was arrested by the Swedish security service SÄPO alongside the Riksbron Bridge in central Stockholm and rolls of film were found at his house in the suburb of Djursholm. Wennerström is believed to have handed over 20,000 pages on the Swedish Air Force's strategy, secret bases, radar defences and mobilisation plans. He was sentenced to life in prison but released on parole in 1974.

79   In April 1962, rumours had reached London that Burgess and Maclean might be coming home to face the music, after a report emerged in Amsterdam that tickets on a KLM flight from Moscow to London had been booked in their names. The British publicly announced that both men would be arrested as soon as they arrived in the country. On the morning they were due to arrive, George Smith obtained warrants for their arrest from a magistrate at Bow Street but the two men never showed up.

seeing British secrets at a Moscow reception in 1961. More recently, a history of Special Branch maintained that "the security service received intelligence from one of their agents which led them to investigate" Vassall, which again suggests that it was MI5 or MI6 ingenuity alone that led to his exposure.

George Smith did indeed have a strong track record. He had been born in Bratton, Wiltshire, in 1905 but soon gravitated to London, joining the Metropolitan Police in 1926 and, like Vassall, lived in a small flat in Pimlico. In his long career in Special Branch he helped to investigate IRA bombers, German spies during the Second World War, members of the Hebrew Legion, Klaus Fuchs and Anthony Wraight in the 1950s, as well as the Portland spies.[80] When Smith retired from Special Branch and returned to Wiltshire at the end of 1962, he received a letter from J. Edgar Hoover, the veteran FBI director, expressing "my appreciation for the co-operation and assistance you have rendered the bureau over the years".

After Smith's death in 1970, Lucas's hagiography claimed that he was "probably the greatest police officer ever to sit at a desk in Scotland Yard's special branch". But the myth was always ahead of the reality. Lucas revealed that he had often drunk with Smith at the Sherlock Holmes pub on Northumberland Street, off Trafalgar Square, and that "when George left the Force many crime reporters lost a good friend. He was never guilty of breaching the Official Secrets Act but he did, from time to time, give expert guidance that prevented many newspapers from producing highly inaccurate

---

80   Anthony Wraight, an RAF flying officer, had a story almost as fascinating as Vassall's. In December 1956 he defected to East Germany after writing to the Society of Cultural Relations (a KGB front), asking to study photography in Moscow. There, he was paid £40 a month for information about the RAF. Wraight then travelled to Poland, but he was denied permission to settle there and in December 1959 he returned to Britain. When Wraight was debriefed by MI5 he said that he had defected after being told that his career as a pilot could be over because of his worsening eyesight. He was dismissed from the RAF but not prosecuted, until an outcry in Parliament forced the government to reconsider. Wraight was arrested by George Smith himself at his parents' home in Eastbourne. In March 1960 he was tried at the Old Bailey and only pleaded guilty to one of three charges under the Official Secrets Act. On 2 April he was sentenced to three years in prison but only served two. In truth, no one really knew exactly what information, if any, Wraight gave the Russians.

reports". Lucas's vague claim that Smith was singlehandedly responsible for unmasking Vassall therefore seemed to owe more to the beer-soaked friendship between an "old-style spycatcher" and a Fleet Street hack than to the truth.

Chapman Pincher, in one of his more lucid moments, once argued that the myth of British police ingenuity was deliberately spread because a defector's life was at risk. "Security agencies preferred to play down the role of defectors and project the wholly fallacious idea that they could identify traitors without external help," Nigel West wrote. "In fact, almost no Cold War spy was caught without that most valuable of commodities, defector information".

Easily the most plausible theory is that Vassall was only detected thanks to information from another defector, a KGB major called Anatoliy Golitsyn (given the codename AE/LADLE by the CIA and KAGO by MI6). In December 1961 Golitsyn turned up on the doorstep of Frank Friberg, the CIA's station chief in Helsinki, and asked for political asylum for himself, his wife and his daughter. Like many defectors, Golitsyn, then aged thirty-five, had both personal and ideological motives: he was thoroughly fed up with the bureaucracy of the KGB. Soon after arriving in Finland, he fell out with his superior, the "Resident" General Zhenikov. When he complained to Moscow about how Zhenikov was running the KGB office he was designated a "conspiring troublemaker". Golitsyn's cover job in Helsinki had been as a humble visa clerk, not unlike Vassall's own job, and like Vassall he was seen as a misfit.

At first, Golitsyn only offered the CIA titbits of information (for example, that a Finnish woman working at the British Council office in Helsinki, Elsa Mai Evans, was in the pay of the Soviets), but once he established his credentials he became a lot more forthcoming. In March 1962 the Americans secretly brought Golitsyn to the CIA headquarters in Langley, Virginia, where he was kept incommunicado for several months and thoroughly "debriefed" by

James Angleton over the next year or two. Golitsyn's English was poor: Angleton found that he had to replay tapes of their conversations to work out exactly what he was trying to say.

Golitsyn did not, as some have claimed, directly identify Kim Philby as a spy – indeed he said that he had never heard the name Philby. But he did talk about "the Ring of Five": the first clue that Philby had, alongside Maclean and Burgess, been part of a network of five Cambridge spies (the others being Anthony Blunt and John Cairncross), not three. He also claimed that the Soviet embassy in London did not need a KGB unit to hunt down traitors because its sources in British intelligence were so good that they were sure they would get advance warning of any defector.

More importantly, Golitsyn confirmed what the FBI had already heard from a source codenamed FEDORA, a Soviet official at the UN building in New York: that the KGB was receiving information from a "homosexual" in the British Admiralty who had been blackmailed while working in Moscow. MI5's files show that by the end of March Jack MacAfee was aware that a credible defector had warned about another spy in the Admiralty, though MI5's director-general Roger Hollis did not tell Admiralty ministers or the Cabinet Secretary Sir Norman Brook, until early April.[81] The Prime Minister was not told this crucial news until 18 April. Sir Harold Caccia, British ambassador in Washington, flew to Chequers to inform Macmillan of Golitsyn's defection, and that he had "spoken of penetration of the British intelligence services, the Foreign Office and the Admiralty".

In the summer of 1962 Golitsyn – with his hair dyed and wearing a false moustache and glasses to alter his appearance – was secretly flown to Britain to be interrogated by Dick White and Arthur Martin of MI5. Martin had a sequence of secret meetings with Golitsyn in Brighton, Coventry, Bournemouth, Liverpool and

---

81   Born in December 1905, Hollis was, like Vassall, a son of the Church of England with strong Somerset roots: his father was Bishop of Taunton from 1931 to 1944.

Edinburgh and showed him secret Admiralty documents. Gradually, through a convoluted experiment, MI5 determined what kind of camera the spy they were looking for was using. Golitsyn was shown twenty-five different versions of the first page of a document about the Clyde nuclear base and was asked to pick out the one most similar to what he had seen at the KGB. Golitsyn chose the image that had been taken with a Praktina camera, illuminated by Anglepoise lamps on both sides.[82]

Christopher Andrew, MI5's authorised historian, wrote that Golitsyn was a "troublesome defector".[83] Golitsyn's credibility was later dented by claims that he thought that the Labour leader Hugh Gaitskell's sudden death in January 1963 was not due to natural causes, as doctors believed, but that the KGB had assassinated him by serving poisoned coffee and biscuits at the Soviet embassy in London, where Gaitskell had gone to obtain a visa a few weeks before his death.[84] Back in the US, Golitsyn "acquired a near guru-like status", and lived on a farm in Upstate New York. He constantly lived in fear of assassination, having been sentenced to death in absentia by the Soviet Union in July 1962. Like Goleniewski, Golitsyn descended into paranoia.

Unlike many defectors, Golitsyn never testified in front of Congress, and nothing written by him appeared in print until the publication of his rambling memoir, *New Lies for Old*, in 1984. The book's "obsessive thesis" was, Nigel West has argued, that "what the West regard as world history over the last 30 years is nothing more than a giant conjuror's trick of KGB disinformation". But it is certain that

---

82   There is no record of Vassall being given a Praktina camera, but one was found in his flat on the day of his arrest. The experiment certainly shows how thorough MI5 were in questioning Golitsyn.

83   In July 1963 Golitsyn visited Britain again, but his visit was brought to a sudden end and the Americans flew him back to Washington, amid a bitter row between MI6 and the CIA. The British had issued a "D-Notice", asking newspapers not to report on the defector's presence or his real name. But several newspapers ignored it and misidentified Golitsyn as Anatoli Dolnytsin, an unrelated bureaucrat working in Moscow for the Soviet Ministry of Foreign Affairs. On top of the Vassall scandal and the defection of Philby, this was a final straw for the Americans..

84   In fact, all Golitsyn had said was that a KGB director of operations had once talked about assassinating an unnamed western opposition party leader. He never said that Gaitskell was a target and he never suggested, or even implied, that Harold Wilson was the Soviet agent anointed to succeed him.

as well as unmasking Vassall, Golitsyn also helped to unmask the British spy Barbara Fell (see Chapter Five), the French spies Georges Pâques and Jacques Foccart, and John Watkins, a former Canadian ambassador in Moscow. Like Vassall, Watkins was the victim of a gay "honey trap" and died in October 1964 of a heart attack in a break between interrogation sessions. Many believe that without Golitsyn's defection in December 1961 and the information he gave to the CIA and MI6, Vassall would never have been unmasked.

A third defector, Yuri Nosenko (codenamed AE/FOXTROT by the CIA) also claimed some of the credit. As a lieutenant-colonel in the KGB's Second Chief Directorate, Nosenko was much more senior than Golitsyn, but his defection seemed to be motivated purely by money. In May 1962 Nosenko approached an American delegate at an arms-control conference in Geneva and told him "I would like you to help me with contact with CIA people. You see, I have some problems. It's a personal matter". It turned out that the "personal matter" was that a sex worker had stolen his wallet. It contained $250 that the KGB had given him for his expenses in Geneva, and he needed to sell information to avoid being out of pocket. Despite this unpromising beginning, Nosenko soon told a CIA officer in Geneva, Tennent H. Bagley, that in the mid-1950s General Oleg Gribanov had recruited a spy codenamed "Serial 3", who was "a pederast and had been acquired by homosexual blackmail". This spy had given the KGB "all NATO" secrets, including atomic documents, from a "Lord of the Navy" (presumably Tam Galbraith, Civil Lord of the Admiralty from 1957–59 or to Lord Carrington, First Lord of the Admiralty in 1959–63).[85] This confirmed what Golitsyn had said, with tantalising new details.

Chapman Pincher, Peter Wright and others argued that Nosenko provided the crucial final piece of the jigsaw and that while Vassall

---

85   The use of the word "pederast" – whose dictionary definition is "a man who engages in sexual activity with a boy or youth" – is another example of Vassall's homosexuality being conflated with paedophilia. There is no evidence, apart from teenage fumblings at Monmouth School, that Vassall ever had sexual relations with anyone under the age of sixteen.

was already on a shortlist of suspects in June 1962, he wouldn't have been put at the top of the list without Nosenko's information. But others, including Angleton, became convinced that Nosenko, who did not defect until he resurfaced in Geneva in January 1964, was "a disinformation agent" who was deliberately sent by the Soviets to undo some of the damage caused by Golitsyn's defection. It has been claimed that Vassall was consciously "blown" to detract attention from another, better-placed naval spy in Britain, who they were more anxious to protect.[86] The theory runs that Vassall may only have been "reactivated" because the Soviets knew that Golitsyn had already given the British clues about his identity. Far from protecting Vassall, the Russians wanted to maximise his chances of being discovered.

Nosenko later admitted that he had exaggerated his seniority in the KGB and had falsely claimed to be a personal friend of General Gribanov. Tennent H. Bagley believed that Vassall would have been caught anyway, based on what Golitsyn had said, without any extra clues supplied by Nosenko. Like Goleniewski, Nosenko ended up feuding with Golitsyn. His claims seemed less far-fetched than the others, and the CIA eventually concluded that he was a genuine defector. But some CIA and MI5 officers always believed that it was "odds on" that he was a Soviet plant intent on misleading the west.[87]

Sixty years on from his conviction, John Vassall remains a pale reflection, caught in a hall of mirrors erected by rival defectors, whose motives are still in doubt.

---

86   Espionage writing is full of accounts of the loyalty Soviet intelligence showed to some of its agents, tinged with ruthlessness towards others. During the Second World War the Red Navy allegedly allowed a boatload of Russian soldiers to be sunk, as calling off the voyage could have exposed one of its informers. Yet while the Rosenbergs' and Lonsdale's handlers were allowed to escape detection by the British, this loyalty was rarely extended to agents like Vassall, who were not Russian.

87   Nosenko told the CIA that he had seen a KGB file on Lee Harvey Oswald, President Kennedy's assassin, but that the KGB had steered clear of recruiting him as an agent because of worries about his mental state, after Oswald had slashed his wrists to try to get their attention. He insisted that there was no Soviet involvement in Kennedy's assassination. But Golitsyn had warned the Americans that any subsequent Russian defectors were not to be trusted. James Angleton and others became convinced that Nosenko's insistence that there was no KGB involvement in the assassination only proved that there must have been.

• • •

Whichever of these competing theories are true, two things are undeniable. The first is that whether it was Goleniewski, Golitsyn or Nosenko, the defector who identified Vassall approached the CIA first, not British intelligence. The Americans could take the most credit for his unmasking.[88] The second is that in the spring or summer of 1962 the net began to close in on Vassall, and it was only a matter of time before he was caught in it.

Chapman Pincher claimed that in the early summer of 1962 Golitsyn told Arthur Martin that the spy they needed to find had a.) been working in the naval attaché's office at the British embassy in Moscow in 1955, b.) was a competent photographer, c.) had later worked in naval intelligence and d.) was still an active spy. It should not have been difficult, based on this information, to narrow the search down to one man: John Vassall. Yet remarkably it still took many months. Vassall was placed at the top of a list of four suspects in the Admiralty (drawn up by Patrick Stewart, head of MI5's research branch) but MI5 then hesitated. Peter Wright recalled that the investigating officer, Ronnie Symonds, believed that "Vassall's Catholicism and apparent high moral character made him a less serious suspect," and Vassall's name was "placed at the bottom of the list instead".

Social class, not actual evidence, appears to be the main reason why Vassall fell down the list, only to be re-elevated to the top that summer. After a while, Vassall's high social standing ceased to be an asset and became a liability, as questions began to be asked about why he seemed to have much more money than a normal Admiralty clerk. Roger Hollis himself put his name to a report on Vassall's membership of the Bath Club and who had sponsored him to become a member there. This all had little to no bearing on

---

88   Neither MI5 nor MI6 had welcomed a Soviet defector since Grigori Tokaev in 1946.

his espionage, but it appeared that Vassall was being charged with breaching another unwritten rule: those who are not gentlemen should know their place.

MI5 discovered that at the Admiralty Vassall was seen as "chippy", and resentful that his social status had not been appropriately recognised. Peter Wright claimed that Vassall's name returned to the top of the list because he was "living way beyond his means in a luxury flat in Dolphin Square". But Vassall's tenancy was not in fact the immediate giveaway: after all, he could have received a legacy from one of his aunts that helped to pay the rent, as he claimed. His rent may have been about half his salary, but this was not unheard of in the early 1960s. Many tabloid journalists used the phrase "Mayfair flats" as shorthand for a secretive, immoral, London elite, playing on the anti-metropolitan prejudices of provincial readers. But while Pimlico was on the up, it was not – and still isn't – on a par with Mayfair. Vassall's superiors at the Admiralty were later lambasted for not asking themselves how Vassall could afford to live there, but the most unusual thing about his flat was its expensive furnishings, not its location. Only in hindsight did they start to wonder.

Instead, the initial focus of MI5's investigation was not Dolphin Square, but the Admiralty building. Some accounts claim that it was searched half-heartedly, and amateurishly: two officers spent three weeks scouring the building at night after all the staff had gone home, looking for evidence against Vassall and other suspects. MI5 then faced a "classic counterespionage problem", argued Wright. Most competent spies leave no traces and it is hard to prove their treachery unless they confess or are caught red-handed. It was decided that it was impractical to search all 9,000 of the Admiralty's staff and the constant stream of visitors. Instead, Wright conceived a technique that seemed straight from the pages of a James Bond novel: marking classified documents with tiny quantities of radioactive material. The theory was that if Geiger counters were set up at the Admiralty's entrances, they would detect any classified documents being removed. This trick failed to yield any results, partly because the Admiralty had too many entrances and exits to cover easily. Another problem, Wright claims, was that the Geiger counters were often "distorted" by luminous wristwatches worn by Admiralty civil servants. Once senior staff began to raise concerns about radiation exposure, the scheme was abandoned.

Before long there was no need for more antics with radioactive paper. After very nearly ordering the arrest of the wrong man – a Russian-born Admiralty officer whose uncle was suspected of being a Soviet spy – by mid-August 1962 MI5 had finally settled on Vassall, who was now on a shortlist of one.

Vassall was an enigma, unknown to anyone at Scotland Yard as there was no record of him ever being prosecuted, or even cautioned, for any crime. Discovering who he was, and who his friends were, would take weeks of intensive legwork. MI5's files show that Charles Elwell – who had led MI5's investigation of the Portland spies – not George Smith of Special Branch, was in the driving seat. On 31 August it was Elwell who told Smith that the spy they were looking for was Vassall, because he fitted the "admittedly vague and contradictory descriptions" given by Golitsyn and that other suspects (whose names are redacted in MI5's files) had been definitively ruled out. It was also Elwell who gave Vassall his short-lived MI5 codename: "VINE LEAF".

Events moved very quickly after that. Nothing suspicious was found in Vassall's Admiralty office: in his locked desk drawers there was nothing more incriminating than an Authentic Atlas, a Geographia map of London, a tube map, shoe cleaning materials, talcum powder, a bottle of scented lotion, soap and a razor.[89] A Trust House Hotels handbook had the names of several upmarket

---

89   In one of the maps, MI5 found handwritten directions to the National Maritime Museum in Greenwich. The museum is adjacent to the Royal Naval College, where Vassall's former boss, Captain Adrian Northey, worked, which suggests that Vassall may have visited him there.

inns – in Chiddingfold, Frensham, Great Bookham, the Bear in Woodstock and the Lygon Arms in Broadway – handwritten on the back.

By late August 1962, Elwell knew that he would not learn who Vassall really was by rifling around drawers but by talking to the two men who had stupidly been overlooked when he was vetted in 1956: Captains Bennett and Northey, who Vassall had worked for when he was believed to have begun spying in Moscow.

On 24 August, Elwell and MacAfee were ushered into Geoffrey Bennett's drawing room at Argyll Road. Bennett said that he and his wife were quickly convinced that Vassall was gay, and that he told Hayter this early on.[90] Bennett added that he had known of two other men in the Moscow embassy who were, "without a shadow of doubt", gay: John Morgan and James Bennett (no relation).[91] But neither Bennett nor his wife had ever suspected that Vassall was a spy. Elwell told Bennett that nothing would go beyond the drawing room's walls – but the entire conversation immediately went into a confidential MI5 file. In a 31 August memo, Elwell wrote that Bennett had been "disappointed by [Vassall's] exaggerated social pretensions", such as his friendship with the Swedish ambassador's wife.

Adrian Northey, who had become Director of the Royal Naval College in December 1961, later told MI5 much the same. He and his wife had regarded Vassall as "a 'pansy' but not a practising one," and a "pleasantly mannered little man". Northey admitted that while in Moscow Vassall could "have removed from the offices whatever he liked".

In the absence of any evidence at his workplace, MI5 had to focus on his home. From 24 August onwards, "letter and telephone

---

90 By now Hayter was no longer pretending that he knew nothing about Vassall's homosexuality. Soon after Vassall's arrest, Bennett wrote to remind him that Vassall had been on the staff during their time in Moscow. Hayter replied saying, "Of course, he did have one serious failing".

91 MI5's files note that Morgan was observed to be "conspicuously disinterested in the junior female staff of the Mission" during a later posting in Peking.

checks" were placed on Vassall's incoming mail and his phone number, TAT 9218. Only on 29 August did Elwell ask for Vassall's work extension – WHITEHALL 9000 Ext. 244 – to be tapped.[92] From 5 September MI5 also had a warrant to intercept post that Vassall received at the Bath Club, which he often used for correspondence (its address was often printed on his Christmas cards).

An "Obs" briefing sheet from 24 August says that Vassall was "almost certainly homosexual", "lives at a rate considerably above what his salary as a junior civil servant would allow" and that he was "outstandingly well dressed". Two sources – codenamed "Towrope" and "Phideas" – were "about to be imposed against Vassall". But MI5 knew surprisingly little about Vassall's private and family life. A report dated 30 August shows that MI5 was unsure whether Vassall's father was still living at Addison House or indeed, whether he was still living at all.

"For twenty days he was shadowed by MI5," a newspaper later claimed. In fact, it was only in early September that full surveillance of Vassall began. It was challenged by an event that was completely unrelated to Vassall's suspected espionage: the discovery of a homemade explosive device outside Dolphin Square, which police believed had been planted by British neo-fascists targeting the square's many Jewish residents. But if anything, the unexploded device was a welcome distraction. Surveillance of Vassall's incoming and outgoing phone calls soon determined that gossip in Dolphin Square was about "the bomb", not about MI5 officers coming and going.

Transcripts of Vassall's phone calls at home and work, painstakingly written up by MI5, revealed many details about his private life. Vassall boasted to a female friend that he had once seen Christian

---

92   Vassall's name, address and telephone number were always in the London phone book: he was never ex-directory. But until July 1962, MI5 files show that the Admiralty mistakenly believed that he lived at 809 Hood House, not 807, and that they did not know his home telephone number, apart from the Dolphin Square switchboard. This suggests that the Admiralty never took much interest in where Vassall lived.

Dior's house in the mountains above Cannes. "Alec" was grateful for Vassall's recent letter and was sadly unable to come and stay the night as planned (Vassall told Alec that he had been to his cousin Jerrold Vassall-Adams's silver wedding anniversary party the night before). At lunchtime on 4 September, Vassall traded office gossip with Jennifer Hall. "Jenny talked of the Admiral having the idea of giving his PA the boot and giving her the job instead", recorded the MI5 eavesdropper. The Admiral "looked like a plumber", Vassall joked, before revealing that he had told Miss Paterson that a bomb was planted near Dolphin Square because "the English were getting fed up with being pushed about by these Jewish landlords". Paterson had snapped, "Well, you ought to join Mosley's gang".[93] That evening, Vassall received a call from his aunt in Pinner to discuss his new curtains. In another conversation with Jennifer, Vassall told her that Simone Galbraith had told him that her husband hated the Scottish Office, which Galbraith described as "a dreary place where they sort of talk about housing in the Glasgow slums … It's a horrible job". Vassall boasted that the Galbraiths would be coming for drinks later in September, once Parliament was sitting.

On 7 September Vassall received a call from David Williams, a neighbour, who told him, "I was just getting out of my bath and saw your light was on". David told Vassall that he was going down to Bournemouth to join "Derek" tomorrow, but their conversation was brief as both were about to go out for dinner, separately. On 8 September Vassall called a carpenter in Dolphin Square's maintenance department and received a call from a friend called Peter, who asked if he could see Vassall before flying to Amsterdam that afternoon (Vassall said he certainly could visit, but only after he'd had a bath and been on a shopping errand to Harrods). On 10 September Vassall called "Nelly" and told her that he was furious that Mary Slater had been over-promoted to a job she could not do, as

---

93   This was not the only anti-Semitic remark attributed to Vassall. His German friend Baumgartel recalled that during a conversation about the Adolf Eichmann case, Vassall had said he "hated Jews".

she did not have "docket experience", before itemising the filing he had to do and complaining about the untidiness of Mr Tupman's office, where Vassall had spent hours looking for information on *HMS Seraph*. Vassall then called his cousin Jerrold to discuss a pair of field glasses that the latter wanted to buy.

Listening to these calls may have given MI5 a voyeuristic thrill but they told them nothing about whether Vassall was spying for the Russians, and if so, how. Vassall may have suspected his phone was being tapped: at 7.19 p.m. on 8 September he called Dolphin Square's switchboard to report that his line "keeps tinkling" and later, he summoned an engineer to examine it.

Vassall's incoming mail provided MI5 with more clues about Vassall's friends. They were an eclectic bunch. MI5 discovered that Vassall had a close friendship with a much older man called Humphrey Hicks, an international croquet player, who lived in Colyford, Devon. Hicks had a wealthy friend called Tingey, an Englishman who had studied at Trinity Hall, Cambridge, but now lived in New Zealand with his wife. The Tingeys, who also played professional croquet, met Vassall in England and suggested that he join Hicks on a trip to New Zealand to visit them. On the night of 31 August 1962, Vassall shared a twin room at the Ingoldisthorpe Manor hotel in Norfolk with Hicks, who paid the bill. Hick's identity was traced because of two insurance claims he made for thefts from his Hillman Minx car, one in 1961 and the other in 1962.

On 4 September Hicks wrote to Vassall from a Norfolk address ("c/o W Lloyd-Pratt Esq, the Oaks, Dersingham") to say "I, too, enjoyed our all-too-rare weekend enormously" and added some royal gossip from the nearby Sandringham estate. Another friend (whose name is redacted in MI5's files) was a county councillor who was, MI5 claimed, "said to be effeminate and connected with the theatre", lived at Ingoldisthorpe, and was one of Vassall's several "queer friends in Norfolk".

MI5 took a closer interest in Pierre Galdi, a Hungarian diplomat based in Dakar, Senegal, who Vassall got to know through another Hungarian – a photographer for "an Italian concern" called Valenciago – who lived at Dolphin Square.[94] On 7 September Galdi called Vassall to say he had just arrived in London and was staying until 9 September. It later turned out, after Vassall's arrest, that his Hungarian neighbour had asked Vassall to put Galdi up but Vassall "had not liked the idea of this" and booked Galdi into one of the square's guest flats instead. But evidence that Vassall was hosting a mysterious Hungarian diplomat seems to have alarmed MI5, who intercepted a call that Galdi made from Amsterdam to a Mr Wilhem in Brussels. Later, when MI5 searched Vassall's flat, they found a bottle of Johnnie Walker Black Label whisky that Galdi had given him.

An unnamed Dolphin Square informant told MI5 "Oh, he's a queer" as soon as Vassall's address was mentioned. The source added that Vassall had a friend, living in Duncan or Beatty House, who owned a Rolls-Royce. "Vassall is a very quiet man, but his friend is just the opposite – noisy, outspoken and fond of liquor". MI5 noted that the source seemed "puzzled to know what the two have in common". Vassall's friends at Dolphin Square included a General Nick Williams, who was retired from the Royal Marines and working as an official at Conservative Party HQ. Another was David Williams (no relation), a professional window-dresser who lived with Derek Webb at 803 Collingwood House. Williams and Webb both worked for an advertising company run by Barbara Brooks of Pont Street Mews SW3, which "employed a number of [Vassall's] friends", MI5 noted. Williams and Webb had introduced Vassall to Brooks at the end of 1961. Since then all four of them had drunk in Vassall's flat two or three times, Vassall regularly visited Webb and Williams's flat, the three of them had dined at the

---

94   Vassall's friendship groups overlapped and he often claimed to know people by several routes. In November 1962, Vassall suggested that he had been introduced to Galdi in Amsterdam by a mutual German friend, Baumgartel.

Mayfair Hotel and they had visited Brooks's cottage in Sussex at least once. When Vassall was arrested in September 1962, Williams and Webb were on holiday in Edinburgh. Despite their friendship, Williams and Webb clearly thought that Vassall was a much more important Admiralty official than he really was: they later told MI5 that Vassall's regular travels were to do with his job.

MI5 also found out – via "Towrope" – that Vassall was due to play bridge on the night of Monday 10 September at Jennifer Hall's flat in Streatham, along with his old Moscow friend Joan Vaughan, who now lived in Enfield (Hall told MI5 in November that in the end they didn't play bridge, as Vassall had not found a "fourth"). "Towrope" said that on 5 September Vassall asked Hall "I don't know, Joan Vaughan – it doesn't matter what we talk about there, does it?" Hall had replied "Oh no, it doesn't matter – she's all right", implying that Vassall was planning to discuss his love life over the bridge table and was checking how discreet Vaughan was. MI5's note of this conversation suggests that it was not on the telephone and that "Towrope" must have had Vassall under very close sur- veillance if a chat in a café or another public place was overheard.[95]

MI5's main concern was Vassall's plans for the following Satur- day, 15 September. On his office phone on 6 September, Vassall told a friend called Derbyshire that he was looking forward to a holiday in Italy and laughed. "This friend of yours?", asked Derbyshire sug- gestively. "Yes", Vassall replied, as if to confirm that he was going to be joined by the man that Derbyshire was thinking of. Vassall said that an uncle (Samuel Vassall) lived in Florence but that he'd only met him once and was not sure he would look him up. Other phone calls suggested that a friend was due to drive Vassall to the airport on the Saturday morning.

Gradually, MI5 pieced together Vassall's plans: he was due to go

---

95   In his 1963 history of MI5, John Bulloch claimed that Vassall was watched for two months before his arrest, that MI5 "bored a peephole in the front door" of his flat and that during the bridge party on 10 September, "two MI5 men were hidden within a yard of him throughout the evening".

on a two-week holiday in Italy, just as he had in September 1960 and September 1961.[96] He would fly to Rome on the 15th, meet one old friend (Francesco Gentile, who now worked at the Italian Ministry of Foreign Affairs) for dinner, and share a double room at the Hotel de la Ville with another: Robert Eiserle, the American he had met at the Tate Gallery earlier that summer.[97] Eiserle – who MI5 originally thought was called "Erdely or some name of that sort" or "Isuli" – booked a flight from Idlewild airport in New York to Rome, arriving at 10.30 on 15 September, roughly the same time as Vassall's plane from London. After three nights in Rome, Vassall and Eiserle would go on to Naples, and then Capri, to stay in Buca Bowinkel's villa. They planned to fly to London on 29 September. Eiserle would then stay with Vassall for a couple of nights at Dolphin Square before returning to New York.

A business card, found later at Vassall's flat, told MI5 that Eiserle was the assistant technical director of Fritzsche Brothers, a chemical company in New York. There was no evidence that he was a spy but the risk of Vassall avoiding arrest by flying to Italy and then defecting to the Soviet bloc was too great. MI5 now had a deadline: amass as much evidence as possible and arrest Vassall before he flew to Rome on 15 September.

Physical "A4 surveillance" – following Vassall on his daily commute between Dolphin Square and Whitehall, on the 24 bus,[98] – revealed nothing untoward. Bugging Room 56A at the Admiralty revealed nothing more exciting than Vassall's dislike of doors being slammed (which he said was "like a form of Chinese torture"), and gossip about a colleague called Keith, who was about to go to Hong Kong to get married. Once, when Vassall was out of the room MI5

---

96 Norman Lucas claimed that an undercover police officer had seen Vassall buy the ticket to Rome at a British European Airways office.

97 Remarkably, the National Archives holds the original letter, posted on 29 August by the Hotel de la Ville's manager, Sergio Pittarello and addressed to "Mr. W. J. C. Vassen", It confirms the reservation of "a double room with bath, room high up with view over Rome if possible".

98 The 24 bus still follows the same route today.

heard Mrs Royal and Miss Paterson discuss his career prospects: "I mean he does himself a disservice with all his pre-occupation with, you know glamorous people. ... He gives the impression that he is rather troubled", the two women said to each other. This suggested that the women knew Vassall was gay, but it provided no insight into his espionage. Royal and Paterson later told MI5 that they had never suspected Vassall was a spy: the only unusual thing about him, Royal said, was that he "bought a lot of toothpaste".

MI5 realised that it needed to find a way of listening to what was going on inside Vassall's flat. They called on the help of a Mr Dobson, a maintenance manager at Dolphin Square, who was temporarily employed as a frontline MI5 operative. Dobson handed over plans, suggested possible observation posts (O.P.s), advised MI5 about Vassall's movements and even offered to get Dolphin Square's nosy porters out of the way if the need arose.

MI5 conducted a detailed survey of Vassall's neighbours at Hood House.[99] The flat directly above Vassall's (number 807) was 908, which was also above 808 next door. Flat 908 was empty in August 1962, but Dolphin Square's thick walls and concrete floors meant that it was deemed impossible to use "probe microphones" to bug Vassall's living room and bedroom from a neighbouring flat. Because of Vassall's regular comings and goings, and visits by his cleaning lady, it was quickly decided that it was impossible to bug Vassall's flat before he went to Italy. Instead, MI5 would attempt to search it while Vassall was out and set up an "O.P." in the window of another flat nearby.

Flats with a direct view of 807 Hood House included 803 Collingwood House but "unfortunately this flat is occupied by

---

99   Number 801 was occupied by a single woman and 802 by a male quantity surveyor. Nothing was known about 803, whose lessee died in 1957, while 804 and 805 had been combined into a single flat, which was occupied by a food importer. Vassall's immediate neighbours were 806 (which was rented by a female catering manager at El Al Israel Airlines and had been sublet since October 1961 to her cousin, Eric Kitchen) and 808, details of which are redacted in MI5's files. Number 809 was occupied by a woman who had lived in Dolphin Square since its construction in 1937.

queers" (David Williams and Derek Webb), MI5 noted. Other options included number 804 and another flat on the floor above, whose occupants were a "gossipy couple", the Hursts. The Hursts had a small child and were expecting another, so they were judged to be less than ideal. Instead, on 30 August, MI5 decided to rent a bedsit, 904 Beatty House, on the other side of the square's garden.[100] But Vassall almost always kept his living room curtains closed and even when they were open, MI5 was looking at the window from 150 feet away.

With no real way of seeing inside the flat, MI5 concentrated on monitoring Vassall's movements outside it – with varying success. On 4 September, a second "O.P." was set up at 2 Chichester Street, from which Dolphin Square's main entrance could be seen. At lunchtime on 4 September, "VINE LEAF" met friends on the steps beside the Foreign Office but MI5's surveillance team did not spot him leave the Admiralty (Vassall may have left via its Spring Gardens exit, which was not being covered at the time). On 6 September he was seen leaving the Admiralty at 6.15 p.m. but a surveillance officer, J. H. R. Orlebar, could not see if he was carrying a briefcase as his umbrella was up. On Saturday 8 September, Vassall was seen leaving Dolphin Square twice: at 11.32 (accompanied by a fifty-year-old man with dark glasses and wearing a chocolate raincoat) and at 5.05 p.m. (with a forty-ish man with a "black bushy Van Dyke type beard", dark hair, a light grey suit and brown shoes). Vassall was not seen returning to the square between these two outings but he may – or may not – have been seen returning by taxi at 6. 40 p.m..

MI5 only achieved a breakthrough on 10 September. It persuaded Eric Kitchen, Vassall's neighbour at 806, to turn a blind eye as it did a "recce" on number 807 using a key cut by Mr Dobson. Dobson also came in with the MI5 officers, in case they ran into a

---

100 MI5 had to take a three-year lease on the bedsit at a rent of £370 a year, which had to be approved by MI5's deputy director general. The service said that it might be possible to sublet the bedsit after the Vassall operation.

suspicious neighbour so that he could claim he was there to deal with an urgent maintenance matter and that the MI5 officers were council officials or contractors. MI5 found that Vassall's sitting room was "luxuriously furnished – Wilton carpet, Persian rug, embroidered damask curtains and antique furniture, together with a pervasive perfume". But there were no signs of espionage.

To modern readers used to Hollywood films featuring drones, cellphone tracking, hidden CCTV cameras and facial recognition software, this surveillance seems erratic, part-time and very last-minute. MI5 only gained access to Vassall's bank accounts in the first few days of September. On the weekend before his arrest, the O.P.s in Dolphin Square were only manned from 8 a.m. to 10.30 p.m., and Vassall was not always followed when he was out. In most cases, Vassall's mail was only "listed" (catalogued) and photographs of unopened envelopes were taken because MI5 was concerned that the Russians were conducting a surveillance operation of their own to check if Vassall's mail was being intercepted. The last thing they wanted was for the Russians to know that Vassall was under surveillance by MI5 as well.

There were several red herrings and last-minute panics. MI5's files reveal that on 28 August the MI5 officer Hugh Winterborn was accosted on a train by a colleague, Ian Carrell, who openly asked him how the investigation into "VINE LEAF" was progressing. On 6 September MI5 heard "a short whirring noise followed by the shuffling of paper" in Vassall's bugged Admiralty office, which they thought could mean a camera was being used. As Vassall's aunt was due to meet him at Dolphin Square that evening, MI5 hoped that Vassall might leave his camera at the office overnight, rather than take it home. But they found nothing.

At 8.30 a.m. on 11 September a man who looked like Vassall was seen leaving Hood House and driving away in an Austin car, registration number 310 CXL. But Vassall did not own a car and it was not him behind the wheel. Later that morning Vassall arrived at the

Admiralty not with a slim document case as usual but with a "well-filled" light tan briefcase. Was he returning a sheaf of documents he had extracted the day before? That evening, Vassall left carrying the briefcase and a cardboard box, roughly six inches by three by one, and a large envelope. He was seen walking towards Birdcage Walk, and he wasn't seen returning to Dolphin Square that night.

There were now signs of desperation in MI5. On 7 September Arthur Martin wrote, "If we had it in mind to attempt to put a homosexual alongside VINE LEAF [I have] a suitable person in mind whose reliability had been tested in the past". Five days before Vassall's arrest, MI5 were planning their own "honey trap" operation.

Why was Vassall arrested on 12 September? To begin with there was no pressing reason to arrest Vassall immediately, as there was no evidence that he was about to give the Russians anything that was more sensitive than what he had already provided. MI5 later discovered that Vassall's final meeting with Nikolai had been on 17 August 1962, when he handed over photographs and was given some money, and that their next "RV" was not due until 30 October, on Abbey Road in Enfield.[101] But once his forthcoming holiday in Italy was discovered, MI5 and Special Branch knew that they had to arrest him before then. The main reason why Vassall was arrested on a Wednesday is that MI5 knew that his cleaning lady, Pamela Hickey, normally came in on Tuesdays or Thursdays. They needed to arrest Vassall on a day when she would not come in, to allow MI5 to conduct a further search of the flat after he had gone to work. The date and time of Vassall's arrest – 6.05 p.m. on Wednesday 12 September, just after he had left the Admiralty – was not determined by Vassall's espionage timetable, but by his upcoming Italian holiday and Mrs Hickey's working hours. MI5's files show that the final decision to arrest Vassall was only reached at 1 p.m. that afternoon, five hours beforehand.

---

101   Abbey Road in Enfield was near the home of Vassall's friend, a Miss Eagles. MI5 soon decided that the proximity of her residence to a rendezvous point was coincidence.

At 5.45 p.m. – just twenty minutes before Vassall's arrest – a second search of his flat began, carried out by six MI5 officers: Winterborn, Colfer, Ronnie Symonds, Catling, Peter Wright and an unnamed photographer.[102] It was much more thorough than the "recce" two days before. In a metal deed box inside Vassall's desk they found records of his credit accounts at Simpsons on the Strand and Harrods, a letter from an Italian lover, a Swedish bank statement and several pieces of old correspondence – including a letter from Tam Galbraith, sent earlier in 1962 – and a note from Vassall's nephew in Pinner, thanking his uncle for a gift of 10 shillings.[103] At the bottom of a bureau, they found a Praktina camera and a smaller Minox one. But they did not find any photographs or films. Films from both cameras, containing images of 176 classified documents, were only found in the hidden compartment of a bookcase that evening after Vassall himself told Special Branch where to look.

● ● ●

Vassall's imminent arrest had not been a very closely guarded secret. Even Geoffrey Bennett, who was so close to Vassall that he had invited him to his son's wedding seven months earlier, seems to have been aware of it before the press was. His daughter-in-law, Perdita, recalls that ten minutes before the news broke, Geoffrey called her and her husband to tell them to be wary of any press interest. The arrest was a complete surprise to both Richard and Perdita.

At about the same moment the director of public prosecutions, Theobald Mathew, called on the Solicitor General, Sir Peter Rawlinson.[104] "Standing rather grandly in front of the fireplace," Rawlinson recalled, Mathew looked "pleased with himself" as he told him

---

102   MI5's search on 12 September does not appear to have taken place in the morning, as some accounts claim.
103   The nephew was in fact his first cousin once removed – one of his cousin Nancy Woodgate's teenage sons.
104   Rawlinson had only been appointed in July 1962. He was deputising for the Attorney General, Sir John Hobson, who was away.

"Sit down, solicitor. You will need to. We have arrested a spy who is a bugger, and a minister is involved". "I duly sat", remembered Rawlinson.

According to Harold Macmillan and Peter Carrington's memoirs, it was Carrington who first gave the Prime Minister news of Vassall's imminent arrest.[105] "On the morning of 12 September 1962 … I received a message that Thorneycroft, the Minister of Defence, and Lord Carrington, the First Lord of the Admiralty, were asking to see me urgently", Macmillan recollected. Sensing the gravity of what they had to announce, Macmillan called his Cabinet Secretary, Sir Norman Brook, into the room. "What they had to tell me was indeed distressing in the present nervous atmosphere. A certain W. J. C. Vassall, an executive officer in the Admiralty, had been arrested as a spy and would shortly come up for trial".[106]

Carrington recalls the moment more happily: "It was with a certain pleasure that I went to the Prime Minister when the security people told me they had nailed Vassall." But Macmillan sighed. "Oh, that's terrible. That's very bad news", he replied. "I was rather crestfallen. The Prime Minister sighed again," Carrington recalled. "Bad news in a way that is," Macmillan said. "It's when we find a spy that there's trouble, more trouble than if we don't. When one catches them it can be most troublesome!"

Later that evening, MI5's director general, Roger Hollis, told Macmillan "I've got this fellow, I've got him!" before adding, dejectedly, "You don't seem very pleased, Prime Minister". Macmillan replied that he'd have preferred Vassall to have either never been caught or caught secretly. "No I'm not at all pleased," the Prime Minister mused. "When my gamekeeper shoots a fox, he doesn't

---

105 Macmillan's recollection is that this conversation occurred on the morning of 12 September, before Vassall's arrest, though the reported speech refers to the event in the past tense. Christopher Andrew claims that Macmillan's memory was playing tricks on him and that he was first told of the Vassall case not by Carrington or Hollis, but by Sir Norman Brook.

106 Vassall might have been pleased to hear he had been promoted by Macmillan: in fact, he had failed to become an executive officer, despite several attempts.

go and hang it up outside the Master of Foxhounds' drawing room; he buries it out of sight. But you just can't shoot a spy as you did in the war."[107] The problem was, Macmillan told Hollis, that during peacetime "You have to try him ... Better to discover him and then control him, but never catch him ... why the devil did you catch him?"

The comment was to have serious long-term consequences. Because of his reception on 12 September, Roger Hollis was, as Alistair Horne puts it, "not over-eager to stick out his neck yet again" and he rarely gave Macmillan security briefings after that. Some have said his slowness in keeping Macmillan informed about developments after Kim Philby's defection, and during the Profumo affair, stemmed directly from Macmillan's unhappiness at being told about Vassall.

That night, a shell-shocked Macmillan wrote in his diary, "There has been another espionage case – and a very bad one – in the Admiralty. An executive officer, homosexual. Entrapped by the Russian embassy spies and giving away material (of varying value) for five or six years. Only caught by the help of a Russian "defector". Macmillan cannily predicted a "great public trial", with the security services "blamed for how hopeless they are" and then "an enquiry [which will conclude] that no one was really to blame ... There will be a row in the press, there will be a debate in the House of Commons. And the government will probably fall". In less than a year, all these prophecies would come true, although downfall only came after the further earthquake of the Profumo scandal. Macmillan, a man who often ended Cabinet meetings by quoting from Horace, seems to have seen himself as a Roman soothsayer, and on the horizon he saw only storm clouds.

---

107 In his diary entry for 15 November 1962, Macmillan used very similar wording: "Unhappily, you cannot bury [a spy] out of sight, as keepers do with foxes". Macmillan's much-quoted comment about foxhunting is sometimes seen as a sign of his pining for retirement, or even senility. In fact, Macmillan was, as ever, making a shrewd point: he sensed that because of the role that CIA's defectors had played in Vassall's detection, a trial could not be avoided.

Why was Macmillan so gloomy that a significant spy had been caught? The main reason for his gloominess – and for the long sentence that Vassall later received – was timing. Nineteen sixty-one had been a disastrous year for British intelligence. On top of revelations about how the Portland spies and George Blake had got away with espionage for years, the last thing that Macmillan needed was the unmasking of another spy, this time at the very heart of the British defence establishment. It would only prompt questions about how many more there must be, undetected.

In a confidential note soon after Vassall's arrest the attorney general, Sir John Hobson, told Macmillan that while his espionage was not quite as serious as that of George Blake, it had, nonetheless, done "exceptionally grave damage to the Nation". Macmillan soon started referring to the "so-called security service". One of his first instincts was to blame Sir William Hayter for not having "kept track" of Vassall at the Moscow embassy. "One should know the private life of a staff in Moscow in a way which is quite impossible in London", Macmillan wrote in his diary. He is said to have once asked Carrington whether British embassies should even employ service attachés and their clerical officers as they only seemed to cause trouble.

On 13 September, Hollis called on the Home Secretary, Henry Brooke, who "showed considerable interest" in the Vassall case. Brooke told Hollis that when he had signed warrants authorising the surveillance of Vassall at Dolphin Square he had assumed that Vassall must be "a senior man" at the Admiralty to be able to afford to live there. All over Whitehall, stable doors were being shut long after the horse had bolted.

•   •   •

For John Vassall, and his captors, there was a sense of relief as he was questioned at New Scotland Yard into the early hours of 13

September. Vassall was not mistreated: tea and sandwiches soon arrived and he happily told the police everything, though he had a niggling feeling that he should really be talking to the security service. After all, he could only make a full confession once. That night was the most exciting of his life.

In some ways Vassall's interrogation was an anti-climax. If anything, Vassall led it: he sensed that the officer in charge did not know what he was doing. Hardened police officers, used to shifty criminals answering 'no comment' to every question, could not believe their luck. In the small hours a "senior official" of some kind entered the room and listened to part of Vassall's testimony, but did not speak. Vassall felt quietly flattered: he was part of an elite group who had been interrogated by both the KGB and MI5.

"Vassall remained remarkably composed throughout this long night, although towards the end he naturally showed signs of strain," the MI5 officer Ronnie Symonds later noted. "He speaks well and is polite and I can understand why some people find him charming. However beneath it all is clearly a man of inferior intelligence as well as of inferior character. I doubt if he realises the enormity of what he has done".

By dawn, Vassall was enjoying the experience less. Special Branch officers flitted in and out, bringing papers that were found during their search of his flat. They seemed to think that Vassall must be part of a huge network of spies. When Vassall said he worked alongside ninety other people in the Admiralty's military division, the officer replied that the eighty-nine others might also be involved. But Vassall was a lone wolf. By the time they drafted a confession for him to sign, he no longer worried about what it contained. As dawn approached through the room's thick net curtains, Vassall leant back in his green leather armchair. He felt nauseous, but also relieved that he had got everything out of his system. He assumed that he would be quietly forgotten about, shunted off to a new job in Canada or elsewhere, out of the Russians' reach. He naïvely believed that his treachery might be brushed under the carpet. How wrong he was.

After he signed his confession Vassall was taken to breakfast, not in a cell, but in the Scotland Yard canteen. He was walked down highly polished corridors and past important looking desks that gleamed inside impressive offices. From the south side of the building he could see the pinnacles of the Palace of Westminster, where a few years earlier he used to rush with papers for Tam Galbraith.

Later that morning, Vassall was taken to Bow Street police station to be fingerprinted. His hat and umbrella went with him: he had to keep everything he had been arrested with. Inside Bow Street he waited in a corridor for a minute, before a perfunctory hearing in the magistrate's court next door. Only then were his possessions taken away from him and was he put in a cell. His father appeared, followed by his brother and a friend. A kind policeman gave Vassall a sweet through the door of his cell before he was driven, in a Black Maria, to Brixton prison. There was no chance of bail – Vassall did not even ask for it – and he was now on remand until his trial. Vassall was escorted past rows of locked cells to Brixton's hospital wing, where he would be kept under constant surveillance for the next five-and-a-half weeks.

As soon as he could, Vassall asked for a Roman Catholic priest to make another, more heartfelt confession: his first since the Russians had ordered him to stop going to confession in Moscow seven years before, in case he spilled the beans. An unnamed friend from Worcestershire, who Vassall had met in the RAF during the war, came to visit. So did his former cleaning lady, Mrs Doris Murray, who "cheered me up with all the local news of Dolphin Square", he later recalled. "It was heartening to be remembered by so many people including the head porter, the woman who ran the cleaners and the bookshop." In truth, Dolphin Square's staff could hardly forget Vassall, who was now at the centre of a media frenzy. Vassall seemed oblivious to his forthcoming trial, and to the fact that Mrs

Murray was telling newspapers all about having worked for him. She later admitted to the Radcliffe inquiry that his letter to her was "borrowed" by the *Daily Mail* and the *Daily Express*.

Vassall had to obtain the governor's permission to write letters.[108] The letter to his father was the most painful, but William replied quickly, and sweetly. On Monday 15 October he wrote to David Peck, the visa officer he had befriended in Moscow in 1954, and his amusing wife. "You must have wondered what on earth one of your friends has done when you heard the news of all the drama that surrounds me now", Vassall began. "I do hope it will make a reconciliation possible in our friendship which I have treasured greatly". But the four-page letter gave no insight into exactly what had happened in Moscow, or since: instead it was a litany of the kindnesses of friends and family, ending with reminiscences of his penultimate weekend of freedom, golfing in Norfolk, where "my partner gave me a handicap of 24 so I just scraped home. The course was at Brancaster, an unspoilt part of the coast". Vassall almost begged the Pecks to write back: "If you can spare a few thoughts for me I shall not forget you. As always your friend, John". There is no record of any reply from the Pecks or of any visit from them.

A happier correspondence was with Geoffrey Bennett, who wrote to Vassall on 20 October to thank him for his recent letter and to say, "I understand a little, at least, of what you must feel". Bennett said he could do no more to help Vassall, but reassured him: "Please remember that I bear you no ill will. ... Man may not be merciful to you on Monday, but God surely will be. Pray that He may give you strength to face the future with courage, and be with you always. Yours sincerely, Geoffrey Bennett". In a separate letter, sent the same day, Rosemary said that Vassall had "been a great friend of ours for years now" and that she and Geoffrey would be at his trial, "feeling affection for you". She added that after a recent

---

108   All of Vassall's correspondence in Brixton was intercepted and copies are still in MI5's archives.

breakdown she had expected to end up in a psychiatric hospital, but had pulled through – and that Vassall could too. She promised to continue writing to him in prison.

On 21 October, the day before his trial, Vassall wrote to Tam and Simone Galbraith. "I know it must have been a great shock to hear of the calamity I have got myself into," it began. But, as usual, Vassall looked on the bright side. He had been re-reading Cardinal Newman's *Apologia Pro Vita Sua* and Evelyn Waugh's *Brideshead Revisited* and he tried to jog Galbraith's memory: "Do you remember the time when I left a copy of this book in your papers at Barskimming … When it is all over I hope I shall be able to come and see you again".

Even if Galbraith's memory of a mislaid copy of *Brideshead Revisited* was jogged, there is no record of any more invitations to Cowley Street or Barskimming once Vassall was released. Galbraith's son, Tom Galbraith (Lord Strathclyde), is certain that his father never sent a reply and indeed there is no record of one, or of any contact with Vassall after the spring of 1962. Vassall found Brixton's warders and prisoners surprisingly sympathetic. He was given "words of encouragement, and smiles" in the hospital ward when he left for the last time to be taken to the Old Bailey for sentencing. But from the former Civil Lord of the Admiralty there was nothing.[109]

•   •   •

Because Vassall had been arrested in such a hurry, MI5 only really pieced together his life after 12 September 1962, not before. Much of MI5's work was ill-informed and speculative. A memo from 10 October, written by Ronnie Symonds and entitled 'The Vassall Case:

---

109 On 13 November 1962 Vassall wrote to Galbraith again, via his solicitors, Wontner & Sons, to convey his "deep distress" that his actions may have led to his resignation and denying that he had authorised the submission of their correspondence to the press. The letter seems to have only been tersely acknowledged by Galbraith's own solicitors a week later. There was no proper reply.

Some Preliminary Comments on C Branch Aspects' asked, "Should a man of weak character who was likely to be a social misfit have been sent to Moscow?". Symonds wondered aloud whether "the rather curious mixture of schools he went to" meant that Vassall had been expelled from some of them. Some of the intelligence that MI5 collected did not even have names attached: one source said that Vassall had been seen at the Rockingham, a gay club on Archer Street in Soho, in the company of a "notorious middle-aged homosexual" who possibly lived near Worcester. He was also said to have been seen drinking in a pub in South Wimbledon with an Englishman teaching Russian at a school in Belgium.

Nothing in Vassall's flat provided any clues about accomplices. In a drawer in Vassall's bedroom, MI5 found two railway tickets: a return from Paddington to Wolverhampton (via Banbury) on 14 November 1961 and a return from King's Cross to Potters Bar and South Mimms[110] on 7 July 1962. Vassall liked to keep trophies of former jobs: among his papers there was an envelope addressed to "Her Britannic Majesty's Ambassador and Lady Hayter, British Embassy, Moscow", dated 23 October 1954. As well as being an "importunate correspondent" himself, Vassall was, Elwell said, a "stamp collector and tuft hunter and I imagine the envelope appealed to both these instincts". MI5 were also intrigued that Vassall had once written to the Bank of England to enquire about how long old £1 notes would remain legal tender for, after the issuing of a new note design. "It will be interesting to see if we find out whether this query was RIS inspired", wrote H. E. D. Cumming on 5 November: it almost certainly wasn't.

MI5 were confronted by many scraps of evidence, none of which suggested that Vassall was part of a wider network of spies, like the Portland ring. This created an information vacuum, but it was

---

110   The station carried this convoluted name from 1923 until 1971, when it reverted to its original name of Potter's Bar.

quickly filled with feverish curiosity about Vassall's family, friends and love life.

A green 1962 diary was found inside his Admiralty desk, which showed that right up until his arrest he had led a hectic social life, dining regularly with "Serge", "Humphrey", "Arthur", "Gordon" and "Aleck". There was the Hon. Vere Eliot, a fellow Bath Club member and a friend of Vassall's mother, who seemed straight from the pages of an Anthony Powell novel. Vassall later told MI5 that Eliot had once bragged that the Russians had offered Lord Montagu of Beaulieu "any amount of money" for a full list of important English homosexuals, and had even offered Montagu asylum in Russia. But Eliot seemed only to be a boastful club bore, not an accomplice in spying.[111]

Neither were Vassall's other London friends likely to be spies. Gisele Hervig ran the rare book department at Hatchards. Dr Hillary James was a psychiatrist and restaurateur who owned La Bicyclette off Sloane Square ("a well-known haunt of queers", MI5 observed) and a pub in Plaxtol, Kent, called The Old Forge, to which Vassall and his friend Aleck Climo had been invited. Vassall had met Alan Tagg (who lived at Whitcomb Street, near Leicester Square, and had been "a set designer for *Job*")[112] in Stratford-up-on-Avon, not Moscow. Dr Gerard Lang, a university lecturer who Vassall had befriended during a course of lectures by the Newman Society at the Cité Universitaire in Paris in December 1952, had been one of his vetting referees in 1956, but did not seem to be a likely candidate for "Admiralty protector". J. Saltzberger, a Lloyds underwriter who shared two "nests" with a man called Morgan (one in London and one in the country) seemed to be a former friend: by 1962 Vassall had fallen out with him after Morgan was "unkind" to him.

---

111 A photograph of a portly Hon. Vere Eliot, in white tie, appeared in *Tatler* on 9 March 1960. Eliot is seen, cocktail in hand, flanked by "Mr and Mrs Tony Prendergast".

112 This was probably *Job: A Masque for Dancing*, a ballet written by Ralph Vaughan Williams in 1931.

Many of Vassall's foreign friends were diplomats, but they seemed to be more familiar with cocktail shakers than Minox cameras. Vassall had met one of them, a thirty-ish Argentinian architecture student called Antuña, in Belgium. He had met Hernando Samper (who worked at the UN in New York and was the nephew of the Colombian chargé d'affaires in London) while swimming in Capri. Vassall had "looked after" another man who worked at the UN, a Brazilian called Gilberto Rizzo, in London in June 1962. In August that year, Vassall had met Bob Smith – a young American man who was secretary to a much older and wealthier one, who Vassall believed had some connection to Kew Gardens – twice in London, including a date at the Berkeley Hotel. There was no evidence that atomic secrets were on their agenda.

Another foreign friend was John Wingstrand, a Swedish diplomat who had been introduced to Vassall by Francesco Gentile in Cairo at Christmas 1959. Wingstrand, like Vassall, "liked to be invited to all the diplomatic parties that are going". The Swedish ambassador in Cairo had disliked Wingstrand so much that he sent him home to Stockholm, though Wingstrand then secured a better job in the West German capital, Bonn. Vassall later told MI5 that Wingstrand had a rich and powerful uncle who lived in France and "mixes in circles close to Princess Margaret".

Another was David Marine, a 35-year-old American bachelor who worked at the Veterans Administration Hospital and as an "instructor of medicines" at Johns Hopkins University, both in Baltimore. Vassall had first met Marine in 1949 or 1950 at a meeting of the Cardinal Newman Association in Rome or at a Parisian café. None of these men looked like accomplices, but MI5 wrote lengthy reports on them all.

They did the same with Humphrey Hicks, Vassall's golfing friend, who had been born in about 1904 and was old enough to be Vassall's father. Hicks, who MI5 described as an "unmarried gentleman of leisure" and "an elderly queer", was brought to MI5's attention by an army captain in Wiltshire called Pemberton, whose mother was a cousin of Hicks, and whose son was Hicks's godson. Pemberton told MI5 that he "was worried about his close connection with Hicks, who was a close friend of a spy", as if Vassall was some kind of infectious disease.

Hicks readily told MI5 that he first met Vassall while staying at Uplands, Vassall's favourite Aldeburgh guesthouse, in early October 1960. In May 1961 Vassall had joined him on a trip to Norfolk. Since then, Hicks had stayed with Vassall at Dolphin Square. Their most recent meeting was only ten days before Vassall's arrest: Hicks had spent the night at Dolphin Square on 30 August and on 31 August he'd driven to Ingoldisthorpe, to which Vassall came by train that evening. After two days of golf Vassall had returned to London by train on 2 September. Hicks had called Vassall on 11 September to make arrangements to meet him for dinner on 14 September, the night before Vassall was due to go to Italy. But when Hicks called again on 13 September to confirm, Vassall's home telephone was answered by a police detective: Hicks had not known that Vassall had been arrested the previous day. "During our friendship I noticed nothing unusual about John", Hicks told MI5. "Politics hardly ever entered into our conversation and I treated him as I would any personal friend".

It was quite clear that Vassall and Hicks had had an uncomplicated love affair in which the young Vassall provided the ageing Hicks with company, and Hicks paid the bills. But the Chief Constable of East Suffolk Police told MI5 that the Uplands guest house's owner, a septuagenarian artist called Connie Winn, had said that Vassall "had a furtive nature to such an extent that she thought he was an English spy". Winn claimed to have been a friend of Sir Vernon Kell, a former head of MI5.[113] East Suffolk police compiled

---

113   Kell was unceremoniously sacked by Churchill on 25 May 1940, a fortnight after he became Prime Minister. He had been MI5's director since its inception in 1909, and had recruited Maxwell Knight, another Hood House resident, in the mid-1920s.

a list of everyone who had stayed at Uplands at the same time as Vassall. Even in November 1966 MI5 were still writing internal memorandums about Hicks's ongoing correspondence with Vassall in prison, even though they concluded that he was not "of any security significance".

MI5 even took an interest in Vassall's old schoolfriends, including a kindergarten friend nicknamed "Dumpy", a Seaford House contemporary called Toby Collyer and W. T. K. Pollard-Williams, an old Monmothian who Vassall once dined with at the Bankers Club. MI5 officers were dispatched to Addison House, the mansion block where Vassall had lived until 1959, to find that the Vassalls' old flat, number one, was now inhabited by a Mr and Mrs Smee. A Mr Roberts, a former Post Office employee living at number three, told MI5 merely that Vassall was "sober ... temperate and a non-smoker". Special Branch even asked Addison House's caretaker whether he had any insights into the Vassall case.

Some of MI5's interviews revealed nothing more than crude homophobia. Mr Marshall, Vassall's superior at the Admiralty in 1962, said that his work was "slipshod" and that he had an "ingratiating smile" which meant that he feared that Vassall might be "making advances on him". A Mr Smith, now working at GEC Engineering in Erith, told MI5 that he had shared an office with Vassall in 1951. For all his "superior" education, Vassall was an "idle and ineffective clerk", Smith complained. "His besetting aim was his social climbing and his homosexuality, which one could easily account for after the event though it was not evident at the time".

Stanley Jennings, Vassall's Moscow flatmate, seems to have known Vassall better than most people, and to have liked him in a distant way. After Vassall's arrest Jennings sent Charles Elwell a thirteen-page handwritten letter from 12 Carlton House Terrace (then used as a satellite of the Foreign Office and only a few yards from where Vassall had been arrested) to say that the news about

Vassall "had come as a devastating surprise". Vassall had never given his flatmate "a single hint that anything was wrong". Jennings feared that his friendships with Volodya Semenov and Boris Khrostov had first led Vassall to seek Russian friendships of his own. Jennings was clearly tortured by the thought that Boris had been involved in compromising Vassall.

Miss Pauline Osman worked at the Treasury, lived in Blackheath and was in her early forties. She had been friendly with Vassall since meeting him in a Treasury canteen in 1947. MI5 were alarmed to note that the canteen had sometimes been used by Burgess and Maclean ahead of their defections in 1951, but Osman assured them that she "cannot remember [Vassall] being part of their clique".

Other friends were less loyal. MI5 concluded that Vassall's "only friend at the Admiralty with whom he was on terms of private acquaintance" was Jennifer Hall, who he had first met in Galbraith's office. Hall later worked for the naval attaché at the British embassy in Copenhagen before returning to London in 1962. She told MI5 that she thought Vassall was a snob who would "often refer vaguely to grand people he knew, including Mr Galbraith". Vassall said that Jennifer must meet Galbraith the next time he came to his flat, though no date was ever suggested. Hall said – probably dishonestly – that she hadn't thought that Vassall was gay, though she reported that a Mrs White, a Moscow contemporary of Vassall's, had told her that he was "said to be a homosexual" there.

When questioned by MI5 William Campbell and Derek Warne predictably denied that they were gay or that they had suspected Vassall of being gay himself. Campbell insisted that Vassall had tracked him down at the end of the war simply to ask for advice on what he should do now that he was demobbed. Warne said that Vassall "was a snob and anxious to give the impression of being a cut above the rest". In September 1963, Vassall's former Moscow flatmate John Richardson, who was now working at the UN in New York, told MI5 that he had "applied to move out as he did not like anything about Vassall or his way of life". But Richardson admitted that he had visited Vassall at Dolphin Square.

There is a pattern in these interviews: Vassall's friends were often derogatory about him and at pains to indicate that someone else knew Vassall much better than they ever did.

Joan Vaughan, one of Vassall's closest friends in Moscow, seemed "very upset" when questioned by MI5 in November 1962, but she insisted that she had only known Vassall for a few months in the summer of 1954 and had only been on Christmas card terms with him since, until they recently met up with Jennifer Hall. Like Hall, Vaughan appeared to be telling MI5 that her friendship with Vassall was more casual than it really was.

As he sat in Brixton prison, Vassall would not have known that some members of his family were already turning their back on him. Nancy Woodgate, a first cousin (and the daughter of his aunt Alma Gooding) worked in the typing pool at an Admiralty depot in Pinner. She told MI5 that she was unhappy about office gossip there about her cousin's arrest. Her husband, Grahame Woodgate, a sales manager at a coatings company, was interviewed on 26 September by Special Branch. Woodgate said that he visited Vassall at Dolphin Square, and that he believed Vassall had a "reasonably high position" in the Admiralty, and that his regular foreign travel was on "official business". Even Vassall's family seem to have been persuaded that his job was a lot more senior than it really was.

In June 1962 the Woodgates had accepted an invitation to join Vassall at the Trooping of the Colour ceremony, which they had watched from an Admiralty window. Also there was a man called Forrester, who Woodgate said "appeared to have no form of livelihood, but always had plenty of money to spend". Woodgate said that he had always suspected that Vassall was gay, and despite accepting his cousin-in-law's hospitality, he was wary of Vassall being "over-friendly with his two teenage sons". Vassall's friends were mostly loyal. But some of his family betrayed him within two weeks of his arrest.

● ● ●

As MI5 searched in vain for evidence of a wider network of spies, it authorised interviews with the two MPs who Vassall said he had known well since 1961.

In November 1962 two government lawyers – Sir Harold Kent and a Mr Chitty of the Treasury Solicitor's Department – interviewed Sir Harmar Nicholls, who recalled meeting Vassall at the House of Commons, as a guest of Fergus Montgomery's, in late 1961. They had gone back to Vassall's flat at Dolphin Square for drinks; he was vague about how the evening had ended. But he categorically denied visiting the flat more than once or having had homosexual relations with Vassall. Nicholls insisted that he had only met Vassall on one other occasion, in the Central Lobby of the Palace of Westminster, when Vassall asked him to pass on his regards to Tam Galbraith.

Montgomery, who was interviewed shortly after Nicholls, was more forthcoming. He confirmed that he had been given Vassall's name by an American mutual friend, though he named him as Mr Molloy (not Dr Bartels, the name that Vassall gave). Montgomery said that he had met Molloy at a New York cocktail party in September 1961 but that Molloy only gave him Vassall's name and number when he came to London that autumn. In the second or third week of November, Montgomery had called Vassall and invited him to dine with him at the Commons.

Why would Montgomery invite a complete stranger to dinner at the Commons, purely on the basis that they had a mutual friend? Montgomery was not asking Vassall for his expertise on the Admiralty, or anything else, and Vassall was not lobbying Montgomery about a political matter. Montgomery didn't openly admit it, but it is clear that this was a simple blind date, or pick-up. Molloy (or Bartels) had told Montgomery that he knew a gay man called Vassall, who he felt would be Montgomery's type.

Montgomery said that he "had already arranged to entertain another guest and he killed two birds with one stone by adding Vassall to the party", an MI5 report noted. Later, Nicholls joined Montgomery's table and the two MPs obtained tickets for their two guests to sit in the Stranger's Gallery while they voted in a division. The other guest then offered to drive everybody home and when they dropped off Vassall, who was the "first port of call", he invited the other three men up to his flat for a drink.

Montgomery added that Vassall was a "sad and lonely character" and was sorry for him. But he admitted meeting Vassall again soon afterwards, for a meal near Leicester Square, and that they'd gone on to the cinema. He and Vassall had six or seven further meetings, three of them at Vassall's flat and the rest of them at cinemas and theatres, including seeing a performance of *Beyond the Fringe*. Montgomery also admitted that he knew Douglas Bushy and had dined with him shortly before Christmas 1961, which Vassall and Bushy spent together in the US.

Vassall later claimed that Montgomery had told him that he had been entertained by "a member of the Soviet embassy" – believed to be the KGB officer Mikhail Lyubimov – whose pregnant wife could not join them for the "evening's entertainment". At the end of the evening, Lyubimov asked Montgomery "When do we meet again?". When Vassall heard about this, he warned Montgomery to be careful. MI5 thus believed that the Soviets may have planned to entrap Montgomery sexually. But in November 1962, Montgomery denied any homosexual activities, with Vassall or anyone else, and said that he had only entered Vassall's bedroom once, to leave his coat there. In May 1962 their association had ended, Montgomery said, because he felt "bored with Vassall", who was "something of a social climber". Montgomery had received three letters from Vassall, but by November 1962 they had conveniently been destroyed.

After seeing transcripts of the interviews with the two MPs, Charles Elwell wrote, "In my view there can be no doubt that

Vassall's friendship with Montgomery was homosexual ... and I think that Montgomery's 'gruff and curt' reaction to Keith's approach may well have been caused by nervousness" ("Keith" is an unidentified MI5 officer). In fact, Vassall later told MI5 that he had a sexual relationship with Nicholls, but not with Montgomery. Nicholls had said less to MI5 than Montgomery, possibly because he had more to hide.

Both MPs were warned that they might have to give evidence to the Radcliffe tribunal. If they ever did, they did so *in camera* – behind closed doors – and neither of their names appear anywhere in Radcliffe's report. Neither MP seems to have been aware of Vassall's espionage, let alone been his accomplices. Nor was there any evidence of a wider network of spies in the Admiralty or the presence of a "spymaster" there who had nurtured Vassall's career. Vassall said that he knew a Mr Shillito, an under-secretary at the Admiralty, on a "minor social plane" before he arrived in Moscow and that Shillito had once "smiled at him in a way", suggesting that he might be gay. But they did not appear to have known each other well. In 1963 MI5 concluded that J. P. L. Thomas (who became Lord Cilcennin in 1956) had probably helped Vassall to "bypass certain security procedures" and secure his Moscow post in 1954. But Cilcennin sems to have done nothing more after that, and he died in 1960. The hunt for Vassall's "protector" in the Admiralty was not over.

In the run-up to Vassall's trial the British press could not say much about his espionage, thanks to Britain's strict contempt of court laws. But speculation about his spying, especially within the Admiralty and the Royal Navy, was spreading like wildfire.

In the middle of 1962, Nick Kettlewell, a young Royal Navy lieutenant, returned to Britain after circumnavigating South America on board *HMS Lion* as her senior communications officer. That October, Kettlewell rented a flat in London and spent several weeks in charge of a team of "watchkeepers" – mostly Royal Navy reservists

– eavesdropping on the Admiralty's internal phone calls. He was taking part in Wintex, a large NATO exercise to ascertain the west's readiness for a hot war, including the security of its telephone and radio communications.[114]

As the Admiralty did not yet have secure lines it knew that it was vulnerable to interception, so all of its staff were always told to be careful with what they said on the telephone. They had been warned that calls would be tapped during the Wintex exercise. Kettlewell and his team overheard people trading gossip about who had known Vassall and what he was like. Some people – doubtlessly being wise after the event – boasted to colleagues that they had long suspected that he was a spy: "Have you heard about Vassall? I knew he was up to no good" was a typical comment, Kettlewell recalls. An exercise that was supposed to ensure that everyone was careful about what they said, over unprotected phone lines which the Russians (at least theoretically) could be tapping, had shown the opposite: far too many people were speaking far too freely.

Every twenty-four hours Kettlewell reviewed the recordings that his team had made. He reported anyone who had spoken too freely about Vassall to his commanding officer, Captain John Trechman, and to Jack MacAfee, the Admiralty's head of security, who Kettlewell remembers as a terrifying figure. MacAfee called everyone who had been heard commenting on the Vassall case into his office and gave them a serious dressing-down. No one was fired or prosecuted as far as Kettlewell can recall: in the wake of the Vassall case the Admiralty, and the Navy, were in no mood for further adverse publicity.

At the end of the exercise the Admiralty decided that those who had been caught telling colleagues that they had known Vassall was a spy were just showing off. Kettlewell's surveillance had not found

---

114   Later in his career Kettlewell served as the Royal Navy's chief naval signal officer, until he retired in 1988 at the rank of commodore.

anyone who had genuinely known Vassall was spying, let alone any accomplices.

There were several other false alarms. On 2 October a "Conseiller Commerce Exterieur" at the French embassy in London contacted the British with possible evidence that Vassall had been sending radio messages from his flat in Dolphin Square, as well as photographing documents there. Pierre Gerard, who lived at 906 Frobisher House, reported that a recent recording he had made of classical music on short wave radio had been marred by signals which may have come from Vassall's flat. Yet MI5 drew a blank: no radio equipment was found there. At the same time MI5 was tapping the phone lines of the British Communist Party's headquarters in Covent Garden. They revealed nothing more than a "sarcastic" conversation on 10 October, on the party's *Daily Worker* line, between a Denis and Sam about Mikhailsky, the "odd bod" Pole who had worked at the embassy at the same time as Vassall. Maybe the British Communist Party had heard some gossip that was not yet in the public domain. But the party did not appear to have been involved in Vassall's spying in any way.

More seriously, MI5 received an anonymous letter alleging that Vassall had been expelled from Monmouth School in 1941 for "gross indecency", having been "corrupted" by its headmaster, Mr Lewin, who the school's governors did not want to see prosecuted for fear of a public scandal. Instead, the letter claimed Lewin was ordered to retire (not called up for military service, as the official story ran). Lewin had subsequently become Vassall's "protector" at the Admiralty and secured his tenancy at Dolphin Square by giving him an "adequate reference". "It also explains the determined efforts of the Admiralty, the Defence Secretary and the Premier to 'play down' the whole affair", the letter concluded. Lewin had risen to be an assistant secretary at the Admiralty but by 1962 he had retired and MI5 concluded that "there was no great point in pursuing him", though the anonymous letter was later passed to the Radcliffe tribunal.[115]

Whatever the distractions caused by these red herrings and false alarms, MI5 knew they had scored a major coup. If Vassall had denied everything, and if no photographic films had been found in his flat, there might not have been enough evidence to prosecute him. But instead he had immediately made a full confession, and they had all the evidence they needed to prosecute. MI5 knew early on who Vassall's handlers had been: photographs of "Gregory", correctly giving his real name as Nikolai Korovin, appeared in newspapers as early as 23 October. Although Vassall had remained strangely loyal to him, and to Nikolai Karpekov, when asked to look through an album of Soviet diplomats in London he identified them both.[116]

But MI5's success was tempered by a mysterious disappearance, which suggested that while Vassall had not been tipped off about his imminent arrest, more important people had been. On 6 September 1962, six days before Vassall's arrest and apparently without his knowledge, Nikolai Karpekov went to Moscow on holiday, never to be seen in London again. From the start it seemed that Vassall was a disposable asset who the Soviets had willingly sacrificed, possibly to protect, or deflect attention away from, a more important spy. There was anger that Karpekov had not been identified and ordered

---

115   In 1963 Lewin told the Radcliffe tribunal that in the late 1940s Vassall, who he barely remembered from Monmouth, had "sought him out at the War Office," where Lewin was then working, and that over the next few years Vassall engineered occasional random meetings. "The relationship was a somewhat equivocal one, although it apparently did not involve any homosexual practices" the Radcliffe report noted. "When Mr Lewin was appointed to the Admiralty in 1950 and realised that Vassall was also serving in that department, he came to the conclusion that it would be better for both of them that their relationship should not be revived". The implication was clear: the oleaginous Vassall had pursued his former headmaster, probably for career advancement rather than a sexual relationship, but had been rebuffed. Vassall seemed to be unaware that Lewin had been deliberately avoiding him, though he said that he once spoke to Lewin when he was working for Galbraith, who Lewin had called to deliver a message. By chance, it was Vassall who picked up the phone and Lewin asked how he was getting on. The memorandum recommending that no further action should be taken against Lewin was written by MI5's deputy director-general Graham Mitchell, who some believed was a Soviet spy himself.

116   Karpekov was also later identified by Giuseppe Martelli, an atomic physicist who was acquitted of espionage in July 1963.

to leave Britain earlier. The press soon discovered Karpekov's flight and in a speech in the House of Commons after Vassall's conviction the Conservative MP Greville Howard asked, "Surely we knew about this man who was going round drawing pink circles on trees in Kensington Park [sic]?[117] For some time he had been known to be a spy. Why cannot we say that he is not persona grata and get rid of him? He skipped within 24 hours of this case coming to light". Like other MPs, Howard was using a pun on "pink circles" to attach as many homophobic tropes as he could to John Vassall. But his real point was clear and valid: although Vassall had been caught, at least one bigger fish had got away.

Karpekov's disappearance was one reason, among many, why the Vassall case further damaged relations between the British and American intelligence agencies. The conviction of Klaus Fuchs in 1950 had already stopped any sharing of nuclear secrets. In 1951 the Americans were annoyed that Kim Philby might have tipped off Guy Burgess and Donald Maclean that they were due to be arrested, prompting them to defect. The special relationship was further damaged by the Blake and Portland cases of 1961.

The British tried to keep the Americans in the loop about the Vassall case. At 16.35 on 12 September – ninety minutes beforehand – a telegram was sent to Richard Helms and James Angleton at the CIA to tell them of Vassall's imminent arrest. On 13 September Vassall had the dubious privilege of being the sole subject of a Joint Intelligence Committee meeting. The meeting's main purpose seems to have been to brief the committee's chairman Sir Hugh S. Stephenson, who was due to go to Washington on 13 October. Arthur Martin, in a note from 18 September, said that he had advised Sir Hugh "not to try to minimise the damage in his report to Washington. It was a serious case". Stephenson himself said that

---

117   The pink circles Vassall was asked to draw as an emergency signal were in fact on a tree on a footpath in Holland Park, not Kensington Gardens.

he was concerned about the potential damage to Anglo-American relations.

On 14 September MI5 wrote to Archibald Bulloch Roosevelt Jr of the CIA (President Theodore Roosevelt's grandson) to thank him for the CIA's help. But then things started to go wrong. In the week after Vassall's arrest, an FBI man in London called Minnich started asking for updates, adding (according to an internal MI5 minute) that he didn't "want to get further into the doghouse because of any discrepancies between what you may tell the bureau and what [Vassall] has seen fit to confess to". It seems that Minnich feared that the British were either embroidering Vassall's confession or withholding information. Martin Furnival Jones (who succeeded Hollis as MI5's director in 1965) wrote on 20 September that "I do not think that [FBI director] Mr Hoover had any grounds for feeling slighted", but the following day G. M. Stone of the British embassy wrote to Furnival Jones saying that Hoover "had expressed himself as very disappointed to say the least" that he had first heard about Vassall from the CIA, not from MI5 or MI6.

In the short term, the Americans were so worried that Macmillan's government might fall that Britain got a face-saving nuclear deal, with the Americans providing them with Polaris missile technology for the Royal Navy's Holy Loch base – the very base that Vassall had given the Soviets sensitive details about. In the long term, however, the Americans never quite trusted the British in the same way again. By 1965, 'British security seemed once again catastrophically bad to American eyes', Peter Wright once claimed. For many Americans, the Vassall case was one of the final straws.

Coverage of Vassall in the American press was, from the start, tinged with mockery of British incompetence. "With his Savile Row suits and ingratiating manner, handsome William John Christopher Vassall liked to move about Britain's nicer resorts, impressing elderly ladies and retired colonels as an outwardly gay blade who was really some sort of secret agent," wrote *Time* on 2 November. "Trouble was, nobody realised just how gay he was – or, for that matter, how secret". US State Department archives show that American diplomats in London knew at once how politically damaging the case was. "The Labor Party, sensing a good issue, persisted in its criticisms ... the matter had shaken not only the House's confidence in the Government's security measures, but also the confidence of the public", the embassy's second secretary Frazier Meade wrote on 9 November. The scandal "provides a welcome, sorely needed and undoubtedly effective cudgel to attack the government."

More seriously, rumours that someone in the Admiralty had protected Vassall from earlier detection reinforced American fears about British intelligence. "England [*sic*] is very conscious of the fact that its series of espionage affairs has weakened U.S. confidence in the effectiveness of British security," the American writers David Wise and Thomas B. Ross said in 1967. "As a result, despite popular belief, British and U.S. intelligence do not work together as harmoniously as they should. Each complains about lack of information from the other".

Nigel West has argued that there was no serious breakdown in Anglo-American relations because of the Vassall case. But there was, from the start, frustration on both sides of the Atlantic that no one really knew exactly what secrets Vassall had divulged. Vassall, who recorded so much about his social life in his diaries and address books, never logged the documents he had photographed. By the end of September 1962, a "Vassall working party" had been set up to "reach an assessment of the damage". But the exact extent of these secrets may never be known.

Opinions still differ about Vassall's importance as a spy. In November 1962 the shadow Defence Secretary, Patrick Gordon Walker, told the Commons that Vassall's "record is hair-raising" and claimed that as personal assistant to the Admiralty's deputy DNI from July 1956 to May 1957 Vassall, "a major spy", had unfettered access to a huge range of valuable defence secrets. This might have been political hyperbole but Chapman Pincher agreed that Vassall provided "information of the highest value to the security and defence chiefs in their successful drive to expand and modernize the Red Navy". The Soviet defector Oleg Gordievsky has claimed that Vassall handed over "thousands of highly classified documents on British and NATO naval policy and weapons development", including plans to expand the Royal Navy's submarine base at Holy Loch. The ex-MI5 spy Peter Wright calculated that of the 200 Soviet spies who were believed to be active in Britain in the early 1960s, "if even 1 per cent were penetrations of the level of Houghton or Vassall, the implications were disastrous".

Important clues lie in the National Archives. From March 1962 onwards the Admiralty was aware that the Russians had received two highly secret documents: a report on the Royal Navy's Mediterranean operations, dated 30 April 1959 and a report dated 8 September 1959 about "the Clyde Base" (Holy Loch). Vassall is also suspected of handing over Joint Intelligence Committee papers from 1957 about eavesdropping devices, NATO papers about force reductions in Germany, telegrams about the supply of arms to Indonesia and the (unpublished) costings exercise for the Defence Estimates for 1958.

Others disagree. When Vassall was first arrested, Harold Macmillan himself was told that the material he was suspected of passing to the Russians was "of varying value". A CIA file from 4 August 1964 asserts that Vassall did not hand over any "US military information". Nick Kettlewell, who conducted surveillance of Vassall's Admiralty colleagues after his arrest, believes that the damage Vassall did was serious but not as consequential as that of other naval spies. John Anthony Walker, a communications specialist in the United States Navy, sold the Soviets information between the late 1960s and early 1980s that meant for a long time they knew the exact locations of the US's submarine fleet.[118] Nor was Vassall's espionage as harmful in human terms as that of George Blake (whose treachery, some have claimed, cost the lives of hundreds of western agents) or the CIA official Aldrich Ames, who gave the KGB names of at least a dozen CIA agents in the 1980s in return for millions of dollars.

The historian Andrew Sinclair has argued that Vassall was punished too harshly, as by the early 1960s the real prize in espionage was not documentation but scientific expertise. "While minor agents like Vassall briefly became household names and served long prison sentences, hundreds of technological spies were undetected or reprimanded without court action." Vassall was not a scientist or a technical expert, merely a junior bureaucrat, but it made political sense to scapegoat him.

•   •   •

John Vassall confessed all. This meant a short sentencing hearing, no formal trial and no jury. There is little courtroom drama in his story.

It was six weeks after Vassall's arrest before he appeared at the Old Bailey: a very short period by modern judicial standards, but to Vassall it must have seemed like an eternity. He had not been charged with treason, for which the death sentence had not yet been officially abolished for those found guilty. Yet he could have faced four decades of imprisonment, the sentence George Blake had been given the year before. Vassall was about to have his most intimate secrets exposed in the most public forum in the land: Court Number One of the Old Bailey. Secrets about his own treachery, and his sexuality. He could not decide which was the most humiliating.

Vassall's solicitor, Derek Muskett, told him at the outset that he

---

118   Walker was only detected, and jailed for life, after his suspicious wife tipped off the FBI. He had received at least $2 million, both in cash and silver bars.

had no option but to plead guilty. Vassall meekly argued that he should plead not guilty, in the hope that he "would not be held totally responsible for his actions". But Vassall had signed a full confession, which he was not willing to withdraw. A more assertive man would have insisted on pleading not guilty and argued in court that his admission of having spied was compatible with a defence of coercion. But assertiveness was not Vassall's style.

On 14 September Vassall appeared for a second time at Bow Street. *The Times* put some facts on the record: a 38-year-old Admiralty civil servant named William John Christopher Vassall had appeared before the Chief Metropolitan Magistrate, Sir Robert Blundell, for a three-minute hearing.[119] Vassall thought that Blundell had seemed kind; later, he was quoted as saying that Vassall's sentence was unduly harsh.

To begin with Vassall faced three charges: that he "for a purpose prejudicial to the safety and interests of the State, did communicate to another person secret official information which is calculated to be, or might be, or is intended to be, directly or indirectly useful to an enemy, contrary to Section 1(i)e of the Official Secrets Act, 1911, as amended", on "a day in 1955", between 1 August 1956 and 31 May 1957 and thirdly, on 17 August 1962. But when Vassall appeared before another Bow Street magistrate, Barraclough, on 9 October, a fourth charge was added: that Vassall had committed the same offence "between August 17 and September 12 1962". Vassall "stood listlessly in the dock", the *Washington Post* reported, as prosecutor Mervyn Griffith-Jones confirmed that the British state now believed that his spying had continued more or less until the moment of his arrest.

Vassall had been told by Blundell that legal aid could not be granted and his solicitor warned that he did not have sufficient funds for his defence if the case lasted any length of time. But by

---

119   Vassall was in fact still thirty-seven at the time: he did not turn thirty-eight until 25 September.

the end of September Vassall had been approached by two tabloid newspapers. The *News of the World* was offering £10,000 for exclusive rights to his story, to be printed after his trial. The *Sunday Pictorial* was only offering £5,000, for a more straightforward story, but that was sufficient to pay Vassall's likely legal costs. He readily accepted, out of desperation.

Vassall had spent most of the money that the Soviets had given him. His flat at Dolphin Square was rented, not owned, so he could not raise a mortgage on it. He simply had no other means of paying for his defence, even though he was pleading guilty. By 9 October – two weeks before his sentencing – the Admiralty knew that Vassall had sold his story but no one could have predicted the political consequences it would have.

At a later committal hearing at the Old Bailey, Vassall recalled being stared at by Admiralty officials who had, until a few weeks earlier, seen him as an inconsequential underling, not a traitor. "The leading prosecuting counsel was a dapper gentleman who read his brief about me with the kind of confidence which showed he thought this case was already in the bag", Vassall said. He had placed great emphasis on the fact that Vassall had been taught photography by the RAF long before he was in the service of the Russians.

Vassall needed a barrister now, not a solicitor. There are varying accounts of how he found one. Some versions say that his distant cousin Jerrold Vassall-Adams[120] "took a leading part" in arranging his defence. But Brigid McEwen, the widow of Vassall's old friend Robin McEwen, recalls that Robin and Vassall reached out to each other spontaneously: a letter from Vassall, asking Robin for help, crossed with a letter from Robin offering such aid. "John could be

---

120   Jerrold Vassall-Adams (known as "Boy") lived in Medmenham, near Marlow, and was the company secretary of the Ottoman Bank in London. He dabbled as an author, writing the foreword to the 1933 *British Legion Annual* and a children's book, *The Book of Dogs*, published in 1950. Born in 1905, Jerrold was almost twenty years older than Vassall, and more like a charitable uncle than a cousin. His grandson, Guy Vassall-Adams, born in 1969, is now a KC in London. He was unaware that he is distantly related to John Vassall or that his grandfather had helped to arrange his defence until this author contacted him.

an awful bore, but he was also a gentle, unassuming and civilised man, without a hint of evil," Brigid, now in her late eighties, recalls, "the Russians watched him all the time and he was putty in their hands." She believes that by 1962, Vassall "wanted to be caught".

Robin, who practised at 2 Hare Court, Inner Temple, readily agreed to help, even though he specialised in commercial cases, not criminal ones. In the event, McEwen was a "junior" to a more illustrious barrister: Jeremy Hutchinson QC, who had only recently taken silk.

Vassall was never over-endowed with self-awareness, and decades later Hutchinson recalled that Vassall "saw his behaviour as a matter of apology rather than shame. He found it difficult to understand that he had been charged at all." Vassall came across as a "weak and rather vain young man who considered himself superior in many ways to those with whom he worked. His job may have been of no great distinction but he thought of himself as a cultured man able to enjoy the most intellectual pursuits of a well-educated gentleman", Hutchinson added. But if Hutchinson regarded Vassall warily, Vassall never noticed: "Mr Hutchinson I admired from the moment I saw him," he recalled in his memoirs.

Hutchinson had the unpleasant task of telling Vassall that there was, as Vassall himself put it, "nothing he could do for me". His trial would not be an opportunity to expose the hypocrisy of the state, which allowed some spies to get off scot-free while jailing others for decades, or to highlight the evils of homophobia. Instead, it was to be an exercise in damage limitation.

John Vassall's trial took place in the Old Bailey's Court Number One on Monday 22 October 1962. Vassall was in the best possible hands: Hutchinson was a veteran of many recent espionage trials. Known in newspapers as the "Blake case QC", he had defended George Blake, in the very same Old Bailey courtroom in 1961. A year later, in July 1963, Hutchinson would defend Dr Giuseppe Martelli, an Italian physicist working at an atomic laboratory in

Culham, Oxfordshire, again in Court Number One. Blake's Old Bailey trial is still well known because of the extraordinary length of his sentence and Martelli's attracted much attention because he was sensationally acquitted. By comparison, it is fair to say that Vassall's, held without a jury and largely *in camera*, was something of a non-event. Technically, it wasn't a trial at all, but a sentencing hearing because he had pleaded guilty. It lasted only two hours.

Ominously, sat alone on the bench was the judge who had sentenced George Blake to forty-two years in jail (at the time, the longest fixed sentence ever handed down) in 1961: the Lord Chief Justice, Lord Parker of Waddington. Vassall's trial had, like many espionage cases, been carefully stage-managed. Papers in the National Archives show that Parker had been especially asked by the Attorney General, Sir John Hobson, to preside over Vassall's trial. Hobson even determined its precise start date: 22 October. Scant details of Vassall's espionage were revealed: both prosecution and defence had agreed in advance what could and could not be said in court.

In some ways Vassall's trial was conducted much like an espionage trial would be today. Court Number One, and its wigs and gowns, has barely changed. But in 1962 government law officers often appeared in court to lead the prosecution at criminal trials (nowadays, the state is represented by a roster of freelance barristers, known as Treasury Counsel). The case against Vassall was outlined by a man who was both a Member of Parliament and the government's chief legal adviser: Sir John Hobson QC MP himself.

Throughout the hearing, Vassall "sat still and expressionless – a slight, pleasant-looking man, in appearance younger than his years, dressed in a dark suit – and he seldom moved his eyes from the Lord Chief Justice," *The Guardian* reported. The only sound that Vassall could hear in Court Number One was the hum of the central heating. "The atmosphere was so quiet that one might have been in the Athenaeum Club," he recalled. When asked for his plea

Vassall suddenly felt an urge to say "not guilty", rather than guilty as in earlier hearings. Only now did it occur to him that he could have mounted a defence based on coercion: as in so many things, Vassall was always one step behind.

Vassall saw himself as a "pawn" and a "pygmy of a spy" compared to George Blake and Klaus Fuchs. Hobson did not agree. He explained that Vassall had been "well rewarded by those who have used him as their tool and has sold some part of the safety and security of the people of this country for cash". "It has been said that you are a known pervert ... that you are a person who has homosexual tendencies? That is right is it not?" asked Hobson in his cross-examination. "Yes," Vassall replied meekly. "And that unhappily you also practise it occasionally?" asked Hobson. "Yes," repeated Vassall. There was, of course, no reference to Vassall having been drugged and raped.

Even these coded references to gay sex were too much for Vassall's father. Brigid McEwen recalls that Reverend Vassall could be seen wandering through the grand halls of the Old Bailey on 22 October, asking Hutchinson and McEwen, "Do you have to mention homosexuality?" But they did: Vassall was in such deep water that for once his homosexuality was an extenuating circumstance, not an incriminating one.

Rather than ascribe any noble motives to Vassall, all Hutchinson could realistically achieve in his speech of mitigation was to persuade Parker to take pity on him. Hutchinson outlined the "grim and squalid background" of his treachery. "We are not here to see this man removed from society as if it were the squashing of a fly", he pleaded. Vassall, Hutchinson argued, had nursed a grievance over the lowly job he held. "His background is a very ordinary, a very unremarkable background; perhaps it is a background which might on the face of it justify a higher rating of a job than the one he has pursued for a number of years now with the civil service".

Throughout his adult life John Vassall had striven to make

himself look like a man of importance. Now, it was Jeremy Hutchinson's job to make Vassall seem like a man of no importance at all. "We cannot hope to tap the spring of sympathy from your Lordship when a man has pleaded guilty to four charges of committing acts which are prejudicial to the security of the State," Hutchinson began. But he did his best.

Vassall hadn't reached a more senior position, Hutchinson implied, because he was "unadult" and "untough", with a "weakness" of latent homosexuality, which "of course brings in its train all the inner turmoil and suffering which we ... know only too well". Vassall was "vulnerable and ... became the victim of a ruthless and pitiless apparatus which has squeezed him into submission". Hutchinson was no homophobe, but he knew that the best chance of securing Vassall a reduced sentence was to portray his homosexuality as an affliction.

Vassall had gone to an ordinary job at the Moscow embassy "in a rather romantic vein", but had found it to be "a cold place, a place where protocol was paramount, and where a junior attaché remained a junior attaché". It was inevitable that he should fall for the "flattery" of Russian men.

Why did Hutchinson not allude to Vassall having been drugged and raped at the "compromise party" in Moscow? To contemporary eyes, these seem to be crucial facts that could, and should, have been mentioned in court to mitigate Vassall's crimes. But Vassall only told the full story about what had happened in the Hotel Berlin many years later, in his 1975 memoirs. Feeling ashamed, he may well not have explicitly told Hutchinson that he had been drugged and raped at all. In 1962 the notion that gay men could be raped was not well understood. Many assumed that gay men were always enthusiastic about sexual interactions of any kind with other men, and thus incapable of withholding consent. Indeed, gay rape was not formally recognised in English law until the passing of the Criminal Justice and Public Order Act in 1994, two years before Vassall's death. But Hutchinson was frank about the "sexual blackmail" that followed, and the Soviets' credible threats of the Lubyanka as well as public disgrace. "My Lord, one does not throw off this conditioning like a dirty garment," Hutchinson argued.

Hutchinson's second tactic was to minimise the scale of Vassall's espionage. There were "no revelations of a master spy for people in search of sensation in this case", he insisted. Vassall was not "a brilliant scientist with a unique and intellectual gift or a rugged ideologist determined to uphold his faith". Instead, Vassall found himself working as a "post office" back in London, in the sense that his job was "fetching and carrying". From 1959 onwards, he had been "dealing with staff technical matters of the dullest kind". Hutchinson, as if to minimise the political import of the Vassall case, stressed that none of the four counts that Vassall faced covered the intervening period when he had worked for Tam Galbraith. He cleverly argued that as a mere clerk Vassall couldn't possibly have had access to information that would do serious damage to national security: "it is quite unacceptable that a clerk in this man's position could have been in a position to pass material which is in a category which would fundamentally harm the safety of this country".

In the end, however, all Hutchinson could really do was to suggest to Parker that there was no case for a sentence of more than twenty years, invoking the warning from the prison reformer Sir Alexander Paterson that "it requires a superman to survive a sentence of more than twenty years with his soul intact". Hutchinson concluded with another plea for pity: "I would ask your lordship, by imposing a just penalty here, to prove once again in this country humanity goes hand in hand with justice".

In his summing-up, Lord Parker asserted that Vassall's "lust" and "selfish greed" had led him to the fateful dinner party at which he had been photographed. These words appalled Vassall: he had not been offered any money until several months later. But he chose not to exercise his right to speak before Parker's sentence was handed down.

It turned out that Hutchinson had achieved something with his skilful mitigation. Parker did hand down a sentence of less than twenty years, if only just. Vassall was sentenced to eighteen years in prison (six years on the first count and twelve on each of the remaining three, running concurrently), making eighteen years in total. This was less than half the sentence given to George Blake in 1961.

Vassall's memoirs make it clear that he resented receiving a sentence of eighteen years, four more than Fuchs had been given in 1950. But many felt he had been lucky not to have got a lot more.[121] Mindful of the public outcry that had greeted the Blake sentence, which had unexpectedly been seen as too harsh rather than not harsh enough, Parker appears to have shied away from giving Vassall such a lengthy one. Eighteen years was long enough to be personally devastating but not long enough to break any records. As a minor cog in the Soviet espionage machine, rather than its linchpin, there was no proof that the documents Vassall had dutifully handed over had given the Soviets any great military or political advantage.

Feeling numb in the dock, Vassall did not hear exactly how many years he had been given: he was only told the length of his sentence by his brother Richard and Robin McEwen in the cells underneath later. But Vassall seemed to regard his sentencing as a relief, regardless of how many years he got. He no longer had nightmares about firing squads and the hangman's noose.

Vassall was driven straight from the Old Bailey to HMP Wormwood Scrubs, then London's most notorious jail, to begin his

---

121 Vassall could have been given a sentence as long as Blake's (which was rumoured to have been fixed at forty-two years because his treachery led to the death of forty-two British agents). Vassall was charged with four counts under the Official Secrets Act, each of which carried a maximum term of fourteen years. If the terms had been made consecutive, not concurrent, he could have been jailed for fifty-six years.

sentence. The van took him along the Embankment on the north bank of the Thames, right past Dolphin Square. "As we passed by I could see that the leaves had turned golden and I knew it would be a long time before I would see my little flat again", Vassall mused. In fact he never saw it again: on 1 December, six weeks after his sentencing, he was "released" from his tenancy and the flat was quickly re-let.

•   •   •

Vassall's trial was not an event that anyone seems to have enjoyed. By chance, it coincided exactly with two important world events that plunged western governments, and the public, into profound gloom. On 22 October 1962 the west lost one of its top agents inside the Soviet Union. Oleg Penkovsky, a military intelligence colonel, who had been handing over invaluable documents to the Americans and British since 1960, was unmasked and arrested. Penkovsky was, Christopher Andrew claims, "perhaps the most important Western agent of the Cold War".

Like Vassall, Penkovsky had taken photographs of documents with a Minox camera. On a visit to London in 1961 he had secretly helped the British to understand the full strength of the KGB's presence at the Soviet embassy – including the importance of its new station chief, Nikolai Karpekov. While Vassall only spent ten years in jail and then the last two decades of his life as a free man, Penkovsky was executed soon after his trial in 1963.

Vassall's trial also coincided with the start of the Cuban missile crisis, which proved just how high the stakes of the Cold War were. Monday 22 October 1962 was, in the Churchillian words of Macmillan's diary, "the first day of the World Crisis" as well as the day of Vassall's trial. For Macmillan, and millions of others, the Cuban crisis "seemed the opening phase of a Third World War". But in his diary a few weeks later, Macmillan confided that "so strangely is the human brain constituted, this terrible danger seemed to distress me less than the personal and human anxieties" of the Vassall affair. Macmillan was scathing about the "sort of mass hysteria worked up by the Press and the less reputable members of the Opposition like [George] Brown and [Richard] Crossman and [Patrick] Gordon Walker". Vassall's long sentence was scant consolation.

Hopes that Vassall's detection, and swift jailing, would be hailed as a British success story would be quickly dashed. Although he may have been a less important spy, Vassall's treachery did much more damage to Macmillan's government than George Blake's had a year earlier. Yet another spy, discovered at the very heart of White-hall, showed how vulnerable Britain was to Soviet infiltration, and it hardly boosted its reputation with the Americans, whose patron-age, expertise and money was vital to Britain's defence.

On 5 October 1962, three weeks after Vassall's arrest, the first James Bond film, *Dr. No,* was shown in British cinemas. But the suave spy portrayed by Sean Connery seemed a far cry from reality. The Vassall case had not made British intelligence seem like a for-midable Cold War adversary, but a bunch of incompetents. Their failure to catch Vassall sooner was seen as a symbol of British ama-teurism and post-war decline.

Lord Carrington's memoirs, published in 1988, explain that "a man named Vassall … had joined the admiralty as a temporary clerk at the age of 17 in 1941 [and] had for a long time been Mos-cow's man." But for several months in late 1962 and early 1963, "John Vassall" needed no introduction: the two words were plas-tered repeatedly on the front pages of newspapers and he became a household name. Vassall finally received the recognition he had craved, but for all the wrong reasons.

As soon as Vassall was arrested meetings were held in the newly formed Ministry of Defence, where it was discussed whether

"D-Notices" should be issued to suppress press coverage.[122] But the days of telling the press what it could and could not report were numbered, and in the end it was decided that Vassall's "story" in the *Sunday Pictorial* should not be stopped because it revealed so little about the secrets that Vassall had handed over and how he had obtained them. Instead, it was just full of sexual titillation.[123]

The days of deference were over. The British press's frenzy over John Vassall was one of the first modern tabloid circuses. The days of British chequebook journalism had arrived and they were here to stay. At least 250 newspaper stories about Vassall appeared in the last ten weeks of 1962 alone. Many of his friends ignored phone calls from the press or doorstep visits from reporters. Ann Miller and Jennifer Hall never spoke to them, and Joan Vaughan only did so after a *Sunday Pictorial* reporter pursued her all the way to Belgium. But others were only too willing to give – or sell – their recollections of Vassall to newspapers.

How had Vassall sold his story? "What seems odd is that this man can write his memoirs and sell them to the Press for an immense sum *after* conviction", a baffled Macmillan mused in his diary. On 5 November Macmillan wrote to the Home Secretary, Henry Brooke, demanding to know how newspapers were printing instalments of Vassall's memoirs, given that he had been held under lock and key ever since his arrest. It later transpired that the *Sunday Pictorial*'s reporters never properly interviewed him. Instead, Norman Lucas and others ghost-wrote stories in Vassall's name. They were only loosely based on Vassall's notes, which were somehow smuggled out of Brixton prison. It is clear that Vassall's lawyers, visitors, the

---

122   A "D-Notice" is "a formal letter of request which is circulated confidentially to newspaper editors" advising them that "publication is considered contrary to the national interest". D-Notices still exist today, but as they have no legal force they are of limited use, particularly now that there are so many online news sources.

123   The British state later found that it had no time to seek a D-Notice to stop the publication of Tam Galbraith's letters and read them at the same time as millions of newspaper readers. Letters that may embarrass a minister, but not endanger national security, could not be suppressed.

police or prison officers had colluded with the press to help Vassall get his story out.

Vassall later claimed that he had been misquoted by the *Pictorial* because he was "ill" in Brixton, as well he might have been as he anticipated a prison sentence of many decades. Drafts of the *Sunday Pictorial*'s articles were supposedly shown to Vassall's solicitor, Derek Muskett. He clearly did a poor job and it seems that Vassall himself was not consulted about how the newspaper embellished his notes. Even if Muskett or Vassall had demanded rewrites, the *Pictorial* would probably have ignored them: Fleet Street has long been known for its skill at putting words in other people's mouths.

The *Pictorial* also managed to secure extraordinary access to Vassall's Dolphin Square flat and everything it contained. Incredibly, 807 Hood House was not properly sealed off as a crime scene after Vassall's arrest – or if it was, the police officers guarding it were very biddable. Norman Lucas later claimed that in the time between Vassall's arrest at 6.05 p.m. on 12 September and the search of his flat about two hours later, he and a photographer broke into – or were let into – the flat and took away numerous items. On 28 September, while Vassall was on remand in Brixton, Lucas somehow obtained a key to the flat and returned to plunder more papers and letters.

"I found it more like the home of a girl than a bachelor," Lucas recalled. "Elegantly furnished with antiques, thick pile carpets and heavy brocade curtains, it had wardrobes full of expensive clothes, a variety of French perfumes on the dressing table, and big, soft cuddly toys propped up in deep armchairs". Lucas added that he rifled through "a miscellany of papers that included catalogues for corsets and newspaper pictures of virile French rugby players".[124] No part of Vassall's life was now off-limits. He had not just sold his story: incredibly, the *Sunday Pictorial* was now the legal owner of

---

124 The photos were presumably from *Le Miroir des Sports*, a magazine that Vassall had been sent from Paris on 21 August, and which had come to light in MI5's surveillance of his incoming post.

his flat's contents. Although the police were present when Lucas returned, there was little they could do to prevent Lucas plundering it. Possession is nine-tenths of the law. After the Radcliffe tribunal was over, the *Pictorial* even pressed the Treasury Solicitors for the return of Vassall's photograph albums, which they had lent to the tribunal but now wanted back. They were the property of the newspaper, not John Vassall or the state.

Before his trial, MI5 had been keen to conceal Vassall's homosexuality. Because his case had been *sub judice*, in theory, the press could report very little other than the name, age and address of the clerk who had been arrested and perfunctory details of his court appearances.[125] At the first ones there had been references to blackmail and "compromising sexual acts", though it was not made clear that they were homosexual ones. But from 9 October onwards, newspaper reports referred to "homosexual acts" at a "Moscow orgy". On 23 October, the morning after Vassall's sentencing, another dam burst. Dozens of stories about his espionage, his lifestyle at Dolphin Square and his foreign travel appeared all over the British newspapers. They made it even plainer that Vassall was gay.

"Arrogance and uncontrollable passion ruined William John Vassall," said the *Daily Telegraph*. The *Daily Express* claimed that Vassall had been in the royal enclosure at Ascot earlier in 1962 and had boasted, "I could have leaned over and touched Princess Margaret". The *Daily Herald* tracked down a lady friend in Brussels, Mademoiselle Sherial Eid, who recalled how she had met Vassall in Cairo at Christmas 1959, at a cocktail party thrown by the Italian consul. "I was a single girl, and he too was single," Eid recalled. "But we never went beyond the platonic stage". The *Daily Mail* carried a huge photograph of Vassall holding hands with an unidentified male "friend" outside the Parthenon in Athens.

---

125 The flow of information between the state and the press wasn't all one way: at 4.20 p.m. on 13 September Charles Davis of the *Evening News* called Special Branch to say he had spoken to a former neighbour of Vassall's, Charles Wakeham of 11 Addison House, who said that Vassall had told him about his regular trips to Europe, but that he had had no inkling that Vassall was a spy.

A few stories did resist the temptation to bombard Vassall with homophobic taunts. "Scrap this law that breeds blackmail," argued Dee Wells, a journalist and broadcaster and wife of the philosopher A. J. Ayer, in a *Daily Herald* column on 25 October. Decriminalisation "won't help the unfortunate Vassall. But it might save others from this ham-handed old pitfall. And it would certainly make the lives of thousands of decent men who happen to be homosexuals less nightmarish than they are now". But such pieces were rare.

Just in case anyone had not got the message, the *Sunday Pictorial* rammed it home again with the first part of its serialisation of Vassall's story on Sunday 28 October. Under the headline "WHY I BETRAYED MY COUNTRY, by John Vassall" its front page carried a photo of Vassall reclining in a bathtub with only his head and shoulders visible. The story underneath exaggerated Vassall's campness and his flat was made to sound like a children's playroom, not a centre of Soviet espionage. "On my dressing table stood a miniature toy white poodle and other furry animals and on my bed my favourite friend – a cuddly toy cheetah. I had a photograph taken in colour of me and my cheetah. I wish I had it with me now," wrote Vassall pathetically.[126]

Vassall's campness was, of course, seen only as further proof of his treachery: since the 1951 defections of Burgess and Maclean, homosexuality had constantly been equated with unreliability and treachery. As if to spread the blame, Vassall dropped hints of a wider scandal, adding that there was an "urgent need for an enquiry into sexual blackmail of people who work in government departments" and that "Many of these types ... are respectable married men holding senior posts".

The *Pictorial*, and other newspapers, gleefully printed descriptions of the wild parties that Vassall was said to have thrown at Dolphin Square and of its expensive carpets and antique furniture.

---

126   Vassall later told the Radcliffe tribunal that the animals were in fact small trinkets of the kind you would put in car windows, not the large soft toys that a child would play with.

By the end of October the British press was in full flow, ridiculing Vassall as a "fawning mediocrity" and a "mother's boy" who had been called "Aunty" by other Admiralty staff. A former schoolmate recalled Vassall as a "sissy and snob", adding that "no one who knew him then would be surprised that he is a homosexual".

These early stories were full of factual inaccuracies. Colonel "Sammy" Lohan, the MOD's deputy director of public relations and secretary of its D-Notice Committee, warned journalists to avoid the "trap" of assuming that Vassall had known about the Portland spy ring or worked with them.[127] But few heeded him. Many stories asserted that Vassall had regularly visited the "House of Secrets" – the Krogers' bungalow in Ruislip – simply because "Gregory" told both Houghton and Vassall how to use Exakta cameras (in fact, Gregory, who was the only link between Vassall and the Portland spies, was always careful to ensure that they knew nothing about each other). Lord Carrington immediately summoned Roger Hollis to explain the stories, which Hollis said were "very misleading" but the damage had already been done.

Other newspapers assumed that "Gregory" (Nikolai Korovin) and "Nikolai" (Nikolai Karpekov) were the same person, simply because they shared the same first name. The *Daily Express* wrongly identified "Gregory" as Grigory Ionesyan, a cultural attaché at the Soviet embassy in London. Ionesyan, who sat on a Whitehall committee to discuss cultural exchanges with the Soviet Union, was horrified when "friends started making jokes at his expense", MI5 noted, and he insisted that he had never met Vassall, let alone been his KGB handler.[128]

---

127 Lohan was evocatively described by the American writers David Wise and Thomas Ross as a "former SOE officers with a handlebar mustache [*sic*], gray hair, a gold-rimmed monocle and Savile Row tailoring". His committee was officially called the "Admiralty, War Office, Air Ministry and Press Committee" in Vassall's day.

128 Not everyone at MI5 believed that Ionesyan was merely a cultural attaché. C. M. James, an MI5 officer, reported that he had once hosted Ionesyan (a "sleek Armenian") and "his very attractive wife" for dinner at his flat in Moscow. Another guest, Evtushenko, later explained that he had been "constrained and prickly" at the party because of the presence of an "MVD man" – Ionesyan – there.

Monmouth School, where John Vassall was educated from 1938 to 1941, was an austere, regimented place, but one where he had his first homosexual experiences in his mid-teens. © Chris Mattison/Alamy Stock Photo

Vassall served as a Leading Aircraftsman (Photography) in the RAF from early 1943 onwards. He soon became skilled at using the Leica cameras he would later use as a spy for the Soviet Union.
© Mirrorpix

Vassall skiing in the Alps, 1949. Even before he started receiving money from the Soviet Union he had expensive tastes in foreign travel. First published in *Vassall: The Autobiography of a Spy* (London: Sidgwick & Jackson Ltd., 1975)

Vassall outside his Moscow flat in April 1954. Little did he know that he would be entrapped by the KGB a few months later. First published in *Vassall: The Autobiography of a Spy* (London: Sidgwick & Jackson Ltd., 1975)

The Hotel Berlin (now the Savoy) in Moscow, where Vassall was drugged, sexually assaulted and photographed in October 1954.

© ruelleruelle/Alamy Stock Photo

Captain Geoffrey Bennett, the naval attaché at the British embassy in Moscow who employed Vassall as his clerk in 1954–55.

© Ann Ward/ANL/Shutterstock

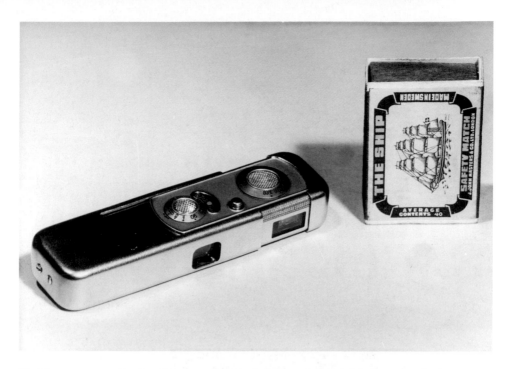

The Minox camera used by Vassall to photograph hundreds, if not thousands, of secret Admiralty documents.
© Mirrorpix

Hood House, Dolphin Square. Vassall rented a flat on the eighth floor from March 1959 until his arrest three-and-a-half years later.

Photograph from author's personal collection

Vassall was very proud of his Dolphin Square flat, with its brocade curtains and antique Queen Anne furniture. His employers never stopped to wonder how a poorly paid clerk could afford to live there. First published in *Vassall: The Autobiography of a Spy* (London: Sidgwick & Jackson Ltd., 1975)

ABOVE The Admiralty
Building on Horse Guards
Parade, where Vassall worked
from the late 1940s until 1954
and again from 1956 until 1962.
© Jeffrey Blackler/Alamy Stock Photo

LEFT Tam Galbraith, the
Civil Lord of the Admiralty,
whose private office Vassall
worked at in 1957–59.
He was forced to resign as a
minister in November 1962
amid hysterical rumours that
he and Vassall had been lovers
who planned to defect to
the Soviet Union together.
©Keystone Press/Alamy Stock Photo

A victorious Fergus
Montgomery at the
Brierley Hill by-election
in 1967. Vassall told
MI5 that he had been
friends with the MP.

© PA Images/Alamy Stock Photo

British Conservative
politician Harmar
Nicholls at his desk
at the Ministry of
Agriculture, Fisheries
and Food in London,
14 April 1955. Vassall
claimed that he had
had a sexual relationship
with Nicholls.

© Fox Photos/Hulton Archive/
Getty Images

Sir Harmar Nicholls and Fergus Montgomery continued their political careers into the 1980s and 1990s, but a third MP, Denzil Freeth, was forced to stand down in 1964 because of rumours that he had attended a party with Vassall. © PA Images/Alamy Stock Photo

The Vassall and Profumo scandals were intertwined. On 15 March 1963 the *Daily Mirror* put unrelated stories about Vassall's spying, Christine Keeler's disappearance and Profumo's possible resignation on its front page. It was a heavy hint that Fleet Street already knew about the connections between Keeler, Profumo and a Soviet naval attaché. © Mirrorpix

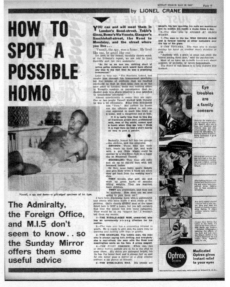

The press's homophobia continued long after Vassall's imprisonment. On 28 April 1963 the *Sunday Mirror* featured an article headlined "How to Spot a Possible Homo": a "short course on how to pick a pervert". © Mirrorpix

THE SUNDAY TIMES *magazine*

JANUARY 7, 1973

VASSALL
the years inside

ABOVE In January 1973, a few weeks after his release, this picture of Vassall appeared on the front page of the *Sunday Times* magazine. He looked much as he had a decade earlier, but with longer hair and sideburns. © Brian Seed

LEFT Vassall in 1984. A colleague described Vassall in his sixties as "delightful, charming and good fun" – but reluctant to talk about the past. © WikimediaCommons, GrindtXX

Most of the journalists' errors and exaggerations stemmed from their crude homophobia. The divide between broadsheet and tabloid newspapers was not as pronounced in the early 1960s as it is today. The *News of the World* was still a substantial paper that carried serious stories alongside salacious tittle-tattle about suburban murders and disgraced vicars. But in 1962 the *News of the World* saw fit to assert that "men like Vassall don't want to be cured", as if being gay was a disease.

Vassall was a dabbler, and nowadays he might be considered a bit of a geek. Alongside his love of opera and ballet, he had a range of hobbies – bridge, model railways, amateur dramatics and Scottish country dancing – which have never been seen as the exclusive preserve of gay men. But the media downplayed any pastimes which did not conform to stereotypes. One journalist wrote that the toiletries in Vassall's flat were like a form of poison: "I washed my hands and they smelt nasty for two days," he commented. "The bedroom was strictly a female's bedroom. I think there were roughly nine or ten bottles of various perfumes and cologne, talc powders of various types ... the display of perfumes one felt that only a fairy queen would have". The press were also strangely coy about the sexuality of its own reporters: when newspapers published a photograph of Vassall and another man at a Venice café, MI5 realised that his companion was John Byrne, a former *Daily Mirror* journalist who now worked at *Ideal Home* magazine and who was, MI5 claimed, "a foppish, very affected Australian who lives with his mother" in Chelsea. Picture captions in newspapers had not identified Byrne.

But while these stories were full of falsehoods, most of them contained a kernel of truth. Although newspapers may have been wrong to assert that the presence of another Admiralty spy had been known about eighteen months earlier, in early 1961, a spy had certainly been known about from March or April 1962 onwards – a good six months before Vassall's arrest. Amid its homophobia, the press did have a valid point that the Admiralty seems to have waived its usual hostility to gay men when it came to Vassall. Cabinet Office files show that in September 1962 Macmillan was told by Carrington that Vassall "earned large sums of money as a male prostitute", which suggests that the Admiralty may have suspected Vassall of selling sexual services before his arrest, not after.

Above all, in early November 1962, MI5 and the police knew that Vassall had one secret that the press had not yet reported. As well as working for the Civil Lord of the Admiralty, Tam Galbraith, Vassall seemed to have developed a friendship with him.

Among the papers found in Vassall's flat, inside a green fibre suitcase, were piles of correspondence, including nineteen letters to Vassall from Galbraith and his wife (mostly the former), sent over the last five years.[129] Once they were examined and photocopied, MI5 decided that they "had no bearing on the prosecution of the case". They were, remarkably, returned to Vassall's flat for the *Sunday Pictorial*'s Norman Lucas to pick up. Other letters from Galbraith to Vassall came into Lucas's possession later, probably thanks to his friends at Scotland Yard.

None of these letters were proof that Tam Galbraith and John Vassall had been gay lovers. But sooner or later they were bound to appear on the pages of the *Sunday Pictorial* or another paper and sooner or later they would extinguish Tam Galbraith's promising political career.

---

129   These included letters from John Robertson, a friend of Vassall's in New York, and David Stewart (who lived at 104 Hood House, seven storeys below Vassall's flat).

CHAPTER FIVE

"THE WRETCHED GALBRAITH"

At first, Thomas Galloway Dunlop Galbraith – known to his friends and family as Tam – was only a footnote in John Vassall's complicated story. Vassall had, on and off, spent twenty years working at the Admiralty and only two of them had been in Galbraith's private office. But before long, Tam Galbraith's name would not be in the footnotes but in scores of newspaper headlines.

Born in March 1917, the eldest of seven children, Tam Galbraith went to Wellington College and then Christ Church, Oxford, to read History. In 1962, Galbraith told MI5 that he had almost been recruited as an MI5 officer by J. C. Masterman, a fellow at Christ Church, and had "got as far as being interviewed by a General or Brigadier in St James' Street".[130] While serving as a lieutenant in the Royal Naval Volunteer Reserve Galbraith unsuccessfully contested Paisley for the Conservatives at the general election of July 1945, and Edinburgh East at a by-election that October. In November 1948, aged thirty-one, he was finally successful at another by-election, in Glasgow Hillhead. Galbraith was quickly tipped for high office, having had a head start over the large influx of

---

130   MI5 had offices at 58 St James's Street during the war, which were used by its Double Cross Committee.

Conservative MPs newly elected at the 1950 and 1951 general elections. Having been an assistant whip since 1950, in 1955 he rose to the key backroom role of Treasurer of HM Household – deputising for the Chief Whip Ted Heath – which he held until his appointment as Civil Lord of the Admiralty in early 1957.

Tam Galbraith came from a powerful Unionist dynasty. His father – another Thomas Galbraith – had become the Unionist MP for Glasgow Pollok, next door to Hillhead, at a by-election in 1940. During Winston Churchill's caretaker government between May and July 1945, Galbraith senior served as Under-Secretary of State for Scotland, a job that his son later held. He remained an MP until he was elevated to the House of Lords as the 1st Baron Strathclyde in 1955.[131] Once in the Lords he served as a more senior Scottish Office minister until 1958.[132] Both Galbraiths – father and son – were well-respected in Glasgow, and in Ayrshire, where their Barskimming estate lay.

While the Galbraiths are an ancient Scottish family, their barony was not an ancient creation. The Galbraiths were "new money": the first Lord Strathclyde had served in the Royal Navy and practised as a chartered accountant, as did his son Tam before he entered Parliament. His grandparents had made their fortunes in shipping, running off-licences or as grain merchants. Although Barskimming was a large estate, Galbraith's great-uncle, Robert Jack Dunlop, had only bought it in the 1910s. Unlike many Scottish lairds, the Galbraiths had not lived in the same castle for centuries, and above all they had made their money not as landowners, but "in trade". It

---

131 Confusingly, although Tam Galbraith was a "Civil Lord" of the Admiralty he never joined his father in the House of Lords. He remained a member of the Commons until his death in 1982, as his father outlived him. After the first baron died in 1985, aged ninety-four, the barony passed to Tam's son, another Thomas Galbraith, who was born in 1960. The 2nd Baron Strathclyde served as Leader of the House of Lords from 2010–12, during David Cameron's premiership. He still lives at Barskimming and the house on Cowley Street, Westminster, where John Vassall visited his father in the late 1950s and early 1960s.

132 As a Minister of State in the Scottish Office Tam Galbraith's father helped kick the Wolfenden Report into the long grass, telling the House of Lords on 4 December 1957 that Wolfenden's committee had not paid enough heed to public opinion regarding the distinction between public law and private morals.

was suggested that some Tory grandees considered them not to be "one of us".

In 1956 Tam Galbraith married Simone du Roy de Blicquy, described by Rebecca West as "a young and beautiful Belgian lady". A daughter was born in 1957 and two sons followed in 1960 and 1962. But some people raised concerns that he had married relatively late, at nearly forty.[133] The historian Michael Bloch has claimed that "some mystery still surrounds" Galbraith's sexuality, and that "it is possible that some unstated mutual attraction existed" between him and Vassall. In 1966 Vassall told MI5 that in the late 1940s or early 1950s he had heard gossip that the newly elected Galbraith might be gay.

At first, MI5 were very concerned about Vassall's work for Galbraith. An MI5 memo from 4 June 1962, when Vassall was first considered as a suspect, claimed that he "would have had access to a very wide range of documents" in his private office. As Civil Lord of the Admiralty Galbraith had responsibility for "works and labour", so in theory few of the reports in his red boxes would have been about military secrets. But in practice, Galbraith spoke on a wide range of issues, as in the late 1950s he was the only Admiralty minister sitting in the Commons rather than the Lords. On the other hand, "Gregory" had been disappointed when Vassall was transferred from naval intelligence to Galbraith's private office in 1957 and relieved when he moved to the Admiralty's military branch. At Vassall's trial Hobson said that while working for Galbraith, only "about 15 per cent to 20 per cent of the documents to which he had access were of the highest importance". Given Whitehall's tendency to unnecessarily classify documents as "top secret" this suggests that few of them were highly sensitive.

Even Rebecca West, who was generally scathing about Vassall's

---

133   Tam Galbraith's son rightly points out that many of his father's male contemporaries married because their twenties had been dominated by wartime service, and that Tam Galbraith had had several girlfriends before meeting Simone in the mid-1950s.

treachery, agreed that his duties in Galbraith's office were little more than "collecting newspaper cuttings, making travel arrangements, meeting distinguished guests at the airport, and bringing in the tea".

But in the feverish weeks of October and November 1962, Vassall's purely administrative role was not yet fully understood. MI5 soon realised however that the working relationship between them had turned into what looked like a friendship. Galbraith was seven-and-a-half years older than Vassall and seems to have taken him under his avuncular wing from the start. When he appeared at the Radcliffe tribunal, Galbraith denied sharing Vassall's interests in music, the theatre or model railways and it seemed that they initially struggled to find anything in common. Galbraith recalled that "It is no good talking about bee-keeping, for example, to Vassall, he was not interested in bee-keeping, or old houses [a topic that Galbraith regularly discussed with his private secretary John Peters]".

In time they did find some common ground: Vassall's extravagant taste in holidays. He once told Galbraith that he was going skiing in Zermatt and was embarrassed when Galbraith asked him if he was going to Gstaad, "which was particularly fashionable at that time, but I had to admit it was Zermatt". Vassall never travelled to Italy with Galbraith as some newspapers suggested but they certainly discussed their shared affection for the Hotel de la Ville in Rome, at which they both stayed – though not at the same time.

Vassall said he had lunched with Galbraith twice at Cowley Street, in the presence of his wife on both occasions. Although Galbraith insisted that he had only visited Vassall's Dolphin Square flat once, along with his wife, MI5 knew that between early 1957 and late 1959 Vassall had visited Barskimming between six and nine times: roughly once every four months. At Barskimming, Vassall was given lunch but he was never offered accommodation. In fact, Vassall told MI5 that after his visits to Barskimming he had often stayed at the Marine Hotel in Troon, sometimes sharing a room with a Glaswegian doctor, Donald Barran, and sometimes visiting two other friends: a Mr Welsh, who lived with his mother in Troon, and David Flanagan, who lived with his own mother in nearby Seamill.

However innocent all this may sound, Vassall had definitely stayed in touch with Galbraith after moving to a new job in October 1959. And Galbraith badly miscalculated his response to the press's enquiries about their relationship. By the time Galbraith and his wife returned from a two-week holiday in Italy on 8 October 1962, their family's nanny had been doorstepped by reporters in London. No doubt irritated by the intrusion, when Galbraith himself was doorstepped at Barskimming by reporters from the *Mail* and *Telegraph* on the day Vassall was sentenced, he decided to set the record straight, rather than ignore them or issue a written statement. "Who's Vassall?" Galbraith asked, before saying that he could not comment because his prosecution was *sub judice*. But he soon loosened up, and told the reporters that, "I felt rather sorry for him – I felt he had a screw loose".

This admission would come to haunt Galbraith, and it prompted an immediate question: if he thought that Vassall had "a screw loose" why had he allowed him to work in his private office at all, and why had he gone out of his way to be kind to him, even serving him lunch at his marital home? Galbraith then tied himself in further knots. "Some people think he was a great buddy of mine, but in my six years as a departmental minister I have had over thirty officials in my house", Galbraith insisted. "My relations with him were not different from those with other civil servants". He then made another striking admission – that he had visited Vassall's Dolphin Square flat – and he appeared to acknowledge that it was an odd place for a junior clerk to live. "The only thing that struck me as strange was his flat. But I believed he had been left money," Galbraith explained.

Galbraith had, as Bill Deedes's biographer Stephen Robinson put it, "witlessly … thrown petrol on the flames". Comments that he assumed were made "on lobby terms" – off the record – (including his observation that Vassall "had a screw loose") were reported *verbatim* in the next day's newspapers. On 23 October the *Daily Mail* claimed, inventively, that "in his 18th-century mansion Mr Galbraith and his assistants waited for Vassall – their trusted courtier a paid servant of Moscow". After arriving at Barskimming Vassall had "mingled" with up to thirty weekend house guests, chatted with them about music, bridge and golf and always wore "the correct clothes for the occasion". The *Mail* seems to have deliberately misinterpreted Galbraith's comment that over thirty officials had entered his homes over the years, and was now claiming that Vassall had been a guest at thirty-strong house parties.

A week after the *Daily Mail*'s story, on 1 November, Galbraith made another miscalculation. In a statement issued via his solicitor he insisted that he had not known Vassall was a homosexual and that Vassall had never stayed the night at his Scottish estate. This only prompted another question: why did Galbraith feel the need to deny overnight stays so strenuously if he had nothing to hide? Cruelly, Galbraith was damned either way.

For the first few weeks after Vassall's conviction, Galbraith was not the main focus of the press's coverage. Newspapers also argued that Lord Carrington should resign. But in Parliament, questions were already being asked about Galbraith's relationship with Vassall. The first mention of it was in the House of Lords, where Herbert Morrison said, "I am personally very worried about the position of the former Civil Lord, who seemed to me to have social relationships with a minor official of the Admiralty which were quite inappropriate". But on 31 October, Carrington did all he could to allay concerns. "No blame can be attached to anybody for the existence … of an individual who was willing to become a spy," he told the Lords. "The real issue of blame, if there is to be blame, is whether he should have been caught sooner". Russian spies at the heart of the British military were seen as a fact of life in the Cold War.

The less deferential House of Commons was having none of it. Labour did all it could to exaggerate the scandal and undermine a government that had already been battered by the exposure of the Portland spy ring and George Blake in 1961. On 30 October, Labour's deputy leader George Brown dropped dark hints that must have set Galbraith's pulse racing: "there are other letters in existence, which I and no doubt others have seen ... which indicate a degree of ministerial responsibility that goes far beyond the ordinary business of a Minister".

The first proper Commons debate on the Vassall affair, on Friday 2 November, sometimes went off track: the heavy-handed policing of recent Campaign for Nuclear Disarmament (CND) demonstrations, and the recent suicide of Robert Soblen, a German national who faced extradition to the US on spying charges.[134] But Galbraith was always in the background. Patrick Gordon Walker, the shadow Defence Secretary, said that the Vassall case, which he referred to as "the official secrets trial", raised "matters that have done great and grievous harm to the nation". Pointedly, Gordon Walker asked why none of Vassall's four charges covered the period when he worked in Galbraith's office. "It may be that there is some technical explanation why no reference was made in the counts to this period ... On the face of it, it certainly looks a little odd", he said.

Peter Thorneycroft, a former Chancellor of the Exchequer who was now Defence Secretary, reminded MPs that "a traitor has been caught and tried and punished, and that is ... a matter for

---

134   Dr Robert Soblen was a prominent member of the pro-Trotsky Left Opposition in Germany in the 1930s. He moved to the United States in 1941 and was arrested there in 1960 on suspicion of being a Soviet spy. Sentenced to life in prison, he fled the US while on bail and sought asylum, first in Israel, then in Britain. He committed suicide by overdosing on barbiturates on 11 September 1962, the day before Vassall's arrest, after his last appeal for asylum in Britain had been denied.

satisfaction on both sides of the House of Commons." But Thorneycroft was forced to concede that Vassall had been "last checked" in 1956, "on his return from Moscow", six years before his arrest. Thorneycroft then dug a deeper hole for himself by adding, "it has been said that this man lived above his income in Dolphin Square. How many of us are not living above our incomes in various squares? One cannot say that because someone is living in Dolphin Square he is obviously getting his money from Moscow."

When it was put to Thorneycroft that Galbraith had told reporters that Vassall "had a screw loose", he attempted a joke – "How often have hon. Members used that expression about other hon. Members?" – which did not land well. And when Gordon Walker interrupted Thorneycroft to ask whether Vassall had a key to Galbraith's red boxes, he had to concede that "He could have done". By trying to limit the damage caused by the Vassall affair, Thorneycroft had only inflicted more. Harold Macmillan wrote in his diary on 5 November that Thorneycroft "took the debate last Friday with too Palmerstonian a touch – in a word, a little flippantly".

It was now time for backbench MPs to have their say. Many of them – both Labour and Conservative – had seen military service during the Second World War and several still preferred to be known by their military rank. Like retired generals discussing old battles they brought their own experiences of the military and intelligence services to bear. But their diagnosis of what had prompted Vassall to start spying, and their prescriptions for how to stop future Vassalls, were based on homophobia, cod psychology and sexism.

John Dugdale (Labour MP for West Bromwich and a former minister in the Attlee administration) asserted that "a cypher is more easily compromised than a woman". Captain John Litchfield, a former deputy DNI who was now Conservative MP for Chelsea, complained that gay civil servants were being "unloaded on to a less highly classified part of their own Ministry or some other Ministry". Instead of being moved they should all be fired. "Character defects are an absolute bar when known in the Armed Services; why, then, are they not in the Civil Service?", he lamented.

Commander Anthony Courtney, Conservative MP for Harrow East, saw fit to boast that he had told his own Russian contacts about his firmly heterosexual tastes: "I have had tremendous fun in Russia — usually late at night, I admit, or after a good lunch — in saying to my Russian opposite number, 'Ivan Ivanovich, you are a friend of mine. We are beginning to know each other very well. It is your duty to watch me, and to record to your superiors everything I say ... Ivan Ivanovich, I will save you some trouble and tell you what my real weakness is – it's blondes'". These were prophetic words: a few years later, Courtney's liking for blondes led to him being smeared by the KGB, apparently in a bid to ensure he lost his seat.[135]

Reginald Paget, Labour MP for Northampton and a former Royal Naval Reserve officer, referred to Vassall – who was thirty-eight years old in 1962 – as "this boy". Paget flattered Anthony Courtney by asking "how long would Master Vassall have lasted if the honourable and gallant Gentleman [Courtney] had been Civil Lord?" By contrast, Galbraith had been "amazingly naïve" not to realise that Vassall was gay, Paget asserted. Greville Howard (Conservative MP for St Ives and a former lieutenant-commander in the Royal Navy) said that British diplomats should be evaluated by "experts, be they police, or psychiatrists, I do not care who"

---

135   Soon after the death of his first wife in 1961, Courtney was in Moscow for a British industrial exhibition and was photographed entertaining a Russian tour guide, Zina Volkova, in his room at the National Hotel. Chapman Pincher claims that Courtney was then warned to tone down his regular anti-Soviet speeches in the Commons and elsewhere. Courtney refused to take the hint and in 1965 the photographs were sent to other MPs, ministers, newspapers and Courtney's new wife. Courtney survived an attempt to deselect him in Harrow East, but in 1966 he was defeated by the Labour candidate, Roy Roebuck, by 378 votes. Although Courtney would probably have lost his seat in the Labour landslide of 1966 anyway, his fate shows that it was not just homosexual men who could be blackmailed.

to identify gay men and exclude them. "I loathe cocktail parties. They are an absolute abomination", he added (newspapers had by now started claiming that Galbraith had attended cocktail parties at Vassall's Dolphin Square flat). Howard even argued that unmarried men should no longer be employed as diplomats ("Is it right that young bachelors should be allowed to go to these Iron Curtain countries?"), which presumed that all married men would magically be immune from sexual blackmail.

Only two MPs resisted the drumbeat of homophobic paranoia. The first was Emrys Hughes, Keir Hardie's son-in-law and the maverick Labour MP for South Ayrshire (in which Galbraith's Barskimming estate lay), who said "I do not want to increase expenditure on the Secret Service. I want to reduce it. I want to abolish it". The other – Anthony Greenwood, Labour MP for Rossendale – was the only one to ponder whether Britain's criminalisation of homosexual activity had made Vassall more vulnerable to blackmail, suggesting that "if the House had been more courageous in its attitude to the Wolfenden Report it would have removed one of the gravest threats to security, namely, the power which the blackmailer has over the homosexual".

The Labour MP Niall MacDermot argued elsewhere that "It is not that homosexuals are more likely to be traitors [but that] homosexuals in this country are peculiarly vulnerable to blackmail … It seems to me that we are paying the price as a country for our attitude to homosexuality". But such voices of sanity were rare in parliamentary debates on the Vassall case. William Shepherd, Conservative MP for Cheadle, said that homosexuals "were dangerous from two points of view: their promiscuity, and second from the fact that they have a grievance against society and are prepared therefore, if necessary, to go against society." Many newspapers and politicians implied that homosexuals were automatically prone to treachery, but few stated their prejudice as explicitly as Shepherd.

Tam Galbraith appeared immune to demands for his resignation as a minister while it seemed that he had not known that Vassal was gay. But on Sunday 4 November, a fortnight after Vassall's conviction and two days after Parliament first debated the case, this immunity ended.

It was the media, not Parliament, that would end up baying for Galbraith's blood. The press's early coverage of Vassall's conviction made relatively little mention of Galbraith, but their reticence did not last long.

On 4 November the *Sunday Pictorial*, in its second instalment of Vassall's story, made more revelations, with the headlines, "The men who came to see me – And the women? They gave me mother love" and "How the Russian Spy Masters Broke Me Down". A photograph of Vassall wearing white bathing trunks left little to the imagination. "For two years I saw him strutting around Moscow like a dressed-up doll," Stanley Johnson, the Associated Press's former Moscow correspondent, was quoted as saying.[136] "More than once I saw his face covered in cream".[137] Unnamed former colleagues and neighbours said that everyone had known of Vassall's "peculiarities". He was a "laughing stock" and his flatmates had wanted "nothing to do with him" and made him sleep on a sofa in the living room.

This speculation about Vassall's attire in Moscow was a prelude to the *Sunday Pictorial*'s more serious allegations that Vassall had been part of a homosexual "conspiracy" across Westminster and Whitehall and that unnamed "Foreign Office perverts" had collaborated with, or been controlled by, him.

---

136   Stanley Johnson is no relation to his namesake, the father of former Prime Minister Boris Johnson.
137   Johnson had been a neighbour of Vassall's and had indeed known him slightly in 1954–56. He later told Radcliffe that his comments had been misquoted, that the cream on Vassall's face was probably "Nivea cream used as a protective in extreme conditions of weather" and that Vassall's appearance as a "dressed-up doll" was, in fact, the sensible attire of a woollen hat and long scarf for an ice-skating expedition. In return, Vassall told MI5 that Johnson was a "homosexual and a drunk". MI5 thought his opinion might be motivated by malice after seeing the comments the newspapers had prompted from Johnson.

An even bigger bombshell was the publication of several letters that Galbraith had written to Vassall over a period of almost five years. Newspapers, and George Brown, had already hinted at their correspondence. The *Daily Mail* had carried a story headlined "Postcard to a Spy", which noted that "Amid the pile of correspondence is a postcard sent during a holiday abroad to Vassall by a leading figure. ... This discovery of the picture postcard from abroad does not mean that there was any sexually improper relationship. It does indicate, the opposition believes, a friendliness which one would not expect to exist between a clerk and a senior colleague".

Although Galbraith was not named, many guessed that he was the subject of the story. And in true Fleet Street style, acknowledging that there may not have been a sexual relationship between him and Vassall only added credence to rumours that there had been.

The letters published by the *Pictorial* on 4 November were innocuous. As the *Annual Register* of 1962[138] said, they contained "nothing more damaging than the former Civil Lord's interest in the office carpets, crockery and paper clips". Galbraith had not opened his soul to Vassall; instead his most heartfelt complaint was about Whitehall bureaucracy. In another letter, Galbraith had authorised Vassall to do some spring cleaning in the office while he was away in Pakistan. "The most that could be said against Mr Galbraith was that he had suffered a socially pressing and plausible junior colleague a trifle too gladly", wrote Rebecca West. Galbraith had done no more than "show patient civility" and his letters were "good-natured and trivial" and "written out of conscientiousness rather than zest ... The waste-paper basket cries out for them". Patrick Higgins has claimed that far from being proof of intimacy, they were just "the sort of letters a man on the move might write to his office in Whitehall". Vassall always addressed Galbraith as "Sir"

---

138   The *Annual Register* was an almanac of British news, then published by Longman and widely read.

or "Civil Lord", and in his letters, Galbraith never referred to Vassall by his first name.

But they also showed a certain chattiness between the civil servant and minister. Vassall sent Galbraith telegrams and sentimental greeting cards when his first two children were born.[139] On 18 September 1957, while Galbraith was on an intercontinental flight, he had written, "Dear Vassall, it isn't often a Civil Lord has the chance to write a note to one of his staff when over the North Pole". And the letters showed that the two men had remained on friendly terms for at least two-and-a-half years after Vassall had left Galbraith's private office. In October 1959, as Vassall was leaving, Galbraith invited him to "come for a meal" at Barskimming if he was ever in Scotland. At Easter 1960 Galbraith had written, "My dear Vassall, Goodness knows what you will think of me for having taken so long to write. We were both delighted to receive your charming card of congratulation and I would have thanked you ages ago except for the fact that the Scottish Office, when Parliament is sitting, keeps me more busy than the Admiralty". Oddly, in late April 1960, Vassall wrote to Galbraith to say he could "walk over to see you" in Barskimming during a ten-day holiday at the Hydro Hotel in Peebles, sixty miles away. As recently as 15 April 1962, five months before Vassall's arrest, Galbraith had written, "Dear Vassall, we much enjoyed your visit and it was good of you to write".

"My dear" was a common salutation in mid-century correspondence, and unlike the "Darling" salutation used by John Profumo in letters to Christine Keeler in 1961, the phrase was no evidence of any sexual relationship. Galbraith only seems to have used the words "My dear Vassall" in two letters: one, just after Vassall left

---

139   The first card, on the birth of Galbraith's daughter, contained these lines: "With her little pink fingers/ And Little pink toes/ And her little pink cheeks/ And a little snub nose/ She must be a darling/ And she's lucky, too/ "Cause not every baby/ Has parents like you". The card to mark the birth of their son contained even worse rhymes: "What makes more noise/ And plays more pranks/ Attracts more dirt/ Deserves more spanks/ Yet who could bring/ More lasting joys/ Than little boys!"

his employ, to thank him and reminisce about a small leaving party Vassall had organised, and the other to console him after his mother's death in 1960. But having reminded readers of Vassall's homosexuality at every opportunity in the preceding days, the *Pictorial* and other papers' implications did not need to be spelt out: The two men had been lovers and Galbraith had been aware of, and possibly complicit in, Vassall's espionage.

The phrase "My dear Vassall" appeared again and again in titillating headlines from 4 November onwards. Taken out of context, "My dear Vassall" could be construed as a lover's term of endearment, not a friendly salutation from a minister to a civil servant. Cleverly, rather than publish all the correspondence in one go, the *Sunday Pictorial* indicated that they wanted to drip-feed it to readers over several weeks. Within one week, the constant repetition of "My dear Vassall" was enough to seal Galbraith's fate.

Vassall was horrified by the publication of Galbraith's letters, which he seemed to have had no advance warning of. On 5 November he asked the MI5 officer, Charles Elwell to tell him "who had authorised this". He insisted that he had not handed the letters to the press, because he would not do anything to "harm the Galbraiths". Vassall later told Elwell that he was "genuinely upset over the ruin of Galbraith's political career".

While other British spies, like George Blake, were accorded some respect for their cunning, all contemporary accounts of Vassall's treachery were soaked in homophobia. By now, many papers were running salacious stories claiming that Vassall had attended "sex parties" and wandered around the West End dressed in women's clothing. Dolphin Square was now rumoured to be a den of homosexuality, as well as espionage.

There had been no mention of Vassall's correspondence with Galbraith at his trial. Again, the Vassall case broke new ground: for the first time the "kiss and tell" revelations of a felon, sold to a newspaper after his conviction rather than aired in court, sealed a politician's fate. As with many later scandals it was tabloid speculation, not legally verified facts, that proved to be a politician's downfall.

In his final ten days as a minister, Galbraith was not preparing to resign but insisting that he had done nothing wrong and begging to keep his job. On 29 October he wrote a fawning letter to Macmillan, apologising for any embarrassment he had caused. He wrote several much longer letters to the Chief Whip, Martin Redmayne, in the days that followed, with convoluted explanations of how and why his innocent friendship with Vassall had developed. But Galbraith only tied himself in yet more knots. He told Redmayne that he kept "more or less open house" at his homes in London and Scotland. He added that his father had had a tenancy at Dolphin Square since the war, firstly in Frobisher House and later in Nelson House, which hardly reassured Redmayne that he couldn't have visited Vassall's flat there more than once.

Later, he told Peter Thorneycroft that "I had no idea what the cost of a flat in Dolphin Square was. My father who has lived there since the Blitz has always said it is cheap and rather slummy, but perhaps these are relative terms". Indeed they are: an address that seemed "cheap and rather slummy" to a wealthy Scottish political dynasty could be the acme of grandeur to the son of a penniless clergyman like John Vassall. Like Thorneycroft himself, Galbraith was too flippant about a man who had been convicted of spying. "I would not say that Vassall quite spoke (to be Snobbish) the King's English absolutely purely, but he very nearly did," Galbraith wrote to Redmayne.

Galbraith had clearly been keen to keep his letters out of the press. The archives reveal that he told Redmayne that he had considered approaching Lady Huntly (the daughter of Lord Rothermere, the press magnate), who he said he vaguely knew, to try to persuade the press to leave the matter alone but had been advised by his solicitors to "leave women out".[140]

On 7 November Tam Galbraith's fate was sealed. Within an hour of Vassall's conviction, Macmillan had set up an internal inquiry, chaired by Sir Charles Cunningham, who had been Permanent Under-Secretary of State at the Home Office (its top civil servant) since 1957. A memo from 7 November from Tim Bligh, Macmillan's principal private secretary, shows that a secret meeting earlier that day agreed that Cunningham's inquiry should publish all the letters from Galbraith to Vassall (twenty-five in total), not just the ones that the *Sunday Pictorial* had quoted from, to call newspapers' (and Labour's) bluff. The letters came out in a white paper (innocuously entitled "Cmnd. 1871"), a document normally used to propose legislation, not to air dirty linen in public.[141]

In the late afternoon of 7 November, Bill Deedes, a minister with unofficial responsibility for press relations, was summoned to see Martin Redmayne at Admiralty House. "We have these letters. Come and look at them," said Redmayne. Deedes joined him and two of Macmillan's private secretaries, Tim Bligh and Philip Woodfield, to discuss whether Galbraith should resign. Deedes "murmured no"' at first, he later maintained, "because it [Galbraith's resignation] implied panic". Deedes then had to leave, to "chair the Chancellor of the Exchequer, Reginald Maudling through a press panel". When he rejoined Redmayne, Bligh and Woodfield at about 7 p.m. he found them in the Cabinet Room with Macmillan. Deedes now changed his mind, having read the full correspondence, which he said was "indeed innocent but open to misinterpretation",

---

140   Galbraith seems to have been exaggerating his friendships in high places: Lady Pamela Huntly's father was in fact another press magnate, Lord Kemsley.

141   Incredibly, files in the National Archives contain original copies of Vassall and Galbraith's correspondence, the original typed copy of Vassall's confession and a host of secret security reports.

"narcissistic"– a common euphemism for homosexual – and that there was "almost certainly impropriety involved".[142]

The press would still sometimes hush up stories about politicians' infidelities and sexuality in the 1960s.[143] The exploits of the bisexual Conservative MP Bob Boothby were suppressed for decades: when the *Sunday Mirror* reported his association with the Kray twins and other underworld figures in 1964, the paper was forced to apologise, sack its editor and pay Boothby £40,000 in an out-of-court settlement.[144] It was only after Boothby's death in 1986 that an even more explosive story came to light; that Boothby had conducted an affair with Macmillan's wife, Dorothy, for several decades until her death in 1966.[145] Boothby may well have been the father of the Macmillans' daughter Sarah, born in 1930 As he pondered whether to fire Tam Galbraith in November 1962, Macmillan must have had his own sexual secret at the back of his mind.

Had circumstances been slightly different Galbraith might well have survived. But his Conservative colleagues now deserted him. On 2 October Macmillan had been reassured by officials that Galbraith's letters were "in every respect wholly innocuous. There is no question of them being put in evidence … and I do not think you need have the slightest anxiety about them". But after they were printed in newspapers, Macmillan became very anxious indeed. It was quickly agreed "that it would be appropriate for Mr Galbraith to offer his resignation and for the Prime Minister to consider on [*sic*] the following morning".

---

142 Deedes's biographer Stephen Robinson has defended him, arguing that Deedes simply wanted to "not rock the boat". Eventually, in 2004, Deedes himself made a sort of apology, conceding that Galbraith's conduct had "in the end … all turned out to be innocent. I made a mistake".

143 The Labour MP Tom Driberg's voracious sexual appetite was widely known in Westminster and Fleet Street but it only came to light publicly when his memoirs were released posthumously in 1977. During his lifetime Lord Beaverbrook and others had refused to publish them (apparently on the orders of MI5, for whom Driberg worked).

144 Boothby was fluent in Russian and regularly visited Russia and Eastern Europe in the 1950s and 1960s, where his sexual appetites left him open to blackmail.

145 The affair had started in 1929, an *annus horribilis* for Macmillan in which he lost both his Stockton-on-Tees seat, and his wife.

As Galbraith's resignation letter was drafted, Macmillan's parliamentary private secretary, Knox Cunningham, served whisky and sodas to all. Lord Carrington was then called in, Deedes recalls, and was "all things considered … in remarkably good humour". As well he might: Galbraith's departure would help to stifle the calls for his own resignation. At 9 p.m. Bligh, Woodfield, Redmayne and Deedes went for a "grisly" supper of oysters at Overton's, a restaurant in St James's, where they made minor changes to the letter that Macmillan had dictated. Redmayne hand-delivered the text to Galbraith's home on Cowley Street shortly after ten.

On the morning of 8 November the press lay in wait outside Galbraith's house and applied yet more pressure. As well as printing additional details of Galbraith's correspondence with Vassall, courtesy of the previous day's white paper, the *Daily Express* ran a story by its chief crime reporter, Percy Hoskins, headlined: "Don't forget they knew for 18 months there was a spy around". Hoskins suggested that a huge cover-up had been underway since the unmasking of the Portland spies in January 1961. Inside the Krogers' bungalow (a "transmitting centre for an entire spy network"), the police had found a "highly secret document [which] had … never left the strong room of the Admiralty", so must have been supplied by another spy. "This one was inside the Admiralty. It was, as we now know, Vassall". Hoskins concluded that "the whole sordid story still needs a lot of explanation."

At 11 a.m. Galbraith signed his resignation letter at his desk at the Scottish Office and at 1 p.m. he arrived at Admiralty House for a "friendly chat" with Macmillan, during which their letters were exchanged.[146] "It is apparent to me that my accustomed manner of dealing with officials and others who serve me has in the circumstances become an embarrassment to you and the government,"

---

146   At least Macmillan met Galbraith face to face to receive his resignation; in Profumo's case it was done remotely, as Macmillan thought that Profumo might not want to speak to a man of nearly seventy about a sexual indiscretion with a woman easily young enough to be Macmillan's granddaughter.

wrote Galbraith, with some understatement. "For this reason alone I feel that my only proper course is to tender my resignation".

To allow Galbraith to retain some dignity, this correspondence contained several lies: that Galbraith was resigning voluntarily and that the Prime Minister would have preferred him to wait until Cunningham's committee had finished its work.

In his memoirs *At the End of the Day*, published in 1973, the wily Macmillan said that allowing Galbraith to resign – he never admitted sacking him – was one of his biggest political regrets. "On looking back … it was a mistake on my part to accept Galbraith's resignation at this stage," Macmillan recalled. "But he was very insistent". Macmillan argued that Galbraith had wanted to resign so he could pursue a libel action and "confound his enemies". Perhaps Macmillan did not want to embarrass Galbraith – who was still an MP in 1973 – by telling the truth: he had ordered Redmayne to sack him.

Harold Evans, Macmillan's press secretary (and no relation to the newspaper editor of the same name), later wrote that Galbraith had insisted on going. Some historians agree: Rebecca West claimed that Galbraith's resignation letter "showed a real desire to crawl away and lick his wounds". Redmayne was more honest, later recalling that Macmillan had reluctantly asked him to tell Galbraith that he had to go. "It was not my happiest moment. Nor were the wolves diverted for more than a moment," said Redmayne.

Exhausted by the Cuban missile crisis – he said that during its thirteen-day duration he was "scarcely sleeping more than one or two hours each night" – and in poor health, Macmillan had been cajoled into making Galbraith the sacrificial lamb. Why didn't he sack Lord Carrington, who had already been weakened by the Portland scandal the previous year? After all, Galbraith had not been an Admiralty minister since October 1959. Carrington, on the other hand, had been First Lord of the Admiralty ever since the reshuffle that had seen Galbraith moved to the Scottish Office. For more than half the time that Vassall had been spying in London, the Admiralty had been Carrington's responsibility and had nothing to do with Galbraith.

But Carrington was the great British political survivor of the second half of the twentieth century.[147] He was also a firm favourite of Macmillan – and many others. Macmillan's premiership was very much an extended "country house party", in which the views of his weekend hosts were deemed as important as public opinion or what the media said. On 5 November 1962 Macmillan wrote to Carrington saying that "if you had been a fly on the wall at Broadlands [Lord Mountbatten's residence] the last weekend you would have heard much to give you pleasure, satisfaction and confidence. Yours ever, H. M.". Sadly, Tam Galbraith did not have quite as many friends in high places. Within three days of Macmillan's letter he had been forced to resign, but Carrington survived.

Carrington himself always peddled the myth that Galbraith's resignation was voluntary, even though he had been at the crucial meeting where it was agreed that he had to be sacked. In his 1988 memoirs he claimed that he had offered to resign if his department had been found to be culpably negligent. "It didn't and I felt under no obligation to resign", he states matter-of-factly. Macmillan seemed to regard Carrington as his protégé and in return, Carrington idolised Macmillan. "He was personally so kind, wholly honourable and generous – he stuck his neck out through thick and

---

147　Carrington had entered the Lords in 1941, aged twenty-one, after the death of his father, the fifth Baron Carrington, in 1938. After serving as a tank commander during the Second World War he held ministerial office in the Churchill and Eden governments. He narrowly survived the Crichel Down affair, a now-forgotten 1954 scandal involving the compulsory purchase of 700 acres of farmland in Dorset. The minister responsible, Sir Thomas Dugdale, resigned, but while Carrington (Dugdale's junior) offered to resign as well, he was told to stay on. Carrington then served as British High Commissioner in Australia before arriving at the Admiralty in 1959. In October 1963 he stepped down as First Lord of the Admiralty and was demoted to be a mere Minister without Portfolio and Leader of the Lords until October 1964 when the Conservatives fell from power. From 1964 to 1970 he was Leader of the Opposition in the Lords. But his career then recovered: he served as Defence Secretary under Heath and as Foreign Secretary under Thatcher until his resignation after the invasion of the Falklands in April 1982. He then had yet another comeback, serving as Secretary-General of NATO from 1984 to 1988. He died in 2018, aged ninety-nine.

thin, and needn't have done so," purred Carrington, who is known to have referred to Macmillan as "Uncle Harold". In return, Macmillan viewed Carrington as "an honourable man in whose word he had absolute confidence".

Carrington regarded Galbraith as an object of pity, not admiration. "The wretched Galbraith, who may have been unduly tolerant of an ingratiating subordinate but was culpable of no more than that, felt that he couldn't carry on, and offered his resignation", he wrote.

Tam Galbraith's son has another explanation: the Labour front bench, and the media, were determined to see an MP resign, rather than a peer like Carrington. Galbraith, as the only Admiralty minister who had sat in the Commons from 1957 to 1959, had to be sacrificed.

One tabloid carried the painful headline "Exit – One Chump", while the *Daily Telegraph* said that Galbraith's resignation was "not obligatory but was plainly to be desired". Yet some broadsheets soon started showing him sympathy. On 11 November, the *Sunday Times* complained of the "most unedifying spectacle" of "a junior minister being sacrificed in a premature resignation before he had even had the chance to justify his conduct before a committee of enquiry". Even *The Observer*, which was normally critical of the Conservative government, said that Galbraith's role was "a minor aspect of a major scandal", the major aspect being the "Admiralty's continuing inability to distinguish Russian spies from Civil servants". Galbraith "has thrown himself gallantly, honourably and obligingly out of the sleigh and into the snow," wrote Mark Arnold-Forster, in a piece entitled "Macmillan shoots the wrong pianist". But by the autumn of 1962 it was tabloids, not broadsheets, that decided politicians' fates.

Everyone who has written about Tam Galbraith's resignation in the six decades since has concluded that he and Vassall did not have a sexual relationship of any kind. And no one has claimed that he was treated fairly. "A wholly innocent man had been destroyed by gossip and rumour", wrote Peter Rawlinson. Labour "had been cultivating innuendoes as assiduously as the Channel Islands cultivate new potatoes" in the run-up to Galbraith's resignation, Rebecca West argued, particularly through a sequence of sanctimonious speeches by George Brown ("a politician who often descended into the gutter", according to Patrick Higgins). Another Labour politician, Richard Crossman, confided in his diary that Brown's speeches, "hinting at queer goings-on in high places", made him "squirm with embarrassment".

Brown was not interested in exposing the Conservatives' hypocrisy and incompetence, but in exploiting the latent homophobia on both sides of the chamber for political advantage. Some claimed that Labour MPs with long memories were simply "getting their own back on the Conservatives", who in 1951 had vilified the Labour minister Hector McNeil for having employed Guy Burgess as his assistant private secretary.[148] Patrick Higgins has drawn parallels between the British Labour Party in the early 1960s and the McCarthyite wing of the American Republican party in the previous decade.[149]

"The Labour Party behaved far below its real intellectual and moral level," Rebecca West argued. She deplored the hypocrisy of Labour frontbenchers like Michael Foot, who immediately "set up a cry that Mr Macmillan was being very unkind to Mr Galbraith" after his resignation. Foot accused Macmillan of "being the most brazen McCarthy of the lot" and that his "capacity for hypocrisy staggers even me": a bit rich, given that for two weeks beforehand Labour had been calling, McCarthy-like, for Galbraith's head on a plate.

---

148   McNeil, who was Deputy Foreign Secretary under Ernest Bevin in the late 1940s and early 1950s, was unmarried and, some have argued, gay. In reality, McNeil probably did little more than save Burgess from dismissal for his frequently drunken behaviour.

149   This is a bold claim: as an American diplomat in London wrote in November 1962, "In the British political vocabulary there is no word lower than 'McCarthyism'".

Even the Labour MP George Wigg, who eagerly exposed the peccadillos of many Tory MPs, agreed that Galbraith was "a kind-hearted, rather inexperienced, junior minister of unimpeachable integrity". Vassall was "a rather simple fellow, Conservative in politics", who had been "victimised by [an] old-fashioned trick". Given that Chapman Pincher (the *Daily Express*'s longstanding defence correspondent) boasted that Wigg "for many years kept me informed almost on a daily basis" about goings-on in Whitehall and Westminster, this suggests that there was no substance in rumours that Galbraith and Vassall had been lovers.[150]

The chapter on Galbraith in Rebecca West's *The Vassall Affair* is aptly subtitled, "A Baffling Nightmare". She pointed out that his trivial correspondence with Vassall was of minuscule significance compared to the bribery and corruption that the Lynskey tribunal had uncovered a decade earlier.[151] Galbraith's "only fault had been to treat his clerk with a certain unworldly kindness". American observers agreed: "On such gossamer evidence as this, the press and the Opposition built a carnival of innuendo that forced Galbraith to resign", wrote David Wise and Thomas B. Ross. Galbraith had been forced out "on totally inadequate grounds, following a spate of nasty gossip", wrote Norman Shrapnel in 1978.

Tam Galbraith was a blameless man whose friendship with Vassall was purely platonic. With hindsight, it seems that his career was unjustly destroyed by a connection with Vassall that may have amounted to little more than a gay crush, unrequited by Galbraith. In his memoirs, Vassall specifically denied that he had ever had a sexual relationship with Galbraith and it seems that Vassall himself

---

150   George Wigg, a pre-war communist who had been an army colonel in the Second World War, was nominally Paymaster General in Wilson's government from 1964 onwards. But he had long been a "licensed rifler in Whitehall dustbins". Wigg's astute use of parliamentary procedure and his forensic intelligence (his "Wiggery pokery", some called it) played a key role in bringing about John Profumo's resignation. Although Wigg was supposedly Wilson's "eyes and ears" on the security services, he never seemed to establish what they were up to and he seemed to generate intrigue rather than end it.

151   The Lynskey tribunal of 1948 found that a junior trade minister in Attlee's government, John Belcher, and a director of the Bank of England, George Gibson, had received money for issuing licences and permissions and withdrawing prosecutions. Belcher was forced to resign, both as a minister and as an MP.

did not believe that Galbraith was gay. The closest equivalent to Galbraith's resignation is not that of Ian Harvey – who was undoubtedly gay – but that of the Labour Cabinet minister, John Strachey, who was forced from office in 1950 after a smear campaign by the Beaverbrook press insinuated that he had known the atomic spy Klaus Fuchs.

Galbraith was cleared, both by Sir Charles Cunningham's internal inquiry and by the Radcliffe tribunal, of having had any relationship with Vassall "that could constitute a security risk". Tam Galbraith was modern Britain's first victim of a tabloid 'sting' and the Vassall affair set the template for a litany of political resignations in the following six decades. If the Vassall scandal is comparable to the Profumo one, then Galbraith is its Stephen Ward: a decent but fallible man, guilty of nothing more than naïveté, who was hung out to dry.[152]

The early 1960s were a golden age for satirists and Galbraith was the butt of many jokes which endured for several months. The BBC television programme *That Was the Week That Was* started its thirteen-month run on 24 November 1962, five weeks after Vassall's conviction. In early 1963 the programme was quick to sink its teeth into the scandal. One sketch mocked Carrington's inability to pronounce his "Rs", while in another a civil servant (David Kernan) presents a draft letter to his superior (Lance Percival). The sketch emphasised the latent *double entendres* in phrases like "Thanking you in anticipation" and "Your obedient servant". It is then agreed that the letter should simply end with the writer's name, which turns out to be "Farey".[153]

---

152   Tam Galbraith was not the first minister to resign over gay sex, either real or imagined. There had been several homosexual scandals alongside the Ian Harvey case in 1958. In 1941, Sir Paul Latham, Conservative MP for Scarborough and Whitby, resigned after being accused of "improper conduct" with three gunners and a civilian. In 1953, William Field, Labour MP for North Paddington, was charged with "importuning men for an immoral purpose" at a public lavatory at Piccadilly Circus tube station. In 1973, two Conservative ministers, Lords Lambton and Jellicoe, were forced to resign after being found to have consorted with sex workers.

153   *That Was the Week That Was* was not homophobic. A more thoughtful sketch in early 1963 gently mocked homophobia by imagining that heterosexuality had been driven underground.

The other pillar of early 1960s satire, *Private Eye* magazine, began publication in October 1961. In March 1963 it ran a spoof of Gibbons's *The History of the Decline and Fall of the Roman Empire*, charting the many crises rocking Macmillan's government, including "clerks and eunuchs". Galbraith's name did not need to be mentioned: he was clearly the butt of all these jokes.

Galbraith's walk in the political wilderness was brief. On 3 May 1963 – eight days after his exoneration in the Radcliffe report – he returned to government as a joint parliamentary secretary at the Department of Transport. It was technically a sideways move from his previous job at the Scottish Office but it felt like a demotion. While Lord Radcliffe had scotched rumours of a homosexual cabal of communist spies in Whitehall, it wasn't enough to save Galbraith's political fortunes in the long term. Despite all the potential he had shown in the 1950s, he returned to the back benches after the Conservatives' defeat in 1964 and remained there until his death eighteen years later.

Although both Carrington and Galbraith had wanted to pursue libel actions against several newspapers in November 1962, they were persuaded to wait until the spring of 1963 to avoid creating more political embarrassment. Carrington and Galbraith hired an aggressive libel lawyer, Helenus "Buster" Milmo, to represent them at the Radcliffe inquiry's hearings.[154] Milmo had been used by MI5 to try to extract a confession from Kim Philby after the flight of Maclean and Burgess, but he was equally unsuccessful in winning damages for Carrington. Carrington told Macmillan that Milmo had advised him that at least three newspaper stories about him were "actionable" and he later claimed that he could have won between £100,000 and £150,000 (a huge sum in the early 1960s) from the *Daily Express*. But he didn't sue, as Macmillan said it would be unwise to antagonise the paper in the run-up to a general election.

---

154   Milmo is the maternal grandfather of the former Labour politician Chuka Umunna, who was briefly tipped as a potential party leader in the 2010s.

In May 1963, Carrington settled and Express Newspapers agreed to pay Milmo's legal costs, which were "seldom modest". But Galbraith pressed ahead with libel writs. In July 1965 both Beaverbrook and Associated Newspapers (publishers of the *Daily Sketch* and the *Mail* titles) offered him a "sincere and deep" apology and paid him undisclosed, but substantial, damages. Neither publisher would have paid any damages if they had been able to substantiate their stories.

At first, Galbraith and his wife put a brave face on things: their son recalls that in the mid-1960s they spent some of their libel settlement on a lengthy trip to the Far East and Australasia. Their son was told about his father's notoriety around 1970, when he was ten, before he left prep school and went to Wellington. Its worldly pupils were likely to ask if Strathclyde – whose name was then Thomas Galbraith, the same as his father – was related to *the* Thomas Galbraith. His father would sometimes talk about the Vassall affair, more in sorrow than in anger, but it was clear that he brooded over his thwarted ambitions and the devious sanctimony of many of his former friends.

Although Strathclyde insists that his father did not have a drink problem, as some have claimed, he accepts that the Vassall scandal was an important factor – though not the only one – in Simone's decision to divorce her husband in 1974. Jonathan Aitken, who entered Parliament as a Conservative MP in February 1974, recalls meeting Galbraith in the 1970s when they both attended a backbench Home Affairs committee, discussing the reform of Section 2 of the Official Secrets Act (OSA).[155] Aitken struck up a conversation with Galbraith, who was by then an angular man, polite but not cosy towards other MPs, Aitken recalls. When Aitken asked Galbraith about his own brush with the OSA and the security services in the wake of Vassall's trial, Galbraith "shifted uncomfortably in

---

155 Aitken was prosecuted in 1970 for passing a secret government report, about British arms sales to Nigeria, to the *Sunday Telegraph* and Hugh Fraser (a pro-Biafran Tory MP). At his Old Bailey trial all the defendants, including Aitken and the editor of the *Sunday Telegraph*, were acquitted. Vassall's barrister Jeremy Hutchinson QC was counsel for the *Daily Telegraph*.

his seat, and seemed to curl up", before lamenting that he had been "completely taken in by" Vassall. Galbraith still seemed to blame Vassall, rather than the press or his fellow ministers, for his political downfall.

Galbraith was always kind to his staff. But after ceasing to be a minister in 1964, he had few staff to be kind to. Backbench MPs had little administrative support in those days: his son recalls that after the 1979 election Galbraith shared one secretary with two other Conservative MPs. In late 1981, Galbraith was diagnosed with an inoperable brain tumour. In the 1982 New Year Honours List he was knighted "for Political and Public Service". He died on 2 January 1982, aged sixty-four, just two days after his knighthood was announced in *The London Gazette* , and before it could officially be conferred. The main consequence of his death was not reflection on his 1962 martyrdom, but the high-profile by-election to fill his Glasgow Hillhead seat.[156]

Galbraith's son believes his father's knighthood was the Thatcher government's way of making amends for Ted Heath's decision to overlook Galbraith for ministerial office. In those days it was more common for backbenchers to get knighthoods after twenty-five or thirty years' service, as long as they stayed out of trouble. Like many political careers, Galbraith's ended in failure. But his knighthood sent a powerful signal: if he had been "in trouble" in 1962 it was now acknowledged that it wasn't trouble of his own making, and that he had been unfairly ordered to resign.

•   •   •

John Vassall's arrest in September 1962 came at a politically awkward time, just as everyone was returning from summer holidays

---

156   In one of the biggest by-election upsets of post-war history, Hillhead, which had been held by the Conservatives since 1918, was won by Roy Jenkins, a former Labour Chancellor, Home Secretary and Foreign Secretary, who had defected to the newly-formed Social Democratic Party (SDP). Jenkins's victory brought him back to Parliament and he was the SDP's undisputed leader until the 1983 general election.

and in the run-up to the party conference season. Yet the fallout from Tam Galbraith's resignation was even more badly timed.

Many people assume that the wheels started to fall off Macmillan's government in 1963. In fact, it had already entered a serious crisis in early 1962. Although the Conservatives had won the 1959 general election with a majority of 100 seats, by 1962 Macmillan seemed old and unwell. After more than a decade of Conservative rule under three Prime Ministers – Churchill, Eden and Macmillan – many felt that its days were numbered. On 8 March 1962, a by-election in the marginal seat of Lincoln (which Labour held by 4,000 votes in 1959) was won by Labour's Dick Taverne with a majority of nearly 8,000.[157] On 14 March a by-election in Orpington, which the Conservatives held with a majority of almost 15,000 in 1959, was sensationally won by the Liberal Eric Lubbock with a majority of almost 8,000. July 1962 also saw the "Night of the Long Knives" when Macmillan sacked seven ministers including the Lord Chancellor, Lord Kilmuir (as David Maxwell Fyfe now was), who as Home Secretary had been fiercely opposed to any reform of the law on homosexuality.

Given this political turmoil, and his private angst about the Vassall affair, it is surprising that Macmillan, as Alistair Horne put it, "treated the matter unduly lightly" at first. His decision to set up Sir Charles Cunningham's committee to look at the security implications of Vassall's conviction, rather than a judicial inquiry, seemed ill-judged. From the start, Labour poured scorn on Macmillan's "extraordinary haste" in appointing a committee "within an hour or so of the end of a trial which lasted only one day," as Patrick Gordon Walker put it. His implication was clear: Macmillan wanted the matter swept under the carpet by "yes men" as quickly as possible. Cunningham's "Committee of Three" – Cunningham

---

157   The by-election was prompted by the resignation of the sitting MP Sir Geoffrey de Freitas to become High Commissioner to Ghana. From 1950 until 1961 De Freitas had lived in Dolphin Square at 906 Hood House, just one floor above Vassall.

himself, Sir Harold Kent (the Procurator-General and Treasury Solicitor) and Sir Burke Trend (the second secretary at the Treasury,
who would succeed Sir Norman Brook as Cabinet Secretary a few
months later) – was mocked as an "odd committee of civil servants". Gordon Walker claimed "it is extraordinary that the case is
being played down in this way".

By the time Galbraith resigned, Labour had tabled a censure
motion to be debated on 14 November, stating that "This House regrets the refusal of the Prime Minister, despite widespread and continuing public concern, to set up an independent enquiry into the
Vassall case". The government had planned to oppose the motion
and defend Cunningham's committee, but a dramatic development, just a few hours after Galbraith's resignation on 8 November,
prompted a change of mind. The government was informed that if
Vassall had not been arrested on 12 September he might have defected to the Soviet Union, with Tam Galbraith.

At the Conservative party conference at Llandudno, in the
second week of October, a young Conservative MP, Peter Tapsell,[158]
had met with the *Daily Sketch*'s political editor Nevill Boyd-
Maunsell (who used the byline Boyd Maunsell) and two Russians: a
journalist and a diplomat from the Russian embassy. Maunsell and
Tapsell had been at Oxford together and they met again in Westminster on 8 November, when Maunsell dropped a bombshell.
Over dinner, he told Tapsell that his paper's crime reporter had
learned from his "considerable" contacts in the police and security
services that Vassall had planned to join Galbraith on a holiday in
Italy, from where they were due to "Do a Pontecorvo"[159] – defect to
Russia together. An astonished Tapsell immediately told the Chief
Whip, who quickly told the Prime Minister.

It was indeed true that Vassall's planned holiday in Italy, from 15

---

[158] He was at the start of a very long career in the Commons: having first been elected in 1959, he lost his
seat in 1964 but he returned in 1966 and stayed there until 2015, becoming Father of the House.

[159] Bruno Pontecorvo, a British-Italian nuclear physicist, had defected to the Soviet Union while on a camp-
ing holiday in Italy in 1949.

to 29 September, would have overlapped with the Galbraiths' own Italian holiday. MI5 files reveal that Galbraith had originally planned to holiday on the French Riviera in late September, but he changed his mind on or before 11 September. On 22 September he and his wife went instead to Elba – an island some 500 miles from Capri, where Vassall would have been had he not been arrested ten days earlier. The official line was that this was coincidence, and indeed it almost certainly was. Vassall himself later told MI5 that the idea he would have met Galbraith in Italy, let alone defected to the Soviet Union with him, was "preposterous". But Vassall also told MI5 that had he known that the Galbraiths were in Italy at the same time "he would certainly have asked them to look him up" there.

Vassall had once sent a postcard to Galbraith from one of his Italian holidays, carrying the words "With memories of Italy", suggesting that the two men might have holidayed together in Italy previously. Vassall later told the Radcliffe inquiry that he'd only been referring to his own Italian memories and that he had never holidayed with Galbraith, in Italy or anywhere else. But the fact that Galbraith had arranged to be in Italy at the same time as Vassall did not help to stop the innuendo.

Intriguingly, unlike Geoffrey Bennett, Galbraith was not contacted by MI5 before Vassall's arrest. Instead, he was only approached on 14 September, two days afterwards. Galbraith was in Edinburgh on Scottish Office business at the time, but he agreed to speak to Charles Elwell when he was back in London. On Friday 21 September he invited Elwell to lunch at Cowley Street. Elwell recorded that "I thought that the luncheon table was not best suited for the business we would be discussing". The meeting was rescheduled for 6 p.m. that evening, but still at Galbraith's home.

Galbraith seems to have done all he could to distance himself from Vassall, telling Elwell that in spite of Vassall's innate kindness, "he had had a horrible time because of Vassall's inefficiency" as his clerk. He had been "rather irritated" by Vassall's vagueness about the kind of job he wanted when he sought careers advice a year before. Galbraith added that Vassall's trips to Barskimming were "really unnecessary", but as "Vassall seemed to have a passion for travelling up to Scotland by train, Galbraith felt that it would be unkind to deny him the opportunity of obtaining an Admiralty rail-pass." Mrs Galbraith told Elwell that "Vassall had become rather a bore by his repeated visits" but it had never occurred to her that he was a "*pederaste*".

Galbraith denied knowing anything about Vassall's planned holiday. But his resignation did not stop the torrent of feverish press speculation: far from it. It now looked like one paper was about to allege that not only was Galbraith Vassall's gay lover, but that they had been on the verge of defecting together.

The days between Galbraith's resignation on 8 November and the Commons debate on 14 November were filled with feverish activity. The panic was so great that a meeting was held at Admiralty House at 2.30 p.m. on Sunday 11 November, just after Macmillan paraded with the royals and other political leaders at the Remembrance Sunday ceremony at the Cenotaph. Deedes found Macmillan with Martin Redmayne and Iain Macleod in the drawing room, reading out a draft speech attacking the press that he intended to deliver in the Commons the following week. Macmillan had "plainly got the bit between his teeth" and seemed pleased to have found a way to meet Labour's demand for a judicial inquiry without looking weak.

As if to pre-empt the *Daily Sketch*'s explosive story, on 14 November Macmillan astonished the Commons by announcing that a *Daily Sketch* journalist "had been told by a member of the police, or the security service, he was not sure which, that had Vassall not been arrested on 12 September it had been his intention to join Mr Galbraith in Italy and that Vassall had intended to 'Do a Pontecorvo'. ... It was also said that my Honourable Friend the former Civil Lord was believed to have spent holidays with Vassall before".

It now suited Macmillan to repeat these incredible claims, to justify an inquiry which he hoped would bring the press into line. After weeks of resisting Labour pressure, Macmillan once again called Labour's bluff. Cunningham's committee would immediately suspend its work and pass the reins to a proper judicial tribunal, to be chaired by a Lord of Appeal, Viscount Cyril Radcliffe.[160]

By establishing a tribunal under a Law Lord, Macmillan could no longer be accused of brushing the affair under the carpet. But, Matthew Parris argues, at the same time he shrewdly added "a sting in the tail". He widened the terms of Radcliffe's inquiry to include the role of the press, rather than just the Admiralty's security failures.

Bill Deedes recalled that after the new tribunal was announced, "for the time being silence fell". The decision to begin an independent inquiry was "Belated, but right" according to *The Times*. But paranoia still stalked the corridors of Westminster, and Admiralty House. In a memo from 16 November, Redmayne recorded that the wife of John Tilney, Conservative MP for Liverpool Wavertree and a junior Foreign Office minister, had been told by her sister, a Mrs Kitto, about a stash of communist weapons.[161] Redmayne interpreted this as a fabrication, aimed at embroiling yet another "minister in a scandal". At the same time, there was no sign that foreign interest in Vassall was abating. Vassall's conviction had received a lot of coverage from American newspapers and on 19 November the British embassy in Washington told London that the *Sunday Pictorial* story was due to be syndicated in them.

In the short term, the electoral verdicts on the Vassall scandal were damning. On 22 November the Conservatives lost two by-elections in supposedly safe seats (South Dorset and Glasgow Woodside, adjacent to Galbraith's Hillhead seat). "Between the

---

160 Radcliffe's inquiry was set up under the Tribunals of Inquiry (Evidence) Act 1921, since repealed, that had been enacted in the wake of a First World War munitions scandal.

161 Mrs Kitto was, Redmayne noted, "not a very respectable character" who lived in Somerset with a group of "pacifists and extreme Socialists". She had boasted to her sister that she had seen an arsenal of rifles, submachine guns, pistols and ammunition in the basement of "what was called Communist Headquarters" in London.

sentencing of the wretched Vassall in October 1962 and the publication of the Radcliffe [report] the following April, Macmillan had
no peace on the security front; the procession of spies continued,"
Alistair Horne wrote. In December, yet another spy case came to
light. Barbara Fell, a 54-year-old woman working at the Central
Office of Information, was jailed for two years for having passed secrets to her lover, the press counsellor at the Yugoslavian embassy
in London. Rebecca West suggested that the Fell case was "far less
sinister" than Vassall's, simply because any sexual manipulation
was of the heterosexual kind. It was "tragic that it had meant ruin
for a human being considered far from mediocre by her friends,"
lamented West (by contrast she did not afford Vassall the same
sympathy, and seemed to consider him as an unreliable homosexual who should never have been hired by the Admiralty).

In his diaries Macmillan wrote that Fell had passed secrets to
her Yugoslavian lover "apparently in the somewhat naïve attempt
to convert him to the Western way of life". Macmillan rationalised that it was "an act of folly rather than treachery". But he was
clutching at straws. By the end of 1962 the dynamic Labour leader,
Hugh Gaitskell, was increasingly seen as a Prime Minister-in-
waiting, having won several bruising battles with the Labour left.
One Labour MP told Alistair Horne that while Macmillan was
"pretty frightening and devastating" in debates on the Vassall case,
"Hugh batted on this wicket absolutely brilliantly ... and turned
the issue away from the Opposition". It was, Horne conceded, "an
extraordinary political performance" by Gaitskell.

Paradoxically, although Gaitskell claimed much of the credit for
Macmillan's decision to set up the Radcliffe inquiry, by the time
its hearings began in earnest Gaitskell was dead, having suddenly
succumbed to lupus on 18 January 1963. Many had expected Macmillan to be succeeded by the considerably younger Gaitskell, but
Macmillan outlived Gaitskell by more than twenty years.

Gaitskell's death was a shock to everyone and if anything, it put the government in more peril in the midst of the Vassall crisis. The volatile George Brown became Labour's acting leader until its MPs had a chance to elect a permanent successor.[162] Brown may not have been a spy, but he was widely seen as a drunken troublemaker and a prolific leaker.[163] He now had a certain right to access security briefings and there were fears that anything Brown was told about the Vassall affair would be immediately leaked to the press.

The National Archives reveal that Brown was suspected of having had advance knowledge, in September and October 1962, of the letters between Vassall and Galbraith, and some even suspected that he somehow orchestrated their leaking to the press himself. Brown was on the *Pictorial*'s payroll as its "industrial adviser" and he had asked questions about Galbraith's letters before they began appearing in the *Pictorial*. As Radcliffe's inquiry was underway, the slim chance of the Conservative government and the Labour opposition forming a bipartisan consensus on security matters vanished entirely.

●   ●   ●

Viscount Cyril Radcliffe was a pillar of the establishment. He was born in 1899 and served as the Ministry of Information's Director General during the Second World War. After the war he chaired two boundary committees established after the Indian Independence Act and was responsible for drawing the borders of India and Pakistan, before becoming a Law Lord and a Reith lecturer in 1951. Throughout the 1950s and 1960s he was one of the British social elite who was repeatedly called upon to chair inquiries, write

---

162   There was clear relief that Brown's tenure as Leader of the Opposition was brief, and at Harold Wilson's election as his successor – defeating Brown – on 14 February. In April 1963 Wilson was briefed about the draft findings of the Radcliffe tribunal "under supervision" and without Brown present because, Tim Bligh explained in a note to Macmillan, "Mr Wilson entirely understands about Mr Brown".

163   In November 1962 Martin Redmayne briefed Tim Bligh that George Brown had, for the last decade, been given £2,000 a year, a house and a car from the *Daily Mirror*.

reports and generally extricate the government of the day from political crises.[164]

Confusingly, in the early 1960s, after the Blake case, Radcliffe had already chaired an inquiry into vetting. His first report, entitled "Security Procedures in the Public Service", was often referenced in discussions about the Vassall case.[165] It was published on 4 April 1962 – the very day that the British received word from the Americans that there was another suspected spy in the Admiralty.

When he first heard about Vassall's arrest, Macmillan thought that the fallout could be dealt with "without the ponderous machinery of an outside tribunal. After all, we had the Radcliffe structure with which to work": following the procedures that Radcliffe specified in his earlier report. But once it became obvious that a judicial inquiry had to be held, Radcliffe was the obvious choice to chair it.

It has been suggested that Cyril Radcliffe had homosexual experiences as a fellow of All Souls College, Oxford, in the 1920s, and that his brother had been imprisoned for homosexual offences. Leslie Rowse's unpublished *Private Lives of Fellows of All Souls* claimed that Radcliffe's "mastery, the impression of cool hard control, conceals a neurotic personality. To begin with, he is a homo; his brother went to prison for it. That helped to form a complex – he made every legal effort to get him off. (The young man was caught with a sailor on the sea-front at Dover)."[166] Rowse added that "In the middle of one night I was awakened by voices in the bedroom across from mine", occupied by the "highly self-conscious and mannered" Radcliffe.[167] "Next day it transpired that Godfrey

---

164 Radcliffe was not only called upon by Conservative governments: in 1967 Harold Wilson asked him to chair yet another inquiry, this time into a story by Chapman Pincher in the *Daily Express*, which claimed that MI5 were routinely reading commercial cables sent from Britain by foreign embassies and businesspeople.

165 Radcliffe's first security inquiry began its work in May 1961.

166 I am grateful to Richard Davenport-Hines for allowing me to see this manuscript.

167 Roger Makins, who was later the British ambassador in Washington who Vassall sent a "begging letter" to in 1953, lived on the same staircase at All Souls at the time.

Winn was Cyril's guest: they did not appear for breakfast, but breakfasted privately in Cyril's rooms".

While Cyril Radcliffe may have been sexually adventurous in his teens and twenties, he was now a judge in his sixties. Despite (or possibly because of) his own gay experiences, his inquiry did not offer any thoughts on the homophobic prejudice that Vassall faced from the media. Nor was his tribunal independent or impartial. Radcliffe and the two other members were carefully handpicked by Macmillan and his staff. The National Archives show that during the harsh winter of 1962–63 Radcliffe wrote lengthy letters to Macmillan, consulting him about his investigation's precise terms of reference.

Alongside Radcliffe sat a high court judge, Sir Patrick Barry, and Sir Edward Milner Holland QC. They were, like Radcliffe, undoubtedly great legal minds and Barry was known for his "no flogging" stance as Chairman of the Advisory Council on the Treatment of Offenders. But like Radcliffe (educated at Haileybury, New College, Oxford and then All Souls) they were both products of top public schools and Oxford University (Barry had gone to Downside, Sandhurst and Balliol College; Holland to Charterhouse and Hertford College, Oxford). Neither was likely to rock the establishment boat.

Their inquiry cannot be accused of being cursory or not talking to enough witnesses.[168] The tribunal was, to all intents and purposes, a court of law: it required witnesses to attend and testify on oath, and anyone who refused faced being accused of contempt. It saw notes on all the debriefing interviews that Charles Elwell of MI5 had so far had with Vassall. The tribunal sat for almost thirty days over a period of three months, questioned 142 witnesses

---

168   Radcliffe's terms of reference were, in theory, wide and very thorough: "(1) the allegations made that the presence of another spy inside the Admiralty was known to the First Lord and his service chiefs after the Portland case eighteen months ago; (2) any other allegations which have been or may be brought to their attention, reflecting similarly on the honour and integrity of persons, who, as Ministers, naval officers and civil servants, were concerned in the case; (3) any breaches of security arrangements which took place; and (4) any neglect of duty by persons directly or indirectly responsible for Vassall's employment and conduct, and for his being treated as suitable for employment on secret work."

and examined vast amounts of documentation. Many witness-es brought their own counsel, meaning that at least twenty-three barristers, ten of them QCs, trooped in and out of the tribunal's sittings. But two-thirds of these sittings were *in camera*, with the press and public excluded.

The inquiry got off to an unpromising start in November 1962. Its public hearings (including the first preliminary session on 21 No-vember) were held in the Board of Trade building on Horse Guards Parade (now part of HM Treasury). The building had been chosen because it had more than five entrances and witnesses could come and go without being ambushed by the press. While the building was huge, the chief conference room that hosted the hearings was so small that reporters overflowed into the forty seats reserved for the public. Public transparency and media scrutiny were never high priorities for Radcliffe.

The proceedings began in earnest in early January 1963 – just before Hugh Gaitskell's death. Another procedural problem soon became apparent: witnesses were often cross-examined by their own counsel, who were unaware of what had been said in previous sessions that had been held *in camera*, and this resulted in much duplication and wasted time.

Despite the galaxy of legal talent, the public hearings gener-ated more heat than light. One of their supposed highlights was Tam Galbraith's appearance on 17 January, and in particular his cross-examination by William Mars-Jones QC, who represented the *Express* titles. Galbraith's candour meant that he was slaugh-tered in the witness box by the merciless Mars-Jones.

"The closest thing I can get to a display of Dad's expertise as a barrister ... is the cross-examining of witnesses he did during the Vassall tribunal," his son, the writer Adam Mars-Jones, recalled.[169]

---

169   Later in 1963 Mars-Jones pulled off a remarkable legal victory when he represented a writer, Kevin Mc-Clory, who claimed that his work on a James Bond screenplay had been plagiarised by Ian Fleming in his novel *Thunderball*. After Mars-Jones's opening speech, which lasted a legendary twenty-eight hours and eight minutes, Fleming settled the case on humiliating terms.

Galbraith argued that there was no difference between the salutation "Dear Vassall" and "My dear Vassall" ("I am therefore going
to eliminate the word 'my' from my vocabulary", was Mars-Jones's
cutting riposte). Galbraith complained that newspaper reports of
his visit to Vassall at Dolphin Square had failed to mention that
his wife had been present. Mars-Jones asked him why he had not
told journalists that she had been, and Galbraith demurred. "But
you still have not answered the question. I have asked you twice.
Perhaps you will be third time lucky," said Mars-Jones. "I will try,"
responded Galbraith. Eventually, Mars-Jones said "That is not an
answer to my question, Mr Galbraith, but I am not going to ask
it again". Galbraith was later reminded that one *Express* title had
changed the wording of a story in a later edition after Galbraith
complained.

At this point, "Dad begins to treat him like a child," Adam Mars-
Jones observed. When Galbraith complained about the wording
of a headline, the QC asked "Do you know what the function of a
headline is?" "Dad could hardly go further in this line of calculated
humiliation if he told Galbraith to stand up straight or to take the
chewing gum out of his mouth" remembered Adam, who had presumably felt his father's wrath. When Galbraith asked Mars-Jones
to repeat a question, his disrespectful reply was "No I am sorry, Mr
Galbraith, but I will not". Even sixty years on, the contempt shown
by a barrister to a former minister is striking. But Mars-Jones's
cross-examination of Galbraith did not yield any new insights into
Vassall's espionage: instead it just seemed unnecessarily cruel.

Colonel Jack MacAfee, the Admiralty's Director of Security, testified that of the 140 enlargements found in Vassall's flat, 17 related
to documents that Vassall would have seen between 24 July and 3
September 1962 – the last day he is believed to have taken documents home. But this had already been aired at Vassall's trial.

Lord Carrington received a bad press in the wake of Vassall's conviction. When the *Daily Express* claimed that he had deliberately

concealed the presence of another spy in the Admiralty from Macmillan, Carrington viewed it as an "accusation of treason". Another paper ran a photograph of Carrington, wearing white tie and drinking at a restaurant that was hosting a Royal Naval Cinematography Association dinner, with the headline "Doesn't Lord Carrington Care?" Carrington's firm view that the press's blows were "well below the belt and entirely without factual justification" meant that he said almost nothing when he testified in front of Radcliffe on 1 February.[170] He said that he had first heard fears of another spy in the Admiralty on 4 April 1962 but he seemed to have shown a curious lack of concern about investigations after that. The first he knew about the spy being pinpointed was after Vassall's arrest, not before. As Richard Deacon put it, Carrington showed a "degree of complacency in high places".

When Roger Hollis, MI5's Director-General, appeared, he did so anonymously and anyone who recognised him was told to keep his name a secret. "The tall doors opened, an impressive figure walked in, and sat down in the witness chair and answered a few questions", Rebecca West reported. "Then he strode out, his anonymity undoubtedly making the spectacle more enjoyable". In the meantime Hollis had said little, but the Radcliffe inquiry began to drag MI5, whose existence was not officially confirmed until early 1963, into the public spotlight. Not long afterwards, on 23 April 1963, the *Daily Mail* ran a story about "Britain's Off-Beat Police" and identified its headquarters as "Leconsfield [*sic*] House, Curzon Street, Mayfair, London W", although it added "the name of their chief is never mentioned."[171]

---

170 Even in Carrington's memoirs, published twenty-five years later, his rage at having to testify at the tribunal was palpable: "The fact of Vassall's betrayal was odious, the misrepresentation and slanders were odious, and the protracted enquiry in a different way was odious".

171 The absurdity was that Hollis's name was in the public domain: the OBE he received at the end of the war, his Companionship of the Bath in 1956 and his knighthood of 1960 were all officially reported, and on the latter occasion *The Times* said that Hollis was "Attached War Office". When he retired, Hollis, "lately attached to the Ministry of Defence", was given a KBE. Chapman Pincher wrote sarcastically in the *Daily Express*, "His identity is known to every foreign agent worth his keep. His name will be banded about today in a score of London clubs ... *Who's Who* reveals his suburban address ... his telephone number is in the London directory. Yet his identity is a secret."

The Portland spy Harry Houghton appeared, gloating that MI5 had turned down his offer of help to hunt down further spies, as they were unwilling to guarantee him a reduced prison sentence in return; Houghton said he would only tell all if he and Ethel Gee were released. Charles Elwell later told the tribunal, "It is never worth asking a liar for information you cannot check". Houghton provided some amusement, but rather than expose Vassall's espionage he made himself look like even more of a crook. Nor did Chapman Pincher reveal anything about the Russian defectors who had helped to identify Vassall. When asked how he had found out about them, Pincher said he had been told by Colonel Lohan. He then boasted that he had received letters of thanks from the heads of both MI5 and MI6, in return for his co-operation. This seems to have been a subtle reminder to Radcliffe to back off. "I later learned that Hollis and Radcliffe had ensured that I would not be pressed ... into revealing any more details about that defector – Golitsin [sic] – who was then secretly in Britain", Pincher later admitted.

On 8 February one of Vassall's fellow Admiralty clerks, Patrick Delahunty, told the tribunal that he had sometimes referred to Vassall as "Miss". Two acquaintances said that Delahunty had told them soon after Vassall's arrest that he had been known as "Miss Vassall" in the office. Again, this shed no light at all on Vassall's espionage, but neither did Vassall's own testimony.

John Vassall had naively high expectations of the Radcliffe tribunal. He seems to have been fixated upon Hugh Gaitskell, to whom he was grateful "for pursuing the background to the case". Vassall somehow believed that Gaitskell had successfully demanded Radcliffe's inquiry as an act of charity towards him. "A friend came to tell me that it was Mr Gaitskell, Leader of the Opposition, who was not satisfied with the way that I had been put away without the public or Parliament knowing what had happened," he wrote in his memoirs. "In the end Mr Macmillan, the Prime Minister, was forced into setting up a tribunal". This shows two misapprehensions:

firstly, that Gaitskell had pushed for an inquiry out of concern for Vassall's welfare, rather than raw politics. Secondly, that Macmillan was forced into setting it up against his will. In fact, Macmillan had deliberately designed it to suit his own ends.

Vassall's appearance at the tribunal, on 29 January 1963, was *in camera*. He was pleased that no one was wearing wigs and gowns, as at the Old Bailey. He was warned that there was a "rather intense woman journalist ... wearing a dark brown outfit" in the room (almost certainly Rebecca West), and that "I must not be put off by her when I entered". In fact, for once, West seemed impressed by Vassall. "Vassall in the witness box was neither timid nor ladyish, but dignified and even formidable," she observed. "In his pale, neat slenderness he recalled a polished flint arrowhead". Vassall even kept his composure when he testified in front of Tam Galbraith, who was sat next to his counsel, Milmo, "looking at me but not wishing to be noticed by me".

Vassall had no chance to play games like Harry Houghton had. The first question he faced – "It has been suggested that it was your perverted appetite that led you to that initial disastrous party in Moscow?" – showed that the inquiry was not an opportunity for him to tell his side of the story. Vassall replied that the party had been a "trap that I could see no way of getting out of" but little else was said about his entrapment or his espionage. Vassall admitted that he had "conceived an admiration" for Galbraith, but he insisted that there was no indication that Galbraith felt a "physical homosexual attraction" towards him, and that they had never been physically affectionate or discussed sexual matters. In the absence of any evidence of a conspiracy to protect Vassall, the tribunal now looked like an inquiry into Vassall's sex life. Most of the questions Vassall faced were about his cross-dressing.

Women's girdles had been found in Vassall's wardrobes (alongside fourteen suits, including one from Harrods which had cost £35). By 5 November 1962, MI5 knew that Vassall had once spent

£30 at Woollands on women's dresses and bras.[172] At Radcliffe's tribunal Vassall admitted that he had purchased a girdle, a slip, a brassiere and a pair of stockings at Woollands. He insisted however that he only wore the items in his flat, at the request of a Mr North or other friends during parties, and that he never wore women's "outer garments". Vassall was a cross-dresser, but it appeared that he only wore women's underwear at home and not on the streets of London or in the office, as some claimed.

Vassall's request for the tribunal to meet his legal costs, as other witnesses' costs had been, was predictably refused. But he was whisked to and from the inquiry in an official car, arriving in the underground garage of the Ministry of Defence building. He never wanted to return to Whitehall again as it "had such bad memories". In a Board of Trade waiting room he bumped into an officer from naval intelligence. They recognised each other but the officer "left immediately, fearing, I suppose, that he might be contaminated in some way", Vassall recalled.

● ● ●

If nothing else, at least the Radcliffe tribunal found that many of the newspapers' more improbable claims about Vassall were base-less. One of the most poignant moments was when it was revealed how Vassall's warm relationship with his cleaning ladies had been destroyed. Doris Murray, Vassall's cleaning lady until March 1962, lived on Colchester Street, very near Dolphin Square.[173] Even after Mrs Murray handed the job to her daughter-in-law, Pamela Hickey, she stayed on good terms with Vassall. He once took Murray out to dinner and then to the Talk of the Town nightclub at the Hippo-drome. Mrs Murray still exercised her Pekingese dog in Dolphin

---

172   Woolland Brothers was a Victorian department store next to Harvey Nichols in Knightsbridge. It closed in 1967 and was demolished in 1969 when it was replaced by the Sheraton Park Tower Hotel.
173   Colchester Street no longer exists. It was demolished later in the 1960s for the construction of Pimlico School.

Square's gardens and Vassall would often ask her into his flat when he saw here there. Soon after his arrest she visited him in Brixton prison.

Vassall also got on well with Mrs Hickey: MI5's files reveal that on 23 August 1962 he left her a cheerful note wishing her a "happy holiday with lots of sunshine" and asking for her advice on house-plants. In an undated note in the week before his arrest, he informed Hickey that "last weekend in Norfolk was wonderful" and invited her to call in for a drink on Friday evening.

After Vassall's conviction, Murray and Hickey were quoted in several newspaper stories. Murray suggested that Vassall had told them that he had once stayed overnight at Galbraith's Scottish estate, that he and Galbraith had travelled around Scotland and stayed together on the Isle of Arran and at Fort William, and that the two men dined together in Chelsea. She also claimed that Galbraith was a regular visitor to Vassall's flat, unaccompanied by his wife, and that she had once seen them enter the bedroom together and emerge from it fifteen minutes later.[174] Murray told journalists that Vassall had clearly idolised Galbraith and that his flat contained a silver-framed photograph of him, which allowed, as Patrick Higgins has put it, "those he knew to believe that they were tied together by more than red tape".[175] She added that Vassall boasted that he had covered his neighbours' front-door spyhole with a newspaper when he had visitors.

But in early October 1962, Murray and Hickey told MI5 that they couldn't "shed any new light on Vassall's background, habits or associates" – and that they had not even known he worked at

---

174 Vassall told the tribunal that he had once gone into his bedroom for fifteen minutes while Mrs Murray was in his flat. He said he could not remember who it was with – possibly his friends Galdi, Webb or Williams – though it certainly was not Tam Galbraith.

175 Vassall had several framed photos in his flat. They were trophies of the important men he had worked with or met, including one of Rear Admiral King, who his parents knew, and a photo of Captain and Mrs Bennett. Galbraith's was not a studio photograph, as some claimed, but a newspaper shot of the minister shaking the hand of a naval captain in Northern Ireland. Newspapers claimed that Vassall had put it on a desk, a chest of drawers or a dresser, but Vassall himself said that it was on a "gateleg table".

the Admiralty. When Murray appeared at Radcliffe's hearing she admitted that she did not know what Galbraith looked like, rendering her claim that she had seen the minister disappear into Vassall's bedroom completely worthless.

It soon became apparent that comments attributed to Hickey had simply been invented by a *Daily Sketch* journalist called Duffy; Hickey said that all she had told reporters was that Vassall sometimes visited Scotland. Murray, meanwhile, was forced to admit that she had fabricated stories, having received a "very considerable amount of money", and had been pressed by "persistent and carefully directed" questioning by John Vass (from the *Daily Express*) and others. It later emerged that some journalists may have posed as police officers to gain titbits of information from Murray and Hickey. Radcliffe's report later said that Murray and Hickey "gave their evidence … in a positive and responsible fashion", but both were, in fact, exposed as either serial liars or pathetic victims of press entrapment.

Many newspapers had run stories about the recent murder of a victualling supplies clerk at the Admiralty, Norman Rickard, who was roughly the same age as Vassall. In February 1962 Rickard's body had been found bound and upside down inside a cupboard in his basement flat on Elgin Avenue, Maida Vale, after he had been missing from duty for a week. A few days later, a 23-year-old "television studio wardrobe boy", Alan Vigar, was found dead in similar circumstances at his flat near Dolphin Square. Their murderer was dubbed "the wardrobe killer" because both bodies had been found stuffed into wardrobes. Both men had been "indulging in sexual practices" at the time of their death, inquests later found.

The *News of the World* described Rickard and Vigar as two men "who lived in the twilight world of the homosexual and … died in the garroter's noose". Vigar was a "slim pretty boy with a weak chest and theatrical ambitions", while Rickard was "a muscle man with a background of civil service respectability". More seriously, the *News*

of the World alleged that Rickard had been recruited as an informer by MI5, to keep an eye on homosexuals in the Admiralty, and
that he had been on Vassall's trail until his death. A *Mirror* journalist, Roy East, alleged that Vassall had known both Rickard and
Vigar, and that they were all regulars at the Alibi club on Berwick
Street in Soho. These stories overlooked the inconvenient truth that
Rickard was killed two months before anyone at the Admiralty had
suspicions about Vassall, but their implication was clear: Rickard
and Vigar had been murdered by Vassall, or on his instructions,
to silence them. Jack Murray, proprietor of both the Alibi and the
Music Box club on Panton Street, testified at the Radcliffe inquiry
that he had never seen Vassall, Rickard and Vigar on his premises,
either separately or together.[176]

These false stories needed to be corrected. But, by the end of its
hearings, the inquiry had become a useful way for the government
to settle scores with the press, and it overreached. Tam Galbraith
was not the only man to feel righteous indignation by the time that
the Radcliffe report was published. In February 1963, while Radcliffe was still in session, two reporters – the *Daily Mail*'s Brendan
Mulholland and the *Daily Sketch*'s Reginald Foster – were jailed for
refusing to reveal their sources for stories they had written about
Vassall. A third only escaped imprisonment by the skin of his teeth.

Brendan Mulholland was in his late twenties and had bylines on
many of the *Daily Mail*'s stories about Vassall. He was one of the
reporters who had doorstepped Tam Galbraith at Barskimming.
Mulholland said he had lost his notebook from the interview,

---

176 MI5's files reveal that Jack Murray told them in January 1963 that he had never seen either man at the
club, though he had told Roy East that Rickard was a member of the Alibi. MI5 noted, however, that
Murray had been "thrown out of Tangier after trying to set up a pederasts' brothel there" and was "a
boaster, myth-maker and a straightforward liar". As Murray was denying everything to MI5's source, one
of the Alibi's customers (a 35-year-old called Jimmy, a "Fleet Street photographer of sorts" who had a line
in blackmail) shouted out, "That was rubbish what they denied at the Tribunal about Rickard. I happen
to know he was murdered by a Russian agent because he was working for the Government. I was told it
by a member of MI5".

though his account of it was corroborated by a *Daily Telegraph* reporter, Harry Miller.[177]

On 5 November Mulholland had written a story alleging that Vassall had had a "protector", a "well-established Admiralty official, who was now retired" and a "man who was to figure prominently in his career at the Admiralty" (Mulholland told the tribunal that the unnamed "protector" in his story was W. R. Lewin, the former Monmouth School headmaster who had subsequently become an Admiralty civil servant).

It was another more frivolous story – claiming that Vassall's office nickname had been "Auntie" and that a female clerk had said that no one could live as Vassall did on a salary of £14 a week – that landed Mulholland in trouble. He refused to reveal his sources, although he implied that some were estate workers at Barskimming.

Reg Foster was a much older Fleet Street legend, originally from Dublin, who had scooped the world by breaking news of the Crystal Palace fire in 1936 (Foster was known as "Fireman Foster" after he wrote about many more big fires).[178] By 1962 he was a freelancer working with a team of six reporters, led by Louis Kirby, at the *Daily Sketch*.

When Foster testified at the Radcliffe tribunal on 15 and 16 January 1963 he admitted that his sources had only told him that Vassall had "bought women's clothing in the West End" but his paper had reported that Vassall "sometimes wore [not purchased] women's clothing on West End trips". Like Mulholland, Foster refused to reveal his sources, one of whom was an Oxford Street shop assistant whose name he didn't even know. When John Donaldson QC, the counsel for the tribunal, made a series of explicit threats that

---

177 Mulholland claimed to have interviewed Galbraith for half an hour, but Galbraith said that they had a frosty interview at Barskimming that lasted five minutes.

178 Foster reported on two of the biggest murder cases of the 1940s and 1950s (the "Acid Bath murderer", John Haigh and the Ten Rillington Place murderer, John Christie) and about the Derek Bentley trial of 1952 (at which Lord Goddard had notoriously sent Bentley to the gallows even though he had not fired the gun which killed a police officer, but had made the ambiguous statement "Let him have it" to the man who did).

Foster could go to jail if he did not reveal them, Foster held firm and the tribunal entered the realm of the surreal.

Foster produced a witness to bolster his claim that Vassall was a cross-dresser. A woman named Ivy Pugh-Pugh, who lived in Herne Bay, Kent, had come forward when she read in the *Sketch* that Foster might face jail. In an *in camera* session on 30 January, Pugh-Pugh testified that during the war she had been married to a former army colonel, working in the theatre, who introduced her to John Vassall in 1944 or 1945. Colonel Pugh-Pugh had revealed himself as a cross-dresser early on in their marriage. They had thrown cocktail parties attended by "gentlemen dressed as ladies". One of them was Vassall, who they knew as "Brenda". After the colonel's death in 1958 Mrs Pugh-Pugh had sold his effects via a personal advertisement in *The Times*, using the pseudonym Major Duval.[179] Vassall had bought the colonel's pink satin corset, while an album of erotic photographs was purchased by a "well-known" man living in Bude, Cornwall. Mrs Pugh-Pugh even produced a handwritten sales note, saying that she had received £5 from Vassall. But Mrs Pugh-Pugh had not contacted the *Sketch* previously and her evidence was not enough to keep Foster out of jail.

A third reporter, Foster's *Sketch* colleague, Desmond Clough, had written less frivolous stories claiming that Soviet surveillance ships disguised themselves as fishing trawlers. Thanks to Vassall's espionage, "Russian trawler fleets managed to turn up with uncanny accuracy in the precise area and on the right date for secret NATO sea exercises". Like the others, Clough refused to reveal his source.

Clough's report could be said to have divulged official secrets but Mulholland and Foster's stories certainly couldn't. Nonetheless, with brutal speed, all three reporters were sent to the High Court to be charged with contempt of court. Clough was sentenced to six

---

179   Such an advert never appeared in *The Times* in 1958. The only comparable one appeared in July 1947, more than a decade earlier, Jeff Hulbert's sleuthing has discovered.

months' imprisonment by Lord Parker, the Lord Chief Justice who had sentenced Vassall four months earlier. Clough only escaped jail after an Admiralty press officer, Neville Taylor, came forward as his source at the end of January, just in the nick of time.[180] On 4 February the high court judge Sir William Gorman (who had previously sentenced the "A6 murderer" James Hanratty to death and jailed the spy Barbara Fell) sent the other two to jail. Despite Foster's fame he was sentenced to three months in Brixton prison – where Vassall had recently been incarcerated – while Mulholland was sentenced to six.

Mulholland and Foster's appeals failed and they were refused leave to appeal to the House of Lords. Although they got out of jail early – Foster was released on 7 May 1963 after thirty-one days and Mulholland on 6 July after ninety days – this did not reduce the press's fury. Their imprisonment had "left Fleet Street seething with anger", Paul Johnson wrote in the *New Statesman*. "It was hitherto unknown for a court to rule that a journalist had no immunity from answering questions on the sources of his information unless, say, the Official Secrets Act had been breached", Richard Deacon explained.

In fact, despite Fleet Street's fury, the three reporters had probably made up the majority of their stories, particularly those about Vassall wearing women's clothing around London and spending evenings "in the West End haunts of perverts". Even Bernard Levin, normally an advocate for a free press, said that at the tribunal's hearings "the press witnesses cut … a poor figure, as, one after the other, they turned out to have got most of what they printed by taking previously printed articles and repeating them with embellishments". 'Churnalism' is nothing new. The press had built "a tower of innuendo on a foundation of rumour and label[led] the result a house of fact", Levin argued.

---

180 It turned out that Taylor had only said that it was possible that Vassall's treachery helped Russian trawlers to track NATO sea exercises, not that it was a certainty. Had Taylor not revealed himself as his source, Clough would have probably joined Mulholland and Foster in jail.

"A great deal of the tribunal's time was spent shooting down the critics", said Richard Deacon. Rather than deflect blame for the Vassall affair away from the government, their harsh treatment of Fleet Street's finest was a miscalculation and immediately backfired. "Such is the path to dictatorship", pontificated the *Daily Sketch*. A leader in *The Times* even argued that it was time for Macmillan to go: "only a change of Prime Minister will persuade people that they are looking at a new ministry". Alistair Horne said that from March 1963 onwards, "open war was declared" between Macmillan and the media.

The perceived injustice of the two reporters' imprisonment provided one motive for the press's dogged pursuit of the Macmillan government over the ensuing Profumo scandal: revenge. Indeed, Mulholland and Foster's appeal against their conviction was rejected on 6 March 1963, just as the first hints about Profumo began to appear.

Foster and Mulholland were soon dubbed the "silent reporters". The National Union of Journalists lobbied twenty-eight MPs and 500 people attended a rally to demand their release. To this day they are regarded as martyrs for being the last journalists sent to jail in Britain for refusing to reveal their sources.[181] Whatever the accuracy of their stories, they were the victims of arbitrary, rough justice. Other reporters who wrote much more inaccurate and homophobic stories were spared punishment.

The journalist who had most annoyed Peter Carrington was not Foster and Mulholland but the *Daily Express*'s Percy Hoskins, who claimed that Carrington had done nothing about reports of another spy lingering in the Admiralty after the Portland spy case.

---

181   There had been few cases of imprisonment for refusal to disclose sources in the decades before the Radcliffe tribunal. In 1933 the writer Compton Mackenzie was tried under the Official Secrets Act after his book, *Greek Memories*, revealed details of his intelligence work in Athens during the First World War. In 1958, two reporters for the Oxford student magazine, *Isis*, were jailed for breaching the Official Secrets Act. Richard Thompson and William Miller had published an edition of *Isis* devoted to the subject of nuclear weapons, their devastating effects and the strong possibility of "nuclear accidents", including earnest articles on "The Moral Responsibility" to disarm.

At the Radcliffe tribunal William Mars-Jones had to formally with-draw Hoskins's allegation but Hoskins himself was not pressed for his source and he escaped unpunished. Norman Lucas also escaped prosecution, even though he had probably written more lies about Vassall than anyone. Not for the last time, reporters were scapegoated while the editors and proprietors who had encouraged them to write their salacious stories got off scot-free. Not once were proprietors required to give evidence, even though Cecil King (the chairman of Daily Mirror Newspapers, which owned the *Sunday Pictorial*) had offered to.

Macmillan never expressed any regret over the jailing of Mulhol-land and Foster. Ten years on he wrote of his fury at the "incipient McCarthyism of the press in their pursuit of Galbraith, and their sanctimoniousness by insisting on 'full protection of their sourc-es'", which Macmillan likened to "claim[ing] the privilege of the priesthood". Macmillan had barely disguised his wish that Radcliffe should get even with the press: according to *The Observer*'s Alan Watkins, he was heard to say during the tribunal, "Now we'll get the journalists". In Parliament, shockingly few MPs championed the freedom of the press. Even Ian Gilmour, a former editor of *The Spectator*, made a spirited attack on the press in his maiden speech.[182] No one in Westminster seemed to consider that the press's worst sin had not been inventiveness, but homophobia, and that even if reporters had misbehaved no democracy should jail them for refusing to reveal their sources.

"The Vassall Tribunal was Britain's mirror image of the Stalin-era show trial", argued Adam Mars-Jones: "not a charade of manufac-tured guilt but a masque of questionable innocence". On 18 January 1963, the actor Kenneth Williams wrote in his diary "The papers are full of this Vassall enquiry. The reporters giving evidence all talk about homosexual intrigue & hint at dark secrets in high places.

182　Gilmour had just arrived in Parliament after winning a by-election in Central Norfolk on 22 November 1962.

All the muck raking is going on [*sic*]. ... Had the government acted on the findings of the Wolfenden report, this whole nasty episode would have never occurred".[183] It is difficult to disagree with Williams. But the question of whether homosexual acts should be decriminalised, to reduce the risk of future Vassalls being entrapped, never arose at the tribunal.

Labour's irresponsible muckraking about Tam Galbraith was never properly exposed. Although Hugh Gaitskell died before the tribunal had barely begun, he had craftily asked Radcliffe in November 1962 (on the advice of Arnold Goodman and Gerald Gardiner) to allow the Labour Party to be represented by counsel throughout its hearings. When Radcliffe predictably refused the request, because Labour was not an "interested party", it only bolstered Labour's argument that the tribunal was a stitch-up by the Conservative government.

Worst of all, John Vassall himself was not given the chance to explain how he had been betrayed by the homophobic press, and particularly by the *Sunday Pictorial*, which repeatedly distorted the truth and printed Galbraith's private letters to him without his prior knowledge or consent. A handwritten draft of his comments to Lord Radcliffe in the National Archives shows that Vassall gave him the names of the two MPs he had befriended in 1961, and details of his relationship with them. But unlike Galbraith, their names were not mentioned in Radcliffe's report or in the press.

Viscount Radcliffe's report was published on 25 April 1963. Harold Macmillan's memoirs later revealed that Radcliffe had shown the Prime Minister a first draft in early April. It was certainly not an independent report, as Macmillan had the final say on what it contained.

The report scotched any hint of official incompetence in the

---

183   Williams is now mostly remembered for his appearances in the *Carry On* films, but in the early 1960s he was also a satirical performer who regularly appeared on *That Was the Week That Was*. His diaries are mostly concerned with showbusiness gossip, but they occasionally comment on political events.

failure to catch Vassall sooner, and both Galbraith and Carrington were exonerated. Rather than sinning, the two ministers had been sinned against. Carrington had been "grossly slandered" by the press. Far from having a sexual relationship with a spy or turning a blind eye to his spying, Galbraith was "not remiss in failing to suspect from his knowledge of Vassall that the latter was a security risk". Galbraith had no reason to disbelieve Vassall's claim that he could afford his lavish lifestyle at Dolphin Square because he had inherited money from a relative.

While this was arguably a fair judgement of Galbraith, the report also asserted that there had been no security failures further down the Admiralty food chain. Radcliffe said that Vassall had only come under suspicion in June 1962 (in fact, Vassall had probably been on a "long list" of suspects before then). "No criticism can be made of the Admiralty, or of the Security Service, for the fact that this arduous and delicate task of identification took about five months to complete", Radcliffe concluded.

"Key control was also less than adequate". Many cupboards in the Military Branch were "suite cupboards, operated by common keys", Radcliffe found. Vassall had his own suite key and classified documents were not segregated and kept in cupboards with "detector or combination locks". But despite all these obvious failings, Radcliffe concluded that "There are no reasonable security arrangements which by themselves could have resulted in Vassall being detected as a spy, nor … did any failure in the security arrangements that were in force within the Admiralty result in Vassall's espionage activities being more extensive or more fruitful than they might otherwise have been".

Of the seventeen points in the "summary of findings" at the end of Radcliffe's report, only three contained criticism of the civil service. Like Lord Denning's report on Profumo, published five months later, Radcliffe found a convenient scapegoat: a recently deceased civil servant, H. V. Pennells, who had been "remiss and lacking in judgement" in approving Vassall's appointment to Moscow in 1954.[184] Vassall had not been positively vetted until late 1956. That he had passed this process was, Radcliffe concluded, a "disquieting thought". But living Admiralty staff who were involved in Vassall's career progression conveniently forgot precise details and were spared censure.

While senior civil servants and ministers were insulated from blame, the British embassy in Moscow was only mildly criticised. From December 1955 onwards, Sigmund Mikhailsky had been "under special rather than general suspicion". He was not dismissed because the embassy feared that "he would only be followed in due course by a successor no less under Russian control". Staff morale seemed to have trumped national security: "They [the embassy] would be unlikely to get another man as useful and obliging as he had been in serving the needs of the staff." British diplomats were "beleaguered forces under a constant and insidious attack": not just from sexual blackmail, but currency offences and black-market operations. But on the question of who was to blame for Mikhailsky not being fired earlier, Radcliffe concluded that the "evidence is not precise enough to enable responsibility to be allocated more closely".

Radcliffe found that Vassall had reported none of his social connections with Russians to the embassy, as he should have done. But Vassall himself had told the tribunal that he couldn't recall being given this instruction until August 1955, nine months after he had first been compromised. A "girl typist" who arrived in Moscow in November 1955 had said that the warnings to steer clear of being compromised by Russians were "very general and rather hurried". But Radcliffe blithely ruled that Vassall's memory must be faulty and that "briefing arrangements were adequately carried out".

The report contained several homophobic descriptions of Vassall.

---

184   Pennells's daughter, Brenda Boyce, told Reuters that her late father was "made a scapegoat because he's dead" and vowed, "They are not going to get away with it". But the criticisms were never withdrawn.

Radcliffe concluded that he was "a bit of a miss" and a "somewhat insinuating young man" with an "insistent cultivation of social contacts", who had bombarded Galbraith with invitations to "come and see his new possession" – his Dolphin Square flat (Radcliffe concluded that Galbraith had only visited it once, in autumn 1959, not after Vassall's mother's death in 1960).

Six months after a trial in which Vassall had been described as an industrious and dangerous spy, Radcliffe's report did all it could to downplay his importance. Radcliffe found that it was only in the spring of 1962 that Vassall had access to very sensitive material, when he had acted briefly as a personal assistant to the head of his section. Radcliffe concluded that Vassall could have handed over more sensitive material had he been "a more adventurous spy", but he had chosen not to. Even when Vassall had worked in the Admiralty's military branch he only had access to documents "of low classification [and] the Russians found his material of little interest," Radcliffe found.[185]

"It is obvious now, with hindsight, that he was a very bad choice for service in a sensitive post behind the Iron Curtain," Radcliffe concluded. "The selection of Vassall, a weak, vain individual and a practising homosexual, can now be seen to be the decisive mistake in the history of the case". But it added that his appointment was "not a mistake for which there must necessarily be blame", because "his weaknesses were not readily apparent and the Admiralty method of selection of staff for appointment as naval attaché's clerks was ill-adapted for assessing ... those defects which the Russians might exploit".

Radcliffe heard from no fewer than twenty-three witnesses who had known, or worked with, Vassall in the Moscow embassy. Although "most men in the junior ranks thought him effeminate and would refer to him among themselves as 'Vera'", Radcliffe noted,

---

185   As paraphrased in a story in *The Times* on 26 April 1963.

he concluded, astoundingly, that "Vassall had no reputation of being a homosexual, either in the Embassy or in diplomatic circles or elsewhere in Moscow. He did not 'flaunt' or otherwise give any indication of his proclivities". "Effeminate" was such a common euphemism for "homosexual" in the 1950s that it is staggering that so many people found Vassall to be "effeminate" without suspecting that he was gay. "The state wanted to show that nobody could know that Vassall was a homosexual," Patrick Higgins has argued – even though many witnesses had stated, or implied, that they had suspected he was gay all along.

More senior staff were somehow incapable of spotting the effeminacy that was so obvious to the junior ranks, Radcliffe concluded. Likewise, the observation that Vassall "took little interest in the opposite sex … would require an excessive degree of suspiciousness [*sic*] on the part of the investigating officer" for them to conclude that this meant Vassall might be gay.

But Vassall's sexuality was immediately obvious to the senior employee he worked with most closely in Moscow: Geoffrey Bennett, who told the tribunal – and MI5 – as such. But the inquiry's report implied that Bennett was merely being wise after the event. "[Bennett] had, we think, gone over his recollection of events again and again in his own mind, until at some point he gave the impression of a precision and clarity of recollection that seemed almost unreal", Radcliffe explained. While Bennett was "essentially an honest witness" he "was faced with the considerable difficulty of trying to make clear to us long after the event, ideas and perceptions that were not so clear at the time of their birth".

In other words, Bennett cannot possibly have consciously believed that Vassall was gay in the mid-1950s; he was merely editing his memories in his eagerness to help the inquiry. "The truth is, we think, that once it was seen that other people were suspecting Vassall, the old doubt recurred to his mind and presented itself afresh as a security consideration", Radcliffe concluded. Bennett had thought that Vassall was gay when he first met him but had then forgotten this suspicion and only recalled it when he told two MI5 officers, just before Vassall's arrest, that Vassall was an "undoubted homosexual". Poor Geoffrey Bennett – an honourable man who had overcome his initial prejudices against Vassall and later became his friend – was made to look like a fool, or a liar.

The "summary of findings" contained several errors that were completely at odds with the evidence that the tribunal had heard. In point 6, Radcliffe said that "There is no truth in the allegation that reports on Vassall made by the Embassy mentioning his homosexual proclivities or his Russian contacts were ignored by the Admiralty. No such reports were made" (in fact, Bennett had given H. V. Pennells such a report in 1954). Point 11 stated, "It is possible that if Captain Bennett had been asked about him some suspicion of Vassall's homosexuality might have come to light" (this implied that Bennett never told anyone that he suspected Vassall was gay: in fact, he had told Sir William Hayter, Adrian Northey, H. V. Pennells and possibly others). Point 17 asserted that there was no truth in the allegation that "the presence of another spy in the Admiralty was known to the First Sea Lord [Carrington] and his Service chiefs for 18 months before Vassall's arrest. The first suspicion of this was conveyed to them in April 1962" (in fact, national newspapers had aired such suspicions in January 1961; Carrington and his staff had either not read the newspapers or had ignored them).

Some of the Radcliffe report's sentences resembled "spoonfuls of blancmange", said Rebecca West, but many other observers had another word for them: whitewash. The report made no mention of Vassall being drugged and raped.

● ● ●

Even John Vassall himself – a man who was always optimistic and often blithely ignored criticisms and insults – realised that he had been done over by Radcliffe's report. "The effect of it was to make me appear a totally insignificant figure playing on my weaknesses, when in fact they knew little about my personality," he reflected a decade later. He failed to realise that the point of the inquiry was not to paint an accurate psychological portrait of John Vassall but to dig the government out of a political hole.

At Admiralty House and on the Conservative benches in the Commons, the immediate reaction to the publication of Radcliffe's report was triumph: Bill Deedes claims that ministers were delighted that the word "fiction" appeared several times in it. Even the American embassy seemed impressed: diplomats told Washington on 7 May, when the report was first debated, that it was a "complete vindication of all ministers". In the short term, the report gave the government some breathing space. After tribunal hearings that "had the British nation throwing up its hands in hypocritical horror", as a reviewer of Vassall's memoirs once put it, Radcliffe's report reassured them that all was now right with British security, and the world. The National Archives reveal that on 28 April 1963 Macmillan wrote to his new Cabinet Secretary, Sir Burke Trend, to say "The great thing is to remain calm ... because Radcliffe has worked out very well from our point of view". Yet this triumphalism soon gave way to hubris: within six months Macmillan was forced to resign after the Profumo scandal.

In the meantime, the Prime Minister continued to brood on the Vassall case. On 12 April 1963, just as Radcliffe was finalising his report, there was an embarrassing leak of civil defence documents to a CND faction called Spies for Peace, who handed out details of where regional seats of government would be located in the event of nuclear war. This stunt was "another security failure", Macmillan wrote in his diary, and "the press – smarting under Vassall – has grasped eagerly at a new chance of attacking me and the Home Secretary".

Not all the newspapers welcomed Radcliffe's report: the *Daily*

Mail said it was "one of the great whitewashing documents of our age". But the press still seemed more interested in peddling homophobic paranoia than attacking the government. This obsession infected the left as well as the right. Even John Freeman, a high-minded former Labour MP who edited the *New Statesman*, wrote that "Somewhere among the senior officials lurks a "Mr Big" who is able to protect homosexuals from the stringent enquiry to which others are subjected when they take over secret jobs". At five feet ten inches Vassall was quite tall, but on 3 May 1963 *The Spectator* wrote, "a small man, described officially as weak and not too bright, fooled all his highly educated superiors and sold his country ... to those who would destroy what is left of our world for seven years. Not seven weeks, before somebody noticed him, but seven years. Nobody is to blame. It just happened. How far can tolerance go?"

As Rebecca West rightly said, "nobody came well out of the Vassall scandal" and the parliamentary debates about it were "redolent of humbug, cruelly irresponsible and silly". Perhaps the silliest of the lot was a debate in May 1963, in which the new Labour leader, Harold Wilson, wondered whether "Our authorities [were] too easily reassured by the school the man went to, the fact that he came of a good family ... the fact that he was personable, had a good accent and manner, and was a member of the Conservative and Bath clubs, as Vassall was? I wonder if the positive vetting of Vassall would have been so casual if he had been a boilermaker's son and gone to an elementary school?" Contemporary newspaper reports recorded that his rhetorical questions were greeted with "Opposition cheers".

Wilson was half right: Vassall had indeed been given his job in Moscow, and sailed through vetting on his return, in part because he was well-spoken and had gone to a minor public school. Wilson's quip that "a hire-purchase firm would have made more searching inquiries over a washing machine account" than the government made about Vassall's suitability was well made. But many on the left knew that Vassall had been the victim of snobbery, not a beneficiary of it. His greatest sin, after his spying and his homosexuality, was that he had "ideas above his station". Wilson seemed to have deliberately misunderstood the Radcliffe report and was opportunistically arguing that Vassall got away with his spying because he was part of the old boys' network, not excluded from it. Worse, Wilson seemed to be recycling the homophobic tropes that all public schoolboys are closet gays and that all gays are willing to turn a blind eye to espionage.

•   •   •

The Radcliffe inquiry was the first of a long string of official inquiries in Britain that ultimately became eviscerations of the media, not candid examinations of governmental failings.

There are many parallels between Radcliffe and the Hutton inquiry of 2004, set up to examine the BBC's allegations that the government had "sexed up" reports of Saddam Hussein's possession of weapons of mass destruction to justify military intervention in Iraq, and the circumstances surrounding the death of the UN weapons inspector David Kelly. But Hutton's report was not a scathing critique of the government's intelligence failures but an assault on the BBC (whose Chairman and Director-General were forced to resign). Similarly, although Radcliffe identified failures in Vassall's vetting, no political heads rolled. None of the civil servants who had failed to spot his treachery for eight years lost their jobs and the only people who ended up in jail were journalists.

Those who had expected the Radcliffe inquiry to end Macmillan's ailing premiership underestimated his cunning: instead, it bought Macmillan more time. But while Hutton's report gave Tony Blair a new lease of life – he was only forced out as Prime Minister three-and-a-half years after its publication – for Macmillan the stay of execution was much shorter.

By the time Radcliffe's report was published, two more scandals were emerging. The first was the defection of Kim Philby, the Harry Houdini of Cold War espionage. Philby had been an acclaimed intelligence officer and was tipped as a future head of MI6 until he resigned in 1951 after Burgess and Maclean's defection. Although theories that Philby had been their "Third Man" were often publicly and privately aired, they were never proven and he was never prosecuted. In 1955, Philby, who was now working as a journalist, was exonerated by Macmillan when he was Foreign Secretary. By the late 1950s the widowed Philby was a "common or garden agent", off the MI6 payroll but still doing occasional assignments. He lived in the Lebanese capital, Beirut, where he wrote stories for *The Observer*, *The Economist* and other British papers, under his own name and the pseudonym Charles Garner.

In 1962 Anatoliy Golitsyn confirmed MI5's suspicions about Philby: despite his official exoneration, he had been a Soviet agent since the 1930s. But Britain had no extradition treaty with Lebanon and the options of kidnapping or assassinating Philby were ruled out. Shortly before Christmas 1962, an old MI6 friend, Nicholas Elliott, was sent to Beirut to extract a confession from Philby and persuade him to come home. Philby is said to have greeted Elliott with the words, "What took you so long?"

In January 1963 Elliott did obtain a confession of sorts, in return for immunity from prosecution, but before London could make its next move, Philby suddenly disappeared.[186] On the night of 23 January he had been due to join his wife Eleanor for dinner with friends, the Balfour-Pauls, but he never showed up. A few days later, Eleanor got a note from her husband, saying "Don't worry, I'm all right and shall write again soon. Say that I have gone on a long tour of the Middle East". Later letters from Philby were postmarked

---

186 In his confession, Philby skilfully shifted suspicion away from another Cambridge spy, Anthony Blunt, and onto the blameless Tim Milne, the Secret Intelligence Service's head of station in Tokyo. Milne had known Philby since their days at Westminster School in the 1920s.

Cairo, but in fact he had been smuggled onto a Russian boat. Philby had the last laugh and achieved what John Vassall was wrongly said to have wanted: "do a Pontecorvo" and defect to Moscow. Some have speculated that Vassall's eighteen-year sentence had helped to convince Philby not to return to England, as he feared he would be prosecuted after all.

Philby's disappearance prompted fresh questions for the British state, which was already reeling from the Vassall case. The credibility of official inquiries, such as Radcliffe's, was reduced by the fact that in the 1950s an internal inquiry had cleared Philby. George Blake (who may have been himself under suspicion from 1955 onwards but was only arrested and charged five years later) is said to have confirmed that Philby was a spy under interrogation in 1961. Why then was a confession only extracted from Philby in January 1963? And why had Philby then been able to flee to Moscow?

Once again, the Americans feared that the British intelligence community was riddled with Soviet agents who had allowed Philby to spy for decades and then escape. After the Vassall and Philby cases "CIA-MI6 co-operation was, regrettably, something less than suggested by the easy relationship of James Bond and Felix Leiter in Ian Fleming's stories", David Wise and Thomas B. Ross concluded. Philby had been the last man that the CIA's James Angleton had suspected of spying for the Soviets. His former friend's treachery fed Angleton's paranoia that the KGB had overseen a "monster plot" to infiltrate western intelligence agencies from the 1930s onwards, prompting the CIA to "turn itself inside out in a quest for a Philby of its own": none was ever found.

By 3 March 1963, Philby's disappearance was common knowledge. On 20 March, Ted Heath (who was then Lord Privy Seal, with responsibility for security matters) had to tell the Commons that his whereabouts was unknown, and on 1 July he admitted that Philby was probably behind the Iron Curtain.

Macmillan's diary from the time referred dismissively to "one

Philby", who had confessed everything "in a drunken fit". In fact, unlike Vassall, Philby was already a sort of celebrity when he was unmasked. His name had appeared in newspapers (both as a potential spy, and as a byline) and been "whispered in the clubs of St James's and the pubs of Fleet Street". By contrast, Vassall's presence in the clubs of St James's had gone unnoticed.

Double standards were clearly at work: MI5 seemed happy to grant Philby immunity from prosecution, as he was too important to put on trial without a fearsome political row that would make the Vassall scandal seem like a municipal boundary dispute. The punishment that MI5 had in mind for Philby was not prosecution but ostracisation and ensuring that he would never find a job in journalism again. Unlike Vassall, Philby knew too much – and crucially, he was "one of us".

The revelations about Philby's defection emerged at exactly the same time as another new scandal. The Vassall affair's sexual dimension, and Tam Galbraith's downfall, became an odd foretaste of the even greater imbroglio that finally doomed Macmillan: Profumo.

The Vassall affair has often been described as a dress rehearsal – or even the "essential prelude", argues Richard Davenport-Hines – to the Profumo one. The two scandals were intertwined from the start. On 15 March 1963, the *Daily Mirror* pulled off one of the most celebrated juxtapositions in the history of British journalism. Under a lead story, headlined "Vassall 'New Evidence' sensation,"[187] the front page carried two more, apparently unrelated, stories: one about the disappearance of Christine Keeler ("The Vanished Model") including a large photograph of her, and the other about

---

187 The Vassall story was a revelation in *Peace News* by Michael Randle, who had befriended Vassall in Wormwood Scrubs in 1962–63. Randle claimed that there, Vassall had told him about his connection to J. P. L. Thomas (later Lord Cilcennin), a former First Lord of the Admiralty. Vassall had apparently heard that Thomas "was a homosexual" before he wrote to him in 1953 to ask for his help in securing a job in Moscow. Despite the "sensation", Thomas was not named in any news stories: he was identified only as "A high official in the Admiralty who was a fellow member of the Bath Club".

the rumoured resignation of John Profumo, headlined "It's completely untrue, says War Minister" with a photo of Profumo and his wife, the actress Valerie Hobson. Thus were Keeler, Profumo's putative resignation and an espionage scandal all on the same page, if not in the same story, for the first time.

Westminster had been awash with rumours about Profumo for several months.[188] While the Labour MP George Wigg was pressing for answers about Vassall, on 11 November 1962 he received an anonymous phone call. "Forget about Vassall. You want to look at Profumo", a mysterious voice said. Famously, Wigg's speech in the Commons on 21 March 1963 was the first to raise the alarm about the connection between "a member of the Government Front Bench ... a Miss Christine Keeler, and Miss [Mandy Rice-] Davies". Although Wigg did not name Profumo, most MPs and journalists knew who he meant. It is often forgotten that Wigg made his speech during a debate on the recent imprisonment of the reporters who had refused to reveal the identity of their sources for stories about Vassall.[189]

If anything, the Profumo scandal was an aftershock of the Vassall one, not the main act that followed the overture. The Profumo affair of 1963 is still seen as the turning point of post-war British history, when the age of deference finally ended and a full-throated modern media first found its voice. History is in fact a year out: the turning point came a year earlier, after Vassall's arrest and conviction in the autumn of 1962.

---

188   The very first, coded, reference to the Profumo scandal in the media was as early as 31 July 1962 in the society magazine *Queen*. Under the headline, "Sentences I Would Like To Hear The End Of..." appeared the words "...called in MI5 because every time the chauffeur-driven Zis [a Russian car] drew up at her *front* door, out of the *back* door into a chauffeur-driven Humber slipped...". The story would only have made sense to people already familiar with Christine Keeler's love life.

189   Wigg's words were as follows: "There is not an hon. Member in the House, nor a journalist in the Press Gallery, nor do I believe there is a person in the Public Gallery who, in the last few days has not heard rumour upon rumour involving a member of the Government Front Bench ... I rightly use the privilege of the House of Commons – that is what it is given me for – to ask the Home Secretary to go on the despatch box – he knows the rumour to which I refer relates to a Miss Christine Keeler and Miss [Mandy Rice-]Davies, and a shooting by a West Indian – and on behalf of the Government, categorically deny the truth of these rumours."

Despite all the attention that Profumo has received in the last six decades, it was essentially a political scandal, not a security one. There is no evidence – apart from Christine Keeler's unreliable memoirs – that John Profumo ever divulged any state secrets to her. There is also scant evidence that Keeler ever spoke to another lover, the Russian assistant naval attaché Eugene Ivanov (nicknamed 'Foxface'), about security matters; some historians believe that they never slept together. Even if they did, Ivanov's intentions were probably only sexual. The idea that Keeler was used by the KGB as a conduit for state secrets is far-fetched indeed. Unlike John Vassall, she never had the opportunity to take photographs of secret Admiralty documents.

There are many parallels between the two cases. John Vassall was the firmly gay naval attaché's clerk who the Russians recruited to spy on his British masters. Eugene Ivanov, meanwhile, was a solidly heterosexual naval attaché who the British wanted to recruit to spy on his Russian masters. Stephen Ward was, like Vassall, the bridge-playing son of a clergyman. The rabid innuendo that accompanied Ward's trial in 1963 was similar to the homophobia that Vassall had faced a year earlier.

There are clear similarities between the way the press reported Profumo's "Darling" letters to Keeler and how it had reported Tam Galbraith's more innocent letters to Vassall a few months before.[190] In the autumn of 1962 Galbraith had been destroyed because of false allegations that he had had a sexual affair with a Dolphin Square tenant, John Vassall; in the summer of 1963 Profumo was brought down by an affair with a former tenant of Dolphin Square, Christine Keeler.

Profumo was luckier than Galbraith at first: when allegations that he had had an "improper" relationship with Keeler were first aired he denied everything. Following Galbraith's departure from

---

190   Macmillan maintained that he was not sure the term "Darling" was necessarily proof of any intimacy, as "I don't live among young people much myself".

the Scottish Office, the War Office did not want to see another ministerial resignation. Many Conservative MPs now felt that Macmillan had overreacted by demanding Galbraith's resignation and few
of them wanted to see Profumo quit.

It was only a stay of execution of course: Labour ruthlessly exaggerated the security implications, constantly referred back to the
Vassall case and by early June, Profumo's ministerial career was
over. The Profumo and Vassall affairs were "the reverse and obverse
of a medal", Rebecca West wrote: on one side an innocent minister
was rapidly forced out, while on the other a culpable minister was
forced out "by accident, and after a long delay".

Many historians have argued that if the press had not been so in-
furiated by the imprisonment of two journalists for stories they had
written about Vassall, they might well have been willing to turn a
blind eye to Profumo's indiscretions. Macmillan was so keen to save
Profumo that by the time he was forced to resign, the scandal had
become a constitutional crisis, not a storm in a teacup about a brief
affair with a topless dancer. Macmillan's "readiness to hope the best
about individuals – which may have owed something to regret at
having too promptly said goodbye to Tam Galbraith ... was derided as naïveté and as evidence of failing powers", said Carrington.
The Vassall affair compelled Macmillan "to move more slowly than
he needed when another scandal hit us all in the following year."
It is thus no exaggeration to say that without Vassall, the Profumo
scandal as we know it would simply not have unfolded as it did.
If the Vassall affair had not happened, it is possible that Profumo
might have resigned much sooner, the press might have called off
the dogs and Christine Keeler's association with Eugene Ivanov
might never have been reported. If so, today, Profumo would only
be half-remembered as a minor footnote, a sexual scandal and
nothing more.

Just as the government thought it had gained the upper hand by
jailing two journalists, an enraged Fleet Street gave the government

no quarter when the Profumo scandal broke. With much understatement, Bill Deedes wrote, "To some extent we were all affected by the outcome of the Vassall affair earlier in the year ... from then on my task of wining hearts and minds in the newspaper world became immeasurably harder". He went on to argue that this "mood of mutual mistrust" was an important precondition of the Profumo affair. "Every part of the Profumo story was used against the government by an exultant Press, getting its own back for Vassall," Macmillan confided to his diary. "The 'popular' Press has been one mass of the life stories of spies and prostitutes. ... Day after day the attacks developed, chiefly on me – old, incompetent [and] worn out."

Richard Crossman's diaries reveal that Labour was initially reluctant to fully exploit the Profumo scandal, as "we'd had the experience of the effect on a Labour Front Bench of George Brown's trying to exploit the charge that Thomas Galbraith had had homosexual relations with Vassall". But the press had no such inhibitions. Profumo was "manna for a vengeful press", says Richard Deacon. Even Vassall himself understood the connection between his own scandal and Profumo: "I realised that as the Prime Minister had been determined to put the press in their place with regard to the Civil Lord and myself, this time they were going to retaliate", he reflected.

"The Vassall case ... lit the fuse that would bring down Macmillan's government in the autumn of 1963" said Patrick Higgins. But few historians have gone so far as to assert that it was really Vassall, not Profumo, that doomed Macmillan. The soundly heterosexual Profumo was afforded more latitude than the possibly gay Tam Galbraith. A Labour MP, Reginald Paget, once said "I understand that the Secretary of War has had a close acquaintanceship with an exceedingly pretty girl. I regard that as a matter for congratulations". In his diary Macmillan wrote of his relief that the Profumo scandal involved "women this time, thank god, not boys".

This explains why the Profumo scandal has always received much more attention from historians, playwrights and film producers than the Vassall affair. Vassall's story lacks one key ingredient: attractive young women. His treachery arose directly from being blackmailed over his sexual activity with other men, not women. Apart from walk-on parts by Galbraith's Belgian wife, a number of Admiralty secretaries and two Dolphin Square charladies, the entire cast of the Vassall case are men.

As with Vassall, the human tragedy at the heart of the Profumo scandal has often been overlooked. The controversy is normally seen as two distinct phases. The first phase occurred in the spring and summer of 1961, when Christine Keeler had a short-lived affair (which may have coincided with her dalliance with the Soviet naval attaché, Eugene Ivanov) with John Profumo, who no doubt believed that the affair would never be made public.[191]

The second phase was two years later, in the spring and summer of 1963, when Profumo's affair and his possible connection to Ivanov were gradually revealed. The drama was amplified by Profumo's insistence that his "acquaintanceship" with Keeler had been entirely proper, until he was sensationally forced to resign on 5 June. The rest is history: after Nigel Birch quoted Robert Browning – "Never glad confident morning again" – in a Commons debate on Profumo in June 1963 and called for Macmillan to go soon, his government appeared doomed (Macmillan finally resigned on 18 October).

Much less attention has been paid to the intervening period, between the autumn of 1961 and the spring of 1963, during which Rice-Davies and Keeler shared a flat at Dolphin Square and were John Vassall's close neighbours. It was at Dolphin Square that

---

191 Nigel West says that the Profumo scandal resulted in part from a misunderstanding – an awkward meeting between Profumo and the Cabinet Secretary Norman Brook in 1961. Profumo thought that he was being gently warned that MI5 knew about his relationship with Christine Keeler and told to steer clear of her; in fact, Brook was trying to suggest that Profumo should use his connection with Ivanov to recruit him as a spy for the British. The powers that be were not aware of Profumo's affair with Keeler until many months later.

Keeler aborted a baby – possibly fathered by Profumo – and it was there that she was held hostage for two days in early 1962, just yards from Vassall's flat.

Keeler's assailant was Aloysius "Lucky" Gordon, a Jamaican jazz singer and small-time drug dealer, who she met in the late summer of 1961 at El Rio, a café in Notting Hill. Gordon was never really Keeler's boyfriend, and he soon began stalking her. He once lured her into his flat in Notting Hill by offering to show her some stolen jewellery but then kept her there at knifepoint for twenty-four hours, raping her at least twice.

In December 1961, Rice-Davies took a tenancy on a flat at Dolphin Square, 501 Duncan House, about 100 yards from Vassall's flat on the other side of the square's courtyard garden. Keeler soon moved in, but in January 1962 she was deserted by Rice-Davies. She lived in the flat alone, her modelling work had dried up and she was penniless, pregnant and frightened. It was all a far cry from the Cliveden swimming pool where she had met Profumo six months earlier.

A few weeks after her abortion, Keeler spotted Gordon at an "All-Nighter" night at the Flamingo club on Wardour Street, Soho. "We tried to avoid him ... but he wouldn't go away," Keeler later recalled. She invited him and a few others back to an impromptu party at 501 Duncan House. Gordon left the flat but promptly returned, carrying an axe, and sat down beside Keeler on a sofa: the party was clearly over. Astonishingly, several other people then left without raising the alarm. One guest, Paul Mann, was told to leave by Gordon, who threatened to kill Mann if he called the police.

Now that everyone else had left, the axe-bearing Gordon was alone with Keeler and another unnamed woman, who was clearly too terrified to leave or intervene. Gordon locked the front door and dragged Keeler into a bedroom. After raping her Gordon hurled the axe, narrowly missing her head, before knocking her "senseless on to the bed" and raping her again. The women were held captive in the flat for two days by Gordon, with Keeler deciding to pretend to yield to his professions of love to survive the ordeal. On the second day, they ran out of food and cigarettes. After trying to persuade Gordon to let the other woman go and buy fresh supplies, Gordon instead agreed to go shopping himself. Only then could the two women call the police, who fortunately arrived by the time Gordon returned and arrested him. Yet Keeler was soon persuaded to drop all charges against Gordon.

In June 1963 Gordon was sentenced to three years in prison for another assault on Keeler, but he overturned his conviction on appeal after serving only two months when witnesses testified that Keeler's evidence was largely false. Keeler then spent six months in Holloway prison after being convicted of perjury. The Profumo affair was full of injustices, but Christine Keeler serving considerably longer in jail than Lucky Gordon must be the greatest of them all.

There is no evidence that John Vassall ever knew, or met, Keeler at Dolphin Square. But both of their tenancies ended miserably. They were both portrayed as promiscuous and lucky to live there at all. In reality, however, they were both prisoners. Christine Keeler was held captive there by a violent rapist, and John Vassall was held captive there by photographs of his own rape.

CHAPTER SIX

"WHY THE DEVIL DID YOU CATCH HIM?": VASSALL IN JAIL

As he began his eighteen-year sentence in October 1962, John Vassall had reasons to be grateful. At least he was alive: many western spies committed suicide after they were unmasked but before they were imprisoned. In 1948 a State Department official, Laurence Duggan, jumped from the sixteenth floor of an office building in New York during, or just after, his questioning by the FBI about involvement in Soviet espionage. In July 1963 Jack Dunlap, a US Army sergeant stationed at the National Security Agency, passed a polygraph test but a suspicious examiner told the FBI that he was uneasy about Dunlap, who was asked to come back for another test the following week. Over the weekend Dunlap killed himself by carbon monoxide poisoning. Only afterwards did the Americans discover that he had been a Soviet spy.

Until a few years earlier the United States had executed spies: in June 1953 Ethel and Julius Rosenberg were killed in the electric chair at Sing Sing prison for having passed atomic secrets to the Soviets. In 1950 Lord Goddard had sentenced Klaus Fuchs to fourteen years in prison – the absolute maximum he could hand down – and made it clear that he would have liked to pass a much longer sentence, or even a capital one.[192] In his summing-up Goddard, who was opposed to the abolition of corporal and capital punishment, said that Fuchs's crimes only "technically" failed to amount to high treason, which then, in theory, still carried the death penalty.

Vassall was also lucky that he was a westerner caught spying for the Soviet bloc, rather than the other way around. Many have noted that any self-pity from Vassall would be misplaced, given that he only served a decade in relatively comfortable English prisons for his crimes. Had he been a clerk in a Russian defence ministry who was caught spying for the west, he would probably have been shot, as Oleg Penkovsky was. The Soviet Union rarely hesitated before executing Russians who it discovered had spied for the West and several Soviet agents were murdered if they tried to retire.

Vassall was a lucky man but not a rich one, despite many newspapers' claims that he had a large stash of Russian gold and had earned a fortune by selling his story. In fact, Vassall seems to have used most of the cash from the Russians to pay for day-to-day expenses. He had saved little money. An analysis of Vassall's finances, carried out by the police and MI5 after his arrest, revealed not how rich Vassall was, but how poor.

From 1956 onwards Vassall was paid between £500 and £700 a year by the Russians, normally in bundles of five pound notes, which almost doubled his meagre salary. According to a memo on "Vassall's Finances and Standard of Living", shown to the Radcliffe inquiry, Vassall's minimum outgoings while living at Dolphin Square were estimated to be £1,750 in 1959, £1,200 in 1960 and £1,250 in 1961. Queen Anne antiques were not cheap in the 1960s. Vassall could only afford them thanks to money from the Russians. Gregory also gave Vassall Christmas presents: a tie pin and cufflinks from Barkers in 1956, dress shirt studs in 1957, half a dozen hock glasses from Harrods in 1958, a martini mixer in 1959 and a pair of gold cufflinks from

---

192   Goddard did not live at Dolphin Square, as several online sources claim, and was never Vassall's neighbour, although he did live close by.

Harrods in 1960. Gregory liked suits from Burberrys and he once urged Vassall to buy one with double-lined trouser pockets, which were ideal for concealing documents. If Vassall did purchase the suit it was presumably bought with Russian money.

Vassall showed no signs of sympathy for communism. But he always insisted that he would still have handed over secrets if he hadn't been paid a penny: it was the fear of blackmail, not monetary reward, that made him continue. "Who on earth would do it for money?" Vassall argued in his memoirs. "One would have to have nerves of steel, to be super-human. ... All money does is give you a false feeling of security and a certain amount of financial freedom. The whole thing is an illusion, a stay of execution, nothing more".

Later, MI5 believed that £500 to £700 a year was an underestimate. In the *Sunday Pictorial* Vassall claimed that he had deposited £3,000 in cash in his bank account in a single year (the account itself suggests otherwise), and that he was given between £50 and £200 at every meeting with his Soviet handler. This suggests that he received thousands of pounds each year, not hundreds.

Dates, facts and figures were never Vassall's strong point. As most, if not all, of the payments were in cash it will never be possible to know how much he received. But if his estimate of £500 to £700 a year is correct and he received about £3,000 in total between 1956 and 1962, only a fraction was saved for a rainy day (in savings accounts and Premium Bonds). The rest was blown on clothes and holidays or on his Bath Club membership, which cost 35 guineas a year. Consciously or unconsciously, Vassall may have retained his membership of the Bath to emulate other spies' forays into clubland: Kim Philby was a member of the Athenaeum and legend has it that during the Second World War he and the other Cambridge spies regularly met at White's (London's oldest gentleman's club). Even with Russian money, Vassall could scarcely afford such an indulgence but he preferred to waste money on transitory things like evening entertainment, holidays and club memberships, rather than saving it for a deposit on his own home. Between 1956 and 1961 Vassall was estimated to have had outgoings at least 30 per cent higher than his modest Admiralty salary. But he was never greedy: he seems to have never dared to ask the Russians for more money than they offered.

After Vassall's trial newspapers claimed that he had often bought cut-price tinned food to eat at home so that he could stretch his budget for going out. Vassall himself said that he had paid for his final American holiday, with Douglas Bushy over Christmas 1961, by selling some Persian carpets that his father had given him. On 8 September 1962 Vassall only had £106 (in a current account with Lloyds Bank and a Post Office savings account) and £500 in Premium Bonds. Two hundred pounds' worth of the bonds were purchased with a legacy from an aunt in 1958 and the rest seem to have been financed by the Russians. All Vassall had to show for seven years of industrious work, aside from some antique furniture and smart suits, was a few hundred pounds' worth of Premium Bonds, guaranteed by the British Exchequer, not the Soviet one.

• • •

For his first twenty-eight days in Wormwood Scrubs prison Vassall was allowed no visitors at all. Instead, he relied on letters. On Monday 22 October, as soon as he returned from being sentenced at the Old Bailey, Vassall wrote to his favourite aunt. "My dearest Aunt Alma, At last it is all over; a thankful release from last night and this morning's ordeal". Rather than wallow in self-pity, Vassall said that "with remission I would only do twelve years". Vassall remembered all the supporters who had been in court to hear his sentence: his "magnificent" cousin (probably a reference to Jerrold), Mrs McNaughten, a friend called Derek Belson and Geoffrey and Rosemary Bennett, who had sat directly behind Robin McEwen and Jeremy Hutchinson.

Vassall's home for the next two years was a grim reminder of his schooldays. Wormwood Scrubs "had that Victorian Protestant Gothic look which is so absolutely soul-destroying", Vassall recalled. Nigel West remarked that the punishment he suffered was no less than the "destruction of his life": not only had the newspapers stripped him of his dignity, he was now deprived of his liberty by the state. But from the very start, Vassall looked on the bright side: at least incarceration at the Scrubs was not as bad as in earlier decades.

Vassall was pleased to see neatly mown grass, and flower beds in the prison's grounds. He was allowed to have a bath on arrival and that afternoon he was sent to the hospital wing, where he would be kept in isolation. He found it "as peaceful as a monastery". The next morning Vassall met the governor, Mr Hayes, who ordered warders to remove him from "escape clothing" once Vassall had assured him that he did not intend to escape. Hayes and Mr Sloane, the prison's education officer, "tried to make my life bearable", Vassall recalled. He appears to have viewed the Scrubs as an unusually benign prisoner-of-war camp, where warders were almost apologetic about keeping their charges incarcerated. Its senior medical officer was "kind and pleasant" and its dentist was "exceedingly agreeable, a gentleman with a beard who behaved as if I was receiving treatment in a Harley Street private practice".

While Vassall had been kept on a hospital wing throughout his time on remand in Brixton, at the Scrubs he was transferred from a hospital wing to a general section after only a few days. It must have been an alarming moment for a high-profile prisoner who had been exposed as gay and jailed for treachery. But Vassall's memoirs insist that "prisoners did not see me in an offensive light" and that he was more the object of curiosity than hostility. For several months he was accompanied by a prison officer wherever he went. He soon became an early riser: he and another prisoner were nicknamed the "greyhounds" because they always raced out of their cells to a washroom where they could shave in private, as soon as their doors were unlocked each morning.

After nine months, Vassall's "special security" was lifted. Poignantly, the most that Vassall wanted to do was sit in a small garden and look at budgerigars in an aviary. In summer 1963 Vassall complained to MI5 that he hadn't been allowed to watch the coronation of the new pope, Paul VI. But Wormwood Scrubs' regime was surprisingly benign in the early 1960s. Vassall was able to take a year's course in English literature, with an Irishwoman called Miss Neal, where he discussed Tennyson, Gerard Manley Hopkins, George Bernard Shaw and T. S. Eliot. He enjoyed other classes in musical appreciation, history, French and even – remarkably – Russian. Lectures on bee-keeping and wild birds were not well-attended but Vassall recalled that jazz band concerts were packed. Once, Vassall went to a variety show featuring the entertainer Dickie Henderson, the Welsh playwright Emlyn Williams narrating *A Christmas Carol* and a jazz sextet, the Savoy Hotel Follies.

Vassall felt that he was not in prison to be punished, but to be kept out of the public eye. "Whitehall was embarrassed by the fact that a homosexual had been found in their midst. I can imagine why – in case they found out more", he observed. Indeed, Vassall suggested that several of his friends inadvertently "outed" themselves by writing to him in prison. One friend told Vassall that others had stopped writing "because they would be afraid for their jobs and careers". "Because of such pressures a whole group of otherwise good friends left me," Vassall remembered.

At least Humphrey Hicks, a wealthy older man with less to lose, carried on writing. On 2 November 1962 Hicks told Vassall that he had "been strongly advised NOT to write to you" and that the press had pursued him all the way from his home in Devon to the Uplands guest house in Suffolk. Hicks was Vassall's first visitor once he was removed from isolation in August 1963. In the meantime, Vassall started receiving fan mail. MI5 intercepted a letter from a patient in Broadmoor Hospital called John Joseph Roberts, who claimed that he had met Vassall at Seaford House prep school in the 1930s, when Vassall had gone by the name "Percy" or "Chris". Roberts also wrote to the Soviet embassy in London to offer his services as a spy.[193] On 9 November 1962 Vassall got a gushing letter from a saner admirer: Mrs Emily Green, who had met him at an English-Speaking Union event in Oxford in the late 1940s. Green clearly had a sort of crush on Vassall and they corresponded for two years or more. "Don't think of me as a silly old woman," she once implored.

At first Vassall worked in the Scrubs' tailor's shop, making jackets for female civil defence officers: "boiler suits and other rather unattractive garments". The tailoring instructor, Mr Millman, was "always trying to be amusing and seeing the funny side of any crazy new regulation that suddenly emanated from the Home Office". Vassall was delighted when Millman later reappeared at his next prison, Maidstone.

Vassall soon became a confirmed Catholic. Despite the Catholic Church's strong opposition to homosexuality of any kind, only a few days after Vassall's arrival at the Scrubs its Catholic chaplain asked him if he wanted to be confirmed. Disarmingly, the priest told Vassall that he "did not agree with something written about me on paper". At some point in late 1963 or early 1964, the Archbishop of Westminster himself, John Heenan, came into the Scrubs to formally receive Vassall into the Catholic Church. Like the other confirmation candidates, Vassall had a private talk with Heenan. Vassall loved the service, which was conducted completely in Latin, with music played by an organist from the Brompton Oratory (as a joke, Heenan asked her how long she was serving; she replied, "Life, but did not want any remission", Vassall recalled).

---

193   Behind Roberts' delusions lay a tragic story: his father had been killed in 1940, when Roberts was still a child and his mother or guardian (he could not decide which) had then taken up with a Canadian army sergeant, who had neglected him.

By the time of Vassall's arrest his widowed father William had left London and was living at Home Farm in Higham, a village near Rochester in Kent, with his younger son, Richard. Despite his ailing health, William wrote to his eldest son frequently and he later visited whenever he could. But Vassall's memoirs say nothing about another family crisis.

In July 1963, nine months after John's conviction, Richard was convicted of indecently assaulting an 11-year-old boy at a cinema in Brentwood, Essex on 30 April. The press reported that Richard, whose profession was given as an "engineering specialist", was also suspected of assaulting two 14-year-olds. "Do you imagine my doing a thing like that?" he had told the police. "My name is Vassall and you realise who I am. My brother was recently sentenced to a long term of imprisonment. Now this, and it would kill my father." Richard was freed on bail pending an appeal, but despite the best efforts of a barrister friend of Robin McEwen's, Tony Lincoln, it was a hopeless case.[194] In January 1964, Richard's appeal failed and he started a three-month sentence. "The poor father," recalls Brigid McEwen. One of William's two sons had been convicted of treachery and now the other one had been jailed for "pinching little boys in a cinema".

In April 1964 a notice appeared in the *London Gazette* announcing that Richard Henry Holland Vassall was now changing his name by deed poll to Richard Henry Holland. One family friend, who has asked not to be identified, says that Richard "discarded his Vassall surname when his brother was convicted of espionage". But it is not clear whether Richard was distancing himself from his brother's crimes or his own: it was probably a bit of both. Vassall did not mention his brother's conviction in his memoirs, published a decade later. When Vassall changed his own name in the early

---

194   Lincoln was a barrister who lived with his father, Samuel Lincoln, a judge, at a house near the King's Road in Chelsea where the McEwens rented rooms as a London base in the 1960s. Robin McEwen and Tony Lincoln jointly wrote a column on legal matters, under the pseudonym R. A. Cline, which regularly appeared in *The Spectator* in the late 1960s.

1970s, after his release from prison, he pointedly did not choose the surname Holland as Richard had.

Richard's crime may have meant that Vassall was relieved that no family or friends were allowed to visit him in jail until August 1963. In the meantime, his only visitors were Treasury Solicitors and MI5 officers who wanted to debrief him.

Under English law Vassall could not be interviewed by MI5, officially at least, ahead of his conviction. Although MI5 sat in on his Special Branch interviews in September 1962, they did so only as observers. Most of his questioning occurred after his conviction, not before. After going to Catholic benediction in the chapel at the Scrubs one Sunday afternoon, Vassall was told that Mr Chitty and Mr Charlton, from the Treasury Solicitors Department, wanted to see him. "They were both suitably dressed in tweeds ... they looked out of place in a prison," Vassall reminisced. He was also questioned by another man ("without any humour whatsoever") about key procedures in the DNI's rooms, which Vassall willingly answered. The only visitor that Vassall did not take kindly to was an Admiralty official who "treated me with contempt". After Vassall walked out of their meeting, the official meekly returned to the Admiralty.

Vassall was more willing to talk to MI5 after "a thoughtful and interesting gentleman whom I rather admired" came knocking. At first, Vassall was worried that a "D-Notice in reverse" had been placed on him and that everything he said would be leaked to the press. It wasn't.

The MI5 officer who Vassall took an instant liking to was none other than Charles Elwell, who had overseen his surveillance.[195] Vassall was still picky about who he spoke to: in November 1962, at one of their first meetings, he told Elwell that while he would see Ted Bridger, he did not want to see anyone who had known him

---

195 When they visited British prisons MI5 officers always used cover names subtly different from their real ones: Elwell told Wormwood Scrubs' warders that his name was Elton.

personally before his arrest or anyone who "would speak to him in the way" that George Smith had.

Vassall soon settled into a routine. In total, Elwell and S. J. France, his successor at MI5, interviewed Vassall twenty-four times between 1962 and 1966. Elwell acted as a kind of social worker while Vassall was not allowed to have visitors: in November 1962, he called Vassall's father to reassure him that his son was all right.

Born in 1919, Elwell was five years older than Vassall. He was, and still is, a controversial figure. After his death in 2008, *The Guardian* lambasted him as a paranoid Cold warrior who had obsessively persecuted "domestic subversives", such as the future Labour ministers Patricia Hewitt and Harriet Harman when they worked at the National Council for Civil Liberties in the 1970s. But Vassall liked him. Given that Elwell had been imprisoned in Colditz during the Second World War, Nigel West says that he was well-placed to get into the mind of a prisoner and gently coax out the information he needed.

Vassall's first meeting with Elwell, on 1 November 1962, lasted for three hours. Vassall told him that far from being motivated by greed, he had been terrified of the RIS, who had sought "to destroy him altogether" if he did not comply. Elwell was sceptical: "I am afraid that Vassall is one who expects that the world owes him kindness and he is aggrieved that his expectations were not fulfilled," he wrote after their first meeting. But the two men established an unlikely rapport, and even a friendship of sorts: in a 1975 interview with the *Sunday Times*, Vassall reminisced fondly about a "very senior member of MI6 [*sic*], who inevitably arrived in a coat with a velvet collar, a bowler hat and a rolled umbrella". Elwell often brought Vassall gifts of confectionery: chocolates from Fortnum & Mason in February 1963 and in March, a box of Bendicks Bittermints. "Vassall ate these with relish", Elwell noted in a minute.

Elwell soon got to know the real John Vassall, and he abandoned some of his earlier prejudices.[196] On 31 August 1962, Elwell had written in a memo that Vassall "may have harboured a grudge against his naval attaché and that this could have contributed to his downfall". Once he started talking to Vassall, however, he realised that the clerk had only become a spy because of the Soviets' blackmail, and that resentment at his treatment by the Moscow embassy was, at most, a secondary factor. Elwell asked Vassall about his family, not because he thought they had known about his spying, but as a piece of "probemanship" to put Vassall at his ease. Vassall is "an inveterate 'picker up' and would strike up an acquaintance with anyone upon the slightest provocation", Elwell observed in October 1962. Once Elwell started visiting Vassall in jail, he gently teased him about his snobbery over his illustrious relatives: Elizabeth Vassall's fame "may have contributed towards Vassall's sense of family prestige and desire for social prominence," Elwell noted.

The MI5 officer also teased Vassall about his good looks, which had attracted several female admirers. Vassall said that he believed that Pauline, one of his late mother's hospital nurses, had developed a "wild passion for him". When Elwell quipped that he seemed to be a "homme fatale", Vassall did not appear amused. But the teasing only seemed to make Vassall like Elwell more: he once said that he had always "enjoyed working for someone like Galbraith, or Bennett, or you" – meaning Elwell himself. Vassall stood up to Elwell's assumptions: when Elwell talked about Vassall's "activities on behalf of the Russians," Vassall corrected him and said, "that he thought we should talk about 'the meetings he was forced to attend'", Elwell noted.

---

196   Elwell often had to put conspiracy theories to Vassall. In March 1963 a man called Alex Shanks, living in a council flat on the White City estate, wrote to the US embassy to say he had had "occasion to speak to Vassall the spy" during a recent stretch in Wormwood Scrubs (Shanks had been jailed for fleecing a firm of money lenders he had worked for, and splashing the cash at Wembley dog track). Shanks claimed that Vassall had told him about a "beautiful tall American blond man" who had experience of photography and had invited him on a holiday to Yugoslavia. This piece of gossip was put to Vassall, who denied all knowledge of Shanks, and Elwell does not appear to have pursued it further.

Elwell had to be cunning to convince Vassall that he would believe what he told him. In September 1963, Vassall was annoyed that Harold Macmillan had told the Commons, in response to a press report about Vassall, that he "could not believe anything that a convicted spy might say to a fellow prisoner". But Elwell reassured Vassall that he had "nothing to lose and a lot to gain" by telling him everything he could remember about his contact with the Russians. An unwritten deal was struck: if Vassall revealed everything, he was more likely to be released well before the end of his eighteen-year sentence.

Vassall did not resist the deal and what MI5 did not already know about Vassall they soon found out. By 1964 MI5 had built up a detailed picture of Vassall's meetings with his Soviet handlers. "Gregory" and "Nikolai" had often used the London Underground to get to their rendezvouses with Vassall. Until then, MI5 had not known much about the KGB's preference for the tube and how they "doubled back" to evade possible surveillance. The only outstanding mystery was the identity of the first "Nikolai", Churanov's sidekick in Moscow. MI5's files reveal that in May 1963, MI5 asked "KAGO" – Golitsyn – to "suggest who Nikolai might be" but KAGO said he could not help. Vassall couldn't help either but he seems to have answered any questions that Elwell put to him as comprehensively as he could.

Between November 1962 and March 1963, Elwell even took an unhandcuffed Vassall on at least three drives around the streets and tube stations of north and west London so that he could show Elwell where he had met his handlers and "make observations", presumably about KGB counter-surveillance techniques. Vassall was told that his "help had been invaluable; this was some consolation", he recalled.

Elwell asked Vassall about the vague claims he had made in the *Sunday Pictorial* about other "vulnerable practising homosexuals" in senior government posts. Vassall readily gave Elwell the names of the two MPs – Fergus Montgomery and Sir Harmar Nicholls – that he had befriended in 1961. But while journalists later speculated that the two unnamed MPs were not only gay but also "friendly with Iron Curtain diplomats", Elwell seems to have done little, if anything, with Vassall's intelligence, and both Montgomery and Nicholls's careers continued unimpeded.

Elwell remained interested in Vassall's friendship with Tam Galbraith: in February 1963 he wrote that he thought "the Press may not have been altogether wide of the mark in their insinuations about Galbraith". He does not, however, seem to have believed that Galbraith, or any other MPs, had known anything about Vassall's espionage. Instead, Elwell soon moved on from Members of Parliament to what, if anything, Vassall knew about other more senior spies at work in the Admiralty.

Ever since Vassall's arrest there had been some niggling doubts. Golitsyn had insisted that Vassall was too junior to have handed over some documents he had seen in a card index in Moscow, such as those about the nuclear submarine base at Holy Loch. In 1964, Vassall told MI5 that he had never seen, or passed to the Russians, some of these atomic secrets. At least two top-secret NATO documents that he had been accused of handing over had never passed his desk. Vassall also denied handing over plans for a Joint Operations Centre in Cyprus. As a prisoner longing to be released early, Vassall was eager to please. He seemed to have told the truth about everything else so there was no reason to disbelieve him now: the hunt for a more senior spy in the Admiralty was back on.

Throughout the 1970s and 1980s several espionage writers – above all, Chapman Pincher in his 1981 book *Their Trade Is Treachery* – claimed that the Portland spies, and Vassall, might have been sacrificed by the Soviets as "chicken feed" to distract the West from a "higher-up", or "Number Two" in the Admiralty. "While Vassall was the most despicable type of traitor, betraying his country through fear and for money, he was convicted of some offences that he had not committed," Pincher acknowledged. In *Traitor: The Labyrinths of Treason*, published in 1987, Pincher claimed that "there seems to be little doubt that Vassall was deliberately 'burned' so that he would be blamed for the activities of a much more senior traitor ... who still has not been exposed".

It later emerged that one senior naval officer was placed under surveillance in the mid-1960s and was spotted making covert visits, on his way home after work, to a basement flat that was sometimes visited by a Soviet intelligence officer. The identity of this "naval officer" took many years to come out. He was Rear-Admiral Colin Dunlop, who was secretary to the First Sea Lord from 1960 until 1963, when Dunlop took command of *HMS Pembroke*. In May 1964 Dunlop was put in charge of the Chatham barracks and the Naval Supply School (a job that took him away from sensitive secrets, some have claimed). He was then promoted to Rear-Admiral before retiring from the navy in 1974.

As late as 2011 Chapman Pincher identified Dunlop only as a "senior naval captain", even though he had died in 2009. Another writer was less cautious: Gordon Brook-Shepherd's 1988 book *The Storm Birds* named Dunlop as a suspected spy, but its first edition had to be withdrawn and reprinted after he threatened a libel writ.[197] Only much later did other writers, including Nigel West, name Dunlop without having to pulp their books.

Controversy surrounds the decision by MI5's head Roger Hollis not to seek Dunlop's prosecution while he was still serving in the navy. Some have argued that Hollis did not intervene: instead, the case officer recommended that the investigation should be discontinued because of the lack of concrete evidence, after which the search for another Admiralty spy was "gradually wound down". Right up until his death in 2014, aged 100, Chapman Pincher argued that Hollis's inaction against Dunlop was further proof that

---

197   Some copies of the first edition still survive: the copy in Cambridge University Library still carries Dunlop's name and has no missing pages.

Hollis himself was a Soviet spy, covering for another. When the KGB's archives were partly opened after the Cold War ended, it was discovered that they contained no file on Hollis. This only seemed to increase Pincher's certainty: the file had clearly been removed and destroyed, he argued.

Others claimed that MI5 had not taken action against Dunlop because they feared that revelations of Dunlop's treachery would only cause further damage to the credibility of the British security services. Like Philby, Blunt and Hollis himself, Dunlop was simply too senior to be put on trial, the theory runs. Whatever the truth, the lack of action against Dunlop certainly fuelled paranoia within MI5, and beyond, that either Hollis, his deputy Graham Mitchell – or possibly both – were Soviet moles. When the Portland spy Gordon Lonsdale was arrested in 1961 he had allegedly asked the police "what had taken them so long", suggesting that he had been tipped off by a KGB agent in MI5 that he was under investigation and liable to be arrested. By April 1963 Graham Mitchell was placed under surveillance. While no evidence was found against him, he retired later that year, two years earlier than planned. Only a few months earlier Mitchell had sent and received many minutes about the investigation into Vassall and regularly travelled between Leconfield House and Admiralty House to brief Macmillan's private secretary, Tim Bligh, about it. Mitchell was eliminated from the investigation after an "impressive performance under interrogation in 1967" but suspicions about Mitchell (who died in 1984) and Hollis (who died in 1973) persist to this day.[198]

There is no evidence that Dunlop's name emerged with Vassall's help: if Dunlop had been a spy, Vassall had never known anything about his espionage. There is also no evidence that Vassall knew anything about Mitchell or Hollis being Soviet spies. It has been

---

198 When Chapman Pincher visited Macmillan at Birch Grove, his country estate in Sussex, shortly before his death in the 1980s, the former Prime Minister described MI5 as "a madhouse" and said that he had never thought Graham Mitchell was a spy – only that Mitchell had been driven mad by MI5, a place where "nobody could work for ten years or more … without losing their reason".

concluded that, at most, Vassall may have been directed towards information that the Soviets could not obtain from Dunlop without being told his identity. The first rule of spying is that spies know as little as possible about what other spies are doing, to minimise the beans they can spill under interrogation.

By autumn 1963 Vassall seemed fed up with constant questions about what he had known about other Admiralty spies. "I think Vassall is pinning his hopes on the return of a Labour government" wrote Elwell in September. In October Elwell told Colonel Higham, Wormwood Scrubs' governor, that Vassall "didn't want any more of that". His regular interviews with Elwell were paused for several months. There is evidence that MI5 gently encouraged Vassall's friends to get him to start talking: its files say that in early 1964 Robin and Brigid McEwen visited Vassall and brought along Douglas Woodruff, the editor of the Catholic magazine *The Tablet*, who urged Vassall to co-operate with MI5 again. Not long afterwards, Elwell moved on and the MI5 officer who replaced him as Vassall's interviewer, S. J. France (who used the alias "Frisby"), does not seem to have had the rapport with Vassall that Elwell enjoyed.

In May 1966 Vassall, who was now in Maidstone prison, let it be known that he did not wish to talk to MI5 again. A few days later, he changed his mind and in June 1966 France visited Vassall and gave him "a box of Newman's continental Assorted Chocolates". But Vassall's co-operation could no longer be easily secured with presents of confectionery, as if he was an uncooperative child. Vassall told France about his hopes for a homosexual law reform bill and said it would remove the threat of blackmail; unwisely, France disagreed and said that the stigma of homosexuality would persist. At the end of the interview, Vassall seemed reluctant to meet France again. France visited him again in September 1966 but he reported that Vassall came out with "a very elaborate series of evasions and red herrings".

If Vassall had lost interest in discussing his spying by 1966, so had the media. After his conviction, media interest in Vassall was intense but short-lived. For a while after Radcliffe's report was published, the press still believed that Vassall had been part of a secret homosexual circle, involving not only Galbraith but other prominent Conservative politicians and possibly centred on Dolphin Square.[199] Once it became known, in 1963, that Christine Keeler had briefly lived at the square after the end of her affair with John Profumo, a steady stream of journalists and photographers trooped in and out of Dolphin Square again, looking for salacious new angles on the Profumo story, just as they had after Vassall's arrest in 1962. In 1963, slides depicting a "homosexual orgy" were found at an address on St George's Square, immediately to the east of Dolphin Square, and ten men aged between thirty-two and fifty-four were arrested at a flat in Stockwell, just across the Thames. Suddenly, the square became a place where truth blurred into fantasy.

Once it became clear that many of the more lurid rumours were fictitious, the media moved on from Dolphin Square, and from John Vassall. Instead, the media reverted to generalised homophobia. On 28 April 1963, three days after the publication of the Radcliffe report, the *Sunday Mirror* (as the *Sunday Pictorial* had just been renamed) carried a story headlined "How to Spot a Possible Homo" with a photograph of Vassall wearing white bathing trunks. The piece proudly boasted that it was a "short course on how to pick a pervert" – both the "obvious" variety (who "could be spotted by a One Eyed Jack on a foggy day in the Blackwall Tunnel") and a "concealed" group that could be betrayed by "an unhealthily strong

---

199   In his memoir, *Mosaic*, Michael Holroyd recalls one Henry Haselhurst, an army officer who had a long-standing affair with Holroyd's aunt, Yolande, before the war. By 1962 Haselhurst lived at Dolphin Square (in a flat in Nelson House). Many of Haselhurst's friends thought he was a spy because he received frequent phone calls from the former Field Marshal Bernard Montgomery and because he owned a schooner, *Black Pearl*, anchored on the Thames nearby. These theories "gained luminous credibility when, in the 1960s, William [*sic*] Vassall was jailed for spying".

affection for their mother", being a "fussy dresser", "over-clean" or "adored by older women".

The article took homophobia to a new level. It implied that gay men were, like spies, devious tricksters who often carefully concealed their true identity. Steve Humphries has argued that, "How to Spot a Possible Homo" did not just trot out old clichés "about limp wrists, suede shoes and frilly shirts". Instead, it warned readers that gay men "play golf, ski and work up knots of muscle lifting weights. They are married, have children. They are everywhere, can be anybody". They were so keen to mask their homosexuality that they would even, the *Sunday Mirror* warned, "give their wives a black eye when they got back from the working men's clubs".

John Vassall was portrayed in several films, plays and novels in the mid-1960s, but only indirectly. *The Creeper*, a 1965 play by Pauline Macaulay, featured an elderly bachelor, Edward Kimberly, living in a flat full of antiques, bows and arrows and other boyish toys, much as Vassall had been portrayed in newspapers two years earlier. Dolphin Square began to crop up frequently in spy fiction, and particularly in John le Carré's novels. The square's environs were well known to him: George Smiley's fictional home is 9 Bywater Street in Chelsea and le Carré's own father, the conman Ronnie Cornwell, lived on Tite Street in his final years (both addresses are within a mile of the square). While le Carré himself never lived or worked in Dolphin Square, his MI5 mentors Maxwell Knight and John Bingham certainly had: before, during and after the war. Le Carré's first novel, *Call for the Dead* (1961), was closely modelled on Bingham's fiction, while Bingham himself was one of his models for George Smiley. Dolphin Square was thus the cradle of a whole genre of post-war espionage fiction, from Bingham's own novels to le Carré and Ian Fleming.

Le Carré's first bestseller, *The Spy Who Came in from the Cold*, published in September 1963 (and made into a film in 1965), makes several knowing nods to Vassall. The novel's anti-hero, Alec Leamas, meets a communist agent called Ashe at a Dolphin Square flat, and the next day he departs for East Germany as a false defector, never to return. In October, a month after *The Spy Who Came in from the Cold* was published, the second film in the James Bond franchise – *From Russia with Love*, based on Fleming's 1957 novel of the same name – was released. Alongside the ludicrous plot and standard orientalist clichés, there seem to be several unsubtle references to the Vassall case. The film's central character is a female Soviet cipher clerk, Tatiana Romanova, who is ordered to seduce Bond so that he can be blackmailed with footage of their frolics: a neat inversion of the Vassall story. In the closing frames Bond is seen throwing the incriminating tape of him and Tatiana into Venice's Grand Canal. If only it had been so easy for John Vassall to dispense with photographs of his own entanglements at the Hotel Berlin.[200]

There are even clearer echoes of Vassall in the *Strangers and Brothers* series of novels by C. P. Snow, who had lived at Dolphin Square in the 1950s. In *Corridors of Power*, published in 1964 but set in 1955–58, the narrator, Lewis Eliot (based on Snow himself), lives in a flat off Bayswater Road. But much of the novel is set in a London that Vassall, and Tam Galbraith, would recognise. Its main character is Eliot's brother-in-law, a young Tory MP called Roger Quaife, who represents part of Kensington and lives on Lord North Street, Westminster (near Cowley Street, where Galbraith lived) Another minister, Lord Houghton (known as "Sammikins" by his friends) is rumoured to be gay and lives on Smith Square, also very near Cowley Street. Quaife's blackmailer, who works for a British defence contractor, is named Hood: the name of the Dolphin Square block in which Vassall had lived.

---

200   There also appears to be a reference to the Portland spy ring. In the briefcase of tricks that Q gives 007 is a tear gas cartridge disguised as a talcum powder tin – one of the ingenious hiding places used in the Krogers' bungalow.

Although the Vassall case featured in many non-fiction books about the febrile political events of the 1960s, only one was solely devoted to it: *The Vassall Affair* by Rebecca West, the most waspish of espionage writers, and published by the *Sunday Telegraph* in July 1963. The Vassall case also merited a long chapter in West's book *The Meaning of Treason*, republished in 1965.

The books may have been considered cutting-edge reportage at the time, but they now seem very dated. Despite their barbs at the hypocrisy of politicians and the "gross inefficiency" of the security services, at heart, they are conservative books which instinctively support the government of the day and do not condone press freedom, sexual emancipation and natural justice. West pilloried Lord Carrington's critics for "carrying out a party manoeuvre", and commented that "cries calling for the resignation of Ministers are animal noises on a par with the mating cry of the moose or the hooting of owls".

West was far less charitable towards Vassall himself. Like other writers, she portrayed his entrapment in a Moscow hotel as a comic moment, not as a traumatic event with life-changing consequences. She claimed that the story of the Moscow party was "a legend" which was "probably engineered so that Vassall might refer to it, should his treachery ever be discovered". West never stopped to consider a more straightforward explanation: having been made to feel ashamed of his homosexuality from an early age, Vassall was terrified of being publicly humiliated, and probably jailed, if he had refused to do the Soviets' bidding.

Preposterously, she argued that if Vassall had been blackmailed, he should have simply reported the incident to his embassy superiors and been posted back to London. She also trotted out the homophobic trope that Vassall could have easily fallen back on a secret network of gay allies to extricate himself from trouble. "He could have looked in his little book for the right address, sent a cable ...

and have been on his way in no time, perhaps a little pale but still neat and polite and not really shattered," West joked.

West was convinced that Vassall had sold secrets because of naïve communism or simply greed. Both of West's books about the Vassall case contain torrents of homophobic language. She described him as "doe-eyed, soft-voiced, hesitant and ephebic [like a Greek youth]" with "a deprecating manner and a tendency to nervous dandyism" and even as a "wretched little pansy boy".

West claimed that like all gay men, Vassall only thought about himself: "He was not a tortured bearer of a cross, flinching under philistine scorn," wrote West. "He was a much-sought-after 'queen', playful and girlish, who loved being courted and appreciated". To West, Vassall was "fascinating and repellent", a "slender figure in sweater and tight jeans, who lurks in the shadow of the wall, just outside the circle of the lamplight, whisks down the steps of the tube-station lavatory, and with a backward glance under the long lashes, offers pleasure and danger".

West proudly announced that she was glad that "inert and latent homosexuals in our society" were in a small minority. She argued that Vassall was not just any old gay but a very dangerous one who did not immediately appear to be gay: "so far as birth, appearance, manners and education are concerned", he was "much like many other people in the civil service". Vassall was therefore damned for appearing camp but also damned for concealing his campness.

Even West's sensible critiques of security failures are soaked in homophobia. The authorities failed to spot Vassall's "homosexual gambols" and that he was "a perfect idiot who should have been detected in five minutes by any security officer worth his salt". Ultimately, West concluded that Vassall never had a "homosexual fairy godfather" in the Admiralty – simply because no sensible person would waste time protecting a "worthless little homosexual". His career couldn't have "been nursed", as it had hardly advanced at all.

Rather than employ huge armies of security officers to spot spies, West concluded that all homosexuals should simply be weeded out of the civil service before they could be promoted.

To date, *The Vassall Affair* is the only book published that is solely devoted to John Vassall: he deserves better.

● ● ●

Vassall's contemporaries in Wormwood Scrubs were not just the usual motley crew of armed robbers, murderers and rapists. Also in the Scrubs was Sir Ian Macdonald Horobin (1899–1976), the former Conservative MP for Oldham East who had served as the parliamentary secretary to the Minister for Power 1958–59.[201] In July 1962, Horobin had been convicted on several charges of indecently assaulting boys aged under sixteen at an East End mission. Horobin was serving a four-year sentence and working in the Scrubs' library, but Vassall was told that he only worked there when no one else was around. Horobin had once described homosexuals as "us poor devils who are born like this; nothing can change me. It is natural for us to love boys in this way," which only reinforced the prejudice that all gay men are potential paedophiles. Vassall did well to keep clear of him.[202]

Leo Abse, the Labour MP whose private members' bill helped to decriminalise many homosexual acts in 1967, once said, "We all know that to send a homosexual to an overcrowded male prison is therapeutically as useless as incarcerating a sex-maniac in a harem". In fact, Vassall seems to have had no sex throughout his ten years in jail. "In some ways it was a painful process being accepted by the tough heterosexual chaps, knowing that I was or could be

---

201   Vassall's memoirs incorrectly state that Horobin had been a minister in the Home Office.
202   After being released from jail, Horobin ended his days in Tangier, a favoured resting place for elderly British gay men of means and a holiday destination for younger men, such as Kenneth Williams, Kenneth Halliwell and Joe Orton.

interested in one or two of them physically," Vassall recalled. But he seems to have resisted making a pass at other prisoners.

Michael Randle, a pacifist who served twelve months in the Scrubs from early 1962 until early 1963 for his role in a "Committee of 100" anti-nuclear demonstration, recalls that Vassall was obviously gay to other prisoners, even if they had not read about his sexuality in the newspapers. Yet, Randle remembers that British prisoners' prejudice against convicted traitors was greater than their prejudice against gay men. He does not recall Vassall being the object of homophobic bullying or ridicule.

Remarkably, Vassall struck up a platonic friendship with an even more notorious convicted spy: George Blake, who in autumn 1962 was barely a year into his forty-two-year sentence.

Whatever the excesses of British security paranoia, it did not seem to extend very far into high-security jails. Vassall had known that Blake was in Wormwood Scrubs before he arrived and yet strangely, for two years the prison service seem to have made no effort to keep the two men apart. The Portland spy Gordon Lonsdale was also in Wormwood Scrubs and he and Blake were supposedly kept apart, but the *Sunday Times* reported that they often met and conversed "in Russian in a low voice".

At first, Vassall was wary of Blake and he "did not dare to invade his circle". But they soon struck up a friendship at a classical music class.[203] "I liked him. He was cultured, with impeccable manners and an open heart," Vassall recalled. Vassall and Blake attended the same English literature class, and for a time they lived in cells directly opposite each other. Vassall quickly told Charles Elwell that he had met Blake and that Blake had been "quite friendly" to him.

On Sunday mornings Blake's cell became a sort of literary

---

203 Vassall also told MI5 that Michael Randle had first pointed out Blake to him. Michael Randle denies this, though he thinks that he, Vassall and Blake did work together in the tailor's shop for a time. There was speculation within MI5 that Randle knew the identity of the "high placed contact in the Admiralty" that Vassall had dropped hints about in his *Sunday Pictorial* serialisation, but Randle does not recall Vassall ever talking in detail about his spying or the identity of other spies.

salon, where he and other members of the prison's "intellectual mafia" listened to BBC radio. Unlike most prisoners, Blake was a non-smoker and he used the money he saved to buy coffee to serve to his guests. A hypochondriac, Blake was a regular visitor to the prison's doctors but he charmed them and sometimes had lunch in the nurses' canteen. MI5 soon concluded that Vassall was trying to emulate Blake's popularity. In November 1962, Elwell wrote: "I got the impression that Vassall is in the process of forming a little salon of some of the elite prisoners" and that Vassall had been "a little hurt that Blake did not introduce himself" at the first opportunity.

"You were one of the victims, and what happened to you was one of the recognised methods used by intelligence or security services throughout the world", Blake told Vassall, according to the latter's memoirs. It is no wonder that Vassall came to like Blake: he told him exactly what he wanted to hear. As Vassall did later, Blake had considered becoming a Catholic priest in early life, only to decide to become a communist instead. Vassall and Blake often spoke about religion in the exercise yard after lunch: Blake told Vassall that his favourite saint was St John of the Cross (a Spanish Carmelite priest who died in 1591) and he borrowed a book from Vassall about the lives of Catholic saints. Vassall even invited Blake to his Catholic confirmation service but Blake declined, saying "it would cause too much comment".

"We talked about travel and the foreign places we had both been to, good food and wine, literature, theatre, cinema and music", Vassall recalled. "Although we held in some cases totally opposite views, we were the best of friends". Like Tam Galbraith, George Blake seems to have been an object of idolatry who was less enthusiastic about the friendship than Vassall was. Michael Randle saw Vassall as a victim of Russian blackmail, pure and simple, rather than an ideological spy like Blake: he does not recall Vassall ever talking about politics.

A few months before Vassall's transfer to HMP Maidstone in

1964, he discussed the Great Train Robbers' escape from Wandsworth jail with Blake, and they pondered the repercussions it might have for security. But Vassall was clearly unaware that Blake had already started conspiring with another prisoner, an Irishman called Sean Bourke, to escape from the Scrubs, a plan that finally came to fruition in October 1966 with Michael Randle's help. Randle thinks that Vassall may have met Bourke but that Vassall was never told anything about Blake's plan to escape. For Vassall, there was no quick release. Although his sentence was less than half the length of Blake's, he was to languish in jail for twice as long.

But Vassall certainly did meet, and talk to, Colin Jordan, "the British tabloids' favourite Neo-Nazi", at Wormwood Scrubs. Jordan had been sentenced to nine months imprisonment in October 1962 for attempting to establish a paramilitary force called 'Spearhead'.[204] Jordan claimed to have spoken to Vassall about six times during exercise periods. In fact, Vassall may have only spoken to Jordan once. Michael Randle was in the Scrubs at the same time as Vassall and spent a lot of time working with him in the tailor's shop, during exercise periods and in English literature classes on Friday evenings. He does not recall ever seeing Vassall and Jordan in each other's company.

Jordan wrote notes on his conversations with Vassall on prison toilet paper and later wrote to Harold Macmillan with a "shocking picture of a still operative homosexual network of corruption, involving Members of Parliament, high civil servants, and even intelligence officers themselves". Jordan also penned a story headlined "Behind the Democratic Curtain" (and subtitled "Homosexual

---

204   Even by the standards of post-war British neo-Nazis, Jordan was a particularly unpleasant specimen. At the 1964 election, Patrick Gordon Walker unexpectedly lost his seat in Smethwick. At the 1965 Leyton by-election he unsuccessfully sought to return to Parliament. During the campaign Jordan organised a gang of thugs to disrupt his meetings with some of them shouting racist slogans and even wearing monkey costumes. Gordon Walker lost the by-election by 205 votes but he had the last laugh: he won in Leyton in 1966 and returned to ministerial office.

Network Endangers National Security") in the August 1963 edition of a fascist magazine, *National Socialist*.

In June 1963, the *Sunday Telegraph* reported that Jordan said that Vassall "certainly seemed to know the Russian in the Profumo affair" and that he had given MI5 the "names of two MPs who had visited [Vassall's] flat at least 12 times," but again neither of them was named.[205]

Macmillan was asked about the Jordan letter in the House of Commons that July, but it was clear that Jordan was trying to trade information, or threaten embarrassing revelations, for early release. Vassall was, not for the first time, guilty of naïveté, but he had not conspired with the far right.

Some writers have scrabbled for evidence of a connection between Bob Boothby and Vassall, but all they have discovered is the word of Jordan, who claimed that "an acquaintance of Vassall kept an establishment catering for those with sexual perversions at an address in London, W8, [and] numbered among his distinguished clients one of our more frequently televised peers, who used to go there to procure chickens [slang for male prostitutes]". Boothby was not named: MI5 simply surmised that he was the peer. In June 1963 Jordan told MI5 that Vassall had told him that he had heard that Boothby had frequented a brothel because he had met the owner, a Mr Ward, in jail. Daniel Jones has suggested that this could have been Stephen Ward, who was briefly on remand in the summer of 1963 (but at Brixton, not Wormwood Scrubs). "The coincidence is striking", says Smith. But there is nothing at all striking about the fact that there are several thousand Londoners with the surname Ward. In his book *The Spy Who Would Be Tsar*, the investigative journalist, Kevin Coogan, excitedly claimed that "one of the leading figures in Vassall's sexual underground was Lord Robert Boothby, a

---

205   Sir Harmar Nicholls was identified only as an "East Anglian Member of Parliament" and Fergus Montgomery as a "north of England" one. Jordan's article claimed that a "top-ranking homosexual " had been "responsible for [Vassall] by-passing normal security screening and debriefing". MI5 assumed that this meant J. P. L. Thomas (later Lord Cilcennin), whose name Jordan had given in a statement to them.

long-time Conservative MP and friend of Fascist leader Sir Oswald Mosley. Lord Boothby was a bisexual, kink-friendly political operative of the highest order, a connoisseur of gay brothels, holder of a KBE, and good pal of the notorious Kray twin gangsters, particularly Ronnie (who was also gay)". [206] Born in 1900, Boothby was old enough to be Vassall's father. In fact, despite lurid claims in the darker reaches of the internet, there is no evidence that they ever met.

H. Montgomery Hyde's book *George Blake Superspy* alleged that as well as Blake, Vassall was friendly with three other prisoners on Wormwood Scrubs' D. Hall: Gordon Lonsdale, the notorious fraudster, Kenneth de Courcy[207] and Sean Bourke, who helped Blake to escape in 1966. Although Blake was not a homosexual, de Courcy wrote a long unpublished memorandum in jail, which claimed that Blake "took a lively interest" in the prison's gay inmates. "Blake took advantage of Vassall's homosexual advances and pumped that young man bone dry", extracting "a full list of everyone in high places who indulged in sexual perversions". In fact, Vassall's memoirs make no mention of de Courcy, Bourke or Lonsdale and MI5's files do not suggest that he knew any of them.

Whatever the truth of these tall tales, MI5 and the Home Office knew from the start that housing Vassall, Lonsdale and Blake together in Wormwood Scrubs was not ideal. A merry dance in Whitehall about which of the prisoners should move, and when and where, ensued. On 14 November 1962 Vassall told Elwell that he had received a message from Winson Green prison in Birmingham, to the effect that Gordon Lonsdale was looking forward to

---

206 Boothby and Mosley had indeed been friends during the 1930s and Boothby had once visited Mosley in prison during the war. But given that Mosley was a member of the Conservatives and then Labour before forming his New Party and then the British Union of Fascists, the list of Mosley's one-time political friends is very long.

207 Rather like Maxwell Knight and Horatio Bottomley, Kenneth de Courcy was one of those mid-century Britons whose colourful career blended far-right politics, celebrity and financial skulduggery. In 1934 he became Secretary of the Imperial Policy Group, and between 1953 and 1964, he was part of the Evangelical Alliance that organised Billy Graham's 'crusades'. In the 1960s he planned a garden city development in Southern Rhodesia but ran off with the funds and was imprisoned for fraud.

meeting Vassall once he arrived at Wormwood Scrubs. In September 1963 MI5 argued that Blake, not Vassall, should be moved out of Wormwood Scrubs, as it was convenient to have Vassall at a London jail where MI5 could access him easily. In hindsight, the Home Office appears very complacent and slow to keep high-profile spies apart from each other. But there were few high-security prisons in the 1960s, so if high-risk prisoners had to be kept apart it was a constant struggle to find prisons to put them in.

Although Wormwood Scrubs' prisoners were supposedly kept under careful lock and key, they were not brutalised. As well as concerts and other performances, in 1964, the prison hosted an unusual event that united two of the "young meteors" of Oxford University and prisoners serving some of the longest sentences in the land. The chairman of the *Daily Mirror*, Hugh Cudlipp, and the paper's gardening correspondent, Xenia Field, brought in two stars of the Oxford Union – Jonathan Aitken and Derek Parfit – to debate whether English private school life was worse than prison.[208] One of the two prisoners who opposed the motion was George Blake. Tellingly, Blake warned in his speech that if his 42-year sentence was not cut, he would cut it himself. He also repeated a joke that the prison's governor had told him after Blake had complained about the excessive length of his sentence: "look on the bright side: you're the only prisoner who might get 14 years remission".[209]

After a lively debate, with much laughter and audience participation, Blake introduced Aitken to John Vassall. Aitken remembers nothing of their short conversation but was left with an abiding impression of how smooth and neat Vassall, with his slicked-back dark hair, looked, compared to the other unkempt inmates.

Someone who had more regular contact with Vassall was one of

---

208 Parfit later became a renowned philosopher and a fellow of All Souls. Aitken became a Conservative MP and minister until a perjury conviction in the late 1990s compelled him to spend seven months in another London prison, Belmarsh.

209 In those days, prisoners who behaved well were often released two-thirds of the way through their sentences; in Blake's case this would have been fourteen years before the end of his 42-year stretch.

Wormwood Scrubs' official visitors, a 45-year-old Dutchman called Leo Vlaanderen. In April 1963 Anthony Foley, a 30-year-old who had served a stretch at the Scrubs for attempted murder and been released in February, claimed to have befriended Vassall at Roman Catholic choir practices. Foley told the Home Office that Vassall had said he had been interviewed by Special Branch and MI5 twice in the year *before* his arrest – but then released without charge to carry on spying. According to Foley, Vassall had told them that he was a homosexual but no further action had been taken. Foley also alleged that he had passed this information to Mr Vlaanderen, who Foley said was a homosexual who had lived at Dolphin Square and known Vassall there. Once out of jail, Foley said he had been invited to Vlaanderen's new flat on Queens Gate Gardens in South Kensington, where he was shown radio transmitting equipment similar to that used by the Portland spies. This raised the fearful prospect that Vassall had been questioned and released many months before his arrest and that he had been part of a larger group of spies centred on Dolphin Square. But if Vlaanderen was a Soviet spy, why would he show a virtual stranger his spying equipment?

In August 1963, newspapers reported that a foreign-born man had been banned from visiting prisoners in Wormwood Scrubs. The next day, 13 August, they revealed the man's name. In fact, Vlaanderann had been forced to resign as a prison visitor in December 1962, not because he was helping spies to escape but because the prison believed that he was using his visits to try and pick up men. Either way, the revelations about Vlaanderen seem to have finally brought the fiasco to an end: Vassall had to be moved from Wormwood Scrubs away from the media limelight.

As early as March 1963 Elwell began pushing for Vassall to be moved to an open prison, "as a reward for having co-operated with us so far [and] as an incentive to co-operate with us further … I recognise, of course, the political objections – fear that Vassall is being favoured by homosexuals in high places – but I think these might be overcome if we are insistent enough". In the end, MI5 were not insistent enough. For the Home Office, moving Vassall to an open prison so early in his sentence was out of the question.

In October 1963, the Home Office asked MI5 for its opinion on moving Vassall to Wakefield prison in Yorkshire. Moving Vassall there would, Elwell warned, only deepen Vassall's "sour mood". MI5 files show that there was discussion in December 1963 about moving Vassall to Maidstone or Chelmsford, but the move was delayed when Vassall began talking to MI5 again, as they did not want to "upset him". In early 1964 Arthur Martin argued that Vassall should stay at the Scrubs, which was more congenial to him, and that the political considerations that kept Blake in the Scrubs should be reassessed: they weren't, with disastrous consequences. Had Blake been moved to Wakefield, it is unlikely that his London accomplices would have helped him to escape from it in 1966.

After just over two years in Wormwood Scrubs and without any warning, Vassall was finally moved to HMP Maidstone on 9 November 1964. He was summoned from the tailor's shop and told to pack immediately. The press knew that Vassall was going to another prison, but not where: the *Daily Mail* said on 11 November that "it is believed he has gone to a jail in the Midlands or the North Country".

Maidstone was not a cushy jail: the Portland spy Harry Houghton, who was a prisoner there in the 1960s, recalled that a "member of the Richardson torture gang" was there and he was attacked several times by "bovver boys or skinheads". Houghton served time in Winchester, Durham, Styal and Nottingham prisons, as well as Wormwood Scrubs, but he said that Maidstone was the only one where he suffered violence.

Vassall's own memoirs say little about his first two years in Maidstone, between 1964 and 1966, but a lot more about his final five-year stretch there from 1967 onwards. He seems to have had a comfortable, if solitary, time at first. He was allowed a portable

Hacker radio in his cell, on which he listened to the BBC's Third Programme. He claimed to have never missed an episode of *A Word in Edgeways* by Marghanita Laski (a high-minded journalist who was the niece of Harold Laski and a regular panellist on *What's My Line?*, *The Brains Trust* and *Any Questions?*). Vassall recalled going to performances by "show-business personalities" such as Adam Faith and Warren Mitchell. As for Maidstone's assistant governor, a Mr Pearson, Vassall only hoped that "the prison service has more governors like him".

Even an encounter with Frank Mitchell – known as the "Mad Axeman" and one of Britain's most notorious convicts – ended happily.[210] Mitchell, "a colossal figure" who "arrived in a white T-shirt and smart slacks, with a chest-expander under one arm and a wireless set and record player under the other", "popped into" Vassall's cell the day after arriving at Maidstone from Dartmoor, to say that he was pleased to meet him and to ask if he was really gay. Vassall replied that he was and to his amazement Mitchell sat on his bed and told Vassall "he had been well provided for at Dartmoor and certainly had not gone without the fruits of life, I knew what he meant", Vassall recalled. Mitchell was "something of a fireball, and if he had stayed I am sure we could have got to know one another well". But soon afterwards, Mitchell told Maidstone's governor that he wanted to go back to Dartmoor, and he did.

Vassall was then moved into a brand-new wing at Maidstone: Thanet House, known to prisoners as the "Hilton Hotel" because of its superior facilities. Vassall liked his new cell and its view of the North Downs. He embarked on one of his favourite pastimes: writing begging letters to old friends. On 18 April 1966, three-and-a-half years after entering prison, Vassall wrote to Sir Harmar

---

210 Mitchell was a henchman of the Kray twins (who later had him murdered, shortly after helping him to escape from Dartmoor in 1966, though Mitchell's body was never found). Mitchell had been sentenced to life imprisonment for robbery with violence in October 1958, having attacked police with two meat cleavers, and was sent to Broadmoor. He escaped, broke into the home of a married couple and held them hostage with an axe, hence his being nicknamed "The Mad Axeman" in the press.

Nicholls MP at the St Stephen's Club on Queen Anne's Gate. It was political fan mail, congratulating Nicholls on another Lazarus-like survival in marginal Peterborough. Even the Labour landslide of 1966 had not unseated him. "When the news came ... of your return to parliament I could not help feeling elated at your spectacular victory..." Vassall gushed. "So much must have happened since we last met ... it would be nice to see your happy and cheerful countenance again; when the House of Commons settles down to its formidable task I hope you will come and see me?" Vassall added that Nicholls could always write to him via his father in Higham, avoiding the prying eyes of prison censors. There is no record of any reply from Nicholls or any visit to Vassall in prison.

On 7 June 1966 Vassall wrote to his Italian diplomat friend, Francesco Gentile. "One does not expect you to talk of the past, though memories of Italy are never out of my mind", Vassall simpered. He virtually begged Gentile to write to him at Higham, where "my father takes an interest in Italian painting and has sent me a head of the School of Botticelli" and a copy of an Egyptian cat bronze, "which reminds me of my travels". Pathetically, Vassall seemed desperate to pretend that he still inhabited his old life and carefree days in museums and art galleries. There is no record of any reply from Gentile.

In November 1965, the *Evening Standard* had run a lighthearted story claiming that Vassall was finding Maidstone "a trifle provincial". But within a year, Vassall was moved further away from London. On 22 October 1966, George Blake sensationally escaped from Wormwood Scrubs. With the assistance of his three friends, the Irishman Sean Bourke, the peace campaigner Michael Randle and another activist, Pat Pottle, he scaled the prison walls using a ladder made of knitting needles. All three men later insisted they were not communists but simply idealists who thought that Blake's 42-year sentence was "inhuman". Again, Vassall was embroiled in another tale of security lapses, official incompetence and over-indulgence of Soviet spies.

When the news reached Maidstone at 10 p.m. on a Saturday evening, Vassall was immediately put on "special watch" and the following Tuesday he was transferred to HMP Durham. He was driven up the M1 motorway (at an average speed of 93mph, Vassall calculated) in a police car, escorted by two others. Vassall loved the excitement: "Royalty would not have been treated better", he recalled. He was fascinated to see that whenever the convoy passed a county boundary a new panda car would join it from a lay-by as another from the outgoing constabulary left. Vassall felt that it was a "perfect operation" but he told his guards that he thought "there was no need for this kind of security". He could have made his own way to Durham by train and would not have absconded. The guards did not agree: with rumours that Blake had been sprung from jail by the KGB still swirling, the prison service was taking no chances.

In late 1965 MI5 had told Maidstone that they no longer needed to see Vassall's correspondence. But every rule was tightened after Blake's escape. Lord Mountbatten's security review led to a rapid crackdown on conditions for prisoners like Vassall. Compared to Maidstone, Durham was a "grim fortress if ever there was one", said Vassall. He was now on its top-security E Wing, "known as Britain's hell-hole, a desperadoes' haunt". Gone was the relative freedom of Maidstone: to begin with, Vassall spent a month in solitary confinement.

Shortly after Vassall moved to Durham his father had a stroke and finally retired as a curate at St James's, Piccadilly. He had visited his son in Maidstone whenever he could, as it was only ten miles from Higham, but the long journey to Durham was now impossible. Six weeks after Vassall's arrival, a serious riot broke out on E Wing and "everything within sight ... lights, windows, doors, furniture" was destroyed. The melee was sparked when a volleyball got stuck in the barbed wire of the prison exercise yard and no one was allowed to retrieve it. For three days many prisoners, including Vassall, barricaded themselves inside their cells for safety. It was probably the most physical danger that Vassall had been in since that night in the Hotel Berlin in October 1954.

Vassall said that after the riot, complaints about brutal treatment at Durham prompted a visit from Professor Leon Radzinowicz, a leading criminologist,[211] which meant that Vassall and others were taken out of their "degrading" escape clothing (brightly coloured uniforms that made it easier to detect prisoners). Vassall was also visited by "a quite exceptional psychiatrist, Dr Westbury" and by the McEwens, whose Marchmont estate was relatively close to Durham.

Brigid McEwen recalls sitting with her husband Robin in a waiting room, in which a fish tank stood incongruously, before being ushered in. Vassall was flanked by warders and sat at a table with a low partition to prevent any hand contact. He was surprisingly upbeat about Durham and told them that there was a "nice crowd of Catholics" there. "Prison seemed to suit Vassall down to the ground," Brigid recalls, as it appealed to his sense of order. He was still able to read *The Times* every day and he learned to weave: he once sent the McEwens a woven square.

Eventually, Vassall got a job examining microfilms: exactly the sort of activity that had landed him in jail in the first place. But this time it was under the auspices of the Durham county librarian, not the KGB. Vassall's job was studying ancient documents and "extracting information to add to local records". Vassall was "delighted" to be working in the prison's chapel behind bullet-proof glass. It has been suggested that he performed this cushy job alongside two other convicted spies – Frank Bossard and Harry Houghton – although a story in *The Sun* in July 1967 claimed that while Vassall

---

211   Radzinowicz's assistant in the early 1960s was Donald West, the academic who wrote *Homosexuality* in 1955.

like sorting through archives, Houghton "preferred painting toy soldiers to sewing mailbags".[212]

In December 1966 a fresh security scare erupted. Vassall began receiving frequent letters from a woman named April Moore, a previously unknown friend. Like Tam Galbraith's, Moore's letters were innocuous. In one, sent from a flat in Hove in January 1967, she moaned about landladies and the hassle of sharing digs. On 17 February she wrote again, from 13 Park View Gardens in Hendon, and in May from the Geneva Guest House, also in Hendon, to say that she had landed a job as an invoice typist at a second-hand car dealership. Her letters seemed naïve: "I wonder if you have any sort of a holiday?" she once asked, before a sequence of disjointed sentences, including the alluring lines "I've finally got my figure correct. About a year before I started writing to you I got a slim girlish figure which only lasted 4 months and then I grew bigger and left it".

Moore's handwriting seemed to differ from letter to letter and MI5 called in graphologists. Was Vassall receiving secret messages? MI5 made enquiries and soon discovered that April Moore was not the pen name of a Soviet accomplice. Instead, she was about forty-five, short, plump and reclusive, and she had been asked to leave her guesthouse in Hove because of her habit of continuously pacing around the room from 2 a.m. to 6 a.m. It transpired that she was a former parishioner of Vassall's father, who may have become an obsessed fan of his son.

In truth, unlike Blake, no one wanted to spring Vassall from jail. The Soviets never showed any sign of wanting to see him released as part of a prisoner exchange. In April 1967, MI5 concluded that it was "highly unlikely that Vassall would wish to escape or that the Russians would have any desire to help him, except possibly as a method of embarrassing the authorities". Vassall was just like any

---

212 Oddly, although they spent time in prison together, neither Vassall nor Houghton mention each other once in their respective memoirs and they do not seem to have been friends.

other prisoner: bored, aching for release and reliant on obsessive fan mail for entertainment.

In the summer of 1967, after nine months in Durham, Vassall was moved – again with no warning – back to Maidstone, along with Harry Houghton. Not long before the move Vassall recalled a visit to Durham by a group of MPs including Renée Short, the left-wing Labour MP for Wolverhampton North-East. Vassall immediately recognised Short, so he must have paid close attention to politics, as she had only been elected to Parliament in 1964. Short's eyes "radiated warmth and understanding" but none of the MPs – even one who knew Vassall's brother – seemed to want to talk to him. Remarkably, Vassall thinks it was due to their visit that he was transferred back to Maidstone shortly afterwards. Vassall received a note from Durham's governor, Major Bride, saying that he was sorry he hadn't said goodbye in person. Perhaps it was his belief in his own importance or cabin fever but by now Vassall saw himself as a visiting VIP on a par with those MPs, not an inmate.

Back at Maidstone Vassall was put in a grim block named Weald and found that security was much tighter. Vassall said his "room" – he does not call it a cell – was "like a small bedsitter in a cottage" despite the fact that it had no lavatory and he had to "slop out".

During his first spell in Maidstone, Vassall became a librarian and was given a "blue band" which gave him greater liberty to wander around. There was no chance of that occurring again. For eighteen months he was back on "special supervision". He was assigned to a job in the printshop, where he worked as a Monotype operator. Once again, Vassall seemed to find a way of making the best of a bad lot. He wrote that the printshop instructor, a Mr Pearce, had much "patience and kindness". Vassall was also allowed to continue weaving, at a class overseen by Mrs Noye, "a dear soul who made everyone feel at home in her presence". Vassall weaved two evenings a week in the winter months and made thirty scarves for friends and relatives ("authentic tartans, they were," he reminisced to the *Sunday Times* in 1973). Under the supervision of a kindly Mr Honey he began gardening at the weekends, he swam in Maidstone's outdoor pool and played badminton in the gym. Although Vassall had never expressed any interest in popular music, he claimed to enjoy watching *Top of the Pops* during his second spell at the prison.

Vassall struck up a friendship with a prison visitor, Captain A. D. B. James, who he said had been Churchill's duty captain during the war. Vassall got to know James's wife when she joined her husband at mass in the prison chapel and he relished giving her flowers that he had cultivated on his allotment.

On 23 July 1968 the *Guardian* reported that Vassall had become a "trustie" and had joint responsibility for running Maidstone's tuck shop. For the last four years of his sentence Vassall had a coveted job, one that a model prisoner gets when he is being prepared for release. "It was a full-time job that I enjoyed thoroughly", he recalled.

He kept it despite two embarrassing scandals that appeared in newspapers. Firstly, Maidstone's printshop was found to be producing false Metropolitan Police warrant cards for underworld criminals to impersonate police officers. Secondly, there were two break-ins at the shop that Vassall helped to manage, in 1970 and 1971, with tobacco and cigarettes stolen. The shop had been fortified after an earlier break-in but the robbers had somehow obtained a circular saw to cut through the security bars. The press seized on the story, reporting that "Admiralty spy John Vassall" had reported one of the break-ins and said "the snout's all gone".[213] After he was cleared of any involvement, Vassall wrote to his former barrister, Jeremy Hutchinson, that "publicity never ceases". Yet Vassall did not seem to mind the attention in the least: for once the press were reporting news, not salacious gossip about his sexuality.

---

213   Snout is archaic slang for tobacco. Vassall said that no one in the prison would dream of him using such a phrase, but the "comment of course became part of prison folklore".

By now some Labour MPs were calling for an improvement in Vassall's prison conditions, though they stopped short of calling for his early release. In early 1968, Anne Kerr (Labour MP for Rochester and Chatham, which covered Higham) called for Vassall to be allowed to visit his father in hospital. Michael Foot, then on the back benches, seems to have called for Vassall to be moved to a lower security classification. In November that year, Home Secretary James Callaghan agreed to Vassall being reclassified from a Category A prisoner to a Category B one, without any objection from MI5. But in a letter to Foot, Callaghan added that Vassall "should not draw any conclusions from ... the result of his recent application for release on licence".

Vassall was a "very good prisoner" whose politics were "if anything right of Centre Socialism", wrote an assistant governor in a memorandum to Maidstone's governor, Major Watson, on 16 December 1969. Vassall's politics seemed impossible to define, but the assistant governor's assessment of him – "the overall impression would seem to be that he was compromised in homosexual activities and for fear of the disgrace of disclosure co-operated with the Russians in passing secret information" – was more generous than the Radcliffe report's.

Yet there were still security scares. By 1968 Vassall's post was being intercepted again and on 6 November an MI5 memo recorded that Vassall had received a letter from Christopher Tremain, of Truro, who announced that he was "a young man interested in getting the authorities to allow you to see your father, who is ill, and to obtain your early release from prison". Tremain, who asked if he could visit Vassall himself, "was probably a homosexual", noted MI5, who returned Tremain's letter without telling Vassall.

At Christmas 1967 Vassall was denied permission to visit his father (who had suffered another stroke) at Joyce Green Hospital in Dartford. But in the spring of 1968 William had a private meeting with his son in the governor's office. Despite his indecent assault conviction, Vassall's brother Richard was also allowed to visit. Vassall wrote to Jeremy Hutchinson in November 1970, saying "whenever my brother is not travelling he is able to visit me in congenial surroundings here". Later, Vassall boasted that he was the first prisoner at Maidstone to obtain lemons and he started drinking his tea with lemon, Russian style. The prisoners held cabaret nights and Vassall recalled a prisoner dressed up as "Stella" and eight prisoners – two of them gay, according to Vassall – competing to become "Miss Thanet". He also played a straight role in a mime routine: a man sitting on a bench reading a newspaper alongside another prisoner in drag.

During his final years in prison, Vassall became a voracious reader. He read *Country Life*, the *Antique Collector*, *Vogue*, *Tatler*. Bertrand Russell's autobiography, Harold Nicolson's diaries, Evelyn Waugh's Sword of Honour trilogy and Lord Longford's *Humility*, which were were sent to him by friends. Soon, Vassall met Longford in person: once he was back at Maidstone the Labour peer visited him several times.

Frank Pakenham (who became Lord Longford in 1961),[214] was a bundle of contradictions. On the one hand he was an Anglo-Irish aristocrat who had briefly served (from May to October 1951) as First Lord of the Admiralty; John Godfrey, a former DNI, was an old friend and regular dining companion.[215] On the other hand he had been secretary to William Beveridge when he wrote the report that became the cornerstone of the welfare state. Longford was passionately opposed to the death penalty and for decades had called for a massive reduction in the prison population, setting up the rehabilitation charity, New Bridge, in the mid-1950s. For four decades he campaigned relentlessly for the release of some of Britain's most sadistic murderers, serial killers and rapists, including the

---

214   He only became the 7th Earl of Longford when his older brother died.
215   John Godfrey, who was director of Naval Intelligence from 1939 to 1943, is another candidate for the model for 'M' in Ian Fleming's James Bond novels. Godfrey recruited Fleming over lunch at the Carlton Grill in May 1939.

"Moors murderer" Myra Hindley. Longford offered unconditional forgiveness and friendship to many prisoners who never denied committing monstrous crimes.

In 1957 Longford instigated the Lords' first debate on the Wolfenden report. He had, like Vassall, been born an Anglican and later converted to Catholicism but his strong faith soon led to a reversal of his early support for gay rights. Longford saw homosexuality as a "painful handicap", like any form of sex outside marriage, and by the late 1960s he saw gay men and women as sinners to be pitied and forgiven, not liberated. He was passionately opposed to abortion and pornography and in the early 1970s he joined Mary Whitehouse's Festival of Light, a religious counterblast against the permissive society.[216]

Vassall's association with Longford is strangely elusive. The frequency, and precise dates, of Longford's visits to Vassall in prison are unknown. Vassall's memoirs make no mention of Longford, other than recollecting hearing him give a talk at the Admiralty about the history of Catholics in the Civil Service in the late 1950s and acknowledging him as someone who had helped him in the book's preface. Any campaigning that Longford did for Vassall's early release is unrecorded. In turn, Vassall is not referenced in Peter Stanford's two biographies of Longford. Only one of the prolific Longford's many books makes any mention of Vassall, and it was published four years after Vassall's death.[217] As with many of the elite people that he encountered, Vassall seems to have mattered less to Lord Longford than Longford did to him.

Maybe Vassall was lucky that he did not become one of Longford's big "causes". Many people saw Longford as nothing more than

---

216   Longford had refused to give evidence for the defence in the *Lady Chatterley's Lover* trial of 1961. "I am afraid I'm a puritan", Longford announced. "But Lawrence was a puritan," a solicitor replied. "Not my sort of puritan," said Longford.

217   The book was Longford's *Prison Diary*, edited by Peter Stanford and published in 2000. It had to be withdrawn by its publisher after an unidentified prisoner, who thought he had spoken to Longford in confidence, objected to that confidence being broken.

a self-righteous old windbag. If Longford had publicly campaigned for Vassall, it may have only made Vassall's crimes seem worse and his early release less likely.[218]

With or without help from Longford, Vassall was determined to seek early release and he began applying to the parole board as soon as he could, in 1967. In 1965 Rebecca West wrote "Vassall is … in prison, and will be there for many years," yet, like Oswald Mosley, the last Dolphin Square resident to be imprisoned for treachery, Vassall spent much less time in prison than he expected to. Within two years of West writing those words, Vassall benefitted from a change in parole rules. He could now apply for early release after serving only a third of his eighteen-year sentence, not two-thirds. In September 1967 the *Evening Standard* claimed that Vassall was hoping to be out by Christmas 1968.

At the end of that year, Vassall sought his former barrister's help. On 19 November 1968 he wrote to Jeremy Hutchinson from Maidstone, praising an "excellent article" that Hutchinson had recently written in *The Times*,[219] adding "may I, in conclusion, render my personal thanks to you, for the care, consideration and time you took in my defence which, though so long ago, I clearly remember". Vassall sent many such obsequious letters to Hutchinson over the next decade. It is clear that this one was an attempt to "butter up" Hutchinson, who Vassall hoped could secure his release.

In January 1969 Special Branch wrote to MI5 expressing concern that if Vassall was given parole he "could cause embarrassment if he went to the USSR". MI5 agreed: on 4 November 1968 they had told the Home Office that while they had no objection to Vassall's release

---

218 Even Myra Hindley asked Longford to stop visiting her in Holloway: although his support was keeping her name in the headlines, it was if anything making her release less likely, not more. His constant demands for the early release of criminal monsters was seen as a perversity, and it did prisoners' chances little good.

219 It was not an article but a letter to the editor, published on 9 November, in which Hutchinson questioned the effect of very long sentences as a deterrent, such as the 42-year sentence handed down to George Blake in 1961, on the grounds that "a few days later John Vassal [*sic*] passed copies of secret documents to the Russians and continued to do so until September, 1962".

on security grounds, "he ... could cause embarrassment to HMG if exploited by the KGB in the USSR for publicity and propaganda purposes. This development would be less probable if Vassall were to keep himself in employment but we foresee that this might not be easy for one who is known to have been a spy and a homosexual."

While technically it was the parole board's decision, an MI5 minute from 29 April 1969 stated that Home Secretary James Callaghan let it be known that he intended "to take a tough line and spies cannot by any means count on getting parole after a third of their sentence". The message was clear: if he was lucky Vassall could hope to be released when he had completed half of his sentence, in 1971, but not before.

On 7 December 1970 Vassall wrote to Hutchinson again, telling him that the new Home Secretary, the Conservative Reginald Maudling, had written to let him know that "having carefully and sympathetically studied all the relevant information available ... [he] has decided that he would not be justified in authorising your release on licence". Vassall's third parole application had been turned down and Vassall wanted Hutchinson's advice on his next steps and his views on whether Home Secretaries had been under "some kind of pressure" to block his release.

Vassall referred to his solicitor, John Bird of Peake and Company, but as always, he wanted the opinion of someone more eminent. By the 1970s, Hutchinson was one of the most famous lawyers in the land, a vice chairman of the Arts Council of Great Britain, a professor of law at the Royal Academy of Arts and a trustee of the Tate Gallery, which he was later Chairman of. It is not clear whether, or how, Hutchinson replied or what steps he took behind the scenes. But from 1970 onwards, MI5's hostility to Vassall's early release softened considerably. The only question was timing, and logistics.[220]

---

220 MI5 were keen to occasionally interview Vassall about intelligence matters right up until his release: on 25 August 1971 Peter Wright requested that the parole board's decision on Vassall's future should be delayed until after he had a chance to visit him at Maidstone.

MI5 was told that Vassall's 1970 parole application had largely been refused because of the negative publicity that may have arisen if he was released from Maidstone soon after Harry Houghton in May 1970.[221] Once Houghton and Ethel Gee were free, however, it seemed that Vassall's next parole application would be looked upon more favourably.

Another question was how much money Vassall had. The £5,000 from the *Sunday Pictorial* did not go to Vassall himself but to his solicitors, Wontner & Sons, from which they deducted around £1,500 in legal fees because Vassall was never granted legal aid. Vassall was taxed on the remaining £3,500 so he cannot have made more than £2,500 from selling his story. Later, he said that much of the remainder was eaten up by more legal fees. Other than that, Vassall only had about £500 in Premium Bonds so there seemed little chance of him gloating after his release about how much money he had made.

The only real obstacles to Vassall's early release after the summer of 1970 were circumstances completely beyond his control. The first was a bizarre coincidence at Vassall's old flat. In June 1970, an MI5 officer, H. D. Wharton, was told, over drinks with Dolphin Square's manager Brain Garrard, that the "DNI [director of naval intelligence] is living in the flat formerly occupied by Vassall". It was true: 807 Hood House, where Vassall had lived from 1959 to 1962, was now the weekday home of Vice-Admiral Louis Le Bailly, the Admiralty's Director of "Defence Staff Intelligence" (the 1970s equivalent of the DNI).

In an MI5 minute Wharton wrote – probably mistakenly – that before his arrest Vassall had entertained "Carrington and the First Sea Lord" in the flat and suggested that the Russians may have bugged their conversations. "There are a thousand flats in Dolphin

---

221 Houghton and Gee were released early after the intervention of their Dorset MP, Evelyn King, who once raised Bunty's health in the Commons. By contrast, no MPs seem to have ever called for Vassall's early release.

Square and many other blocks of flats in S.W.1. The odds against this happening by chance are therefore enormous," wrote Wharton. But senior officials in MI5 brushed aside fears that the Russians had bugged Vassall's flat during his tenancy and that it could be reactivated. A "sweep" of the flat to look for bugs was ruled out, as R. G. Holden felt that "no classified information was at risk". Holden appears to have assumed that unlike Vassall, Le Bailly would never discuss naval secrets, let alone photograph them during his tenancy.[222] Le Bailly's choice of flat was judged to be coincidental and he rented it happily for several years.

The second problem concerned Vassall's probation officer, John Emerson. In August 1970 MI5 was contacted by a Mr Glanville, an assistant secretary at the Home Office, and a parole board member called W. H. Pearce, who had suspicions about Emerson. He had specifically requested to become Vassall's probation officer, they said, and had visited him regularly since 1968. Like George Blake, Emerson had been a prisoner of war in Korea and he had later visited Russia. MI5 believed that he was separated from his Japanese wife and was, Pearce said, a "misfit ... a strange man, authoritarian, ascetic, eccentric – 'just back from *Bridge on the River Kwai*'" – and probably a homosexual.

Pearce concluded that Emerson "had either been attracted to Vassall because of the nature of his particular offence, or that he had deliberately manipulated the situation in order to maintain contact with Vassall should he be granted parole, or that there was a possibility he was working on behalf of a foreign power". By the end of 1970, Emerson told the parole board that Vassall "had had enough of prison and was now getting increasingly bitter with the authorities" and recommended parole.

In January 1971 Emerson was questioned by MI5. He said that

---

222 Le Bailly's memoirs, *The Man Around the Engine*, suggest that he had first reported the connection to Vassall, rather than being told about it. Having discovered that Vassall had been the penultimate tenant, "in some embarrassment I confidentially reported this and quickly discovered the Whitehall capacity for leaks. Within 48 hours the news was in the press."

he had been allocated Vassall and hadn't requested to be his parole officer, although he did admit that he found him "a very stimulating person after the ordinary run-of-the-mill client". Emerson told Vassall that he was "not a spy but a traitor" but he had clearly come to like him. The Home Office was taking no chances: Emerson was quietly moved away from Vassall, who was allocated a new probation officer: the 50-year-old Miss Georgina Stafford.

Once the Le Bailly and Emerson problems were resolved, there seemed to be few obstacles left. Vassall was told by visitors that he could expect to be released in 1972, though others intimated that "political pressures" might mean a delay until 1974. In the summer of 1971, however, Vassall was informed that his fourth parole application had been successful but he had to wait until the autumn of 1972, not 1971, before being let out.[223]

Vassall was intensely honest and a model prisoner. Even throughout his spying career Vassall had rarely lied directly: it was simply that no one ever asked him if he was a Soviet spy. Some believe that Vassall behaved so well in jail that he would probably have been released before 1972 had it not been for the political imperative for the government to look tough.

Being told by Maidstone's new governor, Mr Lister, that his parole application had been successful was a "tremendous moment" but also stressful. The shock prompted a stomach complaint that meant Vassall had to be rushed to hospital for tests, missing a visit to the jail by the Catholic Archbishop of Southwark, Dr Cyril Cowderoy. Another concern for Vassall was his father's deteriorating health. William had resumed his visits to Maidstone, asking warders how John was being treated and thanking the governor for permitting his visits. Relations between father and son were never warm but they appeared to mellow the longer that Vassall was in jail. Yet at

---

223 The decision to finally release Vassall on licence was made by Reginald Maudling. By the time of Vassall's release Maudling he had been forced to resign as Home Secretary in July 1972 because of the Poulson scandal.

around the time that Vassall heard he was to be released, his father became dangerously ill and was confined to hospital. William survived but he remained almost bedridden until his death a year later. Vassall was allowed to visit him, travelling by taxi with two prison officers. A confused William recognised his son but seemed unaware that he was still in prison.

Vassall's prison friends had told him "when the autumn leaves start to fall, John, you will be gone", and he was. In the summer of 1972 Vassall was told that he would definitely be released in October, eight years before the end of his eighteen-year sentence. For once, the press did not go into a frenzy. Over the years opportunistic MPs had voiced concerns about Vassall making more money by selling his story again.[224] But in the end, there was no great media outcry.

Six weeks prior to his release, Vassall was allowed to spend three days outside Maidstone to help him to acclimatise to life after a decade behind bars. Three days of "home leave" was something that all prisoners could request after a certain stage in their sentence but it was not automatic. To Vassall's surprise, his application was approved "without hesitation".

Vassall stayed at the country home of an unnamed friend of his mother's who collected him from Maidstone. As his hostess, "a sympathetic woman", drove him through the countryside, Vassall had to ask her to lower a window: he was so unused to car journeys, other than those from prison to prison, that he felt sick. In a chemist's shop in a small Kentish town, Vassall bought a toothbrush, warily handing over a 50 pence piece: he was still unfamiliar with new decimal coins.

At the house, the family were having sherry in the drawing room. A fire was lit, a dog and an "immaculate white cat" appeared

---

224 These MPs were on the left as well as the right. In September 1968, William Wilson, Labour MP for Coventry South, publicly called on Callaghan not to release Vassall on parole "if substantial proceeds are still around" from his Russian money.

and Vassall chatted to the family's two sons. For dinner, Vassall was served melon and ginger and roast chicken, washed down by a "superb" Saumur. When he went to bed he was delighted to find freshly cut flowers and three books that "my hostess knew I would enjoy": a volume of D. H. Lawrence, Quentin Bell's biography of Virginia Woolf and *The Sun King* (Nancy Mitford's biography of Louis XIV).

Vassall was in raptures. "I could just relax – in a country garden, surrounded by some of the beautiful things of life – a lovely old country house, beautiful silver, good china, comfortable furniture, a cosy snug bed."

After breakfast the next morning he walked around the gardens and went to pick up one of the son's friends from a railway station before lunch, had afternoon tea in the garden and then dinner at the Wife of Bath in Wye, an award-winning restaurant. Over another fine meal, Vassall and his hosts "discussed the Russian and American ways of life – deciding that perhaps England was the best". On the morning of day two, Vassall visited a timber yard, before a walk across "cornfields turned to stubble" with his hostess. After lunch in the garden Vassall said that he wanted to smell sea air and was driven down to Romney Marsh where he swam in the English Channel – his first sea swim for a decade. En route back to Maidstone jail the following morning, Vassall asked to stop at a record shop where he bought his hosts a recording of Brahms's *Variations on a Theme by Haydn*. For Vassall, "three nights in the country had been perfect". For three days, prison had become a distant memory.

Vassall's impending release, scheduled for 24 October 1972 – ten years and two days after he had been sentenced at the Old Bailey – brought logistical challenges. The Home Office was anxious that Vassall would leave jail with more decorum than Harry Houghton, whose release from Maidstone in May 1970 had turned into a media circus. A detailed plan for Vassall's release had been agreed as early as January 1971 and there was no chance of him ending up in a dingy bail hostel, besieged by the media. He would be driven from prison to a solicitor's office for a press conference, as it "was felt that it was no good trying to dodge the press and it was better to get it over as soon as possible". Vassall's probation officer, John Emerson, would drive Vassall to see his ailing father, and then to stay with Emerson's sister in Hastings. Vassall would then spend a few weeks at Quarr Abbey, a Benedictine monastery on the Isle of Wight, and another few weeks with an aunt near Taunton. He would then stay with his brother in Kent for a while before going to London to seek a job in the antiques business. This plan was founded on the hope that keeping Vassall moving, and away from London, would mean that the press would soon give up trying to track him down. But in early 1971, Emerson was taken off Vassall's case and a new plan was needed.

The usual procedure was simply for prisoners to walk out of Maidstone's gates carrying their own luggage to be met by family or friends. But Vassall had at least three suitcases and was worried about being swamped by reporters as he carried them onto the street, given that the BBC had already announced the time and date of his release. The authorities expressly refused to allow cars into the prison grounds to pick prisoners up and they did not make an exception for Vassall.

Luckily, on that day Vassall was escorted through the gate by his solicitor (a Mr Trenner) and Captain James, who helped him to carry his bulky luggage. But Vassall had become so accustomed to prison life that he described his release as "a dreadful day" full of foreboding and he kept himself busy in the prison garden until the last possible moment. As he waited in a holding area, two other prisoners – who Vassall said were gay – told him "Oh John, you must love this publicity". "But I hated it", Vassall insisted. On the drive away from the prison gates he had to ask Captain and Mrs James to stop their car so he could be sick.

• • • •

Vladimir Ilyich Lenin once said "There are decades where nothing happens; and there are weeks where decades happen". The ten years between 1962 and 1972 were certainly not a decade in which nothing happened.

The 1960s, a decade of cultural and sexual liberation, only really got going several months after Vassall landed in jail. The deferential England that he had known had vanished forever: abortion was legalised, divorce was made considerably easier and the Lord Chamberlain no longer censored plays. While Vassall was in jail there had been three Prime Ministers. The sitting Prime Minister was now Ted Heath, a bachelor in his early fifties, while the Liberal leader, Jeremy Thorpe, was married with children but subject to much speculation about his sexuality.

In autumn 1962 the Beatles were still an obscure skiffle band in Liverpool, but by 1972 they had disbanded and were arguably Britain's greatest cultural export since Shakespeare. In 1962 the zebra crossing on Abbey Road in St John's Wood (three minutes' walk from Addison House, where Vassall lived until 1959) was just one of hundreds of such crossings in London. But in 1969 it had become the most famous zebra crossing in the world.

Kennedy had been assassinated, Churchill had died and Khrushchev had been ousted. The Vietnam War had started and was in its death throes by the time Vassall was released. The civil rights movement had transformed the internal politics of the United States, Britain's currency had been decimalised, the Open University had been created and television was now in colour. Although Vassall's beloved Bath Club on Brook Street was still open, the heyday of London gentlemen's clubs was over: many closed in the 1960s and 1970s and the Bath would follow in 1981.

Vassall seemed entirely comfortable in the unfamiliar Britain of 1972. "My first impression is that people today are more humane, not so provincial as they were," he told the *Sunday Times* a few months later. "Life was very rigid in the circle I moved in. If people in high places did understand you, they never let on. Young people now look much more interesting and alive, the clothes are more cheerful and informal".

Alongside shock and surprise, Vassall may also have felt some schadenfreude. While Vassall was in jail, Sir Geoffrey Harrison – one of Sir William Hayter's successors as British ambassador in Moscow – had been ensnared in sexual blackmail, courtesy of "an attractive maid infiltrated into his excellency's residence". In 1968 the maid, called Galya, "indicated her availability for sexual encounters".[225] When she revealed that they had been caught on hidden KGB cameras and told Harrison that they needed to supply secrets to the Russians to avoid the photographs being disseminated he had the good sense to tell the Foreign Office everything and was recalled to London, but not fired.

Harrison soon retired on a full pension in receipt of a top honour, as a Knight Grand Cross of the Most Distinguished Order of St Michael and St George (GCMG). Unlike Vassall's sexual entrapment, Harrison's was voluntary and it was not revealed until 1981. Such is the difference between an ambassador ensnared in a heterosexual honeytrap and a humble clerk entangled in a homosexual one.

The biggest change that occurred while Vassall had been in jail was that most homosexual activities – though not all – had been decriminalised. In the ten years since Wolfenden's recommendations, there were many bumps in the road. In March 1962, six months before Vassall's arrest, the Labour MP Leo Abse put forward a private members' bill to decriminalise homosexuality but it was "talked out" by Conservative MPs. In July 1964 Sir John Hobson – the Attorney General who had led the prosecution of Vassall two years earlier – relaxed the law, telling Parliament that

---

225 The British journalist, John Miller, claimed that the maid's name was Galya Ivanov and that she was the sister of Eugene Ivanov, the Soviet naval attaché who was embroiled in the Profumo affair.

the director of public prosecutions had "advised Chief Constables informally that in order to achieve greater uniformity of enforcement of the law regarding homosexuality in private they should seek his advice before bringing proceedings". This led to a big fall in prosecutions but the Home Secretary, Henry Brooke, closed the door on more substantial reform, asserting that there had been no real change in public opinion since Wolfenden's recommendations had been defeated on a free vote in 1960.

Well into the mid-1960s, and beyond, there was much homophobia in Parliament. In his very last speech in the House of Lords on 24 May 1965, the former Lord Chief Justice, Rayner Goddard, rambled against "coteries of buggers where horrible things go on, and a judge has to listen to stories that make you physically sick".[226] The Conservative MP Humphry Berkeley, who was strongly in favour of decriminalisation, lost his seat at the 1966 election and found that he could not easily return to Parliament given the prejudices of many Conservative associations. Berkeley's defeat stopped his private member's bill to implement Wolfenden's recommendations which he had put forward in 1965. While Hugh Gaitskell's widow Dora was an active supporter of reform (as a member of the Lords from 1964 until her death in 1989) George Brown was always strongly opposed to decriminalisation. "This is how Rome fell!" he once told Barbara Castle.

The case for decriminalisation was largely won with the pragmatic argument that it would lead to a reduction in another crime: blackmail. The Homosexual Law Reform Society ran press adverts featuring a front door marked "Blackmailers Welcome". The society skilfully decided not to focus on the misery that the current law inflicted on gay men and women. Instead it exploited the general

---

226 Goddard had always been a pious bigot. Having been widowed in 1928, he ran as a "purity candidate" in the general election of 1929, standing in South Kensington, whose sitting Conservative MP, Sir William Davison, had been a defendant in a divorce case. It was thought that newly enfranchised young women voters would refuse to support Davison but Goddard, running under the slogan "Purity Goddard", came last in the poll, winning only 15 per cent of the vote.

antipathy towards blackmailers to successfully lobby for Wolfenden to finally be implemented.[227]

Once the homophobic clamour of the Vassall case died down, the case for reform was also aided by more open discussions in the media. Bryan Magee, one of Britain's foremost public intellectuals, made two television documentaries – one about gay men in 1964 and the second about lesbians in 1965 – and in 1966 he wrote a book, *One in Twenty*.[228] These were generally sympathetic and liberal surveys which ended with a call for more "toleration". "The homosexual is not only ... the pansy boy ... it is also the man who sells you your cigarettes over the tobacconist's counter, and the chap with the bowler hat, striped trousers, briefcase and rolled umbrella, or perhaps your doctor," Magee wrote. "It is the labourer on the building site, the lorry driver, the factory workers, the white-collar clerk, the clergyman."

When Leo Abse's latest private members' bill finally got royal assent on 27 July 1967, there was much jubilation. "Ten years is a long time in which to make a decision, but better late than never," mused Ian Harvey. Tellingly, Abse's bill entered the statute book as the Sexual Offences Act 1967, not the Homosexual Emancipation Act or the Sexual Law Reform Act. While it decriminalised private homosexual activity between men aged over twenty-one, it also imposed heavier penalties for "street offences" such as soliciting.

---

227   Many still predicted that if homosexuality was decriminalised the blackmailer's influence would hardly be reduced, as they could still exploit society's inherent homophobia, particularly over bisexual men. Macmillan once mused to his staff, "Would acceptance of the Wolfenden recommendations make blackmail more difficult? Probably not. It was not the avowed and complete homosexual who was vulnerable, but the man who did not go quite so far".

228   Magee's book was very frank about gay sex. "When it comes to bringing each other to orgasm there are three commonplace methods. The first of these, which is also common between the sexes, is masturbation with the hands. The second, likewise common between the sexes, is fellatio, which means taking the penis into the mouth and sucking it. The third – and this, though less common between the sexes, is not so infrequent as many people suppose – is buggery, which means the insertion of the penis of one into the anus of another". But Magee, a liberal humanist who later became a Labour MP, also showed his latent homophobia. "Although I am in favour of changing the existing law, I think the law has become a scapegoat for homosexuals and liberal-minded people," he said in his 1964 documentary. "There is a widespread tendency to ascribe to the law nearly all the things wrong with life for homosexuals, and to assume, or assert, that if the law were changed these basic problems would be solved".

Homosexual activities involving more than two people, or involving an adult man under the age of twenty-one, were still unlawful. Even the activities that Vassall had been photographed engaged in in 1954 would still be unlawful as they involved more than two men.[229] The law did not extend to Scotland or Northern Ireland, where homosexuality was not decriminalised until the early 1980s. It also contained some surprising provisions: a two-year maximum sentence for sex that did not occur in private. Homosexual activity in the armed forces and between merchant seamen on British ships remained a criminal offence. Abse was no homophobe but to get his bill passed in the Commons he pragmatically argued that if homosexuality was decriminalised its prevalence would decline, presumably because it would no longer carry the added thrill of doing something unlawful.

While in jail John Vassall kept an eye on the slow progress of reform. In his memoirs he wrote, "I was on tenterhooks when at last the Wolfenden proposals were finally passed and I gave an enormous sigh of relief that never again could one be blacklisted or fear being prosecuted". Vassall did not appear to wonder whether his own prosecution for spying and the anachronistic "moral panic" it unleashed might have been another factor that had delayed decriminalisation.

• • •

The homophobia that followed the Vassall case was also evident in the courts. Just four weeks after Vassall's conviction, Laurence

---

229 It soon became clear that gay men would still be prosecuted for consensual sexual acts after decriminalisation. Later in 1967 Oliver Ford (a renowned interior designer and a contemporary of Vassall's, who had served in the RAF during the war) was arrested for "indecency" with two soldiers from Knightsbridge Barracks, because he was caught with two men, not one. Ford said he was "ashamed and distressed" but had "honestly believed he was not offending against the law". Nonetheless, he was fined £700 in May 1968. But, in a sign of changing times, Ford received a royal warrant from the Queen Mother in 1976 and was regularly invited to events at Buckingham Palace and Clarence House.

Somers, a 16-year-old 'cellarman', was acquitted because he claimed that the man he murdered had made mild sexual overtures towards him. George Brinham, who had chaired the Labour Party's National Executive Committee in 1959–60, was killed at his basement flat in Kensington on 17 November 1962. Somers was quickly arrested but shortly before Christmas he was cleared of manslaughter at the Old Bailey after employing the "gay panic" defence.[230]

A few months later came yet another reminder of how any suggestion of homosexuality could destroy careers. On 2 March 1963, while the Radcliffe tribunal was underway, *The Times* reported that Mortimer Wilmot Bennett, a 52-year-old under-secretary at the Ministry of Public Building and Works, was fined £25, plus costs, for "persistently importuning male persons for immoral purposes" in a public lavatory in Islington. On 19 February Bennett had had a "very heavy dinner" at the Guildhall involving "sherry in the anteroom, sherry with the soup, hock with the fish, burgundy with the meat and champagne with the sweet. There was also port and finally brandy," *The Times* reported. Later that night two undercover policemen saw Bennett, who was wearing evening dress, entering and re-entering the lavatory three times and smiling and nodding at other men. Bennett, who was defended by Vassall's barrister Jeremy Hutchinson, denied that he was homosexual and insisted that he had kept returning to the lavatory because he felt sick and presumably brought up some of the copious amount of alcohol he had consumed. Nonetheless, he was found guilty, his "great career being snapped by the weakest link in the chain", he was told by a magistrate. Bennett was suspended from his job but mounted a successful appeal in May. It was a lucky escape: had his appeal failed, his career would probably have been ruined.

230　Somers claimed that Brinham had started talking to him outside a gun shop on the Strand and invited him back to his flat to drink beer. Brinham asked if he could kiss him, prompting Somers to hit Brinham with a decanter in a fit of rage. Somers's counsel, Edward Clarke QC, successfully argued that "there is a defence that you are entitled to kill a man, if he is committing an atrocious crime against you". Somers sold his story to the *News of the World*.

The Vassall case was not cited at Somers's or Bennett's trials. Yet in 1965 Lord Boothby cited it when he sued the *Sunday Mirror* for alleging that he was linked to the Kray twins. "Perhaps it is a hangover from the Vassall and Profumo cases," Boothby said. "In recent months I have been uneasily aware of a rise in this kind of witch-hunting atmosphere". Like many gay men of his generation, Boothby's stance was to deny everything, even though most of Westminster and Fleet Street knew that he was gay.

Throughout the 1960s the Vassall scandal was the subject of much banter across the Royal Navy. It was a common jape to sign off letters to senior officers with the words "I remain, Sir, your obedient Vassall" rather than "your obedient servant".[231] More seriously, the Vassall case reinforced institutional homophobia in both the American and British security services and fuelled paranoid conspiracy theories that Vassall was part of a large "fifth column" of gay spies controlled by the Soviets. Only with hindsight, in his ghostwritten stories in the *Sunday Pictorial*, did Vassall come across as a Walter Mitty figure who exaggerated the scale of his love life and the social status of his lovers. At the time, however, there was genuine fear that Vassall had not acted alone.

In November 1962 MI5 heard that Peter Stuhrmann, "a prolific German homosexual who has admitted to having worked for the East German and Russian Intelligence Services", claimed that he had attended "orgies" at 804 Hood House, a flat rented by a woman called Margaret Neale on the same corridor as Vassall's flat. MI5 noted that it was "difficult to divide fact from fiction in his lurid confessions". Then, in August 1963, "French liaison" – France's security services – enquired about Vassall's visits to Paris ("because a fabricator is trying to sell them some yarn linking Vassall to an international RIS network", a minute by G. T. S. Hinton noted), but all of MI5 knew about Vassall's Parisian visits was a single postcard

---

231   I am grateful to John Crossman for providing this information.

that he had sent to the Van Den Borns from Paris on 7 October 1959.

By 1963 at the British embassy in Moscow, which in the mid-1950s had grudgingly tolerated Vassall's homosexuality, a witch-hunt was underway. In a 1998 interview, Dennis Amy, who was put in charge of internal security there a few years after Vassall left, recalled that it was rife with speculation about who was and wasn't gay. "I don't think we had any," said Amy. "In fact I was asked whether the current Admiralty clerk was a homosexual. I said no, he wasn't, but maybe the naval attaché was".[232] Meanwhile, the Soviet bloc's intelligence agencies continued to use homosexual blackmail as a technique well into the 1980s, if not beyond.

Because it could not easily talk to gay civil servants, MI5 relied on the strangest sources to understand what it was like to be blackmailed. In 1969 MI5 officers went to see one of the few public figures who was out and proud: the 2nd Viscount Maugham, the son of a former Lord Chancellor and the nephew of the novelist Somerset Maugham.[233] Viscount Maugham – known to his friends as Robin – is best known for his 1948 novella *The Servant,* which was made into a film starring Dirk Bogarde and James Fox in 1963. MI5 noted that Maugham "makes no attempt to conceal his own homosexual characteristics. In appearance and manner he recalls Max Beerbohm's cartoons of queers".

In 1969 Maugham lived in a flat in Hove, where he was happy to talk to MI5 about Vassall. "Under the stimulus of a second glass of sherry", MI5 said, Maugham confided that if he "had ever found himself in a similar situation he would have had no hesitation whatsoever about reporting the facts to his Ambassador, and he could not imagine why a man with Vassall's social contacts and background should not have done the same." Easily said from an

---

232   See https://archives.chu.cam.ac.uk/wp-content/uploads/sites/2/2022/01/Amy.pdf.
233   No attempt seems to have been made to ascertain the views of Somerset Maugham – who was also gay – before his death in 1965.

armchair in Hove with a glass of sherry at one's elbow. Quite what insight this provided into Vassall's espionage a decade earlier is unclear.

Government training publications from the 1960s were full of references to the Vassall case. In 1964 MI5 produced *Their Trade Is Treachery*, a fifty-page pamphlet given to civil servants in the Foreign Office and other departments.[234] The brochure contained chapters on "How Not to Become a Spy" and "How to Become a Spy". "Spies are with us all the time", the preface warned. "This booklet tells you … how to recognise at once certain espionage techniques and how to avoid pitfalls, which could lead to a national catastrophe or a personal disaster – or both". Alongside the "ideological" spy was the "mercenary spy … motivated by greed. Vassall, the Admiralty spy, claimed that at first he was blackmailed, but later he clearly became a mercenary spy." History was already being rewritten: despite the prosecution accepting Vassall's account of his blackmail at his trial, here MI5 argued that Vassall may have fabricated the story to mask his greed.

No feature-length film has ever been made about the Vassall case. The closest equivalent (other than a single episode of the BBC's 1980 drama series *Spy!*) is a 1964 training film commissioned by the Central Office of Information (COI). *Persona non Grata* was part of a series of films warning civil servants to beware of foreign spies, particularly from the eastern bloc.[235] The films were made, the COI said, with the help of an intelligence officer who is "a successful author in his spare time"– said to be John le Carré.[236]

---

234   Not to be confused with the 1981 book of the same title by Chapman Pincher.

235   A shorter 27-minute film, *It Can't Happen to Me*, was released by the COI in February 1962. Although it was made before Vassall's arrest it contains eerie premonitions. A voiceover warns of the dangers of leaving briefcases in pubs and how innocuous chalk marks on advertising posters can be secret signals to "contacts" that there is information – such as a roll of microfilm – to be collected from a "dead drop" nearby. It depicts the sexual blackmail of a "pretty simple sort of chap … passed over for promotion" who they say is "vain, frustrated, resents authority [and] wants more money and recognition": words that are eerily similar to those said about Vassall a few months later.

236   *Persona non Grata* can, like the other COI films in the series, be viewed on the Imperial War Museum's website at https://www.iwm.org.uk/collections/item/object/1060022073.

In *Persona non Grata*'s opening scene a new second secretary, called Popov, arrives at the Soviet embassy in London, depicted as a mansion in Belgravia. Popov's departing predecessor introduces him to a contact: a sleazy Welsh journalist named Evans, whose money worries are eased by regular cash gifts and free theatre tickets, delivered by the Soviets inside copies of *Exchange and Mart* magazine. At a private viewing at a London art gallery, Evans steers Popov towards a "lost soul" who works at "one of the defence departments" on Horseferry Road, named Cyril Vining.[237] Although Vining's homosexuality is never explicitly stated, he is a combination of stereotypes, both nervous and camp. A bespectacled John Vassall lookalike, Vining dreams of escaping his dull clerical job and becoming a writer but is chided by his boss, a martinet named Ramsay, for penning his creations on ministry notepaper.

Popov is not shown to seduce or entrap Vining, but he certainly flatters him. He takes Vining to the ballet, for expensive dinners and drinks at a fashionable riverside hotel. Vining tells Popov about his dislike of Ramsay ("I don't know what I dislike more, his smugness or his arrogance") and Popov asks Vining to write "cameos of English life" for a Russian magazine, for which he is paid the generous sum of £15 each. Write "whatever you like, whenever you like", Popov tells him enticingly. Vining returns Popov's hospitality by inviting him to a candle-lit dinner in his rented basement rooms, furnished with antiques, in Bloomsbury. After drinking Polish vodka, Vining admits to childhood ambitions to become Prime Minister or Poet Laureate and says it is the first time in four years that he has entertained anyone in his modest digs. But Popov suddenly turns nasty, saying that he knows that the department where Vining works has "plans for the Polaris mixed fleet" and that Vining must help him to "get certain things confirmed". When Vining demurs,

---

237 Vining was played by Frederick Bartman. In 1993 Bartman found himself on trial at the Old Bailey, as Vassall had been. He was charged with the murder of Lady Brenda Cross, the wife of Air Chief Marshal Sir Kenneth Cross, who worked as an assistant at the antique shop that he ran in Pimlico, and who was found bludgeoned to death in its basement. Bartman was acquitted.

Popov says he is "disappointed, even hurt" and reminds him of all the generous hospitality he has received.

Back in the office, Vining reads a memo warning all staff against "social contacts with officials of the Sino-Soviet bloc". He tries to tell the irritable Ramsay all, but the latter is too busy to hear Vining's outpourings and makes a belittling joke about his "artistic temperament". As if in revenge, Vining discovers the combination to Ramsay's safe by reading the impression left on an office notepad. In the next scene, Vining meets Popov for a boating trip and is given another envelope of money and a camera with which to photograph documents. They arrange to meet on the first Saturday of every month, with the first rendezvous at London Zoo.

The pathetic Vining is contrasted with another target of the Soviets: flight sergeant Harry Wilson, an attaché who works in "Sec Ops" at the Air Ministry. To make it abundantly clear that Wilson is heterosexual, he is seen being chided by his wife for his past womanising. But Wilson has another secret: when posted to Moscow a few years earlier he had "made a bit of a mug of myself", as he tells his wife, and fears that he may face jail if his crime is discovered. When later, Soviet diplomats accost Wilson in the street they ominously remind him of "the promise you made in Moscow". The next night Wilson meets his handler – called Nikolai, the same name as Vassall's – who asks him for directions to Charing Cross tube station. Wilson is then given a new rendezvous point – outside Chalk Farm tube station (very close to Frognal station, one of Vassall's meeting places with the real-life Nikolai).

Unlike Vining, Wilson approaches his boss, an amiable man named Scott, and confesses that he had been "on the fiddle" in Moscow until he was caught by the Russians. Scott calls an MI5 officer named Tanner, who puts a tail on Wilson as he goes to his rendezvous with his Soviet handler at Chalk Farm. MI5 also begin to tail Popov, who they suspect is responsible for Wilson's coercion. They see him at the zoo with Vining, who gives Popov an envelope and receives cash in return. Special Branch then follow Vining back to his flat and workplace and he and Popov are swiftly arrested in Hampstead (sardonically codenamed "Redland"). Popov escapes to Moscow, his passport stamped "persona non grata". It is clear that Vining has been ruined, while the sensible Wilson has kept his job and been rewarded for honesty.

Persona non Grata is an obvious fictionalisation of the Vassall case. "Vining" is eerily similar to Vassall's MI5 codename, Vine Leaf.[238] The only real difference between Vassall and Vining is that the latter has never gone to Moscow and the part of the Moscow dupe is played by a heterosexual character, Wilson. *Persona non Grata* implicitly criticises standoffish civil servants who can't establish a proper rapport with their staff, but its main messages are simple: don't give secrets to strange men, particularly those with Russian accents, and if you are compromised by them, tell your boss everything immediately. The question of what you should do if you are a gay civil servant – come out to your boss and risk the sack, or stay in the closet and be sacked anyway if you are ever found out – is sidestepped.

A later COI film which is haunted by the Vassall case was a taut thirteen-minute drama-documentary, also made in black and white. *The Lecture* (1968) opens with a foreign spymaster (clearly a Soviet, though this is never explicitly stated) lecturing an audience of diplomats ahead of their London postings about the quaint British practice of using pouches and briefcases for diplomatic mail. In the next scene, a 34-year-old married Englishman from Birmingham, codenamed Leonid – another bespectacled Vassall lookalike – is befriended by a Russian at an evening class, sexually blackmailed and then "left on ice" for a year before being recontacted. Leonid is compelled to take documents home from work and photograph them with a Minox until he is nearly caught out by the kind of spot

---

238 The film also seems to consciously echo the 1961 film *Victim*: the Salisbury pub, on the corner of Cecil Court and St Martin's Lane in London's West End, appears in both films.

checks that were finally introduced after the Vassall affair. Leonid uses the office photocopier, until access to it is restricted, and then takes the calculated risk of asking to view a file he does not need to see. He is promptly sacrificed by the Soviets because he has "lost his long-term value". *The Lecture* ends with a warning that even banal discussions should be avoided: a Soviet diplomat is seen chatting to a bus conductor, no doubt trying to glean the sensitive secrets of London Transport.

The crude stereotype of Cyril Vining did not reappear in *The Lecture*. It is not specified whether Leonid's blackmail was of the heterosexual or homosexual variety. By the end of the 1960s British government training films had moved on from homophobia. Alongside the Bond films and film adaptations of Len Deighton books (which glorified violence and contained heroes impervious to death and doubt) another genre of spy movie emerged in the late 1960s that depicted British intelligence as a bunch of bumbling amateurs: what Donald McLachlan described (in the *Sunday Telegraph* in 1967) as "a fresh wave of anti-gentleman, down-with-the-old-boy ring" films. Unlike Labour's accusations about decadent old-boy networks in the early 1960s, this "fresh wave", including the 1968 film *A Dandy in Aspic*, was not tinged with obvious homophobia and there were fewer coded references to the Vassall case.

• • •

John Vassall might have been pleased that crude homophobia was becoming rarer on cinema screens by the end of the 1960s. He would have been less enthralled to discover that throughout that decade, many of his gay friends were persecuted for having known him. Several saw their civil service or political careers destroyed, and in at least one case the mere suggestion that they had known Vassall was enough to extinguish their prospects.

Tam Galbraith was not the only Conservative politician whose career was derailed by speculation that he had been Vassall's lover. Another was Denzil Freeth, Conservative MP for Basingstoke. Until the 1950s many gay MPs, such as Tom Driberg and Bob Boothby, "got away with it", but in the 1960s a more combative and less deferential media, along with a new climate of Cold War paranoia, meant that they often didn't.

Born in 1924, Denzil Freeth was exactly the same age as Vassall and was a High Anglican and a successful stockbroker. Like Vassall, Freeth had served with the RAF during the war, training as a pilot in Canada. After Cambridge, where he was president of the Cambridge Union, he entered the Commons in 1955, aged thirty-one, and was soon seen as a "rising star". His vociferous support for implementing Wolfenden's recommendations did not bar him from becoming parliamentary secretary for science in Macmillan's government. Like Galbraith, Freeth found that he often appeared at the despatch box in the Commons because the Minister for Science and Technology, Quintin Hogg, sat in the Lords (as Viscount Hailsham). Hogg was a fervent homophobe but, like the married Ian Harvey, the unmarried Freeth seems to have evaded Hogg's detection. Until 1962 Freeth appeared to be prospering as an ambitious thirty-something destined for high office.

Then, everything started to go wrong for Denzil Freeth. There were two "unfortunate incidents". In the first, Freeth went to empty a dustbin outside his house in Victoria late one night in April 1962, dressed only in his underwear, and was locked out after his front door slammed shut. A passing policeman charged Freeth with being drunk and disorderly, and he was fined £1 (Freeth said variously that wandering around in underwear was either a genuine misadventure or a reaction to worries about his mother's health). The more serious incident was after the Profumo affair of 1963, when Macmillan asked Lord Denning to identify other ministers who might be "security risks". A Sunday newspaper's gossip column had said that a junior minister had once been at a "homosexual party" attended by Vassall and Denning concluded that the minister was Freeth. His disgrace was never made public but when Macmillan retired in late 1963, Freeth was not retained as a minister and he was asked to vacate his safe seat at the 1964 general election. His political career was over, less than ten years after it had begun.[239]

Any connection between Vassall and Freeth is tenuous at best: Freeth is not mentioned anywhere in Vassall's memoirs or in the transcripts of his interviews with MI5. As the Tory party historian Michael McManus has said, Freeth's brutal termination meant that "one of the handful of courageous Tory supporters of gay emancipation was lost to public life".

Officially, the British state does not go in for witch-hunts. In 1961 Radcliffe's first committee said, "Security weaknesses ... are the price we pay for having a social and political system that men want to defend". Harold Macmillan himself once said "we could of course ... run a closely controlled, almost a police state. If you want absolute security you have to do that", before concluding that a police state was anathema to all sensible British values. In 1963, Denning's Profumo report asserted that "The Security Service ... are to be used for one purpose and one purpose only, the Defence of the Realm. They are not to be used to pry into any man's private conduct ... for it would be intolerable to us to have anything in the nature of a Gestapo or Secret Police to snoop into all we do". The reality was very different. In the Vassall case, MI5 quickly amassed a list of all his "unmarried friends in Government service". It continued to investigate them long after the Radcliffe report said – in one of its more sensible conclusions – that Vassall had been a lone spy and not part of a network.

When Charles Elwell started to interview Vassall in the last few weeks of 1962, he told him that while MI5 did not believe that "any of his friends had been involved in his espionage, any friend of a spy

---

239 Freeth went back to stockbroking and lived for another forty-five years before he died in April 2010, aged eighty-five. "He is survived by a great-niece", an obituary noted.

was of some interest to us". Vassall thought he was simply helping MI5 to tie up loose ends by telling them what they did not already know. He did not realise that Elwell was beginning an inquisition. "I have no doubt that a great many of them are [homosexual] and it will not be very difficult to detect them," Elwell wrote in a minute from November 1962.

One of Vassall's friends found himself swiftly dismissed from a glittering military career. Wing Commander Basil Champneys was a senior RAF officer with a Distinguished Flying Cross and had been awarded a "Queen's Commendation for Valuable Service in the Air" in the Queen's Birthday Honours List of 1960. Born in 1920, Champneys was a few years older than Vassall and had first met him during the war at RAF Thorney Island in Chichester Harbour. Vassall was staying there with his father William, who served as an RAF chaplain at Thorney Island for a time. Later, Champneys had married and William christened his daughter. By 1962, Champneys and his wife lived at Bourne End, Buckinghamshire and he was working at the RAF's Joint Welfare Centre.

In November 1962, Elwell wrote to a Group Captain H. D. P. Bisley at the Air Ministry to tell him that Vassall had said he was a friend of Champneys, whose career rapidly fell apart around him. By October 1963, Champneys had been dismissed from the Air Ministry.

Because of Vassall's "frame of mind" and his request "to be excused further visits from officials", MI5 decided not to question him any further about Champneys in July 1963. Later, they tried to conceal that Champneys had lost his job because of rumours about being sexually involved with Vassall. In August 1963, an unidentified MI5 officer wrote a memo saying that when Vassall was ready to talk again, he "would try to insert questions about Champneys but consider it would be unwise to make special visit since V. is sensitive about homo friends".

MI5 seems to have rationalised Champneys's treatment by

pretending that Vassall had willingly betrayed him and would be happy to deliver up more friends. Elwell concluded that if Vassall heard the news of "his friend's misfortune" it "will not necessarily have the effect of sealing his lips forever" because Vassall had given Elwell the impression that "he would welcome action against his homosexual acquaintances. So that if one of them gets the sack, he may be encouraged to tell more about the rest."

In fact there is no evidence in MI5's files, or elsewhere, that Vassall wanted his friends to have their careers ruined. Indeed, El-well's own notes on their meetings say that Vassall had said that he "hoped that a lot of people were not going to get into trouble as a result of anything he said about them". Vassall may well have been motivated by enlightened self-interest, because he knew that help-ing MI5 would increase his chances of early release, but this does not mean that he consciously betrayed his friends.

Far from being glad that Champneys had lost his job, Vassall seems to have been horrified. He confirmed in March 1964 – after Champneys's dismissal – that Champneys had slept with him in his flat and that he "was very much nicer than all the others". Vassall expressed indignation that "a man like Champneys should suffer when Sir Harmar Nicholls, for example, should get away un-scathed".[240] It is small wonder that from late 1963 onwards Vassall was even more reluctant to talk to MI5.

Along with many others, Champneys's name appeared on the list of gay men in public life that Vassall allegedly recited to the fascist Colin Jordan in Wormwood Scrubs in 1963, and which Jordan had sent to Harold Macmillan. When Elwell asked Vassall about Jor-dan's allegations Vassall was vague, and clearly embarrassed about what he had said to Jordan. Champneys was described by Jordan as a "distinguished member of the Joint War Staff" who had once

---

240 Vassall was not the only one to suggest that Nicholls was a sexual predator. In his memoirs, the hotelier Edward Carter recalled going for tea with Nicholls at the House of Commons in 1976. But "as he seemed to be more interested in my thighs than my company ties, I decided to discourage any association". See https://www.theamazinglifeandtimesofedwardcarter-uniqueentrepreneur.com/chapter_eleven_-_1976.

"bellowed in the street" outside Vassall's flat to attract his attention. Vassall told MI5 that Champneys would hardly have done this as his Dolphin Square flat was on the fifth floor (in fact it was on the eighth), but that Jordan's account of Champneys's visit was otherwise accurate. Jordan claimed Vassall had said that Lord Cilcennin had been having a gay affair "with son of Bossom, MP": presumably Clive Bossom, the son of Lord Bossom, and an MP since 1959, who was parliamentary private secretary to the Secretary of State for Air in 1962 (though Lord Bossom also had two other sons who weren't MPs). Jordan claimed that Vassall had said that he and Cilcennin had exchanged "several friendly letters" before his Moscow posting, though Vassall had been coy about whether they had ever met.

Other names on Jordan's list were the MPs Tam Galbraith, Sir Harmar Nicholls and Fergus Montgomery, alongside two Conservative politicians who were widely known to be gay – Ian Harvey and Lord Boothby – and two who weren't: Harold Macmillan's son, Maurice Macmillan, and his son-in-law, Julian Amery. Intriguingly, Jordan claimed that Vassall had told him that he didn't have sexual relations with Montgomery, as he had not "been his type" but that he did with Nicholls. This confirmed what Vassall had told MI5 about the two MPs, although Jordan got a crucial detail wrong: he said it was Nicholls who shared a flat with the TV announcer Kenneth Kendall (who was "known by Vassall to be a homosexual"), not Montgomery.[241]

The list also included some of Vassall's friends and colleagues: Donald Barran, Derek Warne, an unidentified "Mr Shillitode" (presumably Shillito, the under-secretary at the Admiralty who had once smiled at Vassall), along with Commander Geoffrey Marescaux and the Honourable Vere Eliot. This was a pointless list of men who posed no security risk, provided by an evil man who was a self-confessed

---

241   The note made clear that Galbraith's name was included on its list of possible gays, not because of what Jordan had said, but because Vassall had once claimed that Galbraith was a homosexual in a letter to a German friend (Vassall told everyone else that he did not think Galbraith was).

fascist. But MI5 went through every name, noting in a memo who was already believed to be homosexual, and who wasn't.[242]

The most senior civil servant on Jordan's list was Norman Hutchison, an under-secretary at the Scottish Office, who MI5 claimed had first met Vassall in a sweet shop on Old Queen Street. The two had regularly lunched together at the Treasury Solicitor's canteen in the late 1950s and early 1960s. Hutchison had worked in the Scottish Office since 1939, apart from a secondment to the Cabinet Office in 1952–53. He seems to have been of particular interest to MI5 as he had introduced Vassall to Donald Barran, who Vassall had often visited when he delivered red boxes to Tam Galbraith at Barskimming. In the homophobic climate of 1963 one would expect a man of Hutchison's position to deny everything about John Vassall. Instead, on 11 February 1963, Hutchison gave MI5 an extraordinarily detailed statement which laid bare his close friendship with Vassall and his own homosexuality.

"Ever since adolescence I have had to contend with the knowledge of a homosexual propensity in myself, but ... I have succeeded in adjusting myself to the situation," Hutchison began. "I have never indulged physically in anything beyond embracing and, rarely, mutual masturbation, always in private and never promiscuously". Hutchison revealed that he first got to know Vassall in 1957. They were both "late lunchers" in the canteen and Vassall often sat with a senior female mandarin, Lady Fremantle, which made Hutchison believe that Vassall was "a person of standing". For two years Hutchison assumed that Vassall was a private secretary of assistant principal rank: he was amazed to discover in 1959 that he was a mere clerical officer.

Gradually, a friendship had developed. Hutchison used to give

---

242 Speculation about lists of prominent homosexuals Vassall sent to the Russians continued to the end of the 1960s. In November 1968 Norman Lucas gave Special Branch a list, supposedly in Vassall's handwriting, that he had received from a former Wormwood Scrubs inmate, Vilio Olozins. Olozins told Lucas that Vassall had written the list "at the request of the Russians to include particulars of homosexuals known by him to be in 'high' positions".

Vassall lifts home to his flat in St John's Wood and go in for a drink. He later visited him at Dolphin Square about six times and twice invited Vassall to parties at his own flat on Harley Street, which he shared with an American named Jim. They both sensed that the other was gay: early on they discussed the Wolfenden report and Hutchison "became aware that he was attracted to me and felt it was reciprocated". Hutchison showed "sympathetic understanding" and "While not specially attracted, I did not repel him". Hutchison said he had declined an invitation to stay overnight at Dolphin Square, but that he had "on occasion embraced him before leaving".

Hutchison worked closely with Tam Galbraith after he became a Scottish Office minister in 1959. He said that he "politely discouraged" Vassall's fascination with Galbraith's career. But in October 1960, it was Hutchison who had drawn Galbraith's attention to the announcement of Vassall's mother's death in *The Times*, prompting Galbraith to write his "My dear Vassall" letter of condolence. Hutchison said that his last meeting with Vassall was in summer 1962. As Vassall had crossed Pall Mall to greet him, Hutchison stopped to speak to someone else and Vassall looked hurt. Hutchison had to disabuse him of the idea that he had been "'up-staged' for any reason of rank".

Hutchison's statement was strikingly honest and it provided fresh insights into what Vassall's unsuspecting friends had known of his lifestyle. Hutchison believed that Vassall had deliberately avoided promotion because his regular hours and "absence of worries outside office hours" gave him more time for entertaining and holidays. Immediately after Vassall's arrest, Hutchison told his department that he had known him socially. He had, he told MI5, not reported Vassall's "discreet and entirely private homosexuality" earlier, not because he feared "self-disclosure" as a gay man but because he had never suspected that Vassall was a spy. It is not clear how Hutchison was rewarded for his honesty: MI5's files are silent on his subsequent career at the Scottish Office.

MI5 investigated several other current and former civil servants that Vassall had befriended. One was Donald Gowing (ex-Treasury, now working for the Musicians' Benevolent Fund), who MI5 asserted had "homosexual relations" with Vassall at a house at Strand-on-the-Green, west London. Another was Donald Edwards, who worked in the Home Office's press department and often lunched with Vassall. Edwards lived on Upper Montagu Street with a man named Philip. He had met Vassall at Hutchison's flat, though MI5 believed that Vassall and Edwards had not been lovers. A third was Group Captain Leo Wright, who worked at the Air Ministry as a meteorologist. Like Vassall, Wright was an unmarried Roman Catholic convert but was probably not homosexual, MI5 concluded. Like Hutchison's, their employment trajectories are unknown. But what is certain is that another civil servant, who apparently had never known Vassall, found himself in trouble merely for expressing sympathy for him three years after his conviction.

In January 1966 Frederick Cridland, an MOD civil servant, was reported by a clerical assistant for having said that Vassall was "a very nice chap and it was a shame what happened to him" or words to that effect. The MOD wrote to MI5 to specify that in 1964 Cridland's positive vetting found him to be a "fastidious individual who gives the impression of femininity", living alone in a flat in Putney and a cottage in the country. Another MOD civil servant said that Cridland was "an effeminate type who has a very high opinion of himself ... he is a bachelor whose time is fully taken up catering for himself and entertaining friends". There is no record of what action, if any, was taken against Cridland. But the fact that expressing sympathy for Vassall was deemed serious enough to inform MI5 of shows that homophobic paranoia was still in full swing in 1966.[243]

---

243 MI5 was still gathering titbits of gossip about Vassall in December 1966, when it was contacted by an elderly lady who previously ran a chemists. She still possessed prints from a roll of film that Vassall had had developed at her shop shortly before his arrest. The prints showed interior shots of Vassall's Dolphin Square flat and nude shots of him.

Vassall "tried to keep his friends on watertight compartments", MI5 once observed. As well he might: too many of them saw their careers destroyed once their connection with him came to light.

• • •

It was not just British civil servants who saw their careers damaged by their associations with Vassall. On 22 October 1962 – the very day of Vassall's conviction – an MI5 memo recorded that Richard Gardner, an Australian diplomat who had worked in Moscow in the mid-1950s and was now at the Australian High Commission in Ottawa, was a friend of Vassall's.

Gardner, born in Melbourne in 1927, was slightly younger than Vassall and was enjoying a meteoric career, becoming second secretary at the Australian embassy in Washington while still in his early thirties. It was not clear whether Gardner and Vassall had known each other in Moscow: Vassall said the only Australian he knew well there was a man called Keith Prowse. But MI5 discovered that Vassall had met Gardner through their mutual friend John Wingstrand (a Swedish diplomat who Vassall had met in Cairo over Christmas 1959). Gardner later stayed at Vassall's Dolphin Square flat at least once and had written to Vassall in August 1960 to thank him for receiving him "so *amicalement*" for a weekend.

Gardner admitted to his Australian bosses that he was a "compulsive homosexual" who had had an affair with Wingstrand, although he said that the affair he wanted with Vassall never happened. When Gardner came to stay at Dolphin Square, Vassall "did not warm to him". In turn, Vassall always denied having had an affair with Wingstrand and said that he had never particularly liked Gardner, who he thought was "rather selfish and entirely absorbed in his own affairs".

Despite this tenuous connection with Vassall, Gardner was fired with brutal speed just seven weeks after Vassall's conviction. He was interviewed by officials at the External Affairs Department and then by the Australian Security Intelligence Organisation (ASIO), on 2 December. Although ASIO's interviewing officer did not believe that Gardner "was involved in espionage or blackmail in any form" and Gardner even supplied a list of "other homosexuals overseas", by 5 December Gardner had resigned from the Australian diplomatic service "on grounds of ill health", aged only thirty-five.

Vassall insisted that he could not remember anything about many of the Americans he had vaguely known in Moscow. But this did not stop the FBI from conducting detailed investigations into every American in Vassall's diary and address book. Of all the Americans Vassall had known in Moscow, the only ones who seemed to have erred were Captain Paul R. Uffelman, who had been declared 'persona non grata' at the end of his tour for having taken illicit photographs of Russian military installations, and Colonel Frederick Yeager and his wife June. By 1960 Yeager was at the Pentagon and in 1961 their neighbours in a Washington suburb reported that June (who had gone to art classes with Vassall at the US embassy in Moscow) was "on the verge of a nervous breakdown". She was a possible alcoholic who "occasionally had spells during which she screamed in the street". In October 1963 an American diplomat formerly stationed in Moscow, Martin Bowe, told State Department officials in Pretoria that he had known the "well-invited" Vassall through regular games of bingo. There was no evidence that any of these people were spies, or accomplices of Vassall.

Some of these checks appear legitimate. MI5 found letters from J. A. C. Robertson – the United Nations' director of personnel from 1955 to 1958 – in Vassall's flat. Vassall had written to him in 1955 about a possible job at the UN. Robertson was, according to one of the FBI's sources, "definitely pro-Soviet" and he tried to hire as many Soviets and "fellow travellers" as he could to work at the UN Secretariat. The source claimed that Robertson, and his Polish assistant, had been invited in the late 1950s to Moscow where the

Soviets found that while Robertson was not an ideological communist, he was "a drinker and pansy" who they had kept supplied "with plenty of boys and liquor". In return, the Soviets asked for four senior posts in the secretariat, at ambassadorial rank, to be given to their nominees.

It was appropriate for the FBI to make enquiries about letters between Robertson and Vassall, but their other queries seem pointless. They unearthed nothing other than irrelevant details about Vassall's friends' private lives, which had nothing to do with his espionage. The FBI ascertained that Vassall's Hungarian friend Pierre Galdi had once left a New York hotel without paying his phone bill. They tracked down Orville Wilson, the American coding clerk who Vassall had a "homosexual adventure" with at the American Club in Moscow. By October 1962, Wilson was working at the American embassy in Haiti. He told the FBI that he had only known Vassall casually, though he had visited his flat once. Vassall had said that Wilson was the only American that he had "any sort of illicit relations with" in Moscow and the FBI seems to have pursued him for this reason alone. Even after Wilson denied having had sex with Vassall, the FBI – via the US Foreign Service – pestered Charles Elwell to show Vassall a photograph of Wilson so that he could positively identify him.

The FBI also opened files on Robert Eiserle, the New Yorker who Vassall had been due to meet in Italy in September 1962, and his close friend Douglas A. Bushy, who had a clean record apart from an FBI investigation in 1959 over the fraudulent use of Bushy's credit cards after he had lost his wallet. Dr David Marine still worked in Baltimore and the FBI noted that Vassall had stayed with him there, possibly as recently as 1961. Kenneth Rolfe lived in Beverly Hills, where Vassall stayed briefly in 1956 after leaving Moscow. But Rolfe was no movie star, producer or agent: he was a maintenance worker on the Happy Hill estate, which the FBI discovered was known locally as the "Hill of Hell" because of the many stray dogs kept there to control the snake population.

One of Vassall's American friends was "effeminate in his appearance and speech". Another had been arrested for "soliciting for lewd and immoral purposes" in 1954 (the charges had later been dropped). Robert Maluta, who lived in a suburb of Minneapolis, had worked as a salesman for the Fuller Brush Company and then as an auditor at Red Owl Stores. The FBI found nothing more incriminating than the fact that Maluta was a member of "The Society for the Preservation of Barber Shop Quartet Singing".

•   •   •

Back in Britain, Cyril Radcliffe's report on the Vassall case did (at least theoretically) have one useful, and long-lasting, consequence: it ushered in a new era of "positive vetting" (PV) of all civil servants with access to sensitive defence secrets, a system that persists to this day. Although Vassall had supposedly undergone "positive vetting" in 1956, it was very different from the more robust system established in the mid-1960s. After the Vassall case positive vetting as we now know it began: colleagues, family and friends were interviewed by MOD or Special Branch officers to determine as much as possible about a candidate's character and background.

The main consequence of the new PV system seems, simply, to have been a renewed hostility towards gay men. Alongside this, a secret system, misleadingly known as "normal vetting" started, whereby candidates were unaware that they were being vetted. In time, this led to covert blacklists, of BBC employees in particular, who found that they were barred from jobs or denied promotion. In Whitehall, vetting was often used as a way of scoring political points. "Normal vetting" was cited as the reason why some senior trade unionists were not allowed to negotiate on behalf of civil servants, even though only a handful of trade unionists were communists and most of them would have refused to do Moscow's bidding.

Simultaneously, security measures for documents remained less than rigorous. Richard Deacon once collected testimony from Lord Walston, a Labour Foreign Office minister in the late 1960s, which highlighted how complacent British embassies in the Eastern bloc still were. At a British military office in Berlin, Walston saw a senior army officer use two different office bins: one for ordinary waste and the other for "secret waste". As Walston chatted, a German civilian employee emptied both bins: the secret waste was clearly not being shredded or burned.

From now on, any British civil servants returning from a posting behind the Iron Curtain were to be debriefed by MI5 – until the recommendation was vetoed by Harold Caccia, a senior Foreign Office mandarin. Chapman Pincher once condemned this suggestion as "[Roger] Hollis's crass demand". It seems that while gay men were persecuted, sensible security precautions were blocked.

For some espionage writers, such as Ronald Seth, the only lesson to learn from the Vassall case was simply that homosexuals shouldn't be allowed anywhere near sensitive defence secrets. "It is to be hoped that the lessons learnt will be remembered for a very long time," Seth wrote. After Radcliffe's report it was agreed that overseas military attachés, and their clerks, should always be married – a complete reversal of previous practice which had favoured single people, like Vassall, because of lower housing costs. Bachelors were thus often barred from foreign posts because the lack of wives made their sexuality automatically suspect.

MI5's C branch still recommended that gay men should be denied access to sensitive defence secrets because of the risk of blackmail. In 1969, the Institution of Professional Civil Servants (a mandarins' trade union) told Chapman Pincher that the Home Office had told all British police forces to report any criminal offences – other than

minor motoring ones – by civil servants, so that "defects of character" which might render them vulnerable to blackmail would not
go unnoticed. This initiative seems to have primarily been a hunt
for closet gays. Even in 1969, two years after decriminalisation,
nearly half of the "character defect" cases referred to MI5 by government departments involved homosexuality.

Later in his career, Col. "Black Jack" MacAfee (who oversaw the
Admiralty's woeful security at the time of Vassall's prosecution)
was responsible for positive vetting in the MOD. His first question
to candidates was always "Are you queer?", Nick Kettlewell recalls.
Yet the MOD was surprisingly sloppy about basic staff searches,
which could well have stopped Vassall in his tracks. In June 1965,
a Security Commission report found that in five out of six British
spy cases since 1951, British subjects were able to remove classified documents from buildings they worked in. The commission's
recommendation – more spot searches – was another instance of
closing the stable door long after the horse had bolted, and again it
was rarely implemented.

Nowadays staff working in ordinary warehouses, retailers and
offices are routinely subject to random searches, even if their work
has nothing to do with national security. But remarkably, such
searches were rejected by the Radcliffe tribunal on the grounds that
"it could never be wholly effective against a determined person;
because it would be intolerable for those concerned; and because
it would be resented by the staff and have a bad effect on staff
relations." Nick Kettlewell recalls that even in the 1980s, random
checks on personnel entering and leaving the MOD's main building on Whitehall were rare, and normally only occurred during
prearranged official exercises.

Vetting seemed to be primarily concerned with determining
whether candidates had left-of-centre political views, or whether
they were gay, well into the 1970s. In the mid-1970s, Jack Straw
(later a Labour Foreign Secretary) was working as a special adviser

to Barbara Castle, Secretary of State for Health and Social Security. In the course of two interviews – each of them three hours long – Straw's inquisitor leant across the desk, looked Straw in the eye and asked him "Mr Straw, do you like men?". "The system was obsessed with gays under the bed, since some of those who had been discovered to be spies were gay, unsurprisingly blackmailed into betraying their country rather than face the ignominy of a criminal conviction for 'sodomy'", Straw recalled.[244]

In 1982 Lord Diplock's security commission concluded that homosexuality "should not necessarily be treated as an absolute bar to PV clearance, but should be dealt with on a case by case basis, paying particular attention to whether the way in which the individual has indulged in his homosexual tendencies casts any doubts upon his discretion or reliability". But this lenience did not apply to the diplomatic services or armed forces. In 1988 Andrew Hodges, a 20-year-old data processor at GCHQ, openly admitted that he was gay when being vetted, to test the system. The test failed: he was immediately suspended. By then, Maurice Oldfield, head of MI6 from 1973 to 1978 and Alexander Kellar, head of MI5's F Branch in the 1960s, had been "outed" as closet gays.[245] But rather than be lauded as positive role models and proof that gay men can honourably and loyally defend the realm, both men were the subject of fierce debates in Parliament about why and how they had been allowed to continue in service.[246] At the same time, Section 28 (which barred councils and schools from "promoting the teaching of the acceptability of homosexuality as a pretended family relationship")

---

244 Even after six hours of interviews, Straw was summoned to another meeting in Whitehall, where an MI5 officer told him that his sister was believed to have been recruited into the Communist Party in 1961 (Straw maintained that she had only joined because she "fancied" a local CP organiser).

245 Oldfield is often claimed to be a model for John le Carré's spymaster George Smiley. In the 1980s Oldfield told the Cabinet Secretary, Robert Armstrong, that he had only had homosexual relationships as a schoolboy and student, forty years earlier. He believed the rumours that he was still a practising homosexual were a malicious attempt to derail his work in Northern Ireland.

246 The former Labour Foreign Secretary David Owen said that the revelations were "a devastating blow to the credibility of our security services".

meant that another breed of civil servants – teachers – found themselves reluctant to come out as gay men or lesbians.

The government was only forced to end "normal vetting" after the European Commission on Human Rights found that it was a violation of European law, and John Major's government did not lift the *de facto* ban on homosexuals in the diplomatic service until 1991. They also announced that "in the light of changing attitudes" homosexuals were no longer officially barred from access to sensitive documents. Gay men and women were now encouraged to "come out" but in 1994, homosexuality was still listed as one of seven "character defects" that would be considered during vetting (alongside profligacy, alcoholism, drug-taking, unreliability, dishonesty and promiscuity).

At the time of Vassall's death in 1996, gay men and lesbians were still automatically dismissed from the armed forces as soon as their sexuality was discovered or disclosed. In 1997, Duncan Lustig-Prean, a former Royal Navy commander who had been dismissed for revealing he was gay and was now running a pressure group called Rank Outsiders, alleged that MI5 still maintained a "pink list" of homosexuals that was still regularly "used in the gay witch-hunts that continue in the military".[247] Throughout the 1980s and 1990s the rate of dismissal remained steady, at fifty to seventy cases a year, though it dipped slightly during the first Gulf War of 1990–91 as the armed forces needed all the manpower it could get. Even those who were celibate for religious reasons were not exempted. Some men were subjected to painful and intrusive rectal

---

247 Lustig-Prean, who joined the Royal Navy in 1979, was a high-flying young officer who was dismissed in 1995 – when he was on the verge of becoming a military adviser in Downing Street – after telling senior officers that he was gay. Lustig-Prean recalls that even in the 1980s, a confidential "Defence Council Instruction" did not just warn of "honey traps" like the one that had entrapped Vassall. They also ordered personnel to report any suspicious behaviour, such as effeminacy or finding hand cream in lockers to their commanding officers. After Lustig-Prean's dismissal, Rank Outsiders fought to lift the ban on LGBT people serving in the armed forces. After the Labour government was elected in 1997, Rank Outsiders encountered resistance from the new Armed Forces Minister, John Reid, but after a European Court of Human Rights judgement in 1999, Defence Secretary Geoff Hoon finally lifted the ban in January 2000.

examinations to "determine" their sexuality which amounted to torture (in some cases, the men who were examined were pinned down against their will).

Only at the very end of the twentieth century, and the beginning of the twenty-first, did the state's official prejudice against gay men and lesbians disappear. The ban on LGBT people serving in the armed forces was lifted,[248] Section 28 was repealed, LGBT people were given adoption rights and gay men and women were allowed to enter civil partnerships that legally recognised their relationships, and later to marry. In 2001 the age of consent for gay men was finally brought in line with that for heterosexual sex and set at sixteen in England, Scotland and Wales; Northern Ireland followed suit in 2008.

By then John Vassall had been dead for twelve years. He had lived to see many reforms, but at the time of his death in 1996 men and women who were prepared to die for their country were still routinely dismissed from the armed forces because of their sexuality. The prejudice that Vassall had known still lingered.

---

248 There was not much comfort for those who had already been dismissed on grounds of sexuality. After the ban was lifted in 2000, they were invited to apply for compensation for loss of earnings but they could only apply within three years of dismissal so veterans who were released before 1997 were automatically excluded unless they had made a claim at the time. To this day, rates of mental illness, suicide and self-harm are higher among LGBT veterans than heterosexual ones.

CHAPTER SEVEN

"HOPE AND CONFIDENCE": VASSALL AFTER RELEASE

John Vassall's first port of call after he was driven out of Maidstone prison on 24 October 1972 felt strangely familiar. Captain A. D. B. James, the prison visitor he had befriended, drove him to his nearby house, which was so full of naval curios that Vassall felt it was "built just like a ship". When he arrived, Mrs James was the first person to give him a hug.

After breakfast with the Jameses and briefly speaking to the press, Vassall made a courtesy visit to his ailing father in Higham. He then caught a train to London, unmolested by reporters. From London he caught another train to Sussex, getting off at a quiet station where he was met by two unnamed friends driving a Volvo. Vassall had checked that no one had followed him onto the train or off it. Unlike Harry Houghton, he had somehow given the press the slip. "It was a performance which James Bond would have been proud of", he beamed later.

His "sanctuary" for the next few weeks, until Christmas, was April Cottage on Sunset Lane in Pulborough: a thatched cottage hidden amid woodland. Vassall said it was "like a child's fairy tale". A week after his release, on 31 October, Vassall spoke to his former defence barrister, Jeremy Hutchinson, on the telephone and the following day he wrote to say, "My neighbours are the squirrels which race around the trees oblivious of the blackbirds, robins and jays that pop about the lawns".

At first, whenever Vassall went outdoors he felt dizzy. But he soon summoned the courage to visit London and he even walked past the Admiralty. Around Victoria Street Vassall felt that the new office blocks, which had mostly been built after he entered prison, were a "vast improvement". He was "most impressed" by *The Economist*'s new building on St James's Street. The new perfume department at Harrods, in a marbled former banking hall, felt like "fairyland". Vassall went to a jewellers on Old Bond Street to get a watchstrap repaired. It was a jewellers he had used before his arrest and the man behind the counter recognised him. "I'm very pleased to see you are back in circulation", he said, shaking his hand firmly.

Vassall stayed at April Cottage as the guest of two sisters, Doreen and Betty, who he would often talk to by the fire until the small hours. Vassall knew this part of Sussex, having gone to school at Littlehampton in the 1930s, and in 1972 he found that the town of Arundel, and the nearby village of Burpham, had hardly changed in the four decades since. But when the sisters drove Vassall into Worthing to do some shopping, he was amazed by the town's new multi-storey car park – the first he had ever seen – and by its modern Bentalls department store.

In December 1972, Vassall's father William died, aged eighty-seven. By the autumn of 1970 William had entered a convalescent home on the North Downs but it "proved too much" and he returned to hospital, where he barely recognised Vassall when he visited. William had learned all about Vassall's spying, and his homosexuality. But apparently, he had never been told another of Vassall's secrets: his Catholicism. His death seems to have been a relief.

A few weeks after he had lost his father, on 7 January 1973, Vassall appeared on the cover of the *Sunday Times Magazine* with the headline "Vassall: The Years Inside". Vassall looked cheerful and much as he did when he was sentenced ten years earlier, aside from a receding hairline and new sideburns flecked with grey. Vassall's first-person account, a transcription of an interview with Francis Wyndham headlined "The Model Prisoner", was similar to his later memoirs: trite observations about prison life and his desire for a job in the antiques field. His homosexuality, which had been "considered a joke, a sort of entertainment" during his first years in prison, was "no longer something to jeer at" by the end. Vassall said he had benefitted from fifteen months of psychotherapy before his release. But he hardly said anything about the one thing readers wanted to know about: his spying. Perhaps the most intriguing thing was that on the final page of Vassall's interview there was a recruitment advertisement for the Royal Marines – "Become a Royal Marine Officer. It's the sort of life you'll enjoy leading" – which was possibly a joke by the *Sunday Times*'s sub-editors.

Soon after his release Vassall went for a walk with a friend by a harbour, probably on the Sussex coast, and saw a Russian ship docked. He was momentarily tempted "to leave the past behind and forget about it all", he later recalled. "I could have walked aboard, stated who I was and sailed off to far fewer problems than I do by remaining in Britain". But would the Russians have welcomed him back to Moscow? Vassall's usefulness had ended the moment he ceased to work at the Admiralty. Vassall did not really want to go anywhere near Moscow. Other than that he was at a loss. He continued to see a psychiatrist, Dr H. K. Rose, whose therapy was "not so much an in-depth examination of the past as an optimistic look to the future", he remembered. What that future held was anyone's guess but the penniless Vassall needed somewhere to live, and before long he needed a job.

Vassall had abandoned his original plan to spend several weeks at Quarr Abbey on the Isle of Wight but while he was staying at April Cottage in late 1972, he discovered an alternative: a Norbertine monastery, the Our Lady of England Priory at Storrington, five miles south-east of Pulborough. Vassall went into its priory church, a solid brick barn built in 1902, said a prayer of thanks and lit a candle. Vassall soon befriended one of the monks and was invited to help catalogue its library. After spending Christmas at the home of a "Catholic woman friend", Vassall moved into the monastery in early 1973. He had landed on his feet: here was free board and lodging in return for stimulating work, but without the barred windows of prison.

During his six months at the monastery Vassall considered becoming a monk himself. More importantly, whenever his library duties allowed he began to write a memoir. Prisoners were not allowed to keep diaries in those days so Vassall was writing from scratch, but quickly: a first draft was typed out by May 1973. "I am writing a book. It is terribly frank and [I] hope I won't do myself a lot of damage", he wrote to Jeremy Hutchinson in September.

In July 1973 Vassall crossed an adult threshold: he finally passed his driving test in Sussex, having taken lessons since February. And before long he passed another: he became sexually active again. For the first few months after his release he seems to have preferred the company of women. But while living at the monastery Vassall seems to have resumed living a double life. When he wasn't cataloguing the monks' library or penning his memoirs, he befriended yet another gay politician. Thomas Skeffington-Lodge (1905–94) had been Labour MP for Bedford from 1945 to 1950. He is not mentioned in Vassall's memoirs but the novelist Francis King claimed that Skeffington-Lodge, who was then approaching seventy, helped Vassall to pick up a "gay tart" who was brought back to Skeffington-Lodge's house in Brighton and then paid for his services. Apparently, the young man later returned to Skeffington-Lodge's door, after the publication of Vassall's memoirs, to complain "How dare S-L let him go to bed with a spy".[249]

---

249 Francis King and Skeffington-Lodge had a history: Skeffington-Lodge had sued King for libel after King had lampooned Skeffington-Lodge without naming him. Rather than denying everything King made the error of admitting that the derogatory portrait had been based on Skeffington-Lodge, who accepted a settlement. The evidence for his encounter with Vassall lies in a letter from Francis King dated 27 April 1975, among the papers of the English journalist and novelist Kay Dick.

Vassall's memoirs soon secured a publisher: the prestigious Sidgwick & Jackson, where Lord Longford was a director (and later chairman). Vassall claimed that the suggestion of writing a book had first come from friends he corresponded with in prison, not Longford's visits. Vassall appears to have taken his research seriously: MI5 noted that on 16 June 1973 Father Ian McLean, Vassall's mentor at the Norbertines' monastery, wrote to the defector Michał Goleniewski on Vassall's behalf, to seek information about the lead-up to his arrest. But the book had a long gestation period: it was only published on 23 January 1975, almost two years after Vassall began writing it.

Vassall: The Autobiography of a Spy was hardly great literature but it did contain some useful insights. The Lord Montagu scandal of the early 1950s was "yet another witch hunt on the part of the British establishment, cruel and vindictive in the extreme". The Radcliffe report, which at the time Vassall had naively hoped would exonerate him, was a "contrived attempt at character assassination". Vassall clearly resented being described in the report as (in his words) "a social climber and a rich old lady's hanger-on, with an eye to the main chance". To assume that his civil service career "was all in pursuit of sexual gratification, as was suggested in 1962, is as ludicrous as it is hurtful". More importantly, Vassall's memoirs finally explained what exactly had happened in the Hotel Berlin in October 1954: he had been drugged and then raped by at least two other men.

Vassall apologised for the "pain and distress" he had caused his friends and family, but he did not apologise to his country. "Having committed a crime I cannot spend the rest of my life demolishing myself with remorse. I have paid my legal debt to society and I hope that I may seriously feel that I have put that part of my life behind me," he wrote. "I realise that although at the time I felt quite helpless, I should not have allowed myself to become entangled in the deplorable and dreadful world of espionage on behalf of a foreign power ... Of course I regret the past, but I do look forward to the future with hope and confidence".

One of the very few passages in which Vassall did not talk about himself concerned sentencing. He was clearly angry that it seemed to have "as much to do with political opportunism as with reforming and rehabilitating individuals". Even Labour Members of Parliament "fell prey to the security fantasy which was really a means of obscuring the uncomfortable reality of Britain's dwindling military power". These are odd sentences which seem to belong to a very different kind of book. Vassall's description of the Soviet Union as merely a "potentially hostile power" is at odds with the rest of his tale, in which he constantly stresses the Soviets' insatiable appetite for information and how he dreaded being caught and punished. Vassall appeared to be trying to mitigate his actions, but the appeal does not work well.

In truth, he did not seem perceptive enough to realise the full extent of what the Russians had done. At one point he muses, rightly, that "if one is blackmailed into actions of this kind, surely one is not acting freely". But Vassall did not venture further. His book went into more detail about the cocktail parties he attended than about the secrets he gave the Russians. His "friends" are always unidentified and normally faceless: not even his Moscow flatmates are named. The most detailed part is a forensically precise account of the three days of "home leave" he was granted in September 1972, just before his release.

Vassall was certainly not a communist and he saw himself in the "extreme centre", veering more towards liberalism than conservatism. But for all his professed interest in politics, his memoirs never expressed any opinions on Suez, nuclear disarmament, Kennedy's foreign policy, the Hungarian revolution, immigration or any other political issues of the late 1950s and early 1960s. Although CND rallies had been constant events in London in the years leading up to his arrest, they were not mentioned once. And Vassall never pondered the political, diplomatic or security consequences of his actions.

Vassall always had highbrow tastes in music and art. One of the first things he did after leaving prison was to buy a record of Mahler's Symphony No. 5. *Autobiography of a Spy* begins and ends with quotations from T. S. Eliot (*The Family Reunion* at the start and *Four Quartets* at the end). A collection of Baudelaire's poems was one of the few books that Vassall took to Moscow in 1954 and the preface to his memoirs includes lines from Baudelaire's poem "L'Ennemi" (The Enemy) from *Les Fleurs du Mal* (The Flowers of Evil): *Ma jeunesse ne fut qu'un ténébreux orage/ Traversé çà et là par de brillants soleils* (My youth has been nothing but a tenebrous storm/ Pierced now and then by rays of brilliant sunshine).

Yet for all his cultural pretensions, Vassall had little ability to think beyond the here and now. Much of his memoirs are a stream of consciousness account of what he drank, ate and saw. They largely read like a teenage diary, with fatuous comparisons between the "genuine regard" of foreigners and the British "no-nonsense sort of thinking, devoid of understanding and sympathy". Moscow is described as a relief from the "Anglo-Saxon world" in which homosexuality was taboo. Vassall's life, both in Moscow and London, is an endless succession of "delightful parties" at which everyone "danced the night away".

Worst of all, Vassall's book only reinforced homophobic stereotypes of gay men as narcissistic and vain, rather than challenge them. "He constantly referred to famous and semi-famous people that he had the slightest connection to, but he forgot that what readers really wanted to know was who he had slept with and which British public figures, if any, were in the pay of the Russians. On both questions Vassall's book was silent.

Vassall's account of his Admiralty career implied that he was a jet-setting diplomat: the word "clerk" hardly appeared. Before he went to Moscow, "final briefing in London took only ten days", he wrote, as if he had been sent abroad to fill an ambassadorial position. He speculated that secret photographs of him dining with KGB agents were probably taken early on in his acquaintanceship with "the skier" and that they may have been kept "on ice", even if he had never been sexually compromised. This was an interesting theory, but it was ruined by the lines that followed. "For instance, if I had been an official who eventually found himself as a Private Secretary at 10 Downing Street in years to come, it would be more advantageous to the Russians to produce incriminating evidence through an intermediary then, for I would probably have access to documents at Cabinet level, which would surpass anything known to me previously." This said more about Vassall's fantasies than it did about Soviet spycraft.

At one point, he even reinforced the old homophobic trope that gay men are just going through "a phase" and that homosexuality is a "condition" from which it is possible to recover. Approaching fifty, Vassall still mused that "possibly I will be able to reorientate myself eventually and marry". He seemed to have fallen for the argument that homosexuals should be barred from certain jobs, writing that "it does seem to me that the fact that an obvious homosexual (at least to some) should have been appointed to Moscow and allowed to remain there is a serious indictment of our security services". This was not vanity: it was self-loathing.

One writer, Matthew Parris, has described the book as "glutinous" while Thomas Grant said that "it revealed a man who has not yet found adulthood". Contemporary reviews were no more enthusiastic. "It trembles on the edge of that wordy cliché, a 'human document,'" sniffed *The Listener*'s reviewer. It was, the magazine said, a "slightly unnerving" and "bizarre book", to which "understandably enough, no Fleet Street paper has yet sought serial rights". In *The Times*' review of 23 January 1975, headlined "Perfect fall guy", E. C. Hodgkin did not pull any punches. "Mr Vassall was an efficient clerk; he is, alas, no writer. In comment and description, he never rises above an austere level of banality. "Russian ballet is a supreme art"; Capri is "the most beautiful and colourful place I have ever visited"; Cairo "seemed to have preserved so much of the old world ... and so on". Hodgkin concluded that Vassall was "quite astonishingly naïve". "Vassall, who was released from prison in 1972 after serving ten years of his sentence, is now telling all", wrote the *Aberdeen Evening Express*'s reviewer. "Unfortunately his "all" doesn't amount to very much ... His descriptive powers [are] non-existent, his insight into character slight: most of the book [is a] dreary catalogue of names and places". Thus, Vassall's book got terrible reviews not because of homophobic prejudice towards its author, but simply because of its dreariness.

In May 1974, Vassall sent Jeremy Hutchinson a copy of a catalogue in which his book was listed; "The anticipation and reaction of [*sic*] it all is overwhelming", he purred. In September he sent Hutchinson a cutting from *The Bookseller* about its impending publication, which he said had "exceeded all my expectations except that I am very disappointed that the *Sunday Times* who kept my manuscript for many weeks has declined to serialize". Vassall assumed that their refusal was because the press was "afraid" or that the "establishment brought down pressure to bear"; he does not seem to have considered that his book might not have been well-written. Later, he seemed oblivious to bad reviews and boasted that he had turned down an interview with David Frost ("When I saw him on a television interview I was glad I had!" he told Hutchinson).

Vassall did grant *The Times* an interview to help generate interest in the book. The paper reported on 27 January 1975 that "John Vassall ... said yesterday that the two MPs who befriended him while he was in the pay of the KGB are still playing a prominent role in British life". But the story offered no clues to their identity beyond confirming that they were both Conservatives, one was still in the Commons and that Vassall had once slept with the other, who was now in the Lords, at his Dolphin Square flat. As so many former Conservative MPs end up in the Lords, this did not narrow the list down much. Playfully, Vassall did not rule out emigrating to Russia. "I suppose I do not really want to catch 'the last train to Moscow'", he said. "But at least there would be some guaranteed excitement there. I just know that something would be going on".

● ● ●

Back in the real world, Vassall had already left his former identity behind. Although he was interviewed by newspapers as John Vassall and published a book under that name, after his release he used a different name for all day-to-day purposes: John Phillips.[250]

Vassall does not seem to have ever formally changed his name by deed poll but to all intents and purposes he did. From November 1972 onwards, all employment references gave his new name and almost all his letters were signed John Phillips (or "J. P."), not John Vassall. He had good reason to change his name: fear of being hounded by the press. In his memoirs he wrote of his appearance at the Radcliffe tribunal, "I realise the press had a difficult role to play, and in retrospect I still smile at the cartoons and witty remarks made at the time". But "one so-called serious newspaper informed me through a third party that it would 'hound me' even after my release from prison".

For the same reason he chose not to live in London once he left the Norbertines' monastery, but in Kent. In another letter to Jeremy Hutchinson, on 28 May 1973, Vassall said that he was looking for a home in Otford or Shoreham on the North Downs. It is not clear why Vassall chose Kent, but the village of Shoreham has a station, giving Vassall rural seclusion only forty-five minutes from Victoria.

---

250   Why he chose the surname Phillips remains a mystery. The only Phillips who Vassall ever knew seems to be Commander Geoffrey Phillips, the Canadian naval attaché who had been sent home from Moscow for being "pinkish", but Vassall said he barely met him. It is possible that he chose Phillips, which is a common Welsh name, as homage to his schooldays in Monmouth, or simply because it is common across the English-speaking world, and would not attract much attention.

Vassall soon started renting Riverside House in Shoreham, which he said was "perhaps the nicest house and loveliest position here", in a village "miraculously saved from commerce and the motor car". He loved the tranquillity of the North Downs. "Fortunately I have kept my private life away from the press; they do not know where I am still!", he wrote to Hutchinson on 28 September 1973.

In the summer of 1974 Vassall told friends that he wanted to buy somewhere in Shoreham and he had "first refusal" on a "small white house nearby". But it seems that either he could not afford it or the pull of London became too much. By the end of 1974, Vassall was living at 105 Langford Court on Langford Place, just off Abbey Road and five minutes' walk from Addison House, where he had lived in the late 1940s and 1950s.[251] He told Hutchinson that his new flat was a "bedsit", even smaller than his one-bedroom flat in Dolphin Square.[252] Vassall had come full circle. He was, once again, an impecunious bachelor living in St John's Wood, albeit not with his parents.

By now Vassall's letters to Hutchinson had a constant theme: his desperate search for a proper job. In a letter dated 1 November 1972, a week after his release, Vassall added a request he had forgotten to make on the telephone the night before: could Hutchinson help him find "some temporary work with a quiet and discreet antique dealer or someone who likes books"? On 28 April 1973 Vassall wrote from the Norbertines' monastery to ask whether Hutchinson could pass his name on to "anyone in the book world". "If I had an art degree from the Courtauld Institute I could have gone to a gallery in St James's but I have not been in touch, practically speaking, with all this. A pity because I was liked and given sherry," Vassall recalled pathetically.

---

251 Vassall's correspondence shows that he was still living in Shoreham in November 1974. But Janet Foster believes that he was living in St John's Wood by the time she started working with him at the British Records Association in September 1974. It may be that Vassall's two tenancies overlapped.

252 Langford Court is almost a miniature version of Dolphin Square: eight storeys of red brick, albeit with art deco casement windows, not sash ones.

Vassall wrote to Hutchinson again on 22 May to say that he had recently met the personnel director of Blackwell's bookshop in Oxford, a retired vice-admiral called Sir John Parker, who said there was "an outside chance of a post in their Antiquarian book department in the summer, but the chances were not good." (The job at Blackwell's never materialised.) Vassall wrote that he "thought of Oxford or Cambridge as somewhere more soothing than London; or Sussex, Kent or Surrey where there is some life … Everyone tells me or advises me that something to do with books is my best bet. Whether it is selling or with publishers does not worry me". On 21 June Vassall again asked Hutchinson if he had any contacts in the book world, adding that he "could quite easily settle down in a country town from Rye or Tunbridge Wells to Haslemere … In *The Times* there are occasional notices for jobs in art galleries as assistants but nothing has come my way without that elusive introduction".

In a long postscript, an increasingly desperate Vassall listed the responsibilities he'd had in HMP Maidstone's printshop and earnings office, where he had worked "under two civil servants" and "amazed and impressed" the auditors. "I enjoy hard work, getting around, and do not mind long hours if what has to be done is important, or of consequence to my superiors. As you will appreciate I liked working for people in top positions and know and understand their world". In another begging letter on 28 July, Vassall said that he was going to stay with the McEwens at their Scottish estate Marchmont, where "my main preoccupation will be to try and find suitable employment which has eluded me so far". He enclosed a glowing reference from Father Ian McLean, who said that the work Vassall had done in cataloguing the Norbertines' library ("many thousands of books from rare 16th century items to modern works") had "been invaluable and I warmly recommend him for any post in library or archive work". Vassall added that there was "an outside chance" of a job in a large hotel company, but nothing seems to have come of it.

Vassall's constant letters probably annoyed Hutchinson, but they portray a man very different from the vain stereotype that the media had created in 1962. They show genuine gratitude from a man who derived simple pleasure from reading, seeing old friends and country walks, not an oleaginous name-dropper. Vassall once lamented that "When I am asked about my previous career it is extremely difficult to avóid mentioning the dramatic incidents in my former life. Until then no one has the remotest idea that I have lived more than one life".

In the early autumn of 1973 Vassall finally got lucky. "I am now more assured. I have an appointment in the City and I am living in the country and I have made new and valuable friendships," his memoirs announced. He was working as a "researcher in a City company", and only its managing director knew his real identi-ty.[253] He implied that he was working for a large concern, such as a merchant bank or a firm of stockbrokers. In fact, Vassall had found work as a part-time administrator (not as a volunteer, as some ac-counts claim) at the British Records Association (BRA). Then based at the Charterhouse, the BRA is a professional body for archivists which in the 1970s grandly described itself as a charity devoted to "the preservation, understanding, accessibility and study of our re-corded heritage for the public benefit".[254]

Jeremy Hutchinson must have been mightily relieved when Vassall told him, in a letter on 28 September 1973, that he had landed his job at the BRA, where "everyone has been most dis-creet". Vassall later told Hutchinson that the job had come about "quite by chance" when he saw an advertisement in a newspaper. "So [I] wrote at once and the next thing I heard was a telephone call from the Charterhouse to Storrington." It seems that the job

253 The white lie about Vassall being a "researcher in a City company" had legs. "Today he lives quietly under an assumed name", wrote Richard Deacon in 1980. "After a spell in a Catholic monastery, where he wrote his autobiography, he took on research work for a City company" – which went unnamed.
254 Janet Foster recalls that Vassall seemed to work full-time for the BRA in the mid-1970s, but if he did so he was only being paid for three days a week.

was not arranged by Lord Longford, as some have indicated, or the well-connected McEwens: Vassall got it on his own initiative.

In the mid-1970s the BRA was a tiny organisation with only three staff: an archivist, secretary (the job that Vassall filled) and an assistant who helped to sort the archives. Vassall boasted to Hutchinson that his job title was "Administrative Secretary/Manager") and at other times he described himself as "the secretary", implying that he was a member of the BRA's committee or that he occupied a managerial role. In fact he was only ever a secretary at the BRA.

It may have been a lowly job but it was in a wonderful location: in the Master's Court at Charterhouse: a fourteenth-century Carthusian priory that was rebuilt from 1545 onwards as one of Tudor London's great courtyard houses. Charterhouse is one of the most historic, and unknown, corners of central London.[255] The Master's Court had been painstakingly restored after wartime bombing and by the 1970s it was once again a magical place, looking much like a small quadrangle in an ancient Oxford college.

It was, for Vassall, a homecoming. Charterhouse is only a few hundred yards from Bart's Hospital (where he was born in 1924 and where his parents had worked), and from the church of St Bartholomew the Great, where his parents were married. Vassall always loved headed notepaper and many of his personal letters from the 1970s were written on paper with a "Norbertine Canons" letterhead, or on the BRA's elegant headed paper, which proudly recorded that their patron was the Queen Mother, and their president, "The Right Honourable The Master of the Rolls". However humble his job, Vassall used the notepaper to flaunt that he was working at an important institution. He never worried about using his employer's resources, or time, for personal business.

From September 1974 Vassall worked alongside a woman half his

---

255   Until recently Charterhouse was normally closed to visitors, apart from services in its chapel, and it still
      very much feels like a private, cloistered community.

age, who was in her first proper job as an archivist, Janet Foster, who had qualified that summer. At first, Foster thought that the dapper Vassall was in his early forties, not turning fifty. In those days the BRA spent much of its time advising solicitor's firms that were clearing out old cellars before mergers or moving offices, or people whose elderly relatives had died leaving piles of papers in attics. The BRA would help them decide what title deeds, wills and other ancient documents should be discarded and what should be given to records offices.

Janet Foster and Vassall would often go on trips across the country and everyone they met found Vassall charming and very genial. "Vassall was a very good typist, and he did all the work I asked him to do brilliantly," recalls Foster. "John loved being in Charterhouse," she remembers. "Prestige was everything to John, and Charterhouse had prestige in spades. He was very social and always being taken out to swish places by influential friends. But he always talked about the here and now, not the past".

Janet Foster did not listen to most of Vassall's running commentary on his glamorous social life, but she can remember him recounting trips to Scotland – probably to stay with the McEwens. Vassall never told Foster he was gay but it was "understood": like most people who met Vassall, Foster immediately sensed his sexual orientation. Foster is gay herself, and on a trip out of London with Vassall she brought her partner along and the three of them lunched together. But she only knew Vassall as John Phillips. When chatting, Phillips often dropped other people's names, but never his own. While Foster knew that Phillips knew Lord Longford, she had no inkling that they had met through the peer's prison visits.

It was several months before she found out exactly who John Phillips really was – and only by accident. Foster recalls that Vassall always wore an immaculate pinstripe suit, a bright tie and a clean white or striped blue and white shirt. There was a handkerchief in his breast pocket and a gold signet ring on his finger. He always carried a briefcase – probably his old civil service one. The flecks of gold had almost been rubbed off, but four letters – "WJCV" for William John Christopher Vassall, possibly – could just about be discerned, imprinted in the leather. But the mysterious briefcase only aroused interest from Foster, not suspicion.

It was only one morning in early 1975, as Foster travelled into work by train from south-west London, that she saw a photograph of John Phillips in a newspaper being read by another passenger. The story was about the publication of the memoirs of John Vassall, the spy. Foster had known that Vassall was writing a book, having overheard telephone conversations between him and a publisher, but she had no idea what it was about. Vassall was on a week's holiday at the time, to coincide with the book's publication, but when he returned Janet Foster said nothing, as she did not feel it was appropriate to ask him about his book (which was, Foster recollects, "very John" – and not well written). "I had always thought that John was a superficial man because he never talked about his past," Foster recalls. "When I read the book I understood why". Despite his irritating namedropping, Foster liked him, but his real identity was always an elephant in the room.

Most young archivists used the BRA as a springboard to a job as a corporate archivist at a county record office or in academia. Janet Foster moved on at the end of 1975, having worked alongside Vassall for about fifteen months.[256] They had a good working relationship but they didn't stay in touch. Little did she know that Vassall would carry on working there for another two decades. Alongside his part-time job at the BRA Vassall had a second part-time role from the 1970s onwards, working two days a week at a firm of solicitors in Gray's Inn. Vassall may have seen this as another stepping-stone but he never did move on to the kind of job he

---

256 Foster went on to have a long and successful career, first as an archivist at St Bartholomew's Hospital and later at the Wellcome Institute.

craved: in an art gallery, antiquarian bookshop or as private secretary to a person of importance.[257]

As he slowly rebuilt his life, Vassall found that many of his old friends deserted him. Some had stopped writing and visiting him in jail, and he does not seem to have tracked them down after his release. One friendship which had begun in the early 1950s did endure, however: with Robin McEwen, his old Farm Street friend who had helped to defend him in 1962. McEwen had frequently visited Vassall in prison and in 1973 he sent the BRA a reference that helped him secure his job there.

Soon after Vassall's trial Robin had retired from the bar, while still in his thirties, and gone to help run his family's Scottish estate, Marchmont.[258] Marchmont is a Palladian house built by Hugh Hume-Campbell, the 3rd Earl of Marchmont, in 1750 and the McEwens had lived in it since 1912. It has one of the finest country house interiors in Scotland, but because it has rarely been open to the public it is, to this day, scarcely known outside architectural circles.[259] For Vassall this was the perfect place to go for the weekend: an architectural jewel in a large park, unspoilt by the paying public.

Unlike at Barskimming, Vassall was invited to stay overnight at Marchmont, not just for lunch. He seems to have regarded Robin McEwen as a substitute for Tam Galbraith. While Vassall had been in jail, Robin had stood for Parliament twice as a Conservative candidate (one of his candidacies was at the Roxburgh, Selkirk and Peebles by-election of 1965, won by the young David Steel), though he was not elected, possibly because of latent prejudice against his

---

257 He once wrote to Hutchinson to say that that he would appreciate his help in finding something more full-time and permanent. The personnel officer at the Law Society had put Vassall "on her list for a job but there has been no response for some time", lamented Vassall.

258 Robin McEwen and Jeremy Hutchinson also remained in close contact in the 1970s. Hutchinson's papers reveal that in January 1976, McEwen wrote to him to ask for advice on behalf of his first cousin Lady Rose Yorke, who had been arrested in Bermuda a few months earlier on suspicion of involvement in drug smuggling.

259 The house was sold to Sue Ryder Care for use as a nursing home in the 1980s and is now a private home. Brigid McEwen and other members of the family still live on the estate, but not in the main house.

Catholicism. What is more, Robin had recently become a baronet.[260] McEwen was everything that Vassall was not – a wealthy, highly talented figure, a father of six children and a Scottish laird who was brought up in a huge Palladian house that he then inherited – and just the sort of man who Vassall wanted to spend time with.

Vassall stayed at Marchmont at least four times: in summer 1973, February 1974, autumn 1974 and in January 1976. He always arrived without a friend or partner. "Robin felt obliged to look after John after he came out of prison," his widow Brigid recalls. "He felt responsible for him, as John did not seem to have any friends. And he did not want to talk about the past". Vassall seems to have loved his stays at Marchmont: in a letter to Jeremy Hutchinson he recorded that other guests there in summer 1973 were the editor of *The Listener*, a QC named David Hughes and a housemaster at Eton. Robin and Brigid's son John McEwen, then aged about eight, can remember an infestation of frogs on a lawn, which John Vassall enthusiastically helped to remove with rakes, so it could be mowed. John recalls Vassall as a mysterious stranger, made all the more mysterious by his alias, Phillips. But he was not told about his past as a Soviet spy.

Brigid still believes that social class was a key factor in Vassall's failure to report his predicament to his superiors in Moscow. "He had 'minor public school' printed all over him," says Brigid. "Because he was not in the same social class as the ambassador and other senior diplomats, he hadn't the nerve to go to them when he got himself in a spot of bother". Brigid accepts that Vassall would have been sent straight home but she still believes coming clean would have been the best option, even if it meant he was prosecuted for homosexual activity, spying or both. Yet none of these questions were ever discussed when Vassall visited Marchmont in the 1970s:

---

260   Robin McEwen's father, John Helias Finnie McEwen (1894–1962), known as Jock McEwen, was the Unionist MP for Berwick and Haddington from 1931 to 1945. Jock had been made a baronet in 1953 and upon his death in 1962 the baronetcy passed to his eldest son, James. After James's death in 1971 it passed to Robin, as James had three daughters but no sons.

Vassall came there to escape his past, not dwell on it. After Robin's unexpected death in May 1980, aged fifty-three, Brigid never saw Vassall again.

In the late 1970s Vassall forged a new friendship: with the espionage writer Nigel West (whose real name is Rupert Allason). West was the co-author (with Richard Deacon) of *Spy!*, a book about famous espionage cases, including Vassall's, that was published in 1980.[261]

West first met Vassall in about 1977, having been introduced by Lord Longford. It did not seem likely that they would get on: West's father, James Allason, had been a cavalry officer who, during the war, had served on the Joint Planning Staff in the Cabinet War Rooms. This led to an appointment in the War Office's discipline department, providing briefs for the Secretary of State on the sentencing of soldiers found guilty of murder and other serious offences. Allason was Conservative MP for Hemel Hempstead between 1959 and 1974 and became a good friend of John Profumo, as well as his parliamentary private secretary: straight after his resignation Profumo went to stay at the Allason family's second home on the Isle of Wight to lie low.

Allason senior had been unhappy about the way his colleague Tam Galbraith had been "thrown to the wolves" so Vassall may have been wary about meeting his son, who was also trying to become a Conservative MP by the late 1970s. West seemed an unlikely man to win Vassall's trust, given that Vassall had so often been treated badly by writers. But opposites attract and a friendship developed. Vassall even gave West the Minox camera that he had used to photograph Admiralty documents, which had been returned to

---

261 West was not the only espionage writer to use a pseudonym. Richard Deacon was the penname of George Donald King McCormick (1911–98), a journalist and popular historian who had worked for naval intelligence during the Second World War. McCormick worked for the *Sunday Times'* foreign desk and wrote many books (under both McCormick and Deacon), including biographies of Sir Maurice Oldfield and Ian Fleming and histories of the Hellfire Club, Jack the Ripper, the Cambridge Apostles and numerous secret services.

him when he left prison in 1972. West passed it on to an espionage museum in the US.

West entertained Vassall for lunch at his country home in Berkshire in about 1983. Vassall had an unexpected proposition: would West like to employ him as a butler? West, who had stood for Parliament in 1979 and 1983 and was now actively looking for a more winnable seat, politely declined the offer.[262] Although he was fond of Vassall, he understandably drew the line at employing him.

"Vassall felt exploited, and deeply regretted his contact with Lord Longford," West recalls. His autobiographical stories in the *Sunday Pictorial* may have helped to pay his legal bills but they did his rehabilitation no good at all: Vassall had not been strong enough to stop the *Pictorial*'s journalists rewriting his copy. Having been urged to write his autobiography by Longford, Vassall soon regretted it. "He was eager to please, and very pliable," West recalls. "He did not help himself because of certain personality traits, such as his constant name-dropping". But like many others, such as Robin McEwen and Geoffrey Bennett, West found that he liked Vassall more once he got to know him properly.

West's book *Spy!* was a spin-off from a six-part BBC drama series.[263] Its first episode, broadcast on 13 January 1980, was about the Vassall case. Vassall was played by John Normington and Geoffrey Bennett by John Nettleton, best known for playing Sir Arnold Robinson, the Cabinet Secretary in *Yes Minister*.

Spy! was a remarkably restrained account of the Vassall case with a dry, factual voiceover. For once, John Vassall was portrayed as a human being. His promiscuous love life, with regular travel

---

262 In 1979 West stood in Kettering (John Profumo's seat from 1940 and 1945) and lost by 1,500 votes. In 1983 he stood in Battersea but fell 3,000 votes behind Alf Dubs. He became an MP on his third attempt, in Torbay in 1987, holding the seat until 1997.

263 After John Vassall, other episodes featured pre- and post-war espionage cases: the KGB "murder machine" in 1930s Ukraine, the Venlo incident of 1939 and operations in Japan, Nazi Germany and Vichy France. For more details, including clips of the programme, see: https://www.imdb.com/title/tt1397132/?ref_=nm_flmg_act_52 Spy! *Spy!* is not available for streaming or on DVD but a VHS tape of the series can be viewed by appointment at the British Film Institute's archive.

to meet boyfriends across Europe, was glossed over. Vassall came across as a sensitive man, naïve but not evil, and the camp stereotypes (such as wearing a purple satin housecoat while he writes to his mother) are few. Tam Galbraith is not depicted on screen and neither are Vassall's two other "MP friends". Moscow is portrayed as a monochrome, soulless place with archive footage of the Kremlin skyline and the Moscow Metro intercut with interior shots. It is easy to see why the lonely Vassall gravitated towards the flattery of Russian men. Vassall's contact with "the skier" (who he toasts with the words "Here's to gentle slopes and safe falls") was portrayed sympathetically. Sexual relations between them are only implied.

Geoffrey Bennett is portrayed as a genial pipe smoker who proudly announces that "the Stilton's arriving in the diplomatic bag" ahead of a dinner party to which he invites Vassall. But Bennett is clearly annoyed by Vassall from the start: "Rather irritating, not very bright ... they must be scraping the bottom of the barrel in Whitehall!" he complains to a colleague. Bennett's dressing-down of Vassall in *Spy!* is close to the accounts that Vassall and Bennett themselves gave. He chastises Vassall for being "altogether too uppish" and "moving in circles far too exalted for your position here at the embassy". Vassall's "work record here leaves a lot to be desired" and he needs "to be more selective with the invitations you accept". Where dramatic licence is used – Vassall offers to help the ambassador's wife, Lady Hayter, "make up a four" at the bridge table but she immediately walks off saying "I do hate cold soup ... I think we must go into dinner" – is probably not far from the truth.

"Gregory" (Kevin Stoney) reassures Vassall that reports that the British are looking for a spy in the Admiralty are "fairy stories to frighten the children". He introduces Vassall to Nikolai in a London restaurant. That is not quite how Vassall said he met Nikolai but it is not a complete fabrication.

Spy! did, however, contain some howlers. Bennett is shown warning Vassall, on his very first day at the embassy, to minimise social contact with Russians and to report any interactions immediately (in fact, Vassall only received such a warning in 1955 and in the meantime, contact was tolerated or even encouraged). The military officer who Vassall sleeps with in May 1955, just before he was forced to start spying, is given the name Ivan (in Vassall's memoirs, and confession, he was nameless). Admiralty security officers are shown finding a roll of film in Vassall's Whitehall desk (in fact, nothing incriminating was ever found there). John Normington, who was forty-two during filming, was too old to play Vassall (who is only twenty-nine when the action begins in late 1953), but otherwise well-cast.

Spy!'s producers made the elementary mistake of not checking to see which of the real-life characters it portrayed were still alive. One of them was Geoffrey Bennett, who in 1980 was very much alive. In the early 1970s he and his wife Rosemary had moved from Kensington to the seventeenth-century Stage Coach Cottage on Broad Street in Ludlow, Shropshire. Vassall had lost touch with the Bennetts after he had entered prison, despite Rosemary's promises to visit, but Geoffrey sometimes talked to his family about having known Vassall prior to his arrest. He told his children, in-laws and grandchildren that Vassall was "small, neat and inoffensive" and that he had always been surprised that he was only a clerk, given his social background. Bennett had been worried that Vassall was vulnerable to blackmail from the start and he told the Admiralty as much, only for the department to reply that he should not worry.

Geoffrey thought that "he had covered himself", his daughter-in-law Perdita recalls. But he seemed to have felt residual guilt that Vassall's career was allowed to continue on his watch and that if he had acted differently he could have saved Vassall from being entrapped, and stopped him from spying. He also remained annoyed that his warnings about Vassall had gone unheeded by his superiors.

In the 1970s Bennett was still receiving help with his naval research from Russian contacts he had made twenty years earlier. In an interview with the *Ludlow Advertiser*, shortly after Bennett moved to the town, he said "It takes a long time to get information from Russia – sometimes it is a lemon but at other times I get a big surprise". But while he had a ringside seat to one of the twentieth century's biggest naval espionage cases, he never wrote about the Vassall case – either in fictionalised form or as a memoir.[264]

Miles Bennett, Geoffrey's grandson, was born in February 1963, just after Vassall entered Wormwood Scrubs, but until the BBC dramatisation of Vassall's story in 1980, Miles had never known about his grandfather's friendship with the spy. The *Spy!* episode about Vassall happened to be broadcast when Miles, then aged sixteen, was visiting his grandparents in Ludlow. He sat awkwardly alongside his grandfather as the drama unfolded. One scene – in which Admiralty security officers, with torches and blackened faces, search their own building in the dead of night – was a howler too far for Geoffrey. Portraying the search as an SAS-style commando raid was so far from the truth that Bennett lodged a complaint with the BBC for not having told him that the programme was being made (he had only found out about it a few days before it was screened).

It turned out that Bennett had not been consulted because "he was thought to be dead". Bennett received an apology from the programme's producer (Frank Cox) and its director (Ben Rea). But Bennett felt that "I was much more on the ball than the programme showed", and he proceeded to make a more formal complaint, which was only partly upheld. The BBC's Programmes Complaints Commission agreed that the producers had failed "to identify him as a living person or to notify him that the programme was being made" as they should have done. But it "did not consider the

---

264   There is no mention of Vassall in any of Bennett's meticulous scrapbooks, full of correspondence and reviews of his books, which are now held at the Caird Library of the National Maritime Museum in Greenwich.

portrayal was unfair to him or reflected adversely on his reputation as a naval historian". Lady Iris Hayter (whose husband had not been portrayed onscreen) also complained, though she acknowledged that "within its limits" the programme "presented a fair portrayal".[265] To this day, some members of Geoffrey Bennett's family still resent his portrayal on television, three years before his death.[266] "Poor Geoffrey. The BBC did a horrid drama, without consulting the family", his daughter-in-law Perdita remembers.

Spy! may have judged Geoffrey Bennett too harshly. But it is not just the only direct portrayal of John Vassall on screen: it is also an accurate one. His entrapment at the Hotel Berlin was filmed with surprising frankness for a BBC serial of the late 1970s.[267] Vassall is clearly drugged, and virtually unconscious, as three men strip and join him on a sofa while a fourth man starts taking photographs. A pair of naked buttocks is glimpsed on screen and it is clear from the writhing of limbs and torsos that Vassall is being anally raped. A horrified Vassall later tells Mikhailsky that the photographs the Russians have taken show "everything … everything you could possibly imagine".

● ● ●

"This is the beginning", Vassall wrote to Jeremy Hutchinson in May 1974, a few months after he had started his new job at the British Records Association. "I trust that something will finally come out of all this next year. Maybe a job, a house of my own and, I hope, a new circle of friends," he added in another letter a few months later.

By the late 1970s Vassall was keen to find another job. In July

---

265 For more details of the complaints that Bennett and Lady Hayter made, see: https://usir.salford.ac.uk/id/eprint/50417/1/The%20020%20Affair%20submitted%20version.pdf.

266 Geoffrey Bennett died on 5 September 1983, aged seventy-four. His obituary in *The Times* said only this of his Moscow years: "He was largely responsible for organising the visit of the Home Fleet to Leningrad in the autumn of 1955". There was no mention of him being accompanied to Leningrad by John Vassall, one of post-war Britain's most notorious traitors..

267 Although *Spy!* was first broadcast in 1980, its closing credits had a 1979 date stamp.

1979 the BRA gave him a reference that was far more glowing than anything the Admiralty had ever provided.[268] On 24 October 1980 Vassall wrote to Hutchinson with condolences: he had only just read Robin McEwen's obituary after his death in May. Yet Vassall's letter quickly returned to his perennial quest for a better job. "I don't want to bother you again, but should you hear of anything that might possibly suit me I hope you would pass my name on to a friend. In the meantime I still have an office at Charterhouse until I find something else," he added grandly.

On 21 May 1981 Vassall reminded Hutchinson that "Robin McEwen, whose tragic death came as a great shock last year, was hoping to do something on my behalf". Vassall was still working at the BRA part-time but the association seemed unable or unwilling to offer him a full-time job. "With my new reference I wonder whether you could recommend me to someone for another job, however humble, or as a private secretary. It would at least give me hope for the future". In June that year, Vassall wrote to Hutchinson to thank him for putting him in touch with a Mrs Kaspers (apparently a headhunter) who had interviewed him and sent his name to a number of prospective employers, whose application forms Vassall dutifully filled in. By now Vassall felt that his BRA salary "no longer covers the basic requirements of my studio flat" at Langford Court. The final letter from Vassall in Hutchinson's papers, dated 23 December 1981, praised a speech that Lord Hutchinson (who had become a Labour peer in 1978) had made in the House of Lords on penal policy. It added that there was "No luck yet about a job – though I work at Charterhouse and Gray's Inn part-time".

By the early 1980s Vassall seems to have given up on Hutchinson

---

268 Since September 1973 "The Association has been well served by Mr Phillips, who has a pleasant and friendly manner which has made him an amiable colleague", wrote C. D. Chalmers, a principal assistant keeper at the Public Record Office and the BRA's honorary secretary. "He is resourceful and diligent in his work, and is well-fitted by his easy, but precise, manner and his personal appearance ... We should be sorry to lose his services and have no hesitation in recommending him to any future employer". Chalmers provided an identical reference in May 1981: Vassall was still job hunting two years later.

finding him his dream job. His position at the BRA was the end, not the beginning: he carried on working there throughout the 1980s and well into the 1990s. He mostly worked alongside much younger archivists and in the early 1990s his closest colleague was Susan Snell. Like Janet Foster before her, Snell was half Vassall's age, in her early thirties.[269] She remembers him happily bashing away at an old-fashioned typewriter at the BRA's office, which by now had moved from Charterhouse to Padbury Court, a narrow street off Brick Lane in Shoreditch, in a Victorian building overlooking a churchyard. She and Vassall would sometimes visit the nearby Whitechapel Art Gallery at lunchtime. Snell worked full-time but Vassall still only worked for two or three days a week. Vassall managed the BRA's membership database, in those days kept in a card index, received members' annual subscriptions by cheque and banked them at Hoare's Bank on the Strand.

Vassall still called himself John Phillips and it was only after two or three years that Snell discovered his real name, and what a colourful past he had. Like Janet Foster, she found out by accident: as a young woman left alone with a much older man, she discreetly asked a colleague if Phillips was "safe to work with". "Oh, you have no worries on that score", the colleague said, before revealing who Phillips really was. Until then Snell had not definitively known that Vassall was gay, nor that he had spent ten years in jail for espionage. Snell's parents, who were old enough to remember Vassall's trial, were amazed to hear that their daughter was working with him.

"He always enjoyed the company of rich and well-connected people," Snell recalls. Even in his late sixties, Vassall was always immaculately dressed. He loved going to the BRA's annual conference, wearing a smart suit, to mingle with members and distribute literature, Snell recalls. She knew that Vassall had well-off friends, including a family in Sussex who employed him as a sort of butler

---

269   Snell is now the archivist and records manager at the Museum of Freemasonry at Freemasons' Hall.

at house parties, where he wore a red velvet smoking jacket that he once wore to work. The editor of the *Sunday Telegraph*, Donald McLachlan, once wrote that Vassall was "at heart a valet". Robin McEwen's son John even recalls seeing a reference that his father had written for Vassall to become a "gentleman's companion", a butler-cum-valet.

Like Janet Foster twenty years earlier, Snell did not feel comfortable asking Vassall about his past, and he only talked about it tangentially. When she brought Rich Tea biscuits into the office, he referred to them as "prison biscuits" as they had been staples at Brixton, Wormwood Scrubs and Maidstone jails. "John was quite secretive and did not want his quiet life to be disturbed", says Snell. She does not remember any unwelcome phone calls from journalists and Vassall only mentioned Dolphin Square once, in passing, to say how it had been such an exciting place to live.

Vassall's income from the BRA was modest and he did not appear to travel much, other than sometimes staying with friends in France. In 1994 or 1995, around the time of his seventieth birthday, Vassall voluntarily retired from the BRA, once a computer system was introduced. As a clerk Vassall had always been comfortable with the typewriter, carbon paper and card index files, but not with personal computers and Microsoft software. Snell recalls that he was horrified by their arrival. He was always a neat man, with neat handwriting: the many documents handwritten by Vassall that survive are all in fountain pen, not ballpoint, which was common by the early 1960s.

Snell remembers Vassall as "delightful, charming and good fun ... I enjoyed working with John and I was fond of him". After his retirement they stayed in touch. Snell and her husband joined Vassall at a concert of Olivier Messiaen's music in Hampstead and he left them to walk alone on Hampstead Heath after having a drink in a pub. She remembers visiting his flat in St John's Wood for lunch in the 1990s and finding it "old fashioned and in need of decoration and updating" but clean. The last meeting with Vassall that she can remember was at a classical music concert at the Barbican, where Vassall was accompanied by a good-looking, tall and slim young man. "Good for you, John," Snell thought to herself.

Several English spies of Vassall's generation, such as George Blake, Donald Maclean and Kim Philby, spent the rest of their days in Moscow, where they acquired cult status as gentlemen rogues and were highly prized interviewees. Even though they largely refused to talk, they continued to fascinate the British media. Until his death in September 1963 Guy Burgess had lived in a three-bedroom apartment in a garden suburb of Moscow, with a male "sex-companion" (a jazz guitarist called Yasha) and a view of a sixteenth-century monastery. Burgess was a rich man by Soviet standards: his estate was valued at £6,000. In his will he left a bequest of £2,000 and his library of 4,000 books to Philby (by contrast Vassall never received a bequest from another spy).

Maclean (who used the alias Mark Frazer for a while) lived, until his death in 1983, in a more modest flat, but it was right in the middle of Moscow with a view over the Moskva river and close to Kremlin Park. Kim Philby became a senior official at a Soviet news agency and in 1965 he was given the Order of the Red Banner, "for outstanding services over a period of many years to the people of the Union of Soviet Socialist Republics". Until his death in 1988 Philby lived in a large apartment with hand-made furniture, Bokhara and Chivas carpets and an electric icebox, vacuum cleaner, television set and a washing machine with a spin drier – rare luxuries in Soviet Russia. He was given a maid and a bodyguard and his children went to schools normally reserved for senior members of the nomenklatura. Vassall, on the other hand, changed his surname to Phillips and lived quietly in a bedsit in St John's Wood for the rest of his days. He was mostly ignored by historians and journalists.

• • •

On Monday 18 November 1996, John Vassall dropped dead of a heart attack. There is uncertainty over precisely where he died: in some accounts he had his heart attack while on a London bus and in others, it was outside Baker Street tube station, about a mile from his home. He was pronounced dead on arrival at hospital. There was no uncertainty about his funeral arrangements: Vassall had carefully stipulated every detail in advance. Vassall would have probably liked to be buried in an Italian cathedral and his funeral was held at the next-best thing in London: the Brompton Oratory, a grand neo-classical Catholic church in Knightsbridge.[270] The Oratory is half a mile from Vassall's favourite department stores: Harrods and the now defunct Woollands, where Vassall had bought women's clothing.

A few months before Vassall's arrest, the Oratory was the scene of an extraordinary meeting between two spies. On a visit to London in 1961 or 1962, Oleg Penkovsky was taken to the Oratory by an English businessman, Greville Wynne, who acted as his go-between with MI6. Penkovsky "stood for an hour watching those who came with their private prayers", Wynne recalled. "Religion may not give all the answers, Greville," Penkovsky told him. "I'm sure it doesn't. But at least it is true, it is not ordered by the State, and it gives a principle, something to guide our lives. At home we have nothing, only what the State commands". A few months later, on 22 October 1962 – the very day that Vassall was sentenced at the Old Bailey – Penkovsky was arrested in Moscow, and Wynne was arrested in Budapest nine days later. Whether Vassall knew about this part of the Oratory's history or not, it was a fitting place to lay the Cold War to rest, as well as Vassall himself.

---

270   Technically known as the Church of the Immaculate Heart of Mary, the Brompton Oratory was built between 1869 and 1884 from designs by Herbert Gribble. Gribble's building is a competent exercise in the Italian Renaissance style, with echoes of Roman Baroque and Christopher Wren. The Oratory was the largest Catholic church in London until the consecration of Westminster Cathedral in 1903.

"Of course I was terribly upset when the Church decided to stop Latin", Vassall told the *Sunday Times* in 1973. "People say to me, 'Oh John, you are such a traditionalist' but to me I'm afraid it's something that is timeless". Vassall had often worshipped at the Brompton Oratory and he loved its High Church Catholicism. His funeral mass there was conducted entirely in Latin. A horse-drawn hearse delivered Vassall's coffin and transported it to a private cremation afterwards.

Susan Snell recalls being one of about seventy mourners at Vassall's funeral (his solicitor, Peter Kingshill, claimed that there were more than 100). Lord Longford sat in front of Snell but there were no other VIPs that she recognised. She recalls the Brompton Road, the busy street that the Oratory stands on, being closed for the arrival of Vassall's cortège, and thinking how much he would have loved the ceremony of the Latin mass.

"I attended a funeral which aroused many memories – that of John Phillips, as I came to know him," noted Lord Longford in his diary. "I was pleasantly surprised by the good turnout at his funeral ... I was also glad that the press were not there to cross-examine me about my knowledge of him. They soon made up for it, however. The *Evening Standard* made him a front-page story. The *Telegraph* and *Guardian* gave him a lot of attention ... I got to know and like him when he was in Maidstone prison. Later, as chairman of Sidgwick & Jackson, I was responsible for publishing his memoir ... I was asked by more than one newspaper when John became a Catholic. That I couldn't remember, but he was a devout Catholic all the time I knew him."

This was clearly an affectionate recollection of Vassall, though much of it was about Longford himself. Tellingly, Longford did not refer to him as a friend. "John was homosexually inclined when serving as an Admiralty clerk in the British embassy in Moscow," Longford added, implying that Vassall was only slightly gay, and only temporarily. "He was blackmailed by the Russians into passing secrets to them and was eventually sentenced to many years in prison." Even Longford, the supposed champion of the dispossessed, seems never to have realised that Vassall had not just been blackmailed but raped.

It was two-and-a-half weeks after his passing, and two days after his funeral, before the media realised that Vassall had died. "LONDON (AP): John Vassall, who admitted spying for the KGB and was sent to prison in 1962, has died, his lawyer said Thursday. He was 71 ... Vassall was blackmailed into spying for the Soviet Union after being photographed, after an evening's heavy drinking, with a homosexual partner when he was a junior naval attaché in the British Embassy in Moscow in the 1950s", the Associated Press announced on 5 December.[271] "I didn't judge him on his past but I was very fond of him", Longford told the *Evening Standard*. "I admire the way he pulled his life together after what happened to him."

"If I got as long an obituary in the *Telegraph* I should be satisfied," Longford confided to his diary. But most obituaries were unkind and grudging. As David Leitch put it in the *Independent on Sunday*, Vassall's "real downfall was a pernicious and largely extinct English vice: that wistful Pooterish aspiration to being a gentleman, or at least being mistaken for one".

The Times' obituary contained an unforgivable howler: it said that Vassall had been born on 24 September 1920 and had died aged seventy-six, not seventy-two. It saw Vassall as a case study of security failure, not a human being: "He was naive, insecure and socially ambitious, while his homosexuality made him vulnerable to blackmail and his vanity was all too susceptible to greed. ...Vassall was never more than a low-level functionary, but there was nothing low-level about the damage he was able to inflict." To *The Times*, the only remarkable thing about Vassall was that he got

---

271 Vassall was not seventy-one: in fact, he had turned seventy-two eight weeks before his death.

away with it for so long. The paper added that "after his release in 1972 he sought and found obscurity". It did not consider the role that homophobic newspapers may have played in prompting him to do so.

In the *New York Times*, Robert Mcg. Thomas Jr explained that Vassall was "the high-living, low-level British Admiralty clerk whose exposure as a Soviet spy in 1962 created the first of the sex scandals that helped end the political career of Prime Minister Harold Macmillan". But Thomas's balanced piece was ruined by his claim that Vassall had been "blackmailed into becoming a spy after being plied with liquor by KGB agents and photographed in a compromising position with 'two or three men,'" which suggested that he was a willing participant in a drunken orgy, not a victim of sexual assault. The *Guardian*'s obituary, "spy and civil servant", was written by Richard Norton-Taylor and was the kindest. Vassall "gave his name to a spy scandal which caused serious embarrassment to the security services and to the Macmillan government," Norton-Taylor explained. "A prelude to the Profumo affair, it contributed to a growing impression of establishment incompetence and complacency which was to lead in 1964 to the end of 13 years of Tory rule." But Vassall himself was "vain, humourless, self-regarding and naive – a 'perfect fall guy', as he was later to admit", the journalist added. Even *The Guardian* – a liberal newspaper at the vanguard of social reform and firmly opposed to sexism, the trivialisation of rape and homophobia – described Vassall's downfall as being "photographed with three other men in a bed".

In January 1997 Vassall's will was registered, under the name John William Christopher Phillips. As well as changing his surname, Vassall had reshuffled his Christian names. The will (which had been written on 6 August 1991, with Peter Kingshill of 6 Gray's Inn Square as his executor) is a surprising document. Vassall left a reasonably large estate. He pledged £75,000 to various friends and charities, and his bequests were to the most apolitical causes imaginable: the National Trust, a Catholic monastery and a feline charity.

Like Vassall's Dolphin Square flat, his bedsit in Langford Court had been stuffed full of good furniture. All his antiques, mirrors and leatherbound books were left to the National Trust.[272] Surprisingly, Vassall left Monmouth School, which he had not particularly enjoyed going to, his "John Speed map circa 1610 of the County of Monmouthshire". He gave a bequest of £20,000 to the abbot and community of Quarr Abbey on the Isle of Wight and he left £10,000 to the Cats Protection League. He had wanted to bring a cat to Dolphin Square in 1959 but wasn't allowed to because of the square's "no pets" rule. Susan Snell recalls that Vassall was still fond of cats in the 1990s and was sorry that he couldn't have one in Langford Court. She thinks he may have signed up with a charity to "cat-sit" for other people.

Some £20,000 was left to Cristel Wheeler of Shoreham, Kent (where Vassall had lived in 1973–74) and £5,000 each to five others: his brother Richard (with his signet ring and other "personal effects"), Jacqueline Dunell of Beckenham (with his carriage clock and silver cutlery), Doreen Vaughan of London N4 (with his china and linen), Dr Harry K. Rose (Vassall's former psychiatrist) and Anne Ward, who lived in Low Fell, a suburb of Gateshead. Michael Hollidge, of Sevenoaks, was left Vassall's Patek Philippe wristwatch. The residue of Vassall's estate, after debts and funeral expenses, was left to Jean Kentish and Geoffrey Le Serve, who lived at Clee Cottage, near Redhill in Surrey.

None of these people appear on MI5's long lists of Vassall's friends, and possible lovers, in the early 1960s and none of them

---

272 The books were exactly what you would expect to find in John Vassall's library: a mixture of schoolboy light reading, high-minded literature and vanity books about his family history. The National Trust received a book about Marcus Aurelius, a copy of *The Wind in the Willows*, the collected poems of Rupert Brooke, the complete plays and sonnets of Shakespeare, a volume on the drawings of Leonardo da Vinci, John Burke's *History of the Commoners* and a copy of *Lady Holland to Her Son* (a volume of letters sent by Elizabeth Vassall to her son Henry).

are named in Vassall's memoirs, published in 1975. Most, if not all, appear to have befriended Vassall after his imprisonment for espionage, not before. By the 1990s the Cold War was over. The world had moved on, temporarily at least, from Cold War spy stories, and so had John Vassall.

"OUT IN THE COLD"

The John Vassall affair cemented Dolphin Square's reputation as a place of political scandal, which soon eclipsed its earlier reputation for glamour and exclusivity. In the early 1960s Pimlico was very different from swinging Chelsea to the west and posh Belgravia to the north. Like Bayswater and Paddington, Pimlico was still seen as seedy and unfashionable, despite being so close to the centre of London. That began to change in the late 1960s and 1970s, as Pimlico was put on the tube map in 1972, with the expansion of the Victoria line.[273] But the media attention that the Vassall and Profumo scandals had brought to Dolphin Square meant that it was permanently stigmatised.

Dolphin Square now had fewer movie stars but its relative proximity to Westminster overrode the tarnish that Vassall had bestowed upon it, and more and more MPs began renting flats there. Tam Galbraith was far from being the last politician to be brought down by an association with the flats there. Another was the colourful Labour MP Niall MacDermot, a former MI5 officer

---

273   Pimlico did not become very smart until the 1990s. Until the 1980s it was a mixed district with working and lower-middle class residents co-existing happily with the gentrifiers. The acerbic architectural writer Ian Nairn lived a few blocks north of Dolphin Square throughout the 1960s and in 1970, he wrote, "The great thing about Pimlico is its mixture of people and incomes, which had been deliberately encouraged by the council."

who was a staunch supporter of decriminalising homosexuality.[274] As a junior Treasury minister, MacDermot attracted much censure for leaving his wife in 1964 to run off with his half-Italian, half-Russian mistress, Ludmilla Benvenuto. Although MI5 told the Prime Minister, Harold Wilson, that MacDermot's mistress was a security risk, Wilson stood by him and in 1966, Ludmilla became MacDermot's second wife. But MI5 persisted, dredging up evidence that Benvenuto had worked informally for a Russian diplomat in post-war Italy. In 1968 MacDermot, who had been tipped as the next Solicitor General, suddenly resigned as a housing minister "for personal reasons". MacDermot later said that he'd had enough of MI5's vendetta and of their constant bugging of his Dolphin Square flat. Even after his resignation, MacDermot was still subject to a whispering campaign that his wife was being blackmailed by the KGB.

While MacDermot was never suspected to be a spy, it has been claimed that MI5 tried to smear him and his second wife as revenge because MacDermot had raised awkward questions about Kim Philby's defection in 1963. Being a former MI5 officer was seemingly not enough to exempt MacDermot. As with Tam Galbraith, a good minister was forced to resign simply because of the company he had kept at Dolphin Square. But this time it was a Labour politician, caught in the crossfire between Harold Wilson and the security services.

In the early 1970s Wilson himself took turns living at the square with Edward Heath, on their way in and out of No. 10. Wilson first became convinced that MI5 were pursuing a vendetta against him after a mysterious break-in at his flat there. He lived at Dolphin Square from 1971–73, in between his two spells as Prime Minister. He and his wife Mary had lived there briefly during the Second

---

274 MacDermot's early life was not without scandal: in the 1930s he was charged with manslaughter after a fellow Oxford student died of heart failure at a political meeting, but he was acquitted. He subsequently had a respectable career working for MI5 during the Second World War and at the Bar, before becoming an MP in 1957.

World War, while Wilson worked as a statistician and economist at the Ministry of Fuel and Power before becoming an MP. A few months after Wilson unexpectedly lost the 1970 election, they returned there.[275]

Wilson's return to Dolphin Square after an absence of thirty years was full of irony. In June 1963, at the height of the Profumo scandal, Wilson had given a lofty speech in the Commons decrying a "London underworld of vice, dope, marijuana, blackmail, counter-blackmail, violence and petty crime". Little did Wilson know that within a decade he would be living at the scene of one of the Profumo scandal's most terrible events: Dolphin Square, where Christine Keeler had been held captive and raped by Lucky Gordon in early 1962, and where John Vassall had spied after 1962.

Compared to the Macmillan and Douglas-Home governments that preceded it, Wilson's government was remarkably free of public spy scandals in 1964–70. There were no more Vassall cases on Wilson's watch, but behind the scenes MI5 was in turmoil. Its official historian maintains that Roger Hollis was the blameless victim of a vendetta by Peter Wright, a rogue MI5 officer, and Anatoliy Golitsyn (the defector who had helped to unmask Vassall). James Angleton convinced himself that Wilson had been recruited as a Soviet spy in the late 1950s – just as Vassall started spying – and he persuaded some MI5 officers to agree with him.[276] They not only believed that Wilson was a "KGB asset" but also a "Manchurian

---

275   There is some uncertainty about precisely when Wilson lived at Dolphin Square. His authorised biography, by Philip Ziegler, makes no mention of his tenancy there and suggests that when the Wilsons had to leave Downing Street they rented a flat in Vincent Square before moving into Lord North Street before the end of 1970. The Wilsons' interlude in Dolphin Square is skipped over entirely, like an embarrassing secret.

276   Angleton and others alleged that Wilson had been recruited while working, from 1951 onwards, as a consultant to Montague L. Meyer Ltd, a British timber company that did a lot of trade in the Soviet Union. MI5 made much of a photograph showing a moustachioed Wilson walking down a Moscow street with an unidentified female companion in the 1950s, which they cited as evidence that he had been caught in a KGB honey trap. Wilson told MI5, "I can assure you, I kept my trousers buttoned up in Moscow". However, there is evidence that after Wilson met Nikita Khrushchev in early 1956, the KGB gave Wilson the codename 'Olding' in its 'agent development file', presumably in the hope that he might be recruited as a useful informer, if not a spy.

candidate", manoeuvred into the Labour leadership by the hidden hand of Soviet intelligence after Gaitskell's assassination in January 1963.

In 1972, within a few months of moving into Dolphin Square, Wilson had an unshakeable suspicion that MI5 had burgled his flat. Nothing was missing, there was no sign of forced entry and the front door had a five-lever mortice lock that could not easily be picked. But the fastidious Wilson told police that he had found a drawer sticking out from the frame of his desk by a couple of millimetres, not fully closed as usual. Larry Henderson, head of forensics at the Flying Squad, found nothing untoward. But decades later, Henderson said that Wilson may have been the victim of a sophisticated break-in, possibly by the British security services. "His home had been too clean … as if someone had quite deliberately and professionally removed all forensic evidence from the site," Henderson told the *Mail on Sunday* in 2016.

In late 1973 the Wilsons moved from Dolphin Square to a Georgian house on Lord North Street, just off Smith Square. They continued to live there, not at No. 10, during Wilson's final two years as Prime Minister in 1974–76.[277] Much has been written about Wilson's belief that Lord North Street was bugged and that some of his tax papers were stolen from there in the spring of 1974, in a burglary that the police thought MI5 were responsible for. But it was at Dolphin Square that Wilson's paranoia really began.

Only a few months after Harold Wilson left Dolphin Square, Edward Heath arrived. Heath had been defeated by Wilson at the general election of February 1974 after three tumultuous years as Prime Minister. Effectively homeless, Heath spent the next four months living in a flat rented by his friend and fellow MP Timothy Kitson, who obligingly made way for Heath by moving in

---

277　One reason may have been a radical redecoration of No. 10 by Ted Heath. "Gone was the familiar, functional shabbiness," noted Barbara Castle after attending her first Cabinet meeting there in March 1974. "Instead someone with appalling taste had had it tarted up. … it looked like a boudoir".

with another forty-something Tory MP, Spencer Le Marchant, next door.[278] The squatter of Downing Street became the lodger of Dolphin Square. "Cut off from his piano, his stereo and all his cherished mementoes while he fought for his political life, he was a Pooh bear with a very sore head: not an easy tenant", said Heath's biographer John Campbell. Only days before his defeat in February, a Conservative election broadcast had lauded Heath as "an extraordinary man. A private man, a solitary man." Heath was indeed a solitary man now, living alone in a one-bedroom flat at Dolphin Square, much like Vassall's, that was rented in another MP's name.[279]

Ted Heath did not stay at Dolphin Square for very long: in July 1974 he moved to a house on Wilton Street, Belgravia. But many more MPs were equally undeterred by the fact that John Vassall had lived there. They overlooked its growing reputation as a centre for sex work – and two grisly murders, one at the square and the other closely linked to it. In 1964 Hannah Tailford, a west London sex worker believed to have attended parties at Dolphin Square from 1962 onwards, was murdered by an unidentified serial killer. "Jack the Stripper", as they were christened, was believed to have claimed eight victims in and around Hammersmith between 1959 and 1965. Police files on the murder investigation were later suspiciously lost and some contend that the murders were connected to the Profumo scandal.

In 1971 a secret sadomasochistic brothel was uncovered in Duncan House, the block in which Christine Keeler and Mandy Rice-Davies had lived, run by a madam called Sybil Benson. In June 1975 the *Daily Mirror* reported that Michael Shepley, a 39-year-old South African man working as a solicitor at the Greater London

---

278 Kitson, who was a farmer and keen huntsman, represented the North Yorkshire seat of Richmond until 1983, when it was inherited by Leon Brittan. Like Heath, Brittan was later embroiled in false claims of a paedophile ring at Dolphin Square, even though he had never lived there.

279 Heath's stay there has been treated as an embarrassing secret by his biographers. John Campbell placed Kitson's flat in "a functional modern block overlooking Vauxhall Bridge" while Denis MacShane said that Heath had "to camp in a small flat south of the Thames [*sic*]". Philip Ziegler referred to it merely as a "flat near Vauxhall Bridge".

Council, was found in his Duncan House flat "with his head battered and his throat cut".

It emerged that Shepley had picked up a couple of "rent boys" at the railings in Piccadilly Circus (known as the "Meat Rack"), who had then robbed and murdered him. Shepley's mother, who appeared to be in denial that her son had been gay, advanced an alternative theory. Shepley's flat was previously inhabited by a plain-clothes intelligence officer working in Northern Ireland, and Shepley had been murdered by the IRA in a tragic case of mistaken identity. Another theory was that Shepley, who had once drunk at one of the Guildford pubs that the IRA bombed in 1974, was being used by the security services to investigate the bombings. Either way, Dolphin Square was yet again embroiled in a tale of homosexuality and espionage.

In fiction, as in real life, the square was increasingly portrayed as a place of danger. The role it plays in John le Carré's novels changed over the decades, just as the square's fortunes waned.[280] In the opening chapter of *Single & Single*, published in 1999, a corporate lawyer, Alfred Winser, is about to be executed by a Russian-American client and ponders his unhappy marriage: "I should have taken Tiger's advice, set her up in a flat somewhere, Dolphin Square, the Barbican. I should have fired her as my secretary and kept her as my little friend without suffering the humiliation of being her husband", muses Winser. Rather than a glamourous *pied-à-terre* for spies, the square is now just a hypothetical dwelling for a hypothetical mistress. In *A Legacy of Spies*, written in 2017 and set in the recent past, residing at Dolphin Square is portrayed as a form of punishment, not reward. An ageing Peter Guillam, who first appeared as George Smiley's assistant in *The Spy*

---

280 There are several nods to the square in *The Honourable Schoolboy*, published in 1977, about the aftermath of the "Dolphin Case" (the unmasking of an MI5 officer, the Philby-esque Bill Haydon, as a Soviet mole). The novel's villains are two Chinese orphan brothers, "brave sailors" named Nelson and Drake Ko, who share their first names with two of Dolphin Square's blocks. After Nelson Ko is apprehended in Hong Kong he is taken to a safe house in Sussex nicknamed "the Dolphinarium".

Who Came in from the Cold, is summoned from his retirement in Brittany back to London, to be grilled about Operation Windfall, a distant Cold War memory. Guillam stays briefly at "a dismal hotel near Charing Cross Station" but he is soon moved into an MI5 "safe flat": 110B Hood House, in the block where Oswald Mosley, Maxwell Knight and John Vassall had once lived.

In Pimlico it always seems to be raining and Guillam is not happy to be billeted there: "Ever since I had rallied to the secret flag, the place had given me the shivers," he reflects. "Dolphin Square in my day had more safe flats to the cubic foot than any building on the planet, and there wasn't one of them where I hadn't briefed or debriefed some luckless Joe." Like all safe flats, 110B Hood House is a model of "planned discomfort", furnished with a large red fire extinguisher, "two lumpy armchairs with springs gone", a watercolour reproduction of Lake Windermere, a television, a locked minibar and a sign ordering guests not to smoke "EVEN WITH WINDOW OPEN". In the bedroom was a single "iron-hard school bed", a "prison cot". Guillam protests that he is staying in Dolphin Square on "miserly terms".

The only people that Guillam encounters at Dolphin Square are not glamorous actors or politicians but a Hungarian waitress in its restaurant – or "grill room" – and "retired ladies in white hats and croquet skirts" in its courtyard. There is nothing glamorous about the millennial Dolphin Square portrayed in *A Legacy of Spies*.[281] The beaten-up Volvo saloon, into which Christoph (the vengeful son of Alec Leamas) is bundled, is a far cry from the chauffeur-driven cars that would convey many people to the square in the 1950s. And John Vassall never broke down sobbing on Grosvenor Road, as Christoph does: instead, he calmly picked up a camera that Nikolai had left in a phone box there.

---

281 A year after *A Legacy of Spies* was published, the novelist Kate Atkinson wrote *Transcription*, about an MI5 unit based in Nelson House in 1940, eavesdropping on fascist fifth columnists who are plotting in another Dolphin Square flat. Loosely based on Maxwell Knight's real-life activities, *Transcription* also made numerous references to the square's later reputation for sexual transgression and Soviet espionage.

A Legacy of Spies can be seen as nostalgia. It is unlikely that nowadays MI6 would run operations or house assets in such a prominent and expensive block, instead of anonymous semis in the suburbs. Like so much of central London, Dolphin Square has become a valuable real estate commodity, out of reach to all but the wealthy. Its unique rental model, whereby richer tenants indirectly subsidised poorer ones, has been broken. John Vassall could probably not afford to live at Dolphin Square today, even if his remittances from the Russians were uprated with inflation.

Most of the hundreds of MPs who have lived at Dolphin Square over the last eighty years attracted no controversy. David Steel (the Liberal leader who beat Vassall's friend Robin McEwen to enter Parliament in 1965) once said it was "very much a place where you can keep yourself to yourself". But some found that Dolphin Square was their nemesis. Several MPs have died there, in one case by drinking themselves to death, and a judge once jumped to his death from one of the square's windows. Time and time again people have gone to live at Dolphin Square with the highest of hopes, as John Vassall did, only to leave it in disgrace, under arrest or even in a coffin. Few of the many love affairs conducted there seem to have ended happily ever after. Although it can claim to be a sexually emancipated place where gay, lesbian and transgender people could begin to take tentative steps out of the closet, there has also been much tragedy, vice and abuse of power.

In the early 1990s, Raymond Fletcher, a Labour MP who had lived at Dolphin Square in the 1960s and 1970s, was posthumously found to have had another sideline. He was identified as a Soviet spy – codenamed PETER – by the Russian defector Vasili Mitrokhin.[282] Nonetheless, in 1993 the newly-married Princess Anne and

---

282 Many on the left felt that Fletcher (who was MP for Ilkeston from 1964 to 1983) was smeared by the security services. Before his death in 1991, Fletcher called MI5 "a complete bunch of bastards" for having intercepted letters from a Hungarian mistress and passing them to his German wife; his marriage only just survived. His wife died in 1973.

her second husband, Commander Tim Laurence, moved into a large £1,300 a month apartment in Drake House. They moved back to Buckingham Palace a few months later, apparently because the Princess Royal had found Dolphin Square to be "totally naff". She hated "the nosy neighbours, noisy traffic and the sight of hookers plying their trade nearby", a Palace source told the media.

From 1964 onwards the square was run by the Dolphin Square Trust, whose letting policies attracted allegations of cronyism, and in the 1990s it became embroiled in the 'homes for votes' gerrymandering scandal, after which many of Dame Shirley Porter's associates were found to be living at Dolphin Square on very low rents. One 1990s visitor said that Dolphin Square's four miles of corridors had "the lingering aroma of boiled cabbages". In 2002 the journalist, Valentine Low, complained that they were "mile after mile of institutional paint, old carpet and a smell of dust" in urgent need of sprucing up. He added "There is still something irreducibly drab. It lies partly in the buildings, brick monoliths that now look best suited to council housing records. Is Dolphin Square really that special anymore?".

The square remained embroiled in political scandal in the twenty-first century. In 2011, Tony Blair's favourite Catholic priest, Father Michael Seed, was accused of doling out papal knighthoods in return for charitable donations, and of living in a Dolphin Square flat, sublet by one of the people he had arranged a papal knighthood for. The rent that MPs paid for Dolphin Square tenancies, and the windfalls they received for relinquishing them when the square's freehold was bought by an American pension fund, led to several of them becoming enmeshed in the expenses scandal of 2009. The square still had the power to end political careers. One of the most colourful MPs to have lived there in the 1990s and 2000s was the Conservative Michael Mates. In 1993 Mates resigned as a Northern Ireland minister after it emerged that he had given a watch inscribed with "Don't let the buggers get you down" to a suspected fraudster, the businessman Asil Nadir, who had fled from Britain to Northern Cyprus to avoid prosecution.[283]

In July 2015 the Labour peer John Sewel, a deputy speaker of the House of Lords, was caught in a classic tabloid sting with two sex workers in his Dolphin Square flat. Lord Sewel, who had had a respectable career as a senior vice principal of the University of Aberdeen and then as a minister in the Scottish Office during the Blair government, was revealed to be a very different sort of man in the privacy of his Nelson House flat. After welcoming the sex workers at his front door with the salutation "Happy days are here again" and giving one a slap on the backside, he told them, "I just want to be led astray". In footage on the *Sun on Sunday*'s website he was seen snorting cocaine off one of the women's breast and smoking while wearing an orange bra under a leather jacket.[284] Much to the delight of the tabloids, it emerged that six days before his binge Sewel had announced new powers to expel peers from the House of Lords for breaching its code of conduct, writing in the *Huffington Post* that "The actions of a few damage our reputation. Scandals make good headlines." Indeed they did: within two days of the *Sun on Sunday*'s revelations, Sewel resigned both as a deputy speaker and as a peer, heading off an official inquiry. Rarely has a political downfall been so swift. The curse of Dolphin Square had struck again.

In 2014, a few months before Lord Sewel's disgrace, a middle-aged NHS manager and former paediatric nurse, Carl Beech, made

---

283   After stepping down from Parliament in 2010, in 2012 Mates – then aged seventy-eight – tried to revive his political career by being selected as the Conservative candidate for the post of Hampshire's Police and Crime Commissioner. Although Hampshire is a Conservative stronghold and Mates had been one of the county's MPs for more than thirty-five years, he was unexpectedly defeated. One reason was his repeated refusal to answer questions about the £40,000 windfall he had received for vacating his Dolphin Square tenancy while still an MP.

284   Bizarrely, the peer then chose to give his two female companions a running commentary on contemporary British politics, describing David Cameron as "the most superficial prime minister ever", Boris Johnson as "a public-school arsehole" and the Labour leadership election "a fucking mess." Jeremy Corbyn was a "useless ... romantic left-wing idiot".

allegations of a long-running paedophile sex ring, involving a host of establishment figures, at Dolphin Square. Identified at first only as "Nick", Beech claimed that as a child in the late 1970s and early 1980s he had repeatedly been taken to satanic "parties" at the square and other locations, including the Carlton Club, the Elm Guest House in Barnes and a military base on Salisbury Plain.[285]

"Nick's" alleged abusers included Ted Heath. The former Prime Minister's four-month tenancy in 1974 had hitherto attracted no adverse comment. Suspicions about him seemed to rely on the age-old prejudice that an unmarried man must be a closet homosexual, and that a closet homosexual must be a paedophile. But Dolphin Square's long-standing reputation for secrecy and scandal did nothing to dampen the furore over Beech's allegations, which the police described as "credible and true". They were widely leaked to the media and seized on by a new generation of MPs who used parliamentary privilege to make headline-grabbing allegations of an establishment cover-up. Much as Labour's deputy leader George Brown had sought to extract maximum political capital from the Vassall case in 1962, in 2014 Tom Watson (who became deputy leader in 2015) made equally flimsy allegations about another Dolphin Square scandal.

The police appealed for help from anyone who had lived or worked in Dolphin Square during the 1970s and 1980s. By October 2014 the British media, and the internet, was full of lurid accusations of sexual abuse, and even murder, of underage boys. There were far-fetched conspiracy theories about the discovery of a secret film studio, about the square's private water supply and that residents of a children's home in Nottingham had been driven in

---

285   Beech's allegations were not entirely new. In 1994 the satirical magazine *Scallywag* had run a scurrilous article claiming that "'model' agencies providing both young men and women are a thriving industry in Pimlico" and that "the local rent-a-boy agencies provide an almost service industry to the [Dolphin Square] complex". Using a combination of homophobia and anti-Tory sentiment, the story claimed that "Our 'spy' in the building ... has got quite used to young gays wandering around looking for the next rave" and that the "safe Tory enclave of Pimlico" was "nick-named by politico wags as Pimp-lico, for it is here that the rent-a-boy lobby have their headquarters".

Variety Club coaches to be abused at the square. Some even suggested that an MP had been murdered there (in 1991, the Welsh Tory backbencher John Stradling Thomas had been found dead at his Dolphin Square flat).[286]

The Metropolitan Police's investigation into Beech's claims, Operation Midland, was soon overwhelmed by these allegations and became a fiasco. It gradually emerged that Beech was a fantasist. His illustration of Dolphin Square's swimming pool, where abuse had allegedly occurred, turned out not to have been drawn from first-hand knowledge but from the video to Culture Club's 1982 number one single "Do You Really Want to Hurt Me". The video features a pool which is captioned as "Dolphin Square Health Club, 1957" but had in fact been filmed elsewhere.[287] Beech's drawing of Dolphin Square's distinctive trio of entrance arches was hardly proof that he had visited the square, merely that he had once walked past it or looked it up on Google Streetview. Beech's ex-wife said that Beech had told her about abuse by his stepfather but no other men. Emails from a corroborating witness known as Fred were found to have been written by Beech himself.

"Nick's" claims were totally baseless. Worse, Beech was himself found to be a prolific abuser who had committed many offences, including voyeurism. Hundreds of obscene images of children were found on his personal computers. In March 2016 Operation Midland was shut down and Northumbria Police were tasked, not with investigating the men that Beech had named, but Beech himself. Beech was arrested and charged with making and possessing indecent images of children and one count of voyeurism. Later, the

---

286   Although Stradling Thomas had been in poor health and was found to have died of natural causes, conspiracy theorists argued that he had been making enquiries about suspicious deaths at a children's home in Suffolk, and that his own death may have been foul play. Questions were also asked about the 2007 suicide, of a judge, 64-year-old Rodney McKinnon, who had jumped 50ft from the window of his Drake House flat, having suffered from depression and anxiety caused by drugs prescribed for high blood pressure. Mackinnon's brother Warwick McKinnon – also a judge – told his inquest that he doubted it was suicide, as no suicide note was ever found.

287   The video – a tribute to Boy George's relationship with his drummer Jon Moss, and a nod to Dolphin Square's tolerant reputation – can be found at: https://www.youtube.com/watch?v=2nXGPZaTKik.

CPS also charged him with fraud and perverting the course of justice. He was found to have fled to northern Sweden, where he was living quietly on his NHS pension. He was soon extradited back to Britain and in 2019 he was tried at Newcastle Crown Court, convicted, and sentenced to eighteen years in prison: the same length as Vassall's sentence in 1962.

A former police officer, identified only as GB, later told Professor Alexis Jay's Independent Inquiry into Child Sexual Abuse that the police had first investigated allegations of child abuse at Dolphin Square in the 1990s. Complainants had said that from the age of ten upwards "they were abused by 'a politician [and] someone in the Navy' at "a place with Dolphins ... near Westminster Bridge". These details were so tantalisingly vague that it seems that the old media myths about John Vassall and Tam Galbraith were simply endlessly recycled, and heavily embroidered, over the next fifty years, and that "Nick" had only embellished them further.

The writer Henry Porter once wrote that Dolphin Square is "a place as distinct, in its own way, as the Overlook Hotel in *The Shining* or the Bramford Building in *Rosemary's Baby*." If anything, Dolphin Square has become the British equivalent of the Watergate apartment complex in Washington: a byword for deviance and political intrigue. Dolphin Square is not just a block of 1,300 flats. It has long been one of London's most infamous addresses, a decadent place of alcoholic and sexual excess on the borders of respectability. It has been an elusive place where many tenants have come to find love or redemption, to reinvent themselves and enact tantalising fantasises.[288] Like Watergate, it is both a place of genuine scandal and a blank canvas onto which many conspiracy theories have been projected.

---

288 The square still looks and feels much as it did in John Vassall's day. There is still light security: the gates are left open by day and anyone can wander around its garden, the reception area of Rodney House and the shopping arcade. The signage is also much as it would have been in Vassall's day. Even in the 2000s, Dolphin Square vetted its tenants not just in terms of their financial status but in regard to how they comported themselves. These were practices that Vassall would recognise.

Magically, it has been the stage for many of twentieth-century Britain's most important phenomena: the murky interaction between the state and those who betray it, the gradual acceptance of homosexuality, tabloid journalism, celebrity excess and paranoid conspiracy theories. Although Oswald Mosley was arrested there in 1940, he had not been living there long and Maxwell Knight's wartime activities for MI5 came to light much later. It was only in 1962 that Dolphin Square first became known as a place of treachery and espionage. The square's fame, and notoriety, is thus in large part down to one man: John Vassall.

●　●　●

Most people have heard of Dolphin Square and know something of its reputation: not so many have heard of John Vassall. "It is impossible to forget Vassall," wrote Rebecca West in 1963. At first, he seemed to linger in the memory longer than George Blake, who had received a far longer prison sentence. According to E. H. Cookridge in his 1967 book *Shadow of a Spy*, after the Profumo affair it was Blake's story that was soon forgotten and the Vassall scandal was no less important than the Profumo one.

Yet Vassall has largely been forgotten in the six decades since. By the time of his death he was no longer cited in the litany of great shocks that the British psyche underwent in the early 1960s: the Berlin wall, the Cuban missile crisis, the Profumo affair and Kennedy's assassination. Vassall has been submerged by clearer memories of the Profumo scandal. The collective memory is fickle. Rarely has such a long-running news story fallen so far out of the national consciousness within living memory.

Many popular accounts of Profumo make no mention at all of Vassall and to this day, any new revelation about the Profumo case, no matter how trivial, is seized upon by the media. In October 2022

The Guardian devoted half a page to the "revelation" that Ivanov was "a drunken 'lady-killer' [who] MI5 tried to turn", an allegation that was common currency in 1963, some fifty-nine years earlier.[289] Much more significant MI5 files about the Vassall case, released at the same time, received less coverage and much of it was about the confirmation that "KGB spy John Vassall [was] brought down by high living": again, something that was known about sixty years ago.[290]

When Vassall's name is mentioned in history books, he is often subtly dehumanised. Since 1962 his first name has often wrongly been given as William (a name he apparently hated), even years after it became clear that he had always gone by the name John. His surname has also often been misspelt as Vassal or Vassell.

Unlike George Blake and the Cambridge spies – Blunt, Maclean, Philby, Burgess and even Cairncross – no biography of John Vassall has ever been written. The only book devoted solely to him, Rebe-cca West's *The Vassall Affair* of 1963, was not a biography but a short journalistic survey, full of homophobia. Blake appears as a character in Ian McEwan's novel *The Innocent* and in Simon Gray's play *Cellmates* (about his fractious friendship with the Irishman Sean Bourke, who helped him to escape from Wormwood Scrubs). *Cellmates* has been constantly revived since its debut in 1995 and readers, and viewers, have been continuously entertained by the exotic soap opera of Burgess, Maclean and Philby's afterlives in Moscow.

Some have argued that the Cambridge spies were all, with the possible exception of Philby, from quite modest social backgrounds. Blunt, like Vassall, was a parson's son. But unlike Vassall, who dropped out of a minor public school at sixteen, all five of them went to top public schools and then Cambridge (Maclean at Trinity Hall, the other four at Trinity College), where they met each

---

289 See https://www.theguardian.com/uk-news/2022/oct/11/profumo-spy-had-weakness-for-women-and-drink-archives-reveal

290 See https://www.thetimes.co.uk/article/kgb-spy-john-vassall-brought-down-by-high-living-hnxn989gm

other in the early 1930s.[291] They were all considered to be among the brightest of their generation, gaining scholarships, top degrees and often coming top in civil service exams. They all got elite jobs in the expectation of further success. But, by any measure, Vassall was academically and professionally mediocre. He removed files and copied them in much the same way as the Cambridge spies did, but was never anywhere near their level of seniority. Vassall was not part of a spy "group" of any kind, and certainly not one as glamorous and intellectually gifted.

Vassall was also more than a decade younger than the Cambridge Five and crucially, he had not begun spying for the Soviets until he was forced to do so in the mid-1950s. In contrast, the Cambridge Five began spying in the 1930s or during the Second World War, when handing British secrets to the Soviet Union was less morally dubious and many believed that Stalin's Russia was the only real bulwark against fascism in Europe. Vassall's espionage had no such intellectual justification.

As Rebecca West once wrote, Vassall "was not, like Burgess or Maclean, a pampered child of the Establishment". Although middle class, he had not benefitted from a first-class education and he never rose above the clerical ranks. He may have been "Savile Row suited" like Anthony Blunt but unlike Blunt, Vassall had no knighthood to revoke once he was unmasked. The Cambridge spies' social status explains why they have received more attention from historians and film producers, but it also explains why none of them ever served prison terms. When Cairncross was first suspected of being a spy, he was shuffled out of Whitehall and given a job with the UN's Food and Agricultural Organization in Rome rather than prosecuted. Between 1951 and 1964 Blunt was questioned numerous times but there was never definitive evidence that

---

291   John Cairncross went to Hamilton Academy (one of Scotland's most prestigious fee-paying schools), Blunt to Marlborough College, Kim Philby to Westminster School, Maclean to Gresham's, School and Burgess to Eton.

he was a spy. When the Americans presented such evidence to the British in 1964, it was hushed up and Blunt was allowed to continue as Surveyor of the Queen's Pictures and Director of the Courtauld Institute of Art. He was spared humiliation until November 1979 when Margaret Thatcher finally revealed all to a stunned House of Commons.

Rumours persist to this day that the Russians were effectively blackmailing the royal family, with secrets passed to them by Blunt. Some claim that the Russian security apparatus still has a cache of royal secrets, dubbed "the Tony file" in honour of Blunt and collated by the late Yuri Modin (the Cambridge Five's "controller", who later served as Vladimir Putin's mentor in the latter's KGB days). The Russian journalist Gennady Sokolov said in a 2014 interview: "If the letters discovered by Blunt were published in due time, it would lead to a huge scandal, the result of which could be the fall of the dynasty." By contrast, if Vassall ever possessed such powerful secrets, he took them to his grave.

The punishments doled out to proven spies were not proportional to the scale of their treachery. Nigel West has argued that George Blake received a 42-year sentence for espionage that was probably less grave than Philby's. Vassall got an eighteen-year sentence while other spies of his generation, like Melita Norwood, never served a day in jail, even though she had handed over secrets for a far longer period.[292] When Norwood was finally unmasked in 1999 she was spared prosecution because she was eighty-seven and the Cold War was considered ancient history.[293] Unfortunately, Vassall had the misfortune to be caught when the Cold War was still at its height.

---

292   For forty years Norwood provided the Soviet Union with information on the development of nuclear weapons from Tube Alloys and the British Non-Ferrous Metals Research Association. Like Vassall, lowly secretarial jobs had given her access to a wide range of secret documents.

293   Born in 1912 to a British mother and Latvian father, Norwood refused to accept any financial reward from the Soviets and rejected their offer of a pension because she argued that her spying had helped to avoid the possibility of a third world war.

Another reason why Vassall is relatively forgotten is more mundane: unlike Blake, Philby and Maclean, Vassall has no children or grandchildren to defend his legacy or keep his memory alive. Kim Philby's granddaughter, Charlotte Philby – a well-respected espionage novelist in her own right – often appears on television to discuss her grandfather's legacy. After George Blake's death in 2020 there was much speculation about which of his four sons (three by his British wife and the fourth by his Russian one) would attend his funeral (the press gleefully reported that one of the British sons had become a Church of England curate).

By contrast, Vassall had almost no surviving close family at the time of his death. Although his only sibling, Richard, outlived him, he died of cancer in February 2000, aged seventy-four. Because Richard was also childless, John Vassall does not have any nephews, nieces, great-nephews or great-nieces. He had several aunts and uncles, but some of them died childless. He does not seem to have been close to any of his first cousins: none of them are named in his memoirs.[294]

Another reason why Vassall is not so widely remembered is that he cannot be regarded as a gay icon or martyr, like Alan Turing. Technically, he was only jailed for espionage, not for being gay. If anything, the Vassall case was not a milestone on the road to decriminalisation but an obstacle. Many gay men of Vassall's generation, such as the actors Dirk Bogarde and Denholm Elliott, never "came out" even if they worked in fields such as the theatre or publishing, where being gay was seen as less of a hindrance. Elliott (who was born in 1922 and less than two years older than Vassall) kept his bisexuality a secret, was married twice (firstly to the actress

---

294 One of Vassall's first cousins was Anthony Wickham, the son of Vassall's aunt Mary and her husband Reginald Wickham, a Royal Air Force officer and a vicar's son. Anthony was born on 20 May 1919. After graduating from Dartmouth, he joined the Royal Navy and was mentioned in despatches for his role in Operation Torch in 1943. He retired from the navy in 1964 at the rank of lieutenant-commander, but naval sources suggest that this was not related to his cousin John's spying conviction. Anthony died in Taunton on 19 May 2004, the day before his eighty-fifth birthday. Despite strenuous efforts, no living cousins of John Vassall could be traced by this author.

Virginia McKenna from 1954–57) and his HIV diagnosis was only revealed after he died of AIDS-related tuberculosis in 1992. Likewise, Vassall never publicly campaigned for gay rights after he was involuntarily outed. Britain's first gay pride march was in July 1972, a few months before Vassall's release from jail; he did not join any later ones.

It is little wonder that Vassall did not publicly flaunt his gayness after his release: right up to his death, twenty-four years later, he had the clamour of homophobic taunts ringing in his ears. Rebecca West was not the only writer to ridicule and insult him. In Norman Lucas's 1973 biography of Chief Superintendent George Smith, the policeman who caught Vassall, Smith's quarry is infantilised. The chapter about the Vassall case is entitled "The Spy with Cuddly Toys". Lucas acknowledged that Vassall was not "primarily drawn into espionage for financial reward" but he saw being blackmailed as a sign of weakness. "Fastidious, sensitive, weakly vacillating, it is unlikely that he would have found the courage to sell Britain's secrets to the Russians had he not, as he claimed at his trial, been blackmailed into doing so", Lucas wrote.

As well as mocking Vassall as fragile, Lucas subtly doubted whether Vassall was blackmailed at all. George Smith told Lucas that of all the spies he had investigated over the decades, Vassall "was the one who least looked the part". He was, Smith said, a "slim, softly good-looking, dimpled mother's boy". Rather than applaud him for confessing, Lucas claims that "Vassall, as always, was anxious to take the easiest way out of trouble".

Chapman Pincher may have been the doyen of post-war espionage writers, but he poured homophobia all over John Vassall for fifty years. Pincher referred to Vassall as "a classic example whose character weakness was detected by a talent scout", suggesting that his entrapment was a benign photo shoot. The KGB showed him photographs of "previous adventures" – not images of him being gang-raped. Pincher argued that Vassall enjoyed spying, but in fact he only fantasised about a "new world of excitement and danger" before his entrapment, not after. Only a very superficial reading of Vassall's memoirs would give the impression that he enjoyed the reality as much as the fantasy.

The insults were still coming twenty-five years after Vassall's conviction: in a chapter of his 1987 book *Traitors*, entitled "The Homo-Sex Factor", Pincher denounced Vassall as a "type specimen" and a man of "sexual abnormality" and "perversions". The fact that a "passive homosexual ... weak enough to agree to spy" had been "appointed to Moscow and allowed to remain there is a severe indictment of our security services," he wrote. Pincher even likened Vassall to Geoffrey Prime, a GCHQ spy who had committed child sex offences, on the grounds that both men "were the products of unhappy marriages which led to their loneliness".[295]

Two decades later, Pincher's homophobia had not lessened: in his 2011 memoirs he noted that "I eventually met Vassall twice for long interviews over lunch" and concluded that "an obvious homosexual, he should never have been sent to Moscow". Even when Pincher met Vassall in the flesh, he still regarded him as a historic artefact, not a human being. Worryingly, Pincher was not an outlier but an unofficial spokesman for the security services, who leaked stories to him for decades.

Because Vassall did not disclose the full story of what had happened at the Hotel Berlin until 1975, many damaging myths had taken root by then. H. Montgomery Hyde's 1970 book, *The Other Love*, which is broadly sympathetic to Vassall, said that he "became drunk, removed most of his clothes and was photographed on a couch alongside a naked Russian". Hyde added that there was "some

---

295   Geoffrey Prime was found to have spied for the Soviets from 1968 to 1978. Like Vassall, he had passed vetting and even became a personnel security supervisor at GCHQ in Cheltenham. His espionage only emerged when the police investigated sexual attacks on young girls that Prime had committed, which prompted Prime to confess all – about his spying and his sexual offences – to his wife. In 1982 Prime was sentenced to thirty-three years for espionage and three for sexual assaults. He was released from prison in 2001.

plausibility" in Rebecca West's theory that Vassall had become a spy of his own accord and that his "blackmail story" was concocted. Other writers, none of them homophobes, have also unwittingly assumed that Vassall was entrapped during a consensual sexual encounter. Bill Deedes's biographer, Stephen Robinson, said that the "homosexual orgy" where Vassall was ensnared was "staged for his benefit". *The Faber Book of Treachery*, edited by the normally reliable Nigel West, asserted that Vassall "succumbed to blackmail over a brief homosexual relationship he had enjoyed with a Russian youth in Moscow". Even the gay historian Patrick Higgins has intimated that Vassall became a spy of his own free will and "spied because it allowed him to indulge his social fantasies".

All too often, Vassall has been belittled and dehumanised. "A youth drawn too close emotionally to his mother and at the same time somewhat withdrawn from his father is frequently vulnerable in after life," Richard Deacon asserted. "W. John Vassall was a somewhat pathetic figure, almost a case study of a homosexual driven by alienation, rather than by any ideological motivation, to become a traitor", Alistair Horne wrote in his biography of Macmillan. In Beirut in January 1963, Kim Philby is said to have replied to a question from Nicholas Elliott, about spies who had been given long sentences for less than Philby was confessing to, with the words "Ah, well, Vassall – well, he wasn't top league, was he?" Rebecca West once wrote that "People came to think of Vassall not only as a homosexual, but as the homosexual, an archetype". By early 1963 "Vassall" had become a noun, not a name: when a barrister at the Radcliffe tribunal asked Brendan Mulholland, "'Vassall' means a spy who is a homosexual?", Mulholland replied, "Yes".296

---

296 Adam Mars-Jones, whose father represented Express Newspapers at the Radcliffe tribunal, has recalled his confusion, as a young boy in the early 1960s, over whether Vassall "was the name of a person or a role. I knew that to be a vassal was to be an underling, though I don't know how I knew. Perhaps despite my imperviousness to history I had learned something about feudalism at school. From Dad's grim tone when he said the word 'Vassall' I knew not to ask questions, and occasionally absorbed the message that submissiveness was always culpable, though for some people an inescapable destiny". Many other men of the same generation recall the Vassall case as the first time they were told, as schoolboys, about homosexuality.

Vassall is often misunderstood as a man who was led astray, or betrayed, by a gay lover – not a gay man who was raped. Many have contended that Vassall was a libertine who had drunkenly yielded to sexual temptation at the Hotel Berlin. In fact, Vassall was not normally a heavy drinker. He may have gone to many cocktail parties but he drank the cocktails slowly, and unlike most men of his generation he didn't even smoke. Vassall was not an insatiable sex addict who wanted to sleep with any man he could lay his hands on. His memoirs, and MI5's files, are littered with examples of Vassall rebuffing other men's advances. On the first night of his police interrogation Vassall said that he had once declined a "homosexual invitation" from some Americans in a bar in Moscow. Later, Vassall told MI5 that men had sometimes put their hands on his knee at the bar of the American Club, but he had not liked it. Vassall was never as promiscuous as newspapers suggested, and even if he was promiscuous that did not preclude him from being sexually assaulted.

Rebecca West was not the only writer to argue that Vassall was never entrapped at all and that he was motivated by sympathy with communism, class envy or simply greed. George Blake's claims of being brainwashed as a prisoner of war in North Korea in the early 1950s were widely disbelieved: many thought that he had been a committed communist since his involvement with the Dutch resistance in his teens during the Second World War. Likewise, Vassall's claims that he only started spying under duress in 1955 were disbelieved. Some have suggested that the story of Vassall's entrapment was a smokescreen, concealing a plot to inflict maximum political damage on the British state. Kevin Coogan has claimed that "Later events suggest that it was possible that Vassall's arrest was intended to topple the Macmillan government in a new sex scandal and/or to send a threat to other Soviet agents in England that they could be compromised at any time the Russians felt like it". The problem with this theory is that the timing is wrong: the Vassall affair (and the damage done to Tam Galbraith) was the first serious sexual scandal to hit the Macmillan government, not the latest in a long sequence as Coogan claims.

Even Richard Davenport-Hines's otherwise lucid account of the Vassall scandal concludes that his explanations were largely implausible and that "only a weak, helpless fool would have submitted to KGB threats of exposure ... A man who had the nerves for years of high-level espionage would not have been so timid with his blackmailers". Vassall was "a sexually confident young Londoner who attracted prosperous and amusing young men" and "a pert, wily urban survivor whom the official story misrepresented as an inexperienced, vulnerable man open to blackmail". After his arrest, Vassall complained about the rigid embassy hierarchy, the aloof Hayters and the endless protocol, and Davenport-Hines argues that "It seems to have been a KGB instruction for English spies, if caught, to parrot tales of class stigma and subjugation". There is some truth in this: Vassall was certainly sexually experienced long before he got to Moscow and some of his complaints about the embassy rang hollow, but there is no evidence that he had met the Russians before leaving London and been persuaded by them to apply for a job in Moscow.

If Vassall was indeed a vengeful troublemaker and part of a grand conspiracy to bring down the entire British establishment, why did he never publicly name the two Conservative MPs he had slept with (or at least befriended)? Vassall only gave their names to MI5, not newspapers. He told MI5 that when the Russians once asked him for a list of "homosexual acquaintances, particularly those in high places", he refused. In his confession, at the Radcliffe tribunal and in his memoirs, Vassall consistently denied that he had ever had a sexual relationship with Tam Galbraith. He sometimes maintained that he had not even been attracted to Galbraith sexually. And, if Vassall did have a powerful "protector" in the Admiralty, why was he never promoted? The truth is that Vassall was one of le Carré's "bunch of seedy, squalid bastards": a lone wolf at the mercy of the KGB without a network of British allies to mentor him.

Some writers have suggested that Vassall was an accomplice of the far right – simply because he naively spoke to the fascist Colin Jordan in prison – or even a paedophile. This partly explains why Vassall never became a cause célèbre. Instead, he became an embarrassment, both to the gay rights lobby and the security establishment. In the 1980s, politicians and campaigners from the British left took up the causes of several whistleblowers, spies and martyrs who had been harshly treated – the MOD civil servant Clive Ponting, the MI5 officer and Russian spy Michael Bettaney, the MI5 officer Cathy Massiter and the Foreign Office clerical officer Sarah Tisdall. But no one adopted Vassall's case, either to overturn his conviction or to ask the state to issue him an official apology.

Even fifty years on, MI5 seemed embarrassed by the Vassall scandal. Christopher Andrew's authorised history of M15, *The Defence of the Realm* (2009), makes only two passing references to Vassall, chiefly in the context of "the alleged security risks posed by gays". In 2011 Chapman Pincher argued that Andrew only made scant mention of Vassall not because Vassall was an unimportant spy but because of lingering shame. This discomfort also extends to the Royal Navy. When Admiral Sir Jock Slater, a former First Sea Lord, was asked for his memories of the Vassall case by this author, Slater replied that he was "unable to help". This was a curious response, given that Slater was already a Royal Navy lieutenant at the time of Vassall's arrest and the navy was awash with rumours about Vassall at the time.

•   •   •

Television schedules have long been packed with documentaries about Cold War espionage. Recent productions have often repeated hackneyed and inaccurate claims about John Vassall. In the 2022

ITV series, *Secrets of the Spies*, the octogenarian Mikhail Lyubimov, who joined the KGB in 1959 and worked at the Soviet embassy in London from 1961 to 1965, said that Vassall supplied "plenty of material about military questions" and was "considered to be a valuable agent".[297] But Lyubimov has told this author that he "knew nothing of Vassall when in London" as he "worked in the political line". Lyubimov's lack of contact with Vassall has not prevented him from writing about the clerk in a novel, *Dekameron Shpionov* (Decameron of Spies),[298] and discussing him on documentaries as if he had known him.

"Sex between consenting adults is surely a better way of extracting information than torture", the writer Henry Hemming said on *Secrets of the Spies*: but Vassall never gave his consent on the fateful night. Lyubimov claimed that *kompromat* was never employed as a method overseas "but here, in Russia, we did it". Vassall was "treated like a good man", Lyubimov insisted. He made no mention of Vassall being drugged and then raped, only that the "KGB-organised orgy" was "an evening to be forgotten". Afterwards, when confronted with the photographs, Lyubimov claimed that Vassall "nearly collapsed" and "wanted to commit suicide". At first he wanted to report what had happened to his superiors at the embassy but was "soothed" by Mikhailsky and talked out of it.

Lyubimov expressed no remorse for what the KGB had done, and he even suggested that Vassall should have been grateful. Vassall "enjoyed life" and for the first time "was treated as an equal by the creme of the intelligentsia". Lyubimov implied that Vassall's entrapment was a victimless crime, and that his sexual gratification

---

297   Gordon Corera's book, *The Art of Betrayal*, suggests that in the 1960s Lyubimov was an incompetent spy in London. He once took a Foreign Office official, who he thought could become a Russian agent, out to a pub to drink whisky. As soon as the civil servant went to the toilet, two "rough-looking men" from MI5 appeared, sat down next to Lyubimov, said "you are a complete failure" and told him a compromising detail about his own private life – and that they had photographs to prove it. "Mr Lyubimov, either your career is over, or you work for us". Lyubimov skulked back to the Russian embassy. Lyubimov and his family soon returned to Moscow after the British ignored a protest from the Russians about MI5's "barbarous provocation".

298   The novel was published in Russian, and has never been translated into English.

more than recompensed him for having to betray his country. When asked whether the Federal Security Service still carries out honeytrap operations, Lyubimov's response was chilling: "I hope so".

The six-part Netflix series, *Spycraft*, released in 2021, also got key details of Vassall's story wrong. It misleadingly described him as a "young British diplomat" and said that Moscow was one of the "harshest postings" for British civil servants (in fact, Vassall beat off strong competition to get a coveted job there). Vassall "fell in love with his ski instructor", a voiceover announced (in fact, Vassall never saw the "skier" anywhere near a ski slope). Worst of all, Keith Melton (an intelligence historian specialising in American, not British, spy cases) said that Vassall started "partying … at the National Hotel [not the Hotel Berlin]" and that "according to John, he was drugged and filmed in orgies with young boys". This implied that Vassall had consumed a sexual stimulant, not a sedative, and that rather than being taken advantage of he took advantage of underage men: all claims for which there is no evidence whatsoever.

In programmes like these the Vassall story is often told in the same breath as other "honey trap" tales such as those of Mata Hari, James Hudson and Kyle Hatcher.[299] The acronym "MICE"– money, ideology, compromise and ego – is constantly invoked. It is never mentioned that Vassall was not merely "compromised" but raped.

While he is often traduced in documentaries, Vassall has mostly been ignored in recent films and television dramas about 1960s espionage. He was not mentioned at all in *A Spy Among Friends*, ITV's 2022 drama about Kim Philby's interrogation in Beirut, just before he defected to Moscow in January 1963. The drama repeated old claims that Philby identified Roger Hollis and Anthony Blunt as

---

299   In 2009 James Hudson (the British deputy consul general in Ekaterinburg) and Kyle Hatcher (a second secretary and possibly a CIA officer at the American embassy in Moscow) appeared on videos showing them cavorting with Russian sex workers in hotel rooms. Hudson quickly resigned but Hatcher insisted that the footage was fabricated after he had refused a Russian invitation to become a double agent and he kept his job. See: https://www.independent.co.uk/news/world/europe/russian-honeytrap-secrets-lies-sex-and-spies-1742543.html and https://www.dailymail.co.uk/news/article-1205043/U-S-diplomat-caught-video-new-Russian-honeytrap.html.

Soviet agents, and made several references to John Profumo – who makes a fleeting appearance – but none whatsoever to the Vassall case, even though Whitehall was convulsed by it at the time.

Instead, ghostly apparitions of Vassall sometimes appear in dramas loosely inspired by his case. In *London Spy*, a BBC series broadcast in 2015 and set in the present day, Ben Whishaw played Danny, a young gay man who begins a relationship with Alex, an enigmatic MI6 officer, until Alex disappears and is found dead in a locked trunk in the attic of his flat. Jim Broadbent played Scottie, a sixty-something civil servant who delivers a lengthy monologue about the security services' persecution of gay staff. He explains that as a young man he had in fact been an MI6 officer until he was blackmailed by the KGB after an assignation in the gents toilet at Paddington Station. He had then been told that he had been entrapped by MI6 operatives on a "fag hunt". Scottie had to promise not to touch another man – a promise he kept for eleven years – and was shuffled off to a minor job at the Department of Transport. Several of Vassall's civil servant friends were treated even more harshly.

In the 2022 film *My Policeman*, set in the late 1950s, a young married police officer, played by Harry Styles, goes to Venice, which is portrayed as a place of sexual liberation, with his gay lover (Vassall also loved visiting the city in that decade). The policeman's lover, Patrick Hazlewood, works as a curator in a Brighton museum and is played by David Dawson, who bears a close physical resemblance to Vassall. Like Vassall's, Hazlewood's Brighton flat is ostentatiously decorated and full of antiques. Even when he is not mentioned, Vassall seems to lurk in the background of all these dramas.

• • •

As far as is known, the Soviets never dignified Vassall with a codename (he may have had the mundane "Serial 3" but this is not certain). Vassall was not a hero, or even an anti-hero. He had many flaws: he was vain, self-centred, arrogant and snobbish. It is not victim-blaming to point out that in Moscow he was staggeringly naïve to go to parties with Russian men he had never previously met, and without any British company. Even the historian Patrick Higgins, who himself is gay, has argued that Vassall's decision to go to bed with a Russian stranger was foolish: "At no point in this encounter did Vassall think about what he was doing, ... showing levels of naivety in his dealings with his hosts that bordered on the lunatic".

In Wormwood Scrubs Vassall was unforgivably stupid to talk to Colin Jordan, the British neo-Nazi, about his extensive love life. But he was also a loyal and generous friend and a loving son, brother and nephew. Even Rebecca West pointed out that he was known to have shown "long and continued kindness" to a destitute old woman who would never leave him anything in her will. In short, he was a human being, full of strengths and weaknesses, not a stereotype.

He was not a whistleblower, revealing clandestine secrets for what he thought was the greater good. He was not a spy who saved lives, helped to bring about a military victory or misled an enemy into revealing its hand. Instead, he was a glorified photocopier.

Now, Vassall's espionage seems a long time ago. The technological methods that he used – removing paper files from an office and photographing them, giving undeveloped films to his handlers and then returning the files to their cabinets – seem quaint. In Vassall's day there was no cyberwarfare, computer hacking or mass surveillance of emails and mobile communication. When Vassall worked at the Admiralty, "Telegram" was not an end-to-end encrypted communication app but an analogue message, printed out and delivered to its recipient by a uniformed General Post Office messenger. Nowadays, almost everyone has a sophisticated Minox-style camera in their pocket. It is called a smartphone. Treason is now considered a suitable topic for reality television programmes. Yet the moral and sexual hazards that Vassall faced are still with us. In December 2022, the media reported new concerns about entrapment by Russia and other powers, who reportedly arrange for sex workers to greet delegations of British MPs when they go on trips abroad.[300]

Some of Vassall's old London haunts have gone forever. Next door to Claridge's, the former clubhouse of the Bath Club at 41–43 Brook Street is now a "Private Club-style business centre". Many of the places that Vassall knew, such as Dolphin Square, have hardly changed at all however. The Admiralty, where he worked, is now known as the Old Admiralty Building (OAB). Recently restored, it is still used as government offices and houses the new Department for International Trade.

Janet Foster, who worked with Vassall at the British Records Association in the mid-1970s, later qualified as a London tour guide. In 2017 she led a guided Gay Pride walk around Smithfield to mark the fiftieth anniversary of decriminalisation. As she walked her group past Charterhouse, she pointed out the historic building in which she had worked with Vassall four decades earlier. Such acts of commemoration are rare. There are no blue plaques to John Vassall, and there probably never will be.

The only street in London to carry his name is Vassall Road in Kennington, one of several streets of elegant Georgian houses developed in the 1820s by Vassall's distant cousin Elizabeth and her husband, Henry Vassall-Fox, 3rd Baron Holland. For many years, the local electoral ward also carried the name Vassall but when the London Borough of Lambeth's ward boundaries were reviewed ahead of the 2022 elections, Vassall ward (which underwent slight boundary changes) was renamed as Myatt's Fields because

---

300 See https://www.theguardian.com/politics/2022/dec/28/no-10-concerned-mps-engaged-in-sex-and-heavy-drinking-on-trips-abroad.

Elizabeth Vassall and her forebears had owned slaves in Jamaica.[301] The indirect connection to John Vassall played no part in Lambeth Council's decision. In the 1960s the Vassall name was stigmatised because of a Soviet spy; in 2022 it was stigmatised because of his slave-owning ancestors.

At the time of writing, Lambeth Council was considering whether to rename Vassall Road as well. Changing the name of a London street is a long, convoluted and fraught process, but there is an alternative. Keep the Vassall name and make it clear that the street is no longer named after eighteenth- and nineteenth-century slave owners, but after one of the twentieth-century Cold War's most tragic victims.

---

301   See https://brixtonblog.com/2020/09/council-seeks-to-change-slaveholder-ward-names/ and https://www.lambeth.gov.uk/sites/default/files/2021-01/statues-and-memorials-lambeth-united-summary-document.pdf

ACKNOWLEDGEMENTS

This book has relied on many sources. As well as dozens of books that allude to the John Vassall scandal, along with contemporary newspaper stories, it has drawn on interviews with several people who knew Vassall from the 1950s right up to his death in 1996, or were involved in the investigation into his espionage.

I have been blessed with the help of many people who met, or worked with, Vassall. Brigid McEwen (who first met Vassall in the early 1950s and is the widow of his good friend, Robin McEwen) gave me valuable insights into Vassall's life at Dolphin Square and his visits to the Marchmont estate in the 1970s. Thanks are also due to Brigid's son, John, and his wife Rachel. I would like to thank Monus and Jane Rowland for putting me in touch with Miles Bennett, whose mother, Perdita Campbell-Orde, is the daughter-in-law of Geoffrey Bennett, Vassall's boss in Moscow. Perdita met Vassall several times in the early 1960s, including at her wedding and was very helpful with her recollections. Ruth Paley at the British Records Association connected me with Janet Foster and Susan Snell, who worked with Vassall at the BRA from the 1970s to the 1990s. Both women were unfailingly helpful with their recollections of him.

Several other writers on Cold War espionage, and post-war

British history, gave me useful comments on draft chapters. Richard Davenport-Hines and Nigel West have been particularly helpful with their time and expertise. Thanks are also due to Richard Norton-Taylor, Neal Ascherson and Michael Smith.

Several politicians – past and present members of both the Commons and the Lords – gave me useful insights into the career of Tam Galbraith (the minister whose private office Vassall worked in during the late 1950s) and the politics of the time. Simon Mackay (Lord Tanlaw) and Jonathan Aitken shared their memories of Galbraith, and both Jonathan Aitken and Douglas Hogg (Viscount Hailsham) helped me to confirm details of Vassall's incarceration at Wormwood Scrubs. Michael Randle and his wife Anne helpfully provided their memories of Vassall's time at the Scrubs, while Michael was also imprisoned there. My good friends Nick and Alison Raynsford gave me useful advice, as they always have done. Above all, I am very much indebted to Tom Galbraith, (Lord Strathclyde), Tam Galbraith's son, for sharing his insights into a painful period of his family's history.

My father-in-law, Tony Bull, was very helpful in putting me in contact with Royal Navy veterans who had important recollections of the 1962 investigation into Vassall, among them John Crossman and above all, Nick Kettlewell, who was involved in the surveillance of Admiralty staff in the run-up to Vassall's trial. Colin Nicholls KC provided me with valuable insights into the Christopher Swabey affair, which ran concurrently with the Vassall one. John Barrass, Rodric Braithwaite and Tony Humphries gave me useful pointers on the diplomatic service. I am grateful to my aunt, Patricia Howse CBE KC, and my sister-in-law Katharine Broughton, for making strenuous efforts to identify anyone who worked at the British embassy in Moscow in the mid-1950s and who is still living. Their work was ultimately fruitless but it was not for lack of trying. Edward Nicholson helped me with his in-depth knowledge of modern Moscow. I am also indebted to Simon Hall and above all, to Duncan Lustig-Prean, who gave me useful insights into Britain's LGBT history and how the Vassall affair is an important, but largely overlooked, part of it.

My friends and neighbours in Northamptonshire – in Titchmarsh, Oundle and elsewhere – have been a bedrock of support. Mike Lower shared his schoolboy recollections of the Vassall scandal. Mike Greasley gave me helpful comments on draft chapters. Roy Lakey and Sir Ewan Harper provided useful information on Sir Harmar Nicholls, the Conservative MP who John Vassall befriended in the early 1960s and whose former constituency I now (by a neat coincidence) reside in. Tim Haynes and Sue and Hugh Watson gave me generous logistical support. Thanks are also due to Paul Franklin for the pro-bono dog walking and to Huw Roberts for his knowledge of the RAF.

Councillors Joanne Simpson and Paul Gadsby at Lambeth Council provided helpful information about the ongoing debate on whether to rename the only street in London that carries the Vassall name. Martin Heaton gave me useful advice about Vassall's Sussex connections, and Chris Sheffield helped me with the whereabouts of John Vassall's will. I have also been helped by David Castle at Pluto Books, John Clark, Guy Vassall-Adams and Alison Sinclair at the ITV press office. My good friend Ben Rowland kindly let me borrow his home in Streatham over the dog days between Christmas and New Year 2022, during which several chapters were completed. Thanks are also due to my stepson Louis Court, and to Alison Parry, for their research in press archives.

Library and archive research was made much easier by all the staff at the National Archives in Kew; Gareth Bellis at the National Maritime Museum's Caird Library; Kathleen Dixon and her colleagues at the British Film Institute archive; Julie Parry at Bradford University Library; Paul Brown, Nathaniel Patch and Kevin Taylor at the National Archives in College Park, Maryland; Ellie King at the University of Sussex Special Collections at The Keep in Brighton; Clare Anning, Nicola Parker and Thomas Keyton at Monmouth School and Andrew Renwick at the RAF Museum. Much of this book was written in the libraries of Cambridge and I appreciate the help and advice of staff at the University Library, the Radzinowicz Library at the Institute of Criminology and the History Faculty's Seeley Library.

My former agent Martin Redfern has been a tower of strength who gave me much support and encouragement. I am also indebted to his successor at Northbank Talent Management, Matthew Cole, and his colleagues Diane Banks and Natalie Christopher. At Biteback, my editors Olivia Beattie and Lisa Goodrum have been very patient with a lengthy and unwieldy manuscript, as have James Stephens, Suzanne Sangster, Nell Whitaker and Catriona Allon.

Above all, I want to thank my family: my parents, Jane and Neville Grant, my sister Tara and my brother Tom, who have all been steadfast with support and advice. I salute my daughter Alice, to whom this book is dedicated, and my partner Liz Bull, for all their patience. Liz has helped me more than she will ever know, and far more than I deserve.

Alex Grant
Oundle, Northamptonshire
July 2023

SOURCES AND
BIBLIOGRAPHY

In the six decades since it occurred, the Profumo affair has been the subject of dozens, if not hundreds, of books. Post-war British spies such as Donald Maclean, Kim Philby, Guy Burgess and Anthony Blunt have received attention from dozens of biographers. But surprisingly little has been written about the Vassall scandal. Other than Vassall's own memoirs, published in 1975, only one book has focused solely on it: *The Vassall Affair* by Rebecca West, published in 1963, which at 100 pages is arguably more of a pamphlet than a book. It is also long out of print and very difficult to find.[302]

The Vassall case was afforded a lengthy chapter in West's *The Meaning of Treason* in 1965 and since then it has been covered in many books about Cold War espionage and post-war British history (among the better treatments are several books by Nigel West, Patrick Higgins's *Heterosexual Dictatorship* and Richard Davenport-Hines's *An English Affair*). But all too often Vassall is only mentioned in passing, as a prequel to the Profumo scandal, rather than as an important episode in its own right. Tam Galbraith's resignation received an informative chapter in Matthew

---

302   *The Vassall Affair* was published by the *Sunday Telegraph* in July 1963 with a foreword by the paper's editor, Donald McLachlan, a former naval intelligence officer.

Parris's 1995 book *Great Parliamentary Scandals*, but it is fewer than ten pages long and the ensuing chapter about Profumo is more than twice its length.

Jeremy Hutchinson's Case Histories (2015), by Thomas Grant (my brother), contains a good chapter on Vassall's trial but in the context of a biography of Vassall's barrister, not his client. Two recent books – Juliet Nicolson's *Frostquake* and David Kynaston's *On the Cusp: Days of '62* – both examine many of the events of 1962 and the harsh winter that ushered in 1963 in forensic detail, but neither book pays much attention to Vassall.

Even the official historians of Dolphin Square seem curiously reluctant to dwell on its association with Vassall. K. F. Morris's *A History of Dolphin Square* (1995), makes only passing reference to him. "Among the notorious [tenants] was Vassall the spy," Morris wrote. "He had a flat in Hood House which was later unwittingly let to the Director-General of Intelligence at the Ministry of Defence."[303] More than three decades on from Vassall's arrest, the Dolphin Square Trust, which ran the apartment block and published Morris's book, seemed ashamed of him. Terry Gourvish's 2014 book, *Dolphin Square: The History of a Unique Building*, is a much better account but it devotes just two of 400 pages to Vassall, arguably one of the square's most infamous tenants.

Remarkably, while the Vassall case has featured in several books, it has only been dramatised on screen once, in a single episode of a 1980 BBC drama series, *Spy!*, episodes of which are almost impossible to view. As both John Vassall and his sibling were childless, it has been impossible to locate any living relatives (apart from one who was unaware that he was a distant relative until he was contacted by me). I have had much more luck with archives, where I found a treasure trove of material. Vassall's barrister Jeremy Hutchinson (who died in 2017) had a lengthy correspondence with

---

303 Vice-Admiral Louis Le Bailly. See Chapter Six.

him during his imprisonment and afterwards. This correspondence was touched upon in Thomas Grant's *Jeremy Hutchinson's Case Histories* but has been fully examined here for the first time, now that Hutchinson's papers have been given to the University of Sussex.

In the autumn of 2022 the National Archives released thousands of documents on MI5's surveillance of Vassall, on the subsequent investigations by MI5 into everyone he knew (in Britain, the United States and beyond) and on Vassall's ten years in jail. The United States' National Archives and Records Administration also hold a lengthy Federal Bureau of Investigation file on Vassall. These papers offer a fascinating glimpse into the homophobic paranoia that gripped both Britain and America at the time. They confirm for the first time that Vassall had relationships with two Conservative MPs before his arrest – neither of them being the blameless Tam Galbraith. Apart from superficial press coverage in 2022, this newly released and priceless archive material has been examined for the first time in this book.

ARCHIVES

National Archives, Kew
The Security Service (MI5)
KV 2/4576, KV 2/4577, KV 2/4578, KV 2/4579, KV 2/4580, KV 2/4581, KV 2/4582, KV2/4583, KV 2/4584, KV 2/4585, KV 2/4586, KV 2/4587, KV 2/4588.

Foreign Office from the National Archives
FO/953/2108

Treasury Solicitors from the National Archives
TS/58/323/25, TS/58/623, TS/58/626, TS/58/627, TS/58/628, TS/58/629, TS/58/630, TS/58/631, TS/58/632, TS/58/633, TS/58/634,

TS/58/635, TS/58/636, TS/58/637, TS/58/638, TS/58/639, TS/58/640, TS/58/641, TS/58/642, TS/58/643, TS/58/644, TS/58/645, TS/58/646, TS/58/647, TS/58/648, TS/58/649, TS/58/650, TS/58/651 , TS/58/652, TS/58/653 , TS/58/654, TS/58/655, TS/58/656, TS/58/657, TS/58/658, TS/58/661, TS/58/662, TS/58/663 (CEV 21), TS/58/664 (CEV 3), TS/58/665 (CEV 4), TS/58/666 (CEV 5), TS/58/667 , TS/58/668 (CEV 7), TS/58/669 (CEV 8), TS/58/670 (CEV 9), TS/58/671 (CEV11), TS/58/672, TS/58/673 (CEV 13), TS/58/674, TS/58/675 (CEV 15), TS/58/676, TS/58/677, TS/58/678 (CEV 18), TS/58/679 (CEV 19), TS/58/680, TS/58/681 (CEV 21), TS/58/682, TS/58/684 (CEV 24), TS/58/685 (CEV 25), TS/58/686 (CEV 26), TS/58/687 (CEV 27), TS/58/688 (CEV 28), TS/58/689 (CEV 29), TS/58/690 (CEV 321), TS/58/691 (CEV 32), TS/58/692 (CEV 33), TS/58/693, TS/58/694 (CEV 35), TS/58/695 (CEV 36), TS58/696, TS/58/697 (CEV 38), TS/58/698 (CEV 39), TS/58/699, TS/58/700 (CEV 41), TS/58/701 (CEV42).

Admiralty and Ministry of Defence from the National Archives

ADM/1/2808, ADM/1/28016, ADM/1/28026, ADM/1/27370, ADM/1/30091, ADM/1/30092, ADM/116/6385, DEFE/13/261.

Cabinet Office from the National Archives

CAB/21/6076, CAB/128/36/68, CAB/129/113, CAB/129/117, CAB/130/190/GEN793, CAB/301/265, CAB/301/266, CAB/301/267, CAB/301/268.

Miscellaneous from the National Archives

LCO/2/7631, LO/2/1169, BD/52/1/9, T/216/1023 and T/216/1024, PREM/11/3975, PREM/11/4455, CSC/11/258.

Caird Library, National Maritime Museum

MSS/85/098 and MSS/85/132 (Geoffrey Bennett's papers)

The National Archives and Records Administration in College Park, Maryland, United States of America
IRR Personal File on William John Vassell [*sic*] (AA 85 52 09).

University of Bradford Library
Cwl PN/10/179 (The Michael Randle archive)

University of Sussex Special Collections at The Keep, Brighton
Jeremy Hutchinson (Lord Hutchinson of Lullington QC) Archive

BOOKS

Abse, Leo, *Private Member* (London: Macdonald, 1973)

Aldrich, Richard, and Cormac, Rory, *The Black Door: Spies, Secret Intelligence and British Prime Ministers* (London: William Collins, 2017)

Andrew, Christopher, *Her Majesty's Secret Service: The Making of the British Intelligence Community* (London: Penguin Books, 1987)

Andrew, Christopher, and Mitrokhin, Vasili, *The Sword and the Shield: The Mitrokhin Archive and the Secret History of the KGB* (New York: Basic Books, 2000)

Andrew, Christopher, *The Defence of the Realm: The Authorized History of MI5* (London: Allen Lane, 2009)

Ashley, April (with Douglas Thompson), *The First Lady* (London: Blake Publishing, 2006)

Atkinson, Kate, *Transcription* (London: Doubleday, 2018)

Baldwin, James, *Giovanni's Room* (New York: Dial Press, 1956)

Barclay, Theo, *Fighters and Quitters: Great Political Resignations* (London: Biteback Publishing, 2018)

Barnes, Trevor, *Dead Doubles: The Extraordinary Worldwide Hunt for One of the Cold War's Most Notorious Spy Rings* (London: Weidenfeld & Nicolson, 2020)

Beckett, Francis and Russell, Tony, *1956: The Year That Changed Britain* (London: Biteback Publishing, 2015)

Bennett, Geoffrey, *By Human Error: Disasters of a Century* (London: Seeley, Service, 1961)

Berkeley, Humphry, *Crossing the Floor* (London: Allen and Unwin, 1972)

Blake, George, *No Other Choice: An Autobiography* (London: Jonathan Cape Ltd, 1990)

Bloch, Michael, *Closet Queens: Some 20th Century British Politicians* (London: Little, Brown, 2015)

Boothby, Robert, *My Yesterday, Your Tomorrow* (London: Hutchinson, 1962)

Boyle, Andrew, *The Climate of Treason: Five Who Spied for Russia* (London: Hutchinson, 1979)

Bressler, Fenton, *Lord Goddard: A Biography of Rayner Goddard, Lord Chief Justice of England* (London: George G. Harrap & Co. Ltd, 1977)

Brook-Shepherd, Gordon, *The Storm Petrels: The First Soviet Defectors, 1928–1938* (London: Collins, 1977)

Brook-Shepherd, Gordon, *The Storm Birds: Soviet Post-war Defectors* (London: Weidenfeld & Nicolson, 1988)

Bulloch, John, *MI5: The Origin and History of the British Counter-Espionage Service* (London: Arthur Baker Limited, 1963)

Campbell, John, *Edward Heath: A Biography* (London: Jonathan Cape, 1993)

Carrington, Peter, *Reflecting on Things Past: The Memoirs of Peter Lord Carrington* (London: HarperCollins, 1988)

Carter, Miranda, *Anthony Blunt: His Lives* (London: Macmillan, 2001)

Caute, David, *Red List: MI5 and British Intellectuals in the Twentieth Century* (London: Verso, 2022)

Channon, Henry 'Chips', *The Diaries, Volume 2, 1938–43* (London: Hutchinson, 2021)

Channon, Henry 'Chips', *The Diaries, Volume 3, 1943–57* (London: Hutchinson, 2022)

Churchill, Sarah, *Keep On Dancing* (New York: Coward, McCann & Geoghegan, 1981)

Coffield, Darren, *Tales from the Colony Room: Soho's Lost Bohemia* (London: Unbound, 2020)

Coogan, Kevin, *The Spy Who Would Be Tsar: The Mystery of Michal Goleniewski and the Far-Right Underground* (London: Routledge, 2021)

Cook, Matt, *Queer Domesticities: Homosexuality and Home Life in Twentieth-Century London* (London: Palgrave Macmillan, 2014)

Cookridge, E. H., *Shadow of a Spy: The Complete Dossier on George Blake* (London: Leslie Frewin, 1967)

Cookridge, E. H., *The Third Man: The Truth about 'Kim' Philby, Double Agent* (London: Arthur Barker Ltd, 1968)

Corera, Gordon, *The Art of Betrayal: Life and Death in the British Secret Service* (London: Weidenfeld & Nicolson, 2011)

Crossman, Anthony, *The Crossman Diaries: Selection from 'The Diaries of a Cabinet Minister 1964–1970* (London: Magnum Books, 1979)

Danczuk, Simon, *Scandal at Dolphin Square: A Notorious History* (Cheltenham: The History Press, 2022)

Davenport-Hines, Richard, *An English Affair: Sex, Class and Power in the Age of Profumo* (London: William Collins, 2013)

Davenport-Hines, Richard, *Enemies Within: Communists, the Cambridge Spies and the Making of Modern Britain* (London: William Collins, 2018)

Davies, Russell (ed.), *The Kenneth Williams Diaries* (London: HarperCollins, 1993)

Davis, John, *Waterloo Sunrise: London from the Sixties to Thatcher* (Princeton/Oxford: Princeton University Press, 2022)

Day, Peter, *The Bedbug: Klop Ustinov: Britain's Most Ingenious Spy* (London: Biteback Publishing, 2015)

Deacon, Richard, *A History of the British Secret Service* (London: Muller, 1969)

Deacon, Richard, *A History of the Russian Secret Service* (London: Muller, 1972)

Deacon, Richard and West, Nigel, *Spy! Six Stories of Modern Espionage* (London: Mackay, 1980)

Deedes, W. F., *Dear Bill: W. F. Deedes Reports* (London: Macmillan, 2005)

Denning, Lord, *Lord Denning's Report* (Richmond: Her Majesty's Stationery Office, 1963)

Dimoldenberg, Paul, *The Westminster Whistleblowers: Shirley Porter, Homes for Votes and Scandal in Britain's Rottenest Borough* (London: Politico's Publishing Ltd, 2006)

Dorril, Stephen and Ramsay, Robin, *Smear! Wilson and the Secret State* (London: Grafton, 1992)

Drabble, Margaret, *Angus Wilson: A Biography* (London: Martin Secker & Warburg Ltd, 1995)

Draper, Alfred, *Smoke Without Fire: The Swabey Case* (Bromley: Arlington Books, 1974)

Duncan, Ben, *The Same Language* (London: Faber & Faber, 1962)

Dundy, Elaine, *Finch, Bloody Finch: A Biography of Peter Finch* (London: Michael Joseph, 1980)

Edwards, Stephen and Moseley, Keith, *Monmouth School: The First 400 Years* (London: Third Millennium Information, 2014)

Elliott, Sue and Humphries, Steve, *Not Guilty: Queer Stories from a Century of Discrimination* (London: Biteback Publishing, 2017)

Evans, Harold, *Downing Street Diary: The Macmillan Years 1957–63* (London: Hodder & Stoughton, 1981)

Ewing, K. D., Mahoney, Joanna and Moretta, Andrew, *MI5, the Cold War and the Rule Of Law* (Oxford: Oxford University Press, 2020)

Frolik, Josef, *The Frolik Defection: The Memoirs of An Intelligence Agent* (Barnsley: Leo Cooper Ltd, 1975)

Gardiner, Juliet, *From the Bomb to the Beatles: The Changing Face of Post-War Britain, 1945 –1965* (London: Collins & Brown, 1999)

Golitsyn, Anatoliy, *New Lies for Old: The Communist Strategy of Deception and Disinformation* (London: Wheatsheaf, 1986)

Gourvish, Terry, *Dolphin Square: The History of a Unique Building* (London: Bloomsbury, 2014)

Grant, Thomas, *Jeremy Hutchinson's Case Histories* (London: John Murray, 2015)

Grant, Thomas, *Court Number One: The Old Bailey Trials that Defined Modern Britain* (London: John Murray, 2019)

Hall, Simon, *1956: The World in Revolt* (New York: Pegasus Books, 2016)

Hammond, Andrew, *British Fiction and the Cold War* (London: Palgrave Macmillan, 2013)

Harvey, Ian, *To Fall Like Lucifer* (London: Sidgwick & Jackson Ltd, 1971)

Hayter, Teresa, *Hayter of the Bourgeoisie* (London: Sidgwick & Jackson Ltd, 1972)

Hayter, William, *The Kremlin and the Embassy* (Hodder & Stoughton, 1966)

Hayter, William, *A Double Life* (London: Hamish Hamilton, 1974)

Heaps, Leo, *Thirty Years with the KGB: The Double Life of Hugh Hambleton* (London: Methuen, 1984)

Hemming, Henry, *M: Maxwell Knight, MI5's Greatest Spymaster* (London: Arrow Books, 2018)

Hennessy, Peter, *The Secret State: Whitehall and the Cold War* (London: Allen Lane, 2002)

Hermiston, Roger, *Two Minutes To Midnight: 1953 – The Year of Living Dangerously* (London: Biteback Publishing, 2022)

Higgins, Patrick, *Heterosexual Dictatorship: Male Homosexuality in Postwar Britain* (London: Fourth Estate, 1996)

Hobson, Harold, *Indirect Journey: An Autobiography* (London: Weidenfeld & Nicolson, 1978)

Hogan, Peter, *Shirley Bassey: Diamond Diva* (London: André Deutsch Ltd, 2008)

Hollingsworth, Mark and Fielding, Nick, *Defending the Realm: MI5 and the Shayler Affair* (London: André Deutsch, 1999)

Holroyd, Michael, *Mosaic* (London: Little, Brown & Company, 2004)

Hone, Michael, *Christ Has His John, I Have My George* (Scotts Valley: Createspace Independent Publishing Platform, 2016)

Horne, Alistair, *Macmillan 1957–1986* (Macmillan, 1989)

Hosken, Andrew, *Nothing Like a Dame: The Scandals of Shirley Porter* (London: Granta Books, 2006)

Houghton, Harry, *Operation Portland: The Autobiography of a Spy* (London Rupert Hart-Davis Ltd, 1972)

Hyde, H. Montgomery, *The Other Love: A Historical Contemporary Survey of Homosexuality in Britain* (London: William Heinemann Ltd, 1970)

Hyde, H. Montgomery, *George Blake Superspy* (London: Futura Publications, 1988)

Jago, Michael, *The Man Who Was George Smiley: The Life Of John Bingham* (London: Biteback Publishing, 2013)

Jivani, Alkarim, *It's Not Unusual: A History of Lesbian and Gay Britain in the Twentieth Century* (London: Michael O'Mara Books Ltd, 1997)

Jones, Nigel, *Mosley* (London: Haus Publishing, 2004)

Keeler, Christine (with Douglas Thompson), *Secrets and Lies: The Trials of Christine Keeler* (London: John Blake, 2019)

Kuper, Simon, *The Happy Traitor: Spies, Lies and Exile in Russia: The Extraordinary Story of George Blake* (London: Profile Books, 2021)

Kynaston, David, *On The Cusp: Days of '62* (London: Bloomsbury, 2021)

Le Bailly, Louis, *The Man Around the Engine: Life Below the Waterline* (Fareham: Kenneth Mason Publications Ltd, 1990)

Levin, Bernard, *The Pendulum Years: Britain and the Sixties* (London: Jonathan Cape Ltd, 1970)

Longford, Frank Pakenham, *Avowed Intent: An Autobiography of Lord Longford* (New York: Time Warner Paperbacks, 1995)

Longford, Frank Pakenham, and Stanford, Peter, *Lord Longford's Prison Diary* (Oxford: Lion Publishing, 2000)

Lucas, Norman, *Spycatcher: A Biography of Detective-Superintendent George Gordon Smith* (London: W. H. Allen, 1973)

MacCarthy, Fiona, *Last Curtsey: The End of the Debutantes* (London: Faber & Faber, 2006)

McCormick, Donald, *The Master Book of Spies* (London: Hodder, 1973)

Macintyre, Ben, *A Spy Among Friends: Kim Philby and the Great Betrayal* (London: Bloomsbury, 2014)

Macintyre, Ben, *The Spy and the Traitor: The Greatest Espionage Story of the Cold War* (London: Viking, 2018)

Macklin, Graham, Failed Führers: A History of Britain's Extreme Right (Abingdon: Routledge, 2020)

McLaren, Angus, *Sexual Blackmail: A Modern History* (Cambridge, MA: Harvard University Press, 2002)

McManus, Michael, *Tory Pride and Prejudice: The Conservative Party and Homosexual Law Reform* (London: Biteback Publishing, 2011)

Macmillan, Harold, *At the End of the Day: 1961–1963* (London: Macmillan, 1973)

MacShane, Denis, *Heath* (London: Haus Publishing, 2006)

Magee, Bryan, *One in Twenty: A Study of Homosexuality in Men and Women* (London: Secker & Warburg, 1966)

Mars-Jones, Adam, *Kid Gloves: A Voyage Round My Father* (London: Particular Books, 2015)

Masters, Anthony, *The Man Who Was M: The Life of Maxwell Knight, the Real-Life Spymaster Who Inspired Ian Fleming* (London: Grafton Books, 1986)

435

Matthews, Owen, *An Impeccable Spy: Richard Sorge, Stalin's Master Agent* (London: Bloomsbury, 2019)

Miller, Joan, *One Girl's War: Personal Exploits in MI5's Most Secret Station* (Dingle, Co. Kerry: Brandon/Mount Eagle Publications Ltd, 1986)

Milne, Tim, *Kim Philby: The Unknown Story of the KGB's Master-Spy: A Story of Friendship and Betrayal* (London: Biteback Publishing, 2014)

Mitchell, Austin and Wienir, David, *Last Time: Labour's Lessons from the Sixties* (London: Publishing Co. Ltd, 1997)

Morris, K. E., *A History of Dolphin Square* (London: Dolphin Square Trust Limited, 1995)

Mosley, Oswald, *My Life* (London: Thomas Nelson and Sons Ltd, 1968)

Nicolson, Juliet, *Frostquake: The Frozen Winter of 1962 and How Britain Emerged a Different Country* (London: Chatto & Windus, 2021)

Omand, David, *How Spies Think: Ten Lessons in Intelligence* (London: Viking, 2020)

Parris, Matthew, *Great Parliamentary Scandals: Four Centuries of Calumny, Smear & Innuendo* (London: Robson Books, 1995)

Parry-Jones, David, *The Gwilliam Seasons: John Gwilliam and the Second Golden Era of Welsh Rugby* (Bridgend: Seren, 2002)

Penrose, Barrie, and Freeman, Simon, *Conspiracy of Silence: The Secret Life of Anthony Blunt* (London: Grafton, 1987)

Philby, Kim, *My Silent War* (London: MacGibbon & Kee, 1968)

Pimlott, Ben, *Harold Wilson* (London: HarperCollins, 1992)

Pincher, Chapman, *Sex in Our Time: The Frontiers of Modern Research* (London: Weidenfeld & Nicolson, 1973)

Pincher, Chapman, *Inside Story: A Documentary of the Pursuit of Power* (London: Sidgwick & Jackson, 1979)

Pincher, Chapman, *Their Trade Is Treachery* (London: Sidgwick & Jackson, 1981)

Pincher, Chapman, *The Secret Offensive* (London: Sidgwick & Jackson, 1985)

Pincher, Chapman, *Too Secret Too Long: The Great Betrayal of Britain's Crucial Secrets and the Cover-up* (London: Sidgwick & Jackson, 1985)

Pincher, Chapman, *Traitors: The Labyrinths of Treason* (London: Sidgwick & Jackson, 1987)

Pincher, Chapman, *Treachery: Betrayals, Blunders and Cover-Ups: Six Decades of Espionage* (Edinburgh: Mainstream Publishing, 2012)

Pincher, Chapman, *Dangerous to Know: An Autobiography* (London: Biteback Publishing, 2014)

Purvis, Stewart and Hulbert, Jeff, *When Reporters Cross the Line: The Heroes, the Villains, the Hackers and the Spies* (London: Biteback Publishing, 2013)

Radcliffe, Lord Cyril John, *Report of the Tribunal Appointed to Inquire into the Vassall Case and Related Matters* (London: Her Majesty's Stationery Office, 1963)

Radice, Giles and Diamond, Patrick, *Labour's Civil Wars: How Infighting Has Kept the Left from Power (and What Can Be Done About It)* (London: Haus Publishing, 2022)

Randle, Michael and Pottle, Pat, *The Blake Escape: How We Freed George Blake – and Why* (London: Harrap Books, 1989)

Rawlinson, Peter, *A Price Too High: An Autobiography* (London: Weidenfeld & Nicolson, 1989)

Renault, Mary, *The Charioteer* (London: Longman, 1953)

Robinson, Stephen, *The Remarkable Lives of Bill Deedes* (London: Little, Brown, 2008)

Routledge, Paul, *Wilson* (London: Haus Publishing, 2006)

Sandbrook, Dominic, *Never Had It So Good: A History of Britain from Suez to the Beatles* (London: Little, Brown, 2005)

Sandbrook, Dominic, *White Heat: A History of Britain in the Swinging Sixties* (London: Little, Brown, 2006)

Sanders, Lloyd C., *The Holland House Circle* (London: Methuen, 1908)

Seth, Ronald, *Forty Years of Soviet Spying* (London: Cassell, 1965)

Shrapnel, Norman, *The Performers: Politics as Theatre* (London: Constable, 1978)

Sinclair, Andrew, *The Red and the Blue: Intelligence, Treason and the Universities* (London: Weidenfeld & Nicolson, 1986)

Sisman, Adam, *John le Carré: The Biography* (London: Bloomsbury, 2015)

Smith, Michael, *The Anatomy of a Spy: A History of Espionage and Betrayal* (London: The History Press, 2019)

Smith, Michael, *The Real Special Relationship: The True Story of How the British and US Secret Services Work Together* (London: Simon & Schuster, 2022)

Snow, C. P., *The New Men* (London: Macmillan, 1954)

Snow, C. P., *Homecomings* (London: Macmillan, 1956)

Snow, C. P., *The Conscience of the Rich* (London: Macmillan, 1958)

Snow, C. P., *The Affair* (London: Macmillan, 1960)

Snow, C. P., *Corridors of Power* (London: Macmillan, 1964)

Snow, C. P., *The Sleep of Reason* (London: Macmillan, 1968)

Snow, C. P., *Last Things* (London: Macmillan, 1970)

Souhami, Diana, *The Trials of Radclyffe Hall* (London: Weidenfeld & Nicolson, 1998)

Sparrow, Gerald, *How to Become an MP* (London: Anthony Blond, 1959)

Spinetti, Victor, *Up Front...* (London: Robson Books, 2006)

Stamp, Gavin, *Anti-Ugly: Excursions in English Architecture and Design* (London: Aurum Press, 2013)

Stanford, Peter, *Lord Longford: A Life* (London: Mandarin, 1995)

Stanford, Peter, *The Outcasts' Outcast: A Biography of Lord Longford* (Stroud: Sutton, 2003)

Straw, Jack, *Last Man Standing: Memoirs of a Political Survivor* (London: Macmillan, 2012)

Summers, Anthony, and Dorril, Stephen, *Honeytrap: The Secret Worlds of Stephen Ward* (London: Weidenfeld & Nicolson, 1987)

Tate, Tim, *The Spy Who Was Left Out in the Cold: The Secret History of Agent Goleniewski* (London: Bantam Press, 2021)

Taverne, Dick, *Against the Tide: Politics and Beyond, A Memoir* (London: Biteback Publishing, 2014)

Thévoz, Seth Alexander, *Behind Closed Doors: The Secret Life of London's Private Members' Clubs* (London: Robinson, 2022)

Vassall, John, *Vassall: The Autobiography of a Spy* (London: Sidgwick & Jackson, 1975)

West, Donald, *Homosexuality* (London: Gerald Duckworth & Co. Ltd, 1955)

West, Donald, *Gay Life, Straight Work* (Crested Butte, CO: Paradise Publishing, 2012)

West, Nigel, *MI5: British Security Service Operations, 1909–45* (London: Bodley Head, 1981)

West, Nigel, *A Matter of Trust: MI5 1945–72* (London: Coronet, 1985)

West, Nigel, *GCHQ: The Secret Wireless War 1900–86* (London: Weidenfeld & Nicolson, 1986)

West, Nigel, *Molehunt: The Full Story of the Soviet Spy in MI5* (London: Weidenfeld & Nicolson, 1987)

West, Nigel, *The Friends: Britain's Post-war Secret Intelligence Operations* (London: Coronet, 1990)

West, Nigel, *Seven Spies Who Changed the World* (London: Mandarin, 1992)

West, Nigel (ed.), *The Faber Book of Espionage* (London: Faber & Faber, 1993)

West, Nigel (ed.), *The Faber Book of Treachery* (London: Faber & Faber, 1997)

West, Nigel, *Venona: The Greatest Secret of the Cold War* (London: HarperCollins, 2000)

West, Nigel, *Historical Dictionary of Cold War Counterintelligence* (Lanham, MD: Scarecrow Press, 2007)

West, Nigel, *Historical Dictionary of Naval Intelligence* (Lanham, MD: Scarecrow Press , 2010)

West, Nigel, *At Her Majesty's Secret Service: The Chiefs of Britain's Intelligence Service, MI6* (Barnsley: Frontline Books, 2016)

West, Nigel, *Cold War Counterfeit Spies: Tales of Espionage – Genuine or Bogus?* (Barnsley: Frontline Books, 2022)

West, Nigel and Tsarev, Oleg, *The Crown Jewels: The British Secrets at the Heart of the KGB Archives* (London: HarperCollins, 1998

West, Rebecca, *The Vassall Affair* (London: Sunday Telegraph, 1963)

West, Rebecca, *The Meaning of Treason* (London: Penguin Books, 1965)

Wigg, Lord, *George Wigg* (London: Michael Joseph, 1972)

Wildeblood, Peter, *Against the Law* (London: Weidenfeld & Nicolson, 1955)

Williams, John, *Miss Shirley Bassey* (London: Quercus, 2010)

Wilson, A. N., *Our Times: The Age of Elizabeth II* (London: Arrow Books, 2009)

Wilson, Angus, *Hemlock and After* (London: Penguin Books, 1952)

Wilson, Ray, and Adams, Ian, *Special Branch: A History: 1883–2006* (London: Biteback Publishing, 2015)

Wise, David and Ross, Thomas B., *The Espionage Establishment* (London: Jonathan Cape, 1968)

Wright, Peter, *Spycatcher* (Sydney: Heinemann Publishers Australia, 1987)

Wynne, Greville, *The Man from Moscow: The Story of Wynne and Penkovsky* (London: Hutchinson, 1967)

Young, Wayland, *The Profumo Affair: Aspects of Conservatism* (London: Penguin, 1963)

Ziegler, Philip, *Wilson: The Authorised Life* (London: Weidenfeld & Nicolson, 1993)

Ziegler, Philip, *Edward Heath: The Authorised Biography* (London: Harper Press, 2010)

INDEX

Note: JV = John Vassall

Abse, Leo 300–01, 328, 330–31
Aitken, Jonathan 234, 234n155, 306
Amery, Julian 344
Ames, Aldrich 191
Amy, Dennis 47–8, 334
Angleton, James 145, 148, 151, 187, 269, 393
Anglo-American relations 187–9, 269
Anne, Princess Royal 398–9
Ash, Douglas 36
Attwell, W. J. E. 89

Banks, Thomas 29
Barklamb, Arthur 67, 68
Barran, Donald 213, 344, 345
Barry, Sir Patrick 244
Bartels, Dr 132, 181
Bath Club 11, 16–17, 24, 88, 153–4, 156, 281, 327
BBC
    London Spy 417
    Spy! 376–80
    That Was the Week That Was 232
Bedworth, Mr 67, 68
Beech, Carl ("Nick") 400–03
Bennett, Geoffrey
    author 34–6, 139–40, 378–9
    JV's arrest and trial 166, 282
    on JV's sexuality 32–3, 69, 155, 263–4
    naval attaché 31–2
    relations with JV 32–4, 36, 51, 62, 67, 69,
        86, 139, 140–41, 377
    Soviet travels 42, 61–2
    Spy! portrayal 377–80
Bennett, Mortimer Wilmot 332
Bennett, Rosemary 31, 33–4, 61, 172–3, 282

Benvenuto, Ludmilla 393
Berkeley, Humphry 134–5, 329
Blake, George xviii, 85–6, 187, 188, 191, 195–6,
    269, 301–3, 305–6, 310–11, 407, 408
Bligh, Tim 224
Blundell, Sir Robert 192
Blunt, Sir Anthony 108–9, 268n186, 405–6,
    406–7, 416–17
Boothby, Lord (Robert/Bob) 136–7, 225, 304–5,
    333, 344
Bourke, Sean 303, 305, 310, 406
Bowra, Maurice 20
Braithwaite, Rodric 41
Brinham, George 332
British embassy (Moscow)
    colleagues' view of JV 36, 37–8
    embassy life 28, 36–7
    internal security 334
    JV's administrative role 31–3
    JV's interview and appointment 24–5
    JV's living arrangements 29–30
    no suspicion of Soviet infiltration of JV
        64, 65, 67
    Radcliffe report 260–64
Brooks, Barbara 159–60
Brown, George 215, 230, 329
Bulganin, Nikolai 26, 63, 72–3
Burgess, Guy 20, 47, 71, 85, 145, 148, 179, 187,
    230, 384
Bushy, Douglas A. 133, 135, 182, 282, 350

Caccia, Sir Harold 148, 352
Cairncross, John 108n47, 406
Callaghan, James 316, 320
Cambridge Five 148, 405–6
    see also Burgess, Guy; Maclean, Donald;
        Philby, Kim

Campbell-Orde, Perdita (neè Watt) 140–41, 166, 172–73
Campbell, William 17–18, 100–01, 179
Carrington, Lord
  JV's opinion 95
  on JV's spying 167, 201, 214–15
  and Macmillan 228–9
  political survivor 226, 227–9
  press criticism 214, 257–8, 260
  Radcliffe evidence 246–7
  Radcliffe and West exoneration 260, 264, 298
Chamier, Brigadier 51
Champneys, Basil 342–4
Churanov, Vladimir Aleksandrovich (HARRISON) 59–60, 66, 74
CIA 128, 144, 145, 147–8, 149n83, 150, 187–8, 190–91, 269
Cilcennin, Lord (J. P. L Thomas) 24, 183, 270n187, 344
Clough, Desmond 255–7
Cold War 136–7, 200–01
Costakis, Nikolai 44
Courtney, Anthony 217
Crabb, Lionel (Buster) 72
Crankshaw, Edward 47
Cridland, Frederick 347
cross-dressing 249–50, 254, 256
Crossman, Richard 230, 274
Cunningham, Sir Charles 224
  Cunningham inquiry 224, 227, 232

Daily Express 204, 226, 246–7, 252, 257–8
Daily Herald 204, 205
Daily Mail 111, 204, 213, 214, 220, 265–6, 308
Daily Mirror 270
Daily Sketch 252, 254–5
Daily Telegraph 204, 213, 229, 387
Davenport-Hines, Richard 270, 413
Davidson-Houston, Brigadier 67
de Courcy, Kenneth 305
Deacon, Richard 4, 9, 26, 41–2, 48, 98, 256–7, 274, 352, 411
Deedes, Bill 225–6, 265, 274, 411
Delahunty, Patrick 248
Denby, June 37–8
Dolphin Square
  entertaining 104–5, 112, 205, 348
  furnishings and toiletries 105–6, 153, 164, 205, 207
  Galbraith visit (1959) 96, 262
  historical background 107–9
  JV cleaning ladies 171–2, 250–2
  JV neighbours 109–10
  JV surveillance 156–60, 162–6
  JV tenancy 103–4
  Le Bailly tenancy 321–2
  political scandal 295, 391–3, 398–404
  press coverage 205, 207, 295
  sex-work centre 395–6
  in spy fiction 296–7, 396–8

Driberg, Tom 47, 225n143, 340
Dugdale, John 216
Duggan, Laurence 279
Dunlap, Jack 279
Dunlop, Colin 292–4
Dunlop, W. L. 87
Durham Prison 311–14

Edwards, Donald 347
Eiserle, Robert 133–4, 161, 350
Eliot, Hon. Vere 175, 344–5
Elliott, Denholm 408–9
Elliott, Nicholas 268, 412
Elwell, Charles 40, 69, 154–6, 174, 178, 182–3, 222, 244, 248, 287–91, 294, 301, 305–6, 307–8, 341–3
Emerson, John 322–3, 326
Evening Standard 27, 310, 319, 386, 387

Fell, Barbara 150
fiction 296–7, 335–9, 396–8, 405, 414–17
film 296–7, 335–9, 414–17
Fletcher, Raymond 398
Foley, Anthony 307
Foot, Michael 230, 316
Ford, Stanley 30
Foster, Janet 371–2, 419
Foster, Reg 254–6
France, S. J. 288, 294
Francklyn, Agnes 87–8
Freeth, Denzil 340–41
Fuchs, Klaus xvi, 146, 187, 279–80
Furnivall Jones, Martin 188

Gaitskell, Hugh 149, 248–9, 259
Galbraith, Simone 91–2, 131–2, 157, 173, 211, 213, 246
Galbraith, Thomas (later Lord Strathclyde) 210n131, 223
Galbraith, Thomas (Tam)
  background 209–11
  breaks contact with JV 173
  Civil Lord of the Admiralty 80, 89–94, 150, 211–12, 215
  comments to press on JV 213–14
  on JV's homosexuality 214
  letters to JV 208, 220–22, 225, 259
  no sexual relationship with JV 229–32, 249
  Radcliffe tribunal 245–6
  resignation 225–32
  Scottish Office 94, 131, 157
  social relationship with JV 91, 92, 96, 117, 131–2, 166, 208, 212–14, 251, 291, 346
Galdi, Pierre 158–9, 251n174, 350
Gardner, Richard 348–9
Gee, Ethel (Bunty) 123, 124–6, 248, 321
Gentile, Francesco 116–17, 161, 176, 310
Gilmour, Ian 258
Goddard, Lord 279–80
Goddard, Rayner 329

Goleniewski, Michal 143–5, 361
Golitsyn, Anatoliy (KAGO) 59, 147–50, 150, 151, 248, 268, 290, 291, 393
Gordievsky, Oleg 190
Gordon, Aloysius ("Lucky") 276–7
Gordon Walker, Patrick 189–90, 215
Gowing, Donald 347
Greenwood, Anthony 218
"Gregory" (Nikolai Borisovich Rodin) (Korovin)
    JV's London handler 74, 77, 79–84, 93–4, 101, 107, 113, 115, 130, 280–81
    Portland spy ring 126
Gribanov, Oleg (Little Napoleon) 59
Griffith-Jones, Mervyn 192
Guardian, The 195, 288, 315, 388, 404–5

Hall, Jennifer 142, 157, 161, 179, 180, 202
Harrison, Sir Geoffrey 328
Harvey, Ian 119–20, 330, 344
Hauffman, Verner 97
Hay, Frances 65–6, 66–7
Hayter, Lady 30–31, 36, 51, 67
Hayter, Sir William 26–8, 30–31, 51–2, 119–20, 169, 264
Hayward, Harry 36–7
Heath, Edward 50, 269, 394–5, 401
Hickey, Pamela 250–52
Hicks, Humphrey 158, 176–8
Hobson, Sir John 195, 196, 211, 328–9
Hodges, Andrew 354
Holland, Sir Edward Milner 244
Hollis, Roger 148, 152, 167–8, 247, 292–3, 393, 416–17
homophobia 19–21, 178, 204–7, 216–18, 222, 259, 261–2, 266, 267, 295–6, 298–300, 331–4, 409–10
homosexuality
    1950s England 100–103
    decriminalisation 118, 258–9, 300, 328–31
    JV's early life 7, 8–9, 16, 17–18, 19
    JV's London life 110–12
    prosecutions 19–21, 25–6, 102
    Royal Navy 117–18, 333
    security measures 351–6
    terminology 119
    threat of blackmail 120–22
    see also sexual blackmail
Hoover, J. Edgar 146, 188
Horobin, Sir Ian Macdonald 300
Hoskins, Percy 226, 257–8
Houghton, Harry 93, 123–6, 127–9, 144, 145, 248, 308, 312–13, 321, 325
House of Commons, debate on JV 215–18
Howard, Greville 187, 217–18
Hughes, Emrys 218
Hutchinson, Jeremy 194, 196–9, 315, 319, 332, 357–8, 360, 367–70, 380–1
Hutchison, Norman 100, 345–46
Hutton inquiry (2004) 267

Hyde, H. Montgomery 120, 410–11

ITV
    Secrets of the Spies 416
    Spy Among Friends, A 416–17
Ivanov, Eugene 272, 275, 405

James, A. D. B. and Mrs 315, 326, 357
James, Humphrey 68
Jarrett, Sir Clifford 91–2
Jennings, Stanley 29–30, 43–4, 65, 178–9
Johnson, Edward 37
Johnson, Stanley 106, 219, 219n136
Jordan, Colin 303–4, 343–5

Karpekov, Nikolai see "Nikolai" (Nikolai Karpekov) (London handler)
Kavotsov (Khrostov), Boris 43, 179
Keeler, Christine 270–77, 295
Kellar, Alexander 354
Kendall, Kenneth 135, 344
Kerby, Henry 138
Kerr, Anne 315
Kettle, Arnold 20
Kettlewell, Nick 183–5, 190, 353
Khrostov (Kavotsov), Boris 43, 179
Khrushchev, Nikita 71–3
King, John Herbert (MAG) 64
King, R. M. 87
Kitson, Timothy 394–5
Knight, Maxwell 108–9, 177, 296, 305n207, 398n281, 399, 405
Kroger, Peter and Helen 126–8, 144

Labour Party 215, 229, 230, 259, 274
le Carré, John 296–7, 396–8
Le Marchant, Spencer 395
Lecture, The (COI film) 338–9
Levin, Bernard 257
Lewin, W. R. 7, 14, 185, 254
Lewis, Lisa 37
Lewis, P. H. T. 37
Litchfield, John 216–17
Longford, Lord 317–19, 361, 376, 387–8
Lonsdale, Gordon Arnold (Kolon Molody (BEN)) 125–9, 293, 301, 305–6
Lucas, Norman 9, 14–15, 17, 19, 61–2, 96, 145–7, 208, 258, 409
Luck, John Charles 37
Lustig-Prean, Duncan 355, 355n247, 424
Lyubimov, Mikhail 182, 415–16

MacAfee, Jack 142, 148, 155, 184, 246, 353
McCallum, Mary 65–6
MacDermot, Niall 218, 391–2
McEwen, Robin 18–19, 282, 373–4
McEwen, Robin and Brigid 106, 193–4, 196, 312, 373–5
Maclean, Donald 20, 71, 85, 145, 148, 179, 187, 384

Macmillan, Harold
and Carrington 228–9
Galbraith's resignation 224–9
on JV's character 290
on JV scandal 167–9, 200–01
mentions 85–6, 143, 148, 190, 208, 216
on the press 258, 274
Radcliffe tribunal 243, 244, 248–9, 259, 265
resignation 275
Macmillan, Maurice 344
McNaughten, Mrs 105–6, 111, 282
McNeil, Hector 230
Magee, Bryan 330
Maluta, Robert 351
Marescaux, Geoffrey 101, 344–5
Marine, David 24, 75, 100, 176, 350
Mars-Jones, William 245–6, 258
Marshall, Mr 142, 143, 178
Marshall, William 64–5
Martelli, Giuseppe 194–5
Martin, Arthur 148–9, 165, 187, 308
Mates, Michael 399–400
Mathew, Theobald 166–7
Maugham, 2nd Viscount 334–5
Maxwell Fyfe, David 19–20, 117
MI5 241–8, 287–91
    Their Trade Is Treachery 335
    see also Elwell, Charles
Mikhailsky, Sigmund 44–6, 51, 67, 68–9, 185, 261, 415
Miller, Ann 112, 142, 203
Mitchell, Frank 309
Mitchell, Graham 86, 293
Molloy, Mr 181
Monmouth School 6–11, 185, 389
Montagu of Beaulieu, Lord 20–21, 25–6, 175, 361
Montgomery, Fergus 134–5, 136, 181–3, 291, 344
Moore, April 313
Moscow 23–76
    JV's Hotel Berlin entrapment 48–52, 53–7, 118, 197–8, 361, 410–11, 412, 415
    JV's social life 38–42, 52–3, 61, 62, 63, 71, 73, 219, 261
    JV's social life with Russians 41–6
    retired English spies 384
Mosley, Oswald 108, 304, 319, 398, 405
Mulholland, Brendan 253–4, 255–6, 257, 411
Mullett, Michael 67, 68
Murray, Doris 171–2, 250–2
Muskett, Derek 191–2

New Statesman 256, 266
News of the World 193, 207, 252–3
Nicholls, Sir Harmar 135–6, 181, 183, 291, 309–10, 343, 344
"Nick" child abuse scandal 400–03
"Nikki" (Nicolai Korovin) 126
    see also "Gregory" (Nikolai Borisovich Rodin) (Korovin)

"Nikolai" (Moscow handler) 59–60, 74, 290
"Nikolai" (Nikolai Karpekov) (London handler) 129–30, 137–8, 165, 186–7, 200
Northey, Adrian 68, 69, 70, 72, 74, 86, 155, 264
Norwood, Melita 408
Nosenko, Yuri 150–2

The Observer 228, 258, 268
Old Bailey trial 191–200
Oldfield, Maurice 354, 376n261
Operation Fickle 37
Operation Midland 402
O'Regan, Mr 67–8
Orr-Ewing, Sir Charles 48
Osborn, John 138
Osman, Pauline 179

Paget, Reginald 217, 274
Parfit, Derek 306
Park, Daphne 58–9
Parker of Waddington, Lord 195, 198–9
Parrott, Sir Cecil 67
Paterson, Elizabeth 141, 157, 162
Peck, David and Mrs 51, 66, 172
Penkovsky, Oleg 200, 280, 386
Pennells, H. V. 69–70, 260–1, 264
Perry, Olive 37
Persona non Grata (COI film) 335–8
Peters, John 99
Philby, Kim 85, 148, 168, 187, 268–9, 384, 408, 411, 416–17
Pincher, Chapman 147, 150–1, 152, 190, 231, 248, 291–2, 352, 410
Portland spy ring xviii, 123–30, 132, 143–4, 226
positive vetting 85–9, 351–6
Pottle, Pat 310
press
    Dolphin Square 205–6, 207, 295
    homophobia 204–7, 266, 295–6
    inaccuracies 206–7
    JV obituaries 387–8
    Old Bailey trial 188, 195
    Radcliffe report 265–6
    refusal to reveal sources 253–8
    tabloid newspapers 193, 202–07, 208, 226, 229, 232, 251–8
    US press 188–9, 192
    see also titles of individual newspapers
Price, Beryl 38
Prime, Geoffrey 410
Profumo, John 168, 270–6, 395, 404
Pugh-Pugh, Ivy 255

Radcliffe inquiry (1963)
    on British embassy in Moscow 260–4
    Carrington evidence 246–7
    establishment 244–5
    evidence 24, 25, 45, 87, 98, 99, 104–3, 142, 212, 232, 244–50
    Galbraith evidence 245–6

JV's disappointment at outcome 248–9, 361
JV's evidence 249–50, 259
Macmillan 243, 244, 248–9, 259, 265
and the press 250–8
reaction 264–7
report 259–64
Radcliffe inquiry (Security Procedures) (1962) 243, 341
Radcliffe, Lord 242–4
Randle, Michael 187, 270n187, 300, 301, 302, 303, 310, 423
Rawlinson, Sir Peter 166–7, 230
Redmayne, Martin 223, 225, 227
Rice-Davis, Mandy 271, 275–6
Richardson, John 29, 179–80
Rickard, Norman 252–3
Roberts, Elizabeth 87–8
Robertson, J.A.C. 349–50
Rodin, Nikolai Borisovich see "Gregory" (Nikolai Borisovich Rodin) (Korovin)
Rolfe, Kenneth 75, 350–1
Roman Catholic Church 18–19, 25, 39, 63, 302, 386
Rosenberg, Ethel and Julius 279
Rowsell, Ivor 50
Royal, Mrs 141, 162

Sanderson, Amy 63
Schofield, Michael 102
Semenov, Volodya 43, 179
Sewel, Lord 400
sexual blackmail
historical 46–7
JV's Hotel Berlin entrapment 48–52, 53–7, 118, 197–98, 361, 380, 410–11, 412, 415
JV's rendezvous with Soviet handlers 57–9
KGB entrapments 47–8, 328
Shawcross, Hartley 109–10
Shepherd, William 218
Shepley, Michael 395–96
Sherwood, E.S. 88
Short, Renée 314
Skeffington-Lodge, Thomas 360
the "skier" (Aleksey Volkov) 46, 48, 53–4
Smith, Ferguson xvi
Smith, George Gordon xvi, 145–47, 154
Smith, Mr 178
Smith, Roy 31, 37, 70
Snell, Susan 381–83, 386, 389
Snow, C.P., Strangers and Brothers 297
social class 4–6, 10, 32–3, 86, 88, 97, 152–53, 266–7, 374, 406–07
Somers, Laurence 331–32
Spy! (BBC drama) 376–80
Spycraft (Netflix) 416
spying
Cambridge Five 148, 405–06
Dunlop case 292–94
Fell case 241

Fuchs xvi, 146, 187, 279–80
methodology 78–84, 107, 124, 127, 290, 418
Penkovsky case 200
Portland spy ring xviii, 123–30, 132, 143–44, 226, 291
Profumo case 270–77, 395
Soblen case 215
Soviet treatment of Soviet spies 280
suicide after unmasking 279
see also Blake, George; Burgess, Guy; Maclean, Donald; Philby, Kim; Vassall, John (William John Christopher)
Stafford, Georgina 323
Stephenson, Sir Hugh S. 187–88
Stradling Thomas, John 402
Strathclyde, Lord (Tam Galbraith's son) 210n131, 234
Straw, Jack 353–54
Street, John 68
Sun on Sunday 400
Sunday Mirror 225, 295–96
Sunday Pictorial 193, 202–04, 205–06, 208, 219, 220–22, 258, 259, 281, 290–91, 321, 333, 376
Sunday Telegraph 129, 304
Sunday Times 228, 288, 301, 328, 358–9, 365
Swabey, Christopher 117–18
Symonds, Ronnie 152, 166, 170, 173–74
Synott, P. N. N. 89, 94

Thomas, J. P. L. (later Lord Cilcennin) 24, 183, 270n187, 344
Thorneycroft, Peter 115–16, 215–16, 223
The Times 34, 124, 192, 240, 255, 257, 264–5, 312, 319, 364–65, 387–88
Turing, Alan 20, 118n52, 409

Uffelman, Paul R. 349
United States
Anglo-American relations 187–89, 269
JV's American friends 349–51
treatment of spies 279–80
see also CIA

Van Den Born, Bob 39–40, 131
Vassall, John (William John Christopher)
CAREER
Admiralty clerk 12–13, 15–16, 17, 141–43
British Records Association (BRA) 369–73, 381–84
Fleet Section (Admiralty Military Branch) 94–5
job searches 94, 367–69, 381
minister's Admiralty office 89–94
Naval Attaché clerk (Moscow) 21, 24–5, 31, 44
Naval Intelligence Division 84–5, 89
personnel assessments 15, 23, 32–3, 97–9, 142
positive vetting 85–9

RAF 12, 13–15
character 37–8, 78, 417–18
cross-dressing 249–50, 254, 256
death 385
education 6–11
extravagant lifestyle 16–17
family background 1–5
film, television and fictional portrayals
    296–7, 335–39, 396–98, 405, 414–17
finances 60, 280–82, 321
memoirs 360, 361–66
myths and misconceptions concerning
    410–16
name change 366, 371–72, 382, 388
post-prison life 357–60, 366–7
PRISON
Durham 311–14
Maidstone 308–310, 314–21
prison contemporaries 300–08
prison sentence 199–200
release from prison 324–26
Wormwood Scrubs 283–86, 301–08
Roman Catholicism 18–19, 25, 39, 63, 302,
    386
SOCIAL LIFE
foreign travel 40–41, 62–3, 65–6, 70, 73,
    74–5, 87, 112–17, 131, 133, 160–61, 333–34
friends and work contacts 175–80
letters from Galbraith 208, 220–22, 225,
    259
London 110–12, 138–39
Moscow 38–42, 52–3, 61, 62, 63, 71, 73,
    219, 261
M.P. friends 132–36
SPYING
Admiralty security failures 260–61
cameras 114, 130, 137, 149, 166
differing opinions on importance 189–91,
    198
document handovers 59–60, 70
financial rewards 60, 63, 198–99, 280–82
interrogation and confession 169–71
London deactivation (1961-2) 130–31
London reactivation (1962) 136–38
methodology 78–84, 107, 124, 127, 290, 418
MI5 debriefing 287–91, 294
Old Bailey trial 191–200
surveillance and arrest xi–xviii, 153–66, 169
unmasking of JV's identity 143–53
wartime service 12–13
will 388–90
Vassall, Mabel (mother) 4–6, 11–12, 40–1,
    74–5, 80, 95–96, 100, 346
Vassall, Richard Henry Holland (brother) 7–8,
    16, 88, 96, 199, 286–87, 317, 389, 409
Vassall, William (father) 4, 11–12, 95–6,
    99–100, 110, 172, 286, 311, 316–17, 323–24,
    357, 358
Vassall-Adams, Jerrold 157, 158, 193, 193n120,
    424

Vaughan, Joan 160, 161, 180, 202
Vigar, Alan 252–53
Vlaanderen, Leo 307
Volkov, Aleksey (the "skier") 46, 46n, 48, 53–4

Walker, John Anthony 190–91
Ward, Stephen 233, 272, 304
Warne, Derek 100–01, 344
Watkins, John 150
Watson, Tom 401
Webb, Derek 159–60
West, Donald 117
West, Nigel 25, 26, 48, 50, 59, 75, 98, 147, 149,
    189, 288, 375–76, 407
West, Rebecca 65, 68, 88, 98, 107, 132, 211–12,
    220, 227, 230, 247, 249, 264, 266, 273,
    298–300, 319, 404, 405, 406, 418
White, Dick 148–49
Whittaker, Frederick 38
Whyte, David 68
Wigg, George 230, 271
Wilby, William 17–18
Williams, David 159–60
Williams, Kenneth 258–59
Williams, Nick 159–60
Wilson, Angus 109
Wilson, Harold 266–67, 392–94
Wilson, Orville L. 63–4, 350
Wingstrand, John 176, 348
Winn, Connie 177
Winterborn, Hugh 164, 166
Wolfenden Report (1957) 118–19, 120
Woodfield, Philip 224
Woodgate, Nancy and Grahame 180
Wormwood Scrubs 283–85
Wraight, Anthony 146, 146n80
Wright, Leo 347
Wright, Peter 150–51, 152, 166, 188, 190, 393
Wynne, Greville 385
Wynne, M. J. 67

Yeager, Frederick and June 349